The Family Trade

"Charles Stross's *The Family Trade* is an inventive, irreverent, and delightful romp into an alternate world where business is simultaneously low and high tech, and where romance, murder, marriage, and business are hopelessly intertwined—and deadly." —L. E. Modesitt, Jr.

"Quirky, original, and entertaining. *The Family Trade* could be *The Godfather* of all fantasy novels."
—Kevin J. Anderson, *New York Times*
bestselling author of *A Forest of Stars*

"*The Family Trade* is one of those rare delights—a book that is fun, intelligently written, and which leaves a reader breathlessly wondering what will happen next. Readers Beware: Stross weaves a tale that continually builds to an engrossing climax. Once you get into this, you'll find yourself hooked." —David Farland

"*The Family Trade* shows that Charles Stross is no longer a beginner to watch, but a star to watch." —Mike Resnick

"Stross not only creates an alternate world that is fascinating and original, he even does the unheard of, for a fantasist: His depiction of our world is deep and real. His characters behave in ways that make sense. They know all the things they should know, and don't know the things they shouldn't. The result is that we readers can trust this author completely, dive into this story and let it carry us wherever the current flows.

"Not to mention the fact that it's simply a great adventure, full of danger, of plots within plots, of forbidden love, and political murder." —Orson Scott Card

The Hidden Family

"The Hidden Family is a festival of ideas in action, fast moving and often very funny, but underpinned by a rigorous logical strategy. . . . Stross's breezy, almost Heinleinian mode of narration is on fine display." —*Locus*

"Miriam Beckstein, aka Countess Helge Thorold-Hjorth of the Clan, finds her own world to conquer in this fast-moving sequel to *The Family Trade.* . . . Stross continues to mix high and low tech in amusing and surprising ways. . . . [He] weaves a tale worthy of Robert Ludlum or Dan Brown."
—*Publishers Weekly*

"English writer Charles Stross, whose books burst with pop-science ideas, intrigue, strong characters and even romance, continues his Merchant Princes series. . . . Stross is an energetic writer . . . who creates page-turning reads. . . . Readers will be relieved to learn that there is a lot to look forward to in *The Hidden Family,* including a finale that is all Gothic Romance: regrets, a ball and a happy reunion." —*Bookpage*

"These days, finding a science fiction or fantasy novel that *doesn't* feature a kick-ass babe who is either cybernetically enhanced, a martial arts master or a trained ninja killer (or all three) can be hard work. The genres don't lack for Buffyesque role models . . . But there's something different about Miriam, the heroine of Charles Stross' fantasy series 'The Merchant Princes'. . . . It is a tribute to the budding powers of Stross, who works successfully in both the science fiction and fantasy genres, that he pulls off this feat in a fashion both amusing and gripping . . . Miriam is a terrific character, turning the tables on all who would attempt to manipulate her, and setting in motion events that promise to transform the evolution of no less than three separate worlds. For those of us who actually are journalists working on deadline, Stross gives us an escape fantasy that is most seductive, indeed." —*Salon.com*

"Stross effectively keeps all the the plates spinning that he launched into motion in the first volume of this series. . . . Stross is having great fun with these books, and it's contagious."
                                                                                      —Scifi.com

"The sequel to *The Family Trade* continues the adventures of Miriam, the high-tech journalist flung into a fantasy world that really does recall the early volumes of Roger Zelazny's Amber series. . . . Laugh your way to an ending that clearly promises further enjoyable volumes."   —*Booklist*

the HIDDEN FAMILY

TOR BOOKS BY CHARLES STROSS

The Family Trade
The Hidden Family
The Clan Corporate

the HIDDEN FAMILY

BOOK TWO OF THE MERCHANT PRINCES

CHARLES STROSS

TOR®
fantasy

A TOM DOHERTY ASSOCIATES BOOK
NEW YORK

For my parents

NOTE: If you purchased this book without a cover you should be aware that this book is stolen property. It was reported as "unsold and destroyed" to the publisher, and neither the author nor the publisher has received any payment for this "stripped book."

This is a work of fiction. All the characters and events portrayed in this book are either products of the author's imagination or are used fictitiously.

THE HIDDEN FAMILY

Copyright © 2005 by Charles Stross
Teaser copyright © 2006 by Charles Stross

All rights reserved, including the right to reproduce this book, or portions thereof, in any form.

Edited by David G. Hartwell

A Tor Book
Published by Tom Doherty Associates, LLC
175 Fifth Avenue
New York, NY 10010

www.tor.com

Tor® is a registered trademark of Tom Doherty Associates, LLC.

ISBN-13: 978-0-7653-5205-7
ISBN-10: 0-7653-5205-2

First Edition: June 2005
First Mass Market Edition: May 2006

Printed in the United States of America

0   9   8   7   6   5   4   3   2

PART 1

BUSINESS PLANS

LeARNED couNsel

The committee meeting was entering its third hour when the king sneezed, bringing matters to a head. His Excellency Sir Roderick was speaking at the time of the royal spasm. Standing at the far end of the table, before the red velvet curtains that sealed off the windows and the chill of the winter afternoon beyond, Sir Roderick leaned forward slightly, clutching his papers to his bony chest and wobbling back and forth as he recited. His colorless manners matched his startling lack of skin and hair pigmentation: He kept his eyes downcast as he regurgitated a seemingly endless stream of reports from the various heads of police, correspondents of intelligence, and freelance informers who kept his office abreast of news.

"I beg your pardon." A valet flourished a clean linen handkerchief before the royal nose. John Frederick blinked, his expression pained. "Ah-*choo*!" Although not yet in middle age, the king's florid complexion and burgeoning waistline were already giving rise to worries among his physiopaths and apothecaries.

Sir Roderick paused, awaiting the royal nod. The air in the room was heavy with the smell of beeswax furniture polish, and a faint oily overlay from the quietly fizzing gas lamps. "Sire?"

"A moment." John Frederick, by grace of God king-emperor of New Britain and ruler of the territories and dependencies thereof, took a fresh handkerchief and waved off his equerry while anxious faces watched him from all sides. He breathed deeply, clearly battling to control the itching in his sinuses. "Ah. Where were we? Sir Roderick, you have held the floor long enough—take a seat, we will return to you shortly. Lord Douglass, this matter of indiscipline among the masses troubles me. If the effects of the poor grain harvest last year are not mitigated in the summer, as your honorable colleague forecasts"—a nod at Lord Scotia, minister for rural affairs—"then there will be fertile soil for the ranters and ravers to till next autumn. Is there any risk of a *domestic* upset?"

Lord Douglass ran a wrinkled hand across his thinning hair as he considered his reply. "As your majesty is doubtless aware—" He paused. "I had hoped to discuss this matter after hearing from Sir Roderick. If I may beg your indulgence?" At the royal nod, he leaned sideways. "Sir Roderick, may I ask you to rapidly summarize the domestic situation?"

"By your leave. Your majesty?" Sir Roderick cleared his throat, then addressed the room. "Your majesty, my right honorable friends, the domestic condition is currently under control, but there are an increasing number of reports of nonconformist ranters in the provinces. In the past month alone the royal police have apprehended no less than two cells of Levelers, and uncovered three illicit printers—one in Massachusetts, one in your majesty's western New Provinces, and one in New London itself." A whisper ran around the table: It was an open secret that the cellar press in the capital could print whatever they liked with only loose control, except for the most blatantly slanderous rumors and Leveler sedition. For there to be raids, the situation must be far worse than normal. "This ignores the usual rumbling in the colonies and dominions. Finally, police operations uncovered a plot to blow up the Western Summer Palace at Monterey—I would prefer not to discuss this in open cabinet until we have resolved the situation. Someone or something is stirring up Leveler activists, and there have been rumors of French livres greasing the wheels of treason. Certainly it takes money to run subversive presses or buy explosives, and it must be coming from somewhere."

Sir Roderick sat down, and Lord Douglass rose. "Your majesty, I would say that if adventures are contemplated overseas, and if this should coincide with a rise in the price of bread, the introduction of new taxes and duties, *and* an outburst of Leveler ranting, I should not like to face the consequences without the continental reserves at Fort Victoria ready to entrain for either coast, not to mention securing the loyalty of the local regiments in each parliamentary district."

"Well, then." The king frowned, his forehead wrinkling as if to withstand another fit of sneezing: "We shall have to see to such measures, shall we not?" He leaned forward in his chair. "But I want to hear more on this matter of where the homegrown thorns in our crown are obtaining their finances. It seems to me that if we can snip this odious weed in the bud, as it were, and demonstrate to the satisfaction of our peers the meddling of the dauphin at work in our garden, then it will certainly serve our purposes. Lord Douglass?"

"By all means, your majesty." The prime minister glanced at his minister for special affairs. "Sir Roderick, if you please, can you see to it?"

"Of course, my lord." The minister inclined his head toward his monarch. "As soon as we have something more than rumor and suspicion I will place it before your majesty."

"Now if we may return to the agenda?" The prime minister suggested.

"Certainly." The king nodded his assent, and Lord Dou-

glass cleared his throat, to continue with the next point on
the afternoon-long agenda. The meeting continued, and in
every way beside the sneezing fit it seemed a perfectly normal session of the Imperial Intelligence Oversight Committee, held before his imperial Majesty John the Fourth, king
of New Britain and dominions, in the Brunswick Palace on
Long Island in the early years of the twenty-first century.

Time would show otherwise . . .

On the other side of a flipped coin's fall, in an office two
hundred miles away in space and perhaps two thousand
years away from the court of King John in terms of historical divergence, another meeting was taking place.

"A shoot-out." The duke's tone of voice, normally icily
deliberate, rose slightly as he abandoned his chair and began
to pace the confines of his office. With close-cropped gray-
ing hair, and wearing an immaculately tailored dark suit, he
might have been mistaken for an investment banker or a
high-class undertaker—but appearances were very decep-
tive. The duke, as head of the Clan's security apparat, was
anything but harmless. He paused beneath a pair of steel
broadswords mounted on the wall above a battered circular
shield. "In the summer palace?" His tone hardened. "I find it
hard to believe that this was allowed to happen." He looked
up at the swords. "Who was supposed to be in charge of her
guard?"

The duke's secretary—his keeper of secrets—cleared his
throat. "Oliver, Baron Hjorth is of course responsible for the
well-being of all beneath his roof. In accordance with your
orders I requested that he see to Lady Helge's security." A
moment's pause to let the implication sink in. "Whether he
complied with your orders bears investigation."

The duke stopped pacing, standing in front of the broad
picture windows that looked out across the valley below the
castle. Heavily forested and seemingly empty of human
habitation, the river valley ran all the way to the coast, marking the northern border of the sprawling kingdom of Gruin-

markt from the Nordmarkt neighbors to the north. "And the lady Olga?"

"She protests in the strongest terms, my lord." The secretary shrugged slightly, his face expressionless. "I sent Roland to attend to her personally, to ensure she is adequately protected. For what it's worth, there were no identifying marks on the bodies. No tattoos, no indications of who they were. Not Clan. But they had weapons and equipment from the other side and I am—startled—that Lady Olga, even with help from our runaway, survived the incident."

"Our *runaway* is my niece, Matthias," the duke reminded his secretary. "A rather extraordinary woman." His expression hardened. "I want tissue samples, photographs, anything you can come up with. For the hit squad. Get them processed on the other side, run them across the FBI most-wanted database, pull whatever strings you can find, but I want to know who they were and who they thought they were working for. And how they got there. The palace was supposed to be securely doppelgängered. Why wasn't it?"

"Ah. I have already looked into that." Matthias waited.

"Well then?" The duke clenched his hands.

"About three years ago, Baroness Hildegarde ordered our agents on the other side—via the usual shell company—to let out one side of the doppelgänger facility to a secondary Clan-owned shipping company she was setting up. It was all aboveboard and conducted in public at Beltaigne, approved in full committee, but the shipping company moved away a year later to more suitable purpose-built facilities, and they in turn sub-let the premises. It was walled off from the original bonded store and converted into short-lease storage, leaving it wide open. Purely coincidentally, it covered the New Tower, and parts of the west wing of the palace were left undoppelgängered. Helge wouldn't have known enough to recognize this as unusual, but it left most of her suite wide open to attack by world-walkers from the other side."

"And where was Oliver, Baron Hjorth while this was going on?" the duke asked, deceptively mildly. A failure to doppelgänger the palace correctly—to ensure that it was

physically collated with secure territory in the other universe
to which the world-walking and occasionally squabbling
members of the Clan had access—was not a trivial oversight, not after the blood feud or civil war that had killed
three out of every four members of the six families only a
handful of decades ago.

"He was worrying about roofing costs, I imagine."
Matthias shrugged again, almost imperceptibly. "If he even
knew about it. After all, what does security matter if the
building caves in?"

"If." The duke frowned. "That slime-weasel Oliver is in
Baroness Hildegarde's pocket, you mark my words. An unfortunate coincidence that they can both deny responsibility
for, and Helge, Miriam as she calls herself, is left facing assassins? It's almost insultingly convenient. She's getting
slack—we shall have to teach her a lesson in manners."

"What are your orders regarding your niece, my lord?
Since she appears to have run away, like her mother before
her, she could be found in breach of the compact—"

"No, no need for that just yet." The duke walked slowly
back to his desk, his expression showing little sign of the
stiffness in his joints. "Let her move freely for now." He lowered himself into his chair and stared at Matthias. "I expect
to hear about her movements by and by. Has she made any
attempt to get in touch?"

"With us? I've heard no messages, my lord." Matthias
raised one hand, scratched an itch alongside his nose. "What
do you think she'll do?"

"What do *I* think?" The duke opened his mouth, as if
about to laugh. "She's not a trained security professional,
boy. She might do anything! But she *is* a trained investiga-
tive journalist, and if she's true to her instincts, she'll start
digging." He began to smile. "I really want to see what she
uncovers."

Meanwhile, in a city called Boston in a country called the
United States:

"You know something?" asked Paulette. "When I told you to buy guns and drive fast I wasn't, like, expecting you to actually *do* that." She put her coffee cup down, half-drained. There were dark hollows under her eyes, but apart from that she was as tidy as ever, not a hair out of place. Which, Miriam reflected, left her looking a bit like a legal secretary: short, dark, Italianate subtype.

Miriam shook her head. *I wish I could keep it together the way she does,* she thought. "You said, and I quote from memory, 'As your attorney I am advising you to buy guns and drive fast.' Right?" She smiled tiredly at Paulette. Her own coffee cup was untouched. When she'd arrived at the other woman's house with Brilliana d'Ost in tow, the release of tension had her throwing up in the bathroom toilet. Paulette's wisecrack was in poor taste—Miriam had actually killed a man less than twenty-four hours ago in self-defense, and now things were starting to look *really* messy.

"What's an attorney?" asked Brill, sitting up on the sofa, prim and attentive: nineteen or twenty, blond, and otherworldly in the terrifyingly literal way that only a Clan member could be.

"Not me, I'm a paralegal. Just in case you'd forgotten, Miriam. I'd have to study for another two years before I can sit for the bar exams."

"You signed up for the course like I asked? That's good."

"Yeah, well." Paulette put her empty mug down. "Do you want to go through it all again? Just so I know where I stand?"

"Not really, but . . ." Miriam glanced at Brill. "Look, here's the high points. This young lady is Brilliana d'Ost. She's kind of an illegal immigrant, no papers, no birth certificate, no background. She needs somewhere to stay while we sort things out back where she comes from. She isn't self-sufficient here—she met her very first elevator yesterday evening, and her first train this morning."

Paulette raised an eyebrow. "R-i-i-ght," she drawled. "I think I can see how this might pose some difficulties."

"I can read and write," Brill volunteered. "And I speak

English. I've seen *Dynasty* and *Rob Roy,* too." Brightly: "And *The Godfather,* that was the duke's favorite! I've seen that one three times."

"Hmm." Paulette looked her up and down then glanced at Miriam. "This is a kind of what you see is what you get proposition, is it?"

"Yes," Miriam said. "Oh, and her family wants her back. They might get violent if they find her, so she needs to be anonymous. All she's got are the clothes on her back. And then there's this." She passed Paulette a piece of paper. Paulette glanced at it, then raised her other eyebrow and did a double take.

"This is valid?" She held up the check.

"No strings." Miriam nodded. "At least, as long as Duke Angbard doesn't cut off the line of credit he gave me. You've got the company paperwork together, ready to sign? Good. What we do is, we open a company bank account. I pay *this* into it and issue myself with shares to the tune of fifty grand. We write you up as an employee, you sign the contract, I issue you your first paycheck—eight thousand, covers your first month only—and a signing bonus of another ten thousand. You then write a check back to the company for that ten thousand, and I issue you the shares and make you company secretary. Got that?"

"You want me as a director?" Paulette watched her closely. "Are you sure about that?"

"I trust you," Miriam said simply. "And I need someone on this side of the wall who's got signing authority and can run things while I'm away. I wasn't kidding when I told you to set this up, Paulie. It's going to be big."

Paulette stared at the banker's draft for fifty thousand dollars dubiously. "Blood money."

"Blood is thicker than water," Brill commented. "Why don't you want to take it?"

Paulette sighed. "Do I tell her?" she asked Miriam.

"Not yet." Miriam looked thoughtful. "But I promised myself a few days back that anything *I* start up will be clean. That good enough for you?"

"Yeah." Paulette turned toward the kitchen doorway, then paused. "Brilliana? Is it okay if I call you Brill?"

"Surely!" The younger woman beamed at her.

"Oh. Well, uh, this is the kitchen. I was going to make some fresh coffee, but I figure if you're staying here for a while I ought to start by showing you where things are and how not to—" She glanced at Miriam. "Do they have electricity?" she asked. Miriam shook her head minutely. "Oh sweet Jesus! Okay, Brill, the first thing you need to learn about the kitchen is how not to kill yourself. See, everything works by electricity. That's kind of—"

Miriam picked up a bundle of official papers and a pen, and wandered out into the front hall. *It's going to be okay,* she told herself. *Paulie's going to mother-hen her. Two days and she'll know how to cross the road safely, use a flush toilet, and work the washing machine.* Two weeks, and if Paulie didn't kill her, she'd be coming home late from nightclubs with a hangover. *If* she didn't just decide that the twenty-first century was too much for her, and hide under the spare bed. Which, as she'd grown up in a world that hadn't got much past the late medieval, was a distinct possibility. *Wouldn't be a surprise; it's too much for* me *at times,* Miriam thought, contemplating the stack of forms for declaring the tax status of a limited liability company in Massachusetts with a sinking heart.

That evening, after Paulette and Miriam visited the bank to open a business account and deposit the checks, they holed up around Paulie's kitchen table. A couple of bottles of red wine and a chicken casserole went a long way toward putting Brill at her ease. She even managed to get over the jittery fear of electricity that Paulie had talked into her in the afternoon to the extent of flipping light switches and fiddling with the heat on the electric stove. "It's marvelous!" she told Miriam. "No need for coal, it stays just as hot as you want it, and it doesn't get dirty! What do all the servants do for a living? Do they just laze around all day?"

"Um," said Paulette. One glance told Miriam that she was

suffering a worse dose of culture shock than the young transportee—her shoulders were shaking like jelly. "Like, that's the drawback, Brill. Where would *you* have the servants sleep, in a house like this?"

"Why, if there were several in the bedchamber you so kindly loaned—oh. I'm to drudge for my keep?"

"No," Miriam interrupted before Paulette could wind her up any further. "Brill, ordinary people don't have servants in their homes here."

"Ordinary? But surely this isn't—" Brill's eyes widened.

Paulette nodded at her. "That's me, common as muck!" she said brightly. "Listen, the way it works in this household is, if you make a mess, you tidy it up yourself. You saw the dishwasher?" Brill nodded, enthused. "There are other gadgets. A house this big doesn't *need* servants. Tomorrow we'll go get you some more clothes—" She glanced at Miriam for approval."—then do next month's food shopping, and I'll show you where everything's kept. Uh, Miriam, this is gonna slow everything up—"

"Doesn't matter." Miriam put her knife and fork down. She was, she decided, not only over-full but increasingly exhausted. "Take it easy. Brill needs to know how to function over here because if it all comes together the way I hope, she's going to be over here regularly on business. She'll be working with you, I hope." She picked up her wineglass. "Tomorrow I'm going to go call on a relative. Then I think I've got a serious road trip ahead of me."

"You're going away?" asked Brill, carefully putting her glass down.

"Probably." Miriam nodded. "But not immediately. Look, what I said earlier holds—you can go home whenever you want to, if it's an emergency. All you have to do is catch a cab around to the nearest Clan safe house and hammer on the door. They'll have to take you back. If you tell them I abducted you, they'll probably believe it—I seem to be the subject of some wild rumors." She smiled tiredly. "I'll give you the address in the morning, alright?" The smile faded. "One thing. Don't you *dare* bug out on Paulie without telling her first. They don't know about her and they might do something about her if they learn . . . mightn't they?"

Brill swallowed, then nodded. "I understand," she said.

"I'm sure you do." Miriam realized Paulette was watching her through narrowed eyes. "Brill has seen me nearly get my sorry ass shot to pieces. She knows the score."

"Yeah, well. I was meaning to talk to you about that, too." Paulette didn't look pleased. "What the hell is happening over there?"

"It's a mess." Miriam shook her head. "First, Olga tried to kill me. Luckily she gave me a chance to talk my way out of it first—someone tried to set me up while I was visiting you, last time. Then the shit really hit the fan. Last night I figured out that my accommodation was insecure, the hard way, then parties unknown tried to rub out Olga and me, both. *Multiple parties.* There are at least two factions involved, and I don't have a clue who this new bunch are, which is why I'm here and brought Brill—she's seen too much."

"A second gang? Jesus, Miriam, you're sucking them up like a Hoover! What's going on?"

"I wish I knew, believe me." She drained her wineglass. "Hmm. This glass is defective. Better fix it." Before she could reach for the bottle, Paulette picked it up and began to pour, her hand shaking slightly. "Had a devil of a time getting here, I can tell you. Nearly put my back out carrying Brill, then found some evil son of a bitch had booby-trapped the warehouse. Earlier I phoned Roland to come tidy up—someone murdered the site watchman—but instead someone put a bomb in it."

"I *told* you that smoothie would turn out to be a weasel," Paulette insisted. "It's him, isn't it?"

"No, I don't think so." Miriam shook her head. "Things are messy, very messy. We ran into one of Angbard's couriers on the train over, so I gave him a message that should shake things loose if it's anyone on his staff. And now . . . well." She pulled out the two lockets from her left pocket. "Spot the difference."

Paulette's breath hissed out as she leaned forward to study them. "Shit. That one on the left, the tarnished one—that's yours, isn't it? But the other—"

"Have a cigar. I took it off the first hired gun last night. He won't be needing it anymore."

"Mind if I? . . ." Paulette picked the two lockets up and sprang the catch. She frowned as she stared at the contents, then snapped them closed. "The designs are different."

"I guessed they would be." Miriam closed her eyes.

Brill stared at the two small silver disks as if they were diamonds or jewels of incalculable value. Finally she asked, timidly, "How can they be different? All the Clan ones are the same, aren't they?"

"Who says it's a Clan one?" Miriam scooped them back into her pocket. "Look, firstly I am going to get a good night's sleep. I suggest you guys do the same thing. In the morning, I'm going to hire a car. I'd like to be able to go home, just long enough to retrieve a disk, but—"

"No, don't do that," said Paulette.

Miriam looked at her. "I'm not stupid. I know they're probably watching the house in case I show up. It's just frustrating." She shrugged.

"It's not that bad," Paulette volunteered pragmatically. "Either they got the disk the first time they black-bagged you—or they didn't, in which case you know precisely where it is. Why not leave it there?"

"I guess so," Miriam said tiredly. "Yeah, you're right. It's safe where it is." She glanced at Brill, who mimed incomprehension until she was forced to smile. "Still. Tomorrow I'm going to spend some time in a museum. *Then*—" She glanced at Paulette.

"Oh no, you're not going to do *that* again," Paulie began.

"Oh yes, I am." Miriam grinned humorlessly. "It's the only way to crack the story wide open." Her eyes went wide. "Shit! I'd completely forgotten! I've got a feature to file with Steve, for *The Herald*! The deadline's got to be real soon! If I miss it there's no way I'll get the column—"

"Miriam."

"Yes, Paulie?"

"Why are you still bothering about that?"

"I—" Miriam froze for a moment. "I guess I'm still thinking of going back to my old life," she said slowly. "It's something to hang onto."

"Right." Paulette nodded. "Now tell me. How much money is there on that platinum card?"

Pause. "About one point nine million dollars left."

"Miriam?"

"Yes, Paulie?"

"As your legal advisor I am telling you to shut the fuck up and get a good night's sleep. You can sort out whether you're going to write the article tomorrow—but I'd advise you to drop it. Say you've got stomach flu or something. Then you can take an extra day over your preparations for the journey. Got it?"

"Yes, Paulie."

"And another thing?"

"What's that?"

"Drink your wine and shut your mouth, dear, you look like a fish."

The next day, Miriam pulled out her notebook computer—which was now acquiring a few scratches—and settled down to pound the keyboard while Paulette took Brill shopping. It wasn't hard work, and she already knew what she was going to write, and besides, it saved her having to think too hard about her future. The main headache was not having access to her Mac, or a broadband connection. Paulie, despite her brief foray into dot-com management, had never seen the point of spending money to receive spam at home. Finally she pulled out her mobile and dialed *The Herald*'s front desk. "Steve Blau, please," she said, and waited.

"Steve. Who's this?"

"Steve? It's Miriam." She took a deep breath. "About that feature."

"Deadline's this Thursday," he rumbled. "You needing an extension?"

She breathed out abruptly, nearly coughing into the phone. "No, no, I'm ready to e-mail you a provisional draft, see if it fits what you were expecting. Uh, I've had a bit of an exciting life lately, got a new phone number for you."

"Really?" She could almost hear his eyebrows rising.

"Yeah. Domestic incident, big-time." She extemporized hastily. "I'm having to look after my mother. She's had an incident. Broken hip. You want my new details?"

"Sure. Hang on a moment. Okay, fire away."

Miriam gave him her new e-mail and phone numbers. "Listen, I'll mail in the copy in about an hour's time. Is there anything else you're looking for?"

"Not right now." He sounded amused. "They sprang a major reorg on us right after our last talk, followed by a guerilla page-plan redesign; looks like that slot for a new columnist I mentioned earlier is probably going to happen. Weekly, op-ed piece on medical/biotech investment and the VC scene, your sort of thing. Can I pencil you in for it?"

Miriam thought furiously. "I'm busier than I was right after I left *The Weatherman,* but I figure I can fit it in. Only thing is, I'll need a month's notice to start delivering, and I'd like to keep a couple of generic op-ed pieces in the can in case I'm called away. I'm going to be doing a lot of head-down stuff in the next year or so. It won't stop me keeping up with the reading but it may get in the way of my hitting deadlines once in a blue moon. Could you live with that?"

"I'll have to think about it," he said. "I'm willing to make allowances. But you're a pro. You'd give me some warning wherever possible, right?"

"Of course, Steve."

"Okay. File that copy. Bye."

She put the phone down for a moment, eyes misting over. *I've still got a real life,* she told herself. *This shit hasn't taken everything over.* She thought of Brill, trapped by family expectations and upbringing. *If I could unhook their claws, I could go back to being the real me. Really.* Then she thought about the rest of them. About the room at the Marriott, and what had happened in it. About Roland, and her. *Maybe.*

She picked the phone up again. It was easier than thinking.

Iris answered almost immediately. "Miriam, dear? Where have you been?"

"Ma?" The full weight of her worries crashed down on her. "You wouldn't believe me if I told you! Listen, I'm onto a story. It's—" She struggled for a suitable metaphor. "It's as big as Watergate. Bigger, maybe. But there's people involved who're watching me. I'd like to spend some time with you, but I don't know if it would be safe."

"That's interesting." She could hear her adoptive mother's mind crunching gears even on the end of a phone. "So you can't come and visit me?"

"Remember what you told me about COINTELPRO, Ma?"

"Ah, those were the days! When I was a young firebrand, ah me."

"Ma!"

"Stuffing envelopes with Jan Six, before Commune Two imploded, picketings and sit-ins—did I tell you about the time the FBI bugged our phones? How we got around it?"

"Mom." Miriam sighed. "Really! That student radical stuff is so *old,* you know?"

"Don't you *old* me, young lady!" Iris put a condescending, amused tone in her voice. "Is your trouble federal, by any chance?"

"I wish it was." Miriam sighed again.

"Well then. I'll meet you at the playground after bridge, an hour before closing time." *Click.*

She'd hung up, Miriam realized, staring at her phone. "Oh sweet Jesus," she murmured. *Never, ever, challenge a one-time SDS activist to throw a tail.* She giggled quietly to herself, overcome by a bizarre combination of mirth and guilt—mirth at the idea of a late-fifties Jewish grandmother with multiple sclerosis giving the Clan's surveillance agents the slip, and guilt, shocking guilt, at the thought of what she might have unintentionally involved Iris in. She almost picked up the phone to apologize, to tell Iris not to bother—but that would be waving a red rag at a bull. When Iris got it into her mind to do something, not even the FBI and the federal government stood much chance of stopping her.

The playground. That's what she'd called the museum, when she was small. "Can we go to the playground?" she'd asked, a second-grader already eating into her parents' library cards, and Iris had smiled indulgently and taken her there, to run around the displays and generally annoy the old folks reading the signs under the exhibits until, energy exhausted, she'd flaked out in the dinosaur wing.

And *bridge.* Iris *never* played card games. That must mean . . . yes. The bridge over the Charles River. More confirmation that she meant the Science Museum, an hour before closing time. Right. Miriam grinned mirthlessly, remembering Iris's bedtime stories about the hairy years under FBI surveillance, the times she and Morris had been pulled in for questioning—but never actually charged with anything. When she was older, Miriam realized that they'd been too sensible, had dropped out to work in a radical bookstore and help with a homeless shelter before the hard-core idiots began cooking up bombs and declaring war on the System, a System that had ultimately gotten tired of their posturing and rolled over in its sleep, obliterating them.

Miriam whistled tunelessly between her teeth and plugged her cellular modem card back into the notebook, ready to send in her feature article. Maybe Iris could teach her some useful techniques. The way things were going, she needed every edge.

A landscape of concrete and steel, damp and gray beneath a sky stained dirty orange. The glare of streetlamps reflected from clouds heavy with the promise of sleet or rain tomorrow. Miriam swung the rental car around into the parking lot, lowered her window to accept a ticket, then drove on in search of a space. It was damply cold outside, the temperature dropping with nightfall, but eventually she found a free place and parked. The car, she noted, was the precise same shade of silver-gray as Iris's hair.

Miriam walked around the corner and down a couple of flights of stairs, then through the entrance to the museum.

Warm light flooded out onto the sidewalk, lifting her gloom. Paulette had brought Brill home earlier that afternoon, shaking slightly. The color- and pattern-enhanced marketing strategies of modern retail had finally driven Brill into the attack of culture shock Miriam had been expecting. They'd left Brill hunched up in front of the Cartoon Network on cable, so Paulette could give Miriam a lift to the nearest Avis rental lot. And now—

Miriam pushed through the doors and looked around. Front desk, security gates, a huge human-powered sailplane hanging from the ceiling over the turnstiles, staff busy at their desks—and a little old lady in a powered wheelchair, whirring toward her. Not so little, or so old. "You're late! That's not like you," Iris chided her. "Where have you been?"

"That's new," Miriam said, pointing to the chair.

"Yes, it is." Iris grinned up at her, impishly. "Did you know it can outrun a two-year-old Dodge Charger? *If* you know the footpaths through the park and don't give the bastards time to get out and follow you on foot." She stopped grinning. "Miriam, you're in *trouble*. What did I teach you about trouble?"

Miriam sighed. "Don't get into it to begin with, especially don't bring it home with you," she recited, "never start a war on two fronts, and especially don't start a land war in Asia. Yes, I *know*. The problem is, trouble came looking for me. Say, isn't there a coffee shop in the food court, around the corner from the gift shop?"

"I think I could be persuaded—*if* you tell me what's going on."

Miriam followed her mother's wheelchair along the echoing corridor, dodging the odd family group. It took them a few minutes, but finally Miriam got them both sorted out with drinks and a seat at a table well away from anyone else. "It was the shoe box," Miriam confessed. Iris had given her a shoe box full of items relating to her enigmatic birthmother, found stabbed in a park nearly a third of a century ago. After all those years gathering dust in the attic the locket still worked, dumping Miriam into a world drastically unlike her own. "If you hadn't given it to me, they wouldn't be staking out your house."

"Who do you think *they* are?"

Miriam swallowed. "They call themselves the Clan. There are six families in the Clan, and they're like this." She knotted her fingers together, tugged experimentally. "Turns out I'm, uh, well, how to put this? I'm not a *Jewish* princess. I'm a—"

"She was important," Iris interrupted. "Some kind of blue blood, right? Miriam, what does the Clan do that's so secret you can't talk but so important they need you alive?"

"They're—" Miriam stopped. "If I told you, they might kill you."

Iris raised an eyebrow. "I think you know better than that," she said quietly.

"But—"

"Stop trying to overprotect me!" Iris waved her attempted justification away. "You always hated it when I patronized you. So what is this, return-the-favor week? You're still alive, so you have something on them, if I know you. So it follows that you can look after your old mother, right? Doesn't it?"

"It's not that simple." Miriam looked at her mother and sighed. "If I knew you'd be safe . . ."

"Shut up and listen, girl." Miriam shut up abruptly and stared at her. Iris was watching her with a peculiar intensity. "You are by damn going to tell me *everything*. Especially who's after you, so that I know who to watch for. Because anyone who tries to get at you through me is going to get a very nasty surprise indeed, love." For a moment, Iris's eyes were icy-cold, as harsh as the assassin in the orangery at midnight, two days before. Then they softened. "You're all I've got left," she said quietly. "Humor your old ma, please? It's been a long time since anything interesting happened to me—interesting in the sense of the Chinese proverb, anyway."

"You always told me not to gossip," Miriam accused.

"Gossip is as gossip does." Iris cracked a smile. "Keep your powder dry and your allies briefed."

"I'll—" Miriam took a sip of her coffee. "Okay," she said, licking her dry lips. "This is going to take a long time to tell, but basically what happened was, I took the shoe box home and didn't do anything with it until that evening. Which probably wasn't a good thing, because . . ."

She talked for a long time, and Iris listened, occasionally prompting her for more detail but mostly just staring at her face, intently, with an expression somewhere between longing and disgust.

Finally Miriam ran down. "That's all, I guess," she said. "I left Brill with Paulie, who's looking after her. Tomorrow I'm going to take the second locket and, well, see if it works. Over here or over there." She searched Iris's face. "You believe me?" she asked, almost plaintively.

"Oh, I believe you, kid." Iris reached out and covered her hand with her own: older, thinner, infinitely familiar. "I—" She paused. "I haven't been entirely honest with you," she admitted. "I had an idea this was going to get weird before I gave you the box, but not like this. It seemed like a good time to pass it on when you began sniffing around their turf. Large-scale money laundering is exactly the sort of thing the, this Clan, would be mixed up in, and I suspected—well. I expected you to come back and ask me about it sooner, rather than simply jumping in. Maybe I should have warned you." She looked at Miriam, searchingly.

"It's okay, Ma." Miriam covered Iris's hand with her other.

"No, it's *not* okay," Iris insisted. "What I did was wrong! I should have—"

"Ma, shut up."

"If you insist." Iris watched her with a curious half-smile. "This second knotwork design—I want to see that. Can you show me sometime?"

"Sure." Miriam nodded. "Didn't bring it with me, though."

Her mother nodded. "What are you going to do next?"

"I'm—" Miriam sighed. "I warned Angbard that if anybody touched a hair on your head, he was dead meat. But now there's a second bunch after me, and I don't have a hot-line to their boss. I don't even know who their boss *is*."

"Neither did Patricia," murmured Iris.

"What did you say?"

"I'd have thought it was obvious," Iris pointed out quickly. "If she'd known, they wouldn't have gotten near her." She shook her head. "A really bad business, that." For a moment she looked angry, and determined—the same expression Miriam had glimpsed in a mirror recently. "And it hasn't gone away." She snorted. "Give me your secret phone number, girl."

"My secret—what?"

Iris grinned at her. "Okay, your dead-letter drop. So we can keep in touch when you go on your wanderings. You *do* want to keep your old mom informed of what the enemies of freedom and civilization are up to, don't you?"

"Ma!" Miriam smiled right back. "Okay, here it is," she said, scribbling her new, sanitized mobile number down on a piece of paper and sliding it over to Iris.

"Good." Iris tucked it away quickly. "This locket you found—you think it goes somewhere else, don't you?"

"Yes. That's the only explanation I can come up with."

"To another world, where everything will of course be completely different." Iris shook her head. "As if two worlds wasn't already one too many."

"And mystery assassins. Don't forget the mystery assassins."

"I'm not," said her mother. "From what you've been telling me . . ." She narrowed her eyes. "Don't trust *any* of them. Not the Clan, not even the one you bedded. They're all—they sound like—a bunch of vipers. They'll screw you as soon as you think you're safe."

"Ma." Miriam began to blush. "Oh, I don't *trust* them. At least, not to do anything with my best interests at heart."

"Then you're smarter than I was at your age." Iris pulled on her gloves. "Give an old lady a lift home? Or at least, back to the woods? It's a cold and scary night. Mind you, I may have forgotten to bring your red cloak, but any wolves who try to lay hands on this old granny will come off worse."

PAWNBROKER

It's no good," said Miriam, rubbing her forehead. "All I get is crossed eyes, blurred vision, and a headache. It doesn't *work*." She snapped the assassin's locket closed in frustration.

"Maybe it doesn't work here," Brill suggested. "If it's a different design?"

"Maybe." Miriam nodded. "Or then again, it's a different design and it came through on the other side. How do I know where I'd end up if I *did* get it to work here?" She paused, then looked at the locket. "Maybe it wasn't real clever of me to try that here," she said slowly. "I really ought to cross over before I try it again. If there's really a third world out there, how do we know there isn't a fourth? Or more? How do we know that using it twice in succession brings you back to the place you departed from—that travel using it is commutative? It raises more questions than it answers, doesn't it?"

"Yes—" Brill fell silent.

"Do you know anything about this?" Miriam asked.

"No." She shook her head slowly. "I don't—they never spoke about the possibility. Why should they? It was as much as anyone could do to travel between this world and the other, without invoking phantoms. Would testing a new sigil not be dangerous? If it by some chance carried you to another world where wild animals or storms waited . . ."

"Someone must have tried it." Miriam frowned. "Mustn't they?"

"You would have to ask the elders," Brill offered. "All I can tell is what I was told."

"Well, anyway," Miriam rubbed her forehead again, "if it works, it'll be one hell of a lever to use with Angbard. I'll just have to take this one and cross over to the other side before I try to go wherever its original owner came from. Then try from there."

"Can you do that?" Brill asked.

"Yes. But just one crossing gives me a cracking headache if I don't take my pills. I figure I can make two an hour apart. But if I run into something nasty on the far side—wherever this one takes me—I'll be in deep trouble if I need to get away from it in a hurry."

Malignant hypertension wasn't a term she could use with Brill, but she'd seen what it could do to people. In particular she'd seen a middle-aged man who'd not bothered to follow the dietary guidelines after his HMO doctor prescribed him an ancient and dubious monoamine oxidase inhibitor. He'd flatlined over the cheese board at a birthday party, the glass of sparkling white wine still at hand. She'd been in the emergency room when the ambulance brought him in, bleeding from nose and eyes. She'd been there when they turned the ventilator off and filled out the death certificate. She shook her head. "It'll take careful planning."

Miriam glanced at the window. Snow drifted down from a sky the color of shattered dreams. It was bitterly cold outside. "What I *should* do is go across, hole up somewhere and catch some sleep, then try to cross over the next day so I can run away if anything goes wrong. Trouble is, it's going to be just as cold on the other side as it is here. And if I have to run away, I get to spend two nights camping in the woods, in winter, with a splitting headache. I don't think that's a really great idea. And I'm limited to what I can carry."

When's Paulie due back? she wondered. *She'll be able to help.*

"What about a coaching-house?" Brill asked, practical-minded as ever.

"A coaching—" Miriam stopped dead. "But I can't—"

"There's one about two miles down the road from Fort Lofstrom." Brill looked thoughtful. "We dress you as a, an oracle's wife, summoned to a village down the coast to join your husband in his new parish. Your trap broke a wheel and—" She ran down. "Oh. You don't speak hoh'sprashe."

"Yup." Miriam nodded. "Doesn't work well, does it?"

"No." Brill wrinkled her nose. "What a nuisance! We could go together," she added tentatively.

"I think we'll have to do that," said Miriam. "Probably I play the mute mother and you play the daughter—I try to look older, you to look younger. Think it would work?"

From Brilliana's slow nod she realized that Brill did—and wasn't enthusiastic about it. "It might."

"It would also leave you stranded in the back of beyond up near, where was it, Hasleholm, if I don't come back, wouldn't it?" Miriam pointed out. "On the other hand, you'd be in the right place. You could make your way to Fort Lofstrom and tell Angbard what happened. He'd take care of you," she added. "Just tell him I ordered you to come along with me. He'll swallow that."

"I don't want to go back," Brilliana said evenly. "Not until I've seen more of this wonderful world."

Miriam nodded soberly at her. "Me too, kid. So we're not going to plan on me not coming back, are we? Instead, we're going to plan on us both going over, spending the night at a coach-house, and then walking down the road to the next one. They're only about twenty miles apart—it's a fair hike, but not impossible. Along the way, I disappear, and catch up with you later. We spend the night there, then we turn back—and cross back here. How does that sound?"

"Three days?" Brill looked thoughtful. "And you'll bring me back here?"

"Of course." Miriam brooded for a moment. "I think I want some more tea," she decided. "Want some?"

"Oh yes!" Brilliana sat up eagerly. "Is there any of Earl Grey's own blend?"

"I'll just check." Miriam wandered into Paulette's kitchen, her mind spinning gears like a car in neutral. She filled the kettle, set it on the hob to boil, began searching for tea bags. *There's got to be a way to make this work better,* she thought. The real problem was mobility. If she could just arrange how to meet up with Brill fifteen miles down the road without having to walk the distance herself—"Oh," she said, as the kettle began to boil.

"What is it?" asked Brill, behind her.

"It's so obvious!" Miriam said as she picked the kettle up. "I should have figured it out before."

"Figured? What ails you?"

She poured boiling water into the teapot. "A form of speech. I meant, I've worked out what I need to do." She put the lid on the pot, moved it onto a tray, and picked it up to carry back into the living room. "Go on."

"You've hatched a plan?"

"Yes." Miriam kicked the kitchen door shut behind her. "It's quite simple. I've been worrying about having to camp in the woods in winter, or make myself understood, or keep up appearances with you. That's wrong. What I should have been thinking about is how I can move *myself* about, over there, to somewhere where there's shelter, without involving anyone else. Right?"

"That makes sense." Brilliana looked dubious. "But how are you going to do that, unless you walk? You couldn't take a horse through. Come to think of it, I haven't seen any horses here—"

Miriam took a deep breath. "Brill, when Paulie gets back I think we're going to go shopping. For an all-terrain bicycle, a pair of night-vision goggles, a sewing machine, and some fabric . . ."

* * *

The devil was in the details. In the end it took Miriam two days to buy her bicycle. She spent the first day holed up with cycle magazines, spokehead Web sites, and the TV blaring extreme sports at her. The second day consisted of being patronized in successive shops by men in skintight neon Lycra bodysuits, to Brill's quietly scandalized amusement. In the end, the vehicle of Miriam's desire turned out to be a Dahon folding mountain bike, built out of chromed aluminium tubes. It wasn't very light, but at thirty pounds—including carrying case and toolset—she could carry it across easily enough, and it wasn't a toy. It was a real mountain bike that folded down into something she could haul in a backpack and, more importantly, something that could carry herself and a full load over dirt trails as fast as a horse.

"What *is* that thing?" Brill asked, when she finished unfolding it on a spread of newspapers on Paulette's living room carpet. "It looks like something you torture people with."

"That's a fair assessment." Miriam grimaced as she worked the allen keys on the saddle-post, trying to get it locked at a comfortable height. "I haven't ridden a bike in years. Hope I haven't forgotten how."

"When you sit on that thing, you can't possibly be modest."

"Well, no," Miriam admitted. "I plan to only use it out of sight of other people." She finished on the saddle and began hunting for an attachment place for the toolkit. "The Swiss army used to have a regiment of soldiers who rode these things, as mounted infantry—not cavalry. They could cover two hundred miles a day on roads, seventy a day in the mountains. I'm no soldier, but I figure this will get me around faster than my feet."

"You'll still need clothing," Brill pointed out. "And so will *I*. What I came across in isn't suitable for stamping around in the forest in winter! And we couldn't possibly be seen wearing your camping gear if we expect to stay in a coaching inn."

"Yup. Which is where this machine comes in." Miriam pointed to the other big box, occupying a large chunk of the floor. "I take it there's no chance that you already know how to use an overlocker?"

The overlocker took them most of the rest of the day to figure out, and it nearly drove Paulette to distraction when she came home from the errand she'd been running to find Miriam oiling a bicycle in the hall and Brill puzzling out the manual for an industrial sewing machine and a bunch of costume patterns Miriam had bought. "You're turning my house into an asylum!" she accused Miriam, after kicking her shoes off.

"Yeah, I am. How's the office hunt going?"

"Badly," snapped Paulette. Her voice changed: "Offices, oy, have we got offices! You should see our offices, such wonderful offices you have never imagined! By the way, how long have you been in business? There'll be a deposit if it's less than two years."

"Uh-huh." Miriam nodded. "How big a deposit?"

"Six months rent," Paulie swallowed. "For two thousand square feet with a loading bay and a thousand feet of office above it, that comes to about thirty thousand bucks. Plus municipal tax, sewer, electric and gas. And the broadband you want."

"Hmm." Miriam nodded to herself, then hit the quick-release bolts. The bike folded in on itself like an intricate origami sculpture and she locked it down in its most compact position, then eased the carrying case over it.

"Hey, that's real neat," Paulette said admiringly. "You turning into a fitness freak in your old age?"

"Don't change the subject." Miriam grunted, then upended the case and zipped it shut. Folded, the bike was a beast. She could get the thing comfortably on her back but would be hard put to carry anything else. *Hmm.* "Back in a minute." She shouldered the bike pack and marched to the back door that opened on Paulette's yard. "Here goes nothing," she muttered, and pulled out her locket.

Half an hour later she was back without the bike, staggering slightly, shivering with cold, and rubbing her sore fore-head. "Oh, I really don't need to do that so fast," she groaned.

"If you *will* do that with no preparation—" Paulette began to say waspishly.

"No, no." Miriam waved her away. "I took my pills, boss, honest. It's just *really* cold over there."

"Where did you stash it?" Paulie asked practically.

"Where your back wall is, over on the other side, where there's nothing but forest. *Brrr.* Up against a tree, I cut a gash in the bark." She brandished her knife. "Won't be hard to find if we go over from here: Main thing will be walking to the road, the nearest one is about half a mile away. Better go in the morning."

"Right," Paulette said skeptically. "About the rent."

"Yeah." Miriam nodded. "Look, give me fifteen minutes to recover and I'll get my coat. Then we can go look over that building, and if it's right we'll go straight on to the bank and move another whack of cash so you can wave a deposit under their nose." She straightened up. "We'll take Brill. There's a theatrical costume shop we need to check out; it might speed things up a bit." Her expression hardened. "I'm tired of waiting, and the longer this drags on the harder it'll be to explain it to Angbard. If I don't get in touch soon, I figure he'll cut off my credit until I surface. It's time to hit the road."

Two days later, a frigid morning found Miriam dozing fitfully on a lumpy, misshapen mattress with a quietly snoring lump to her left. She opened her eyes. *Where am I?* she wondered for a moment, then memory rescued the day. *Oh.* A pile of canvas bags before her nose formed a hump up against the rough, unpainted planks of the wall. The snoring lump twitched, pushing her closer to the edge. The light streamed in through a small window, its triangular tiles of glass uneven and bubbled. She'd slept fully dressed except for her boots and cloak, and she felt filthy. To make matters worse, something had bitten her in the night, found her to its taste, and invited its family and friends along for Thanksgiving.

"Aargh." She sat up and swung her feet out, onto the floor. Even through her wool stockings the boards felt cold as ice. The jug under the bed was freezing cold too, she discovered as she squatted over it to piss. In fact, the air was so chilly it leached all the heat out of any part of her anatomy she exposed to it. She finished her business fast and shoved the pot back under the bed to freeze.

"Wake up," she called softly to Brilliana. "Rise and shine! We've got a good day ahead!"

"Oh, my head." Brill surfaced bleary-eyed and disheveled from under the quilt. "*Your* hostelries aren't like this."

"Well, this one won't stay like this for long if I get my way," Miriam commented. "My mouth tastes like something died in it. Let me get my boots on and warm my toes up a bit."

"Hah." Brilliana's expression was pessimistic. "They let the fire run low, I'd say." She found the chamber pot. Miriam nodded and looked away. *So much for en suite bathrooms,* she thought mordantly. "You stand up, now," Brill ordered after a minute.

"Okay. How do I look?" asked Miriam.

"Hmm. I think you will pass. Don't brush your hair until we are out of sight, though. It's too clean to be seen in daylight, from all those marvelous soaps everyone uses on the other side, and we don't want to attract attention. Humph. So what shall we do today, my lady?"

"Well, I think we'll start by eating breakfast and paying the nice man." *Nice* was not an adjective Miriam would normally use on a hotelier like the one lurking downstairs—back home she'd be more inclined to call the police—but standards of personal service varied wildly in the Gruinmarkt. "Let's hit the road to Hasleholm. As soon as we're out of sight, I'm going to vanish. You remembered your pistol?"

Brill nodded.

"Okay, then you're set up. It *should* just be a quiet day's walk for you. If you run into trouble, first try to get off the road, then shoot—I don't want you taking any chances, even if there isn't much of a bandit problem around these parts in winter. Luckily you're more heavily armed than anyone you could possibly meet except a Clan caravan."

"Right." Brill nodded uncertainly. "You're sure that strange contraption will work?"

Miriam nodded. "Trust me."

Breakfast below consisted of two chipped wooden bowls of oatmeal porridge, salted, eaten in the kitchen under the watchful (if squinting) eyes of the publican's wife—which made it harder for Miriam to palm her pills. She made a song and dance of reciting some kind of grace prayer over the bowls. Miriam waited patiently, moving her lips randomly—her mute and incomprehending condition explained by Brill, in her capacity as long-suffering daughter.

Barely half an hour later, Miriam and Brill were on the road again, heading toward the coast, breath steaming in the frigid morning air. It was bitterly dry, like an icy desert. A heavy frost had fallen overnight, but not much snow. Miriam hunched beneath a heavy canvas knapsack that held her bicycle and extra supplies. Brill, too, bore a heavy bag, for Miriam had made two trips through to cache essential supplies before they began this trip. Although they'd come only two miles from Paulette's house, they were centuries away in the most important way imaginable. Out here, even a minor injury such as a twisted ankle could be a disaster. But they had certain advantages that normally only the Clan and its constituent families would have—from their modern hiking boots to the hefty automatic pistol Brill carried in a holster concealed beneath her Thinsulate-lined cloak.

"This had better work." Miriam's teeth chattered slighly as she spoke. "I'm going to feel *really* stupid if it turns out that this locket doesn't work here, either."

Brill said pragmatically, "my mother said you could tell if they're dead. Have you looked at it since we came through?"

"No." Miriam fumbled in her pouch for it. It clicked open easily and she shut it at once. "Ick. It'll work, alright, if I don't spill my guts. It feels *rougher* than the other one."

Frozen leaf skeletons crunched beneath their boots. The

post house was soon out of sight, the road empty and almost untraveled in winter. Bare trees thrust limbs out above them, bleak and barren in the harsh light of morning. "Are we out of sight, yet?" asked Miriam.

"Yes." Brill stopped walking. "Might as well get an early start."

Miriam paused beside her. She shuffled her feet. "Don't wait long. If I don't return within about five minutes, assume it means everything's alright. Just keep walking and I'll join you at the post house. If you hear anyone coming on the road, hide. If I'm late, wait over for one day then buy a horse or mule, head for Fort Lofstrom, and ask to be taken to Angbard. Clear?"

"Clear." For a moment Brill froze, then she leaned forward and embraced Miriam. "Sky Father protect you," she whispered.

"And you," said Miriam, more surprised than anything else. Abruptly she hugged Brill back. "Take care." Then she pulled away, pulled out the assassin's locket, and stood in the middle of the road staring into its writhing depths.

It was twelve o'clock, and all the church bells in Boston were chiming noon.

The strange woman received nothing more than covert glances as she walked along The Mall, eyes flickering to either side. True, she wore a heavy backpack—somewhat singular for a woman—and a most peculiar cap, and her dress was about as far from fashionable as it was possible to be without street urchins harassing her with accusations of vile popery; but she walked with an air of granite determination that boded ill for anyone who got in her way.

Traffic was light but fast, and she seemed self-conscious as she looked both ways repeatedly before crossing the street. An open Jolly-car rumbled past behind her, iron wheels striking sparks from the cobblestones. There was a burst of raucous laughter from the tars within, returning to the North Station for the journey back to the royal dockyards. She dodged nimbly, then reached the safety of the sidewalk.

The pedestrian traffic was thicker near the fish market and the chandlers and other merchant suppliers. The woman glanced at a winter chestnut seller, raised her nose as she sidestepped a senescent pure-collector mumbling over his sack of dogshit, then paused on the corner of The Mall and Jefferson Street, glancing briefly over one shoulder before muttering into her scarf.

"Memo: This is *not* Boston—at least, not the Boston I know. All the street names are wrong and the buildings are stone and brick, not wood or concrete. Traffic drives on the left and the automobiles—there aren't many—they've got chimneys, like steam locomotives. But the signs are in English and the roads are made of cobblestones or asphalt and it *feels* like Boston. Weird, really weird. It's more like home than Niejwein, anyway."

She carried on down the street, mumbling into the tie-clip microphone pinned inside her scarf. A brisk wind wheezed down the street, threatening to raise it from her head: She tugged down briskly, holding it in place.

"I see both men and women in public—more men than women. Dress style is—hmm. Victorian doesn't describe it, exactly. Post-Victorian, maybe? Men wear cravats or scarves over high collars, with collarless double-breasted suits and big greatcoats. Hats all round, lots of hats, but I'm seeing suit jackets with yellow and blue stripes, or even louder schemes." She strode on, past a baroque fire hydrant featuring cast-iron Chinese dragons poised ready to belch a stream of water. "Women's costume is all tightly tailored jackets and hems down to the ground. Except some of the younger ones are wearing trousers under knee-length skirts. Sort of Oriental in style." A woman pedaled past her on a bicycle, back primly upright. The bike was a black bone-shaker. "Hm. For cycling, baggy trousers and something like a Pakistani tunic. Everyone wears a hat or scarf." She glanced left. "Shop prices marked in the windows. I just passed a cobbler's with a row of metal lasts and leather samples on display and *Jesus Christ*."

She paused and doubled back to stare into the small, grimy windows of the shop she'd nearly passed. A distant buzzing filled her ears. "A mechanical adding machine—electric motor drive, with nixie tubes for a display. That's a divide key, what, nineteen-thirties tech? Punched cards? Forties? Wish I'd paid more attention in the museum. These guys are a *long* way ahead of the Gruinmarkt. Hey, that looks like an Edison phonograph, but there's no trumpet and those are tubes at the back. And a speaker." She stared closer. The price . . . "price in pounds, *shillings,* and pennies," she breathed into her microphone.

Miriam paused. A sense of awe stole over her. *This* isn't *Boston,* she realized. *This is something else again.* A whole new world, one that had vacuum tubes and adding machines and steam cars—a shadow fell across her. She glanced up and the breath caught in her throat. *And airships,* she thought. "Airship!" she muttered. It was glorious, improbably streamlined, the color of old gold in the winter sunshine, engines rattling the window glass as it rumbled overhead, pointing into the wind. *I can really work here,* she realized, excitedly. She paused, looking in the window of a shipping agent, Greenbaum et Pty, "gateways to the world."

"'Scuse me, ma'am. Can I help you with anything?"

She looked down, hurriedly. A big, red-faced man with a bushy moustache and a uniform, flat-topped blue helmet—*oops,* she thought. "I hope so," she said timidly. *Gulp. Try to fake a French accent?* "I am newly arrived in, ah, town. Can you kind sir direct me to a decent and fair pawnbroker?"

"Newly arrived?" The cop looked her up and down dubiously, but made no move toward either his billy club or the brass whistle that hung on a chain around his neck. Something about her made up his mind for him. Maybe it was the lack of patching or dirt on her clothes, or the absence of obvious malnutrition. "Well now, a pawnbroker—you'll not want to be destitute within city limits by nightfall, hear? The poorhouse is near to overflowing this season and you wouldn't want a run-in with the bench, now, would ye?"

Miriam bobbed her head. "Thank you kindly, sir, but I'll

be well looked after if I can just raise enough money to contact my sister. She and her husband sent for me to help with the children."

"Well then." He nodded. "Go down Jefferson here, turn a left into Highgate. That'll bring you to Holmes Alley. *Don't* go down the Blackshaft by mistake, it's an odious rookery and you'll never find your way out. In Holmes Alley you can find the shop of Erasmus Burgeson, and he'll set you up nicely."

"Oh *thank* you," Miriam gushed, but the cop had already turned away—probably looking for a vagrant to harass.

She hurried along for a block then, remembering the cop's directions, followed them. More traffic passed on the road and overhead. Tractors pulling four or even six short trailers blocked the street intermittently, and an incongruous yellow pony trap clattered past. Evidently yellow was the interuniverse color of cabs, although Miriam couldn't guess what Boston's environmentalists would have made of the coal burners. There were shops here, shops by the dozen, but no department stores, nor supermarkets, or gas-burning cars, or color photographs. The advertisements on the sides of the buildings were painted on, simple slogans like BUY EDISON'S ROSE PETAL SOAP FOR SKIN LIKE FLOWER BLOSSOM. And there were, now she knew what to look for, no beggars.

A bell rang as Miriam pushed through the door of Erasmus Burgeson's shop, beneath the three gold spheres that denoted his trade. It was dark and dusty, shelves racked high with table settings, silverware, a cabinet full of pistols, other less identifiable stuff—in the other side of the shop, rack after rack of dusty clothing. The cash register, replete with cherubim and gold leaf, told its own story: And as she'd hoped, the counter beside it displayed a glass lid above a velvet cloth layered in jewelry. There didn't seem to be anybody in the shop. Miriam looked about uneasily, trying to take it all in. *This is what people here consider valuable,* she thought. *Better get a handle on it.*

A curtain at the back stirred as a gaunt figure pushed into

the room. He shambled behind the counter and turned to stare at her. "Haven't seen you in here before, have I?" he asked, quizzically.

"Uh, no." Miriam shuffled. "Are you Mr. Burgeson?" she asked.

"The same." He didn't smile. Dressed entirely in black, his sleeves and trousers thin as pipe cleaners, all he'd need would be a black stovepipe hat to look like a revenant from the Civil War. "And who would you be?"

"My name is Miriam, uh, Fletcher." She pursed her lips. "I was told you are a pawnbroker."

"And what else would I be in a shop like this?" He cocked his head to one side, like a parrot, his huge dark eyes probing at her in the gloom.

"Well. I'm lately come to these shores." She coughed. "And I am short of money, if not in posessions that might be worth selling. I was hoping you might be able to set me up."

"Posessions." Burgeson sat down—perched—on a high, backless wooden stool that raised his knees almost to the level of the counter-top. "It depends what type of posession you have in mind. I can't buy just any old tat now, can I?"

"Well. To start with, I have a couple of pieces of jewelry." He nodded encouragingly, so Miriam continued. "But then, I have in mind something more substantial. You see, where I come from I am of not inconsiderable means, and I have not entirely cut myself off from the old country."

"And what country would that be?" asked Burgeson. "I only ask because of the requirements of the Aliens and Sedition Act," he added hastily.

"That would be—" Miriam licked her lips. "Scotland."

"Scotland." He stared at her. "With an accent like that," he said with heavy irony. "Well, well, well. Scotland it is. Show me the jewelry."

"One moment." Miriam walked forward, peered down at the countertop. "Hmm. These are a bit disappointing. Is this all you deal in?"

"Ma'am." He hopped down from the stool. "What do you take me for? This is the common stock on public display, where any mountebank might smash and grab. The better class I keep elsewhere."

"Oh." She reached into her pouch and fumbled for a moment, then pulled out what she'd been looking for. It was a small wooden box—purchased from a head shop in Cambridge, there being a pronounced shortage of cheap wooden jewelry boxes on the market—containing two pearl earrings. Real pearls. Big ones. "For starters, I'd like you to put a value on these."

"Hmm." Burgeson picked the box up, chewing his lower lip. "Excuse me." He whipped out a magnifying lens and examined them minutely. "I'll need to test them," he murmured, "but if these are real pearls, they're worth a pretty penny. Where did you get them?"

"That is for me to know and you to guess." She tensed.

"Hah." He grinned at her cadaverously. "You'd better have a good story next time you try to sell them. I'm not sticking my neck in a noose for your mistress if she decides to send the thief-takers after you."

"Hmm. What makes you think I'm a light-fingered servant?" she asked.

"Well." He looked down his nose at her. "Your clothes are not what a woman of fashion, or even of her own means, would wear—"

"Fresh off the boat," Miriam observed.

"And earrings are among the most magnetic of baubles to those of a jackdaw disposition," he added.

"And wanting a suit of clothes that does *not* mark me out as a stranger," Miriam commented.

"Besides which," he added with some severity, "*Scotland* has not existed for a hundred and seventy years. It's all part of Grande Bretaigne."

"Oh." Miriam covered her mouth. *Shit!* "Well then." She mustered up a sickly smile. "How about this?"

The quarter-kilogram bar of solid gold was about an inch wide, two inches long, and half an inch thick. It sat on the display case like an intrusion from another world, shimmering with the promise of wealth and power and riches.

"Well now," breathed Burgeson, "if this is what ladies of means pay their bills with in Scotland, maybe it's not such an unbelievable fiction after all."

Miriam nodded. *It had better cover the bills,* she thought, *the damn thing set me back nearly three thousand dollars.* "It all depends how honest you aren't," she said briskly. "There are more where this one comes from. I'm looking to buy several things, including but not limited to money. I need to fit in. I don't care if you're fiddling your taxes or lying to the government, all I care about is whether you're honest with your customers. You don't know me, and if you don't want to, you'll never see me again. On the other hand, if you say 'yes'—" she met his eyes—"this need not be our last transaction. Not by a very long way."

"Hmm." Burgeson stared right back at her. "Are you in French employ?" he asked.

"Huh?"

Miriam's fleeting look of puzzlement seemed to reassure him. "Well *that's* good," he said genially. "Excuse me while I fetch the aqua regia: If this is pure I can advance you, oh, ten pounds immediately and another, ahum—" He picked up the gold bar and placed it on the balance behind him. "—sixty two and eight shillings by noon tomorrow."

"I don't think so." Miriam shook her head. "I'll take ten today, and sixty tomorrow—plus five full pounds' credit in your shop, here and now, for goods you hold." She'd been eyeing the price tags. The shilling, a twentieth of a pound, seemed to occupy the same role as the dollar back home, except that they went further. Pounds were *big* currency.

"Ridiculous." He stared at her. "Three pounds."

"Four."

"Done," he said, unnervingly rapidly. Miriam had a feeling that she'd been had, somehow, but nodded. He strode over to the door and flipped the sign in the window pane to CLOSED. "Now by all means, let me test out this bar. I'll just take a sample with this scalpel, mind . . ." He hurried into the back room. A minute later he re-emerged, bearing a glass measuring cylinder full of water into which he dropped the gold bar. Scribbled measurements followed. Finally he nodded. "Oh, most satisfying," he muttered to himself before looking at her. "Your sample is indeed of acceptable purity," he said, looking almost surprised. Reaching into an inner pocket he produced a battered wallet, from which he plucked improbably large banknotes. "Nine one-pound notes, milady, the balance in silver and a few coppers. I hope these are to your satisfaction; the bank across the street will happily exchange them, I assure you." Next he produced a fountain pen and a ledger, and a wax brick and a candle and a metal die. "I shall just make out this promissory note for sixty pounds to you. If you would like to select from my wares, I can work while you equip yourself."

"Do you have a measuring tape?" she asked.

"Indeed." He pulled one down from a hook behind the counter. "If you need any alterations making, Missus Borisovitch across the way is a most excellent seamstress, works while you wait. And her daughter is a fine milliner, too."

Over the next hour, Miriam ransacked the pawnbroker's shop. The range of clothing hanging in mothballs from rails all the way up to the ceiling, a dizzying twenty feet up, was huge and strange, but she knew what she wanted—anything that wouldn't look too alien while she realized her liquid assets and found a real dressmaker to equip her for the sort of business she intended to conduct. Which would almost certainly require formal business wear, as high finance and legal work usually did back home. For a miracle, Miriam discovered a matching jacket, blouse, and long skirt that was in good condition and close enough to her size to fit. She changed in Burgeson's cramped, damp-smelling cellar while he reopened the shop. It took some getting used to the outfit—the jacket was severely tailored, and the blouse had a high stiff collar—but in his dusty mirror she saw someone not unlike the women she'd passed on her way into town.

"Ah." Burgeson nodded to her. "That is a good choice. It will, however, cost you one pound fourteen and sixpence."

"Sure." Miriam nodded. "Next. I want a history book."

"A history book." He looked at her oddly. "Any particular title?"

She smiled thinly. "One covering the past three hundred years, in detail."

"Hmm." Burgeson ducked back into the back of the shop. While he was gone, Miriam located a pair of kidskin gloves and a good topcoat: The hats all looked grotesque to her eye, but in the end she settled on something broad-brimmed and floppy, with not too much fur. He returned and dumped a hardbound volume on the glass display case. "You could do worse than start with this. *Alfred's Annals of the New British.*"

"I could." She stared at it. "Anything else?"

"Or." He pulled another book up—bound in brown paper, utterly anonymous, thinner and lighter. "This." He turned it to face her, open at the fly-leaf.

"The Hanoverian Exodus Reconsidered"—she bit her lip when she saw the author. "Karl Marx. Hmm. Keep this on the bottom shelf, do you?"

"It's only prudent," he said, apologetically closing it and sliding it under the first book. "I'd strongly recommend it, though," he added. "Marx pulls no punches."

"Right. How much for both of them?"

"Six shillings for the Alfred, a pound for the Marx—you *do* realize that simply being caught with a copy of it can land you a flogging, if not five years exile in Canadia?"

"I didn't." She smiled, suppressing a shudder. "I'll take them both. And the hat, gloves, and coat."

"It's been a pleasure doing business with you, madam," he said fervently. "When shall I see you again?"

"Hmm." She narrowed her eyes. "No need for the money tomorrow. I will not be back for at least five days. But if you want another of those pieces—"

"How many can you supply?" he asked, slipping the question in almost casually.

"As many as you need," she replied. "But on the next visit, no more than two."

"Well then." He chewed his lower lip. "For two, assuming

this one tests out correctly and the next do likewise, I will pay the sum of two hundred pounds." He glanced over his shoulder. "But not all at once. It's too dangerous."

"Can you pay in services other than money?" she asked.

"It depends." He raised an eyebrow. "I don't deal in spying, sedition, or popery."

"I'm not in any of those businesses," she said. "But I'm really, truly, from a long way away. I need to establish a toe-hold here that allows me to set up an import/export business. That will mean . . . hmm. Do you need identity papers to move about? Passports? Or to open a bank account, create a company, hire a lawyer to represent me?"

He shook his head. "From *too* far away," he muttered. "God help me, yes to all of those."

"Well, then." She looked at him. "I'll need papers. *Good* papers, preferably real ones from real people who don't need them anymore—not killed, just the usual, a birth certificate from a babe who died before their first birthday," she added hastily.

"You warm the cockles of my heart." He nodded slowly. "I'm glad to see you appear to have scruples. Are you sure you don't want to tell me where you come from?"

She raised a finger to her lips. "Not yet. Maybe when I trust you."

"Ah, well." He bowed. "Before you leave, may I offer you a glass of port? Just a little drink to our future business relationship."

"Indeed you may." She smiled, surreptitiously pushing back her glove to check her watch. "I believe I have half an hour to spare before I must depart. My carriage turns back into a pumpkin at midnight."

PART 2

❧

POINT OF DIVERGENCE

hISTORY LESSON

You are telling me that you *don't know* where she is?"
The man standing by the glass display case radiated disbelief, from his tensed shoulders to his drawn expression.

Normally the contents of the case—precious relics of the Clan, valuable beyond belief—would have fascinated him, but right now his attention was focused on the bearer of bad news.

"I told you she'd be difficult." The duke's secretary was unapologetic. He didn't sneer, but his expression was one of thinly veiled impatience. "You are dealing with a woman who was born and raised on the other side; she was clearly going to be a handful right from the start. I told you that the best way to deal with her would be to coopt her and move her in a direction she was already going in, but you wouldn't listen. And after that business with the hired killer—"

"That *hired killer* was my own blood, I'll thank you to remember." Esau's tone of voice was ominously low.

"I don't care whether he was the prince-magistrate of Xian-Ju province, it was dumb! Now you've told Angbard's men that someone outside the Clan is trying to kill her, and you've driven her underground, *and* you've ruined her usefulness to me. I had it all taken care of until you attacked her. And then, to go after her but kill the wrong woman by mistake when I had everything in hand . . . !"

"You didn't tell us she was traveling in company. Or hiding in the lady Olga's rooms. Nor did we expect Olga's lady-in-waiting to get nosy and take someone else's bait. We're not the only ones to have problems. You said you had her as good as under control?" Esau turned to stare at Matthias. Today the secretary wore the riding-out garb of a minor nobleman of the barbarian east: brocade jacket over long woolen leggings, a hat with a plume of peacock feathers, and riding boots. "You think forging the old man's will takes care of anything at all? Are you losing your grip?"

"No." Matthias rested his hand idly on his sword's hilt. "Has it occurred to you that as Angbard's heir she would have been more open to suggestions, rather than less? Wealth doesn't necessarily translate into safety, you know, and she was clearly aware of her own isolation. I was trying to get her under control, or at least frightened into cooperating, by lining up the lesser families against her and positioning myself as her protector. You spooked her instead, before I could complete the groundwork. You exposed her to too much too soon, and the result is our shared loss. All the more so, since *someone*—whoever—tried to rub her out with Lady Olga."

"And whose fault is it that she got away?" Esau snarled quietly. "Whose little tripwire failed?"

"Mine, I'll admit." Matthias shrugged again. "But I'm not the one around here who's blundering around in the dark. I really wanted to enlist her in our cause. Willingly or unwillingly, it doesn't matter. With a recognized heir in our pocket, we could have enough votes that when we get rid of Angbard . . . well. If that failed, we'd be no worse off with her dead, but it was hardly a desirable goal. It's a good thing for you that I've got some contingency plans in hand."

"If the balance of power in the Clan tips too far toward the Lofstrom-Thorold-Hjorth axis, we risk losing what leverage we've got," warned Esau. "Never mind the old bat's power play. What did she think she was up to, anyway? If the council suspected . . ." He shook his head. "You have to get this back under control. Find her and neutralize her, or we likely lose all the ground we have made in the past two years."

"I risk losing a lot more than that," Matthias reminded him pointedly. "Why did your people try to kill her? She was a natural dissident. More use to us alive than dead."

"It's not for the likes of you to question our goals." Esau glared.

Matthias tightened his grip on his sword and turned slowly aside, keeping his eyes on Esau the whole time. "Retract that," he said flatly.

"I—" Esau caught his eye. A momentary nod. "Apologize."

"We are partners in this," Matthias said quietly, "to the extent that both our necks are forfeit if our venture comes to light. That being the case, it is essential that I know not only what your organization's intended actions are, but *why* you act as you do—so that I can anticipate future conflicts of interest and avoid them. Do you understand?"

Esau nodded again. "I told you there might be pre-existing orders. There was indeed such an order," he said reluctantly. "It took time to come to light, that's all."

"What? You mean the order for—gods below, you're still trying to kill the mother and her *infant*? After what, a third of a century?"

It was Esau's turn to shrug. "Our sanctified elder never rescinded the command, and it is not for us to question his word. Once they learned of the child's continued existence, my cousins were honor-bound to attempt to carry out the orders."

"That's as stupid as anything I've ever heard from the Clan council," Matthias commented dryly. "Times change, you know."

"*I* know! But where would we be without loyalty to our forefathers?" Esau looked frustrated for a moment. Then he pointed to the glass display case. "Continuity. Without it, what would the Clan be? Or the hidden families?"

"Without—that?" Matthias squinted, as against a bright light. A leather belt with a curiously worked brass buckle, a knife, a suit of clothes, a leatherbound book. "That's not the Clan, whatever you think. That's just where the Clan began."

"My ancestor, too, you know."

Matthias shook his head. "It wasn't clever, meeting here," he murmured.

"We're safe enough." Esau turned his back on the Founder's relics. "The question is, what are we to do now?"

"If you can get your relatives to stop trying to kill her, we can try to pin the blame on someone else," Matthias pointed out. "A couple of candidates suggest themselves, mostly because they *have* been trying to kill her. If we do that then we can go back to plan A, which you'll agree is the most profitable outcome of this situation."

"Not possible." Esau draw a finger across his throat. "The elders spoke, thirty-three years ago."

Matthias sighed. "Well, if you insist, we can play it your way. But it's going to be a lot harder, now. I suppose if I can get my hands on her foster-mother that will probably serve as a lure, but it's going to cost you—"

"I believe I can arrange a gratuity if you'd take care of this loose end for us. Maybe not on the same scale as owning your own puppet countess, but sufficient recognition of your actions."

"Well, that would be capital. I'll set the signs and alert my agents. At least here's something we can agree on."

"Indeed."

Matthias opened the door into the outer receiving room of the cramped old merchant's house. "Come on."

Esau followed Matthias out of the small storeroom and down a narrow staircase that led out into the courtyard of the house. "So what do you propose to do once she's dead?"

"Do?" Matthias stopped and stared at the messenger, his expression unreadable. "I'm going to see if I can salvage the situation and go right on as I was before. What did you expect?"

Esau tensed. "Do you really think you can take control of the Clan's security—even from your current position—without being an actual inner family member and Clan shareholder?"

Matthias smiled, for a moment. "Watch me."

Gathering twilight. Miriam hid from the road behind a dead-fall half buried in snow while she stripped off her outer garments. Her teeth chattering from cold as she pulled on a pair of painfully cold jeans. She folded her outfit carefully into the upper half of her pack, then stacked the disguise she'd started out wearing in the morning on top. Then she unfolded and secured the bike. Finally she hooked the bulky night-vision glasses around her face—*like wearing a telescope in front of each eye,* she thought—zipped the seam in the backpack that turned it into a pair of panniers, slung them over the bike, and set off.

The track flew past beneath her tires, the crackle of gravel and occasional pop of a breaking twig loud in the forest gloom. The white coating that draped around her seemed to damp out all noise, and the clouds above were huge and dark, promising to drop a further layer of fine powdery snow across the scene before morning.

Riding a bike wasn't exactly second nature, but the absence of other traffic made it easier to get to grips with. The sophisticated gears were a joy to use, making even the uphill stretches at least tolerable. *Seven-league boots,* she thought dreamily. The other town, whatever it was called, not-Boston, was built for legs and bicycles. She'd have to buy one next time she went there, whenever that was. Despite her toast to the prospects of future business with Burgeson, she had her reservations. Poor Laws, Sedition Acts, and a cop who obligingly gave directions to a clearly bent pawnbroker—it added up to a picture that made her acutely nervous. *It's so complex! What did he mean, there's no Scotland? Until I know what their laws and customs are like it's going to be too dangerous to go back.*

The miles spun by. After an hour and a half Miriam could feel them in her calf muscles, aching with every push on the pedals—but she was making good speed, and by the time darkness was complete the road dipped down toward the coast, paralleling the Charles River. Eventually she turned a corner, taking her into view of a hunched figure squatting by the roadside.

Miriam braked hard, jumped off the bike. "Brill?" she asked.

"Miriam?" Brill's face was a bright green pool in the twilight displayed by her night goggles. "Is that you?"

"Yes." Miriam walked closer, then flicked her goggles up and pulled out a pocket flashlight. "Are you okay?"

"Frozen half to death." Brill smiled shakily. "But otherwise unharmed."

A vast wave of relief broke over Miriam. "Well, if that's *all* . . ."

"This cloak lining is amazing," Brill added. "The post house is just past the next bend. I've only been waiting for an hour. Shall we go?"

"Sure." Miriam glanced down. "I'd better change, first." It was the work of a few minutes to disassemble the bike, pull on her outfit over her trousers, and turn the bike and panniers into a backpack disguised by a canvas cover. "Let's get some dinner," Miriam suggested.

"Your magic goggles, and lantern." Brill coughed discreetly.

"Oh. Of course." Together they fumbled their way through the darkness toward the promise of food and a bed, be it ever so humble.

Almost exactly twenty-four hours later, Paulette's doorbell chimed. "Who is it?" she called from behind the closed door.

"It's us! Let us in!" She opened the door. Brill stumbled in first, followed by Miriam. "Trick or treat?"

"Trick." Paulette stood back. "Hey, witchy!"

"It is, isn't it." Miriam closed the door. "It itches, too. I don't know how to put this discreetly—have you got any flea spray?"

"Fleas! Away with you!" Paulette held her nose. "How did it go?"

"I'll tell you in a few minutes. Over a coffee, once I've made it to the bathroom—oh shit." Miriam stared up the staircase at Brilliana's vanishing feet. "Well at least that's sorted." She dropped her pack onto the carpet; it landed with a dull thump." 'Scuse me, but I am going to strip. It's an emergency."

"Wait right there," said Paulie, hurrying upstairs.

By the time she returned, bearing a T-shirt and a pair of sweats from the luggage, Miriam had her boots off and was down to outer garments. "Damn, central heating," she said wonderingly. "There's nothing to make you appreciate it like three days in a Massachusetts winter without it. Well, two and a half."

"Did you got where you wanted to go?" Paulie asked, pausing.

"Yeah." Miriam cracked a wide, tired grin.

"Give me five, baby!"

High fives were all very well, but when Miriam winced Paulette got the message. "Use the living room," she said. "Get the hell out of those rags and then go up to my bedroom, okay? You can use the bedroom shower."

"You're a babe, babe." Miriam nodded. She pulled a face. "Oh shit. I think I'm coming on."

"That's no fun. Look, go. I'll sort the mess out later, 'kay?"

An hour later Miriam—infinitely warmer and cleaner—sat curled at one end of Paulette's living room sofa with a mug of strong tea. Brill, wrapped in a borrowed bathrobe, sat at the other end. "So tell me, how was your walk in the woods?" Paulette asked Brill. "Meet any bears?"

"Bears?" Brill looked puzzled. "No, and a good thing—" she caught Miriam's eye. "Oh. No, it was uneventful."

"Well then." Paulie focused on Miriam. "You had more luck, huh? *Not* just a walk in the woods?"

"Well, apart from Brill half freezing to death while I was trying not to get arrested, it was fine."

"Getting. Arrested." Paulette picked up the teapot and poured herself a mug. "You're not getting away with that, Beckstein. Didn't they accept your press pass or something?"

"It's Boston, but not as we know it," Miriam explained. "Uh, about two miles southeast of here I found myself on the edge of town. They speak English and they drive automobiles, but that's about as far as the similarities go." She pulled out her dictaphone and turned the volume up: *"zeppelin overhead, with a British flag on it! Uh, four propellers, sounds like diesel engines. There goes another steam car. They seem to make them big deliberately, I don't think I've seen anything smaller than a fifty-eight Caddy yet."*

Paulette closed her mouth with a visible effort. "Did you take photographs?" she asked.

"Uh-huh." Miriam grinned and held up her wrist. "You'll have them just as soon as I get my Casio secret agent watch plugged into the computer. I *knew* those Inspector Gadget toys would come in handy sooner or later."

"Toys." Paulette rolled her eyes.

"Well, now we've got a whole new world to not understand," said Miriam. "Any constructive suggestions?"

"Yep." Paulette put her mug down. "Before you go over again, girl, we work out what you're going to do. You need a lawyer or business manager over there, right? And you need money, and somewhere to live, and we need to find a place on the far side that's away from human habitation in Brill's world and we can rent on our own side. Right? And we need to understand what you're messing with before you get yourself arrested. So spill it!"

Miriam reached into her bag and pulled out two books then dumped them on the table with a bump. "History lesson time. Watch out for the one with the brown paper cover," she warned. "It bites."

Paulette opened that one first, looked at the flyleaf, and sucked in her breath. "Communist?" she asked.

"Nope, it's much weirder than that." Miriam picked up the

other book. "I'll start with this one, you start with that one, then we'll swap."

Paulette glanced at the window. "It's nearly eleven, for Pete's sake! You want I should pull an overnighter?"

"No, that won't be necessary." Miriam put her book down and looked at her. "I've been meaning to raise this for a while. I've been staying here, and I didn't mean to. I really appreciate you putting Brill up, but two guests is two too many and—"

"Shut up," Paulette said fiercely. "You're going to stay here till you've told me what you've seen and gotten your act together to move out properly! And hit the deadline," she muttered under her breath.

"Deadline?" Miriam raised an eyebrow.

"The Clan summit," Brill explained tonelessly. She yawned. "I told Paulie about it."

"You can't let them do it!" Paulette insisted.

"Do what?" Miriam blinked.

"Move to declare you incompetent and make you a permanent ward of whoever the Clan deems appropriate," Brill explained. She looked puzzled. "Didn't you know? That's what Olga said Baron Oliver was muttering about."

Iris raised the cup of coffee to her lips with both hands. She looked a little shaky today, but Miriam knew better than to make a fuss. "So what did you do next?" she asked.

"I went to bed." Miriam leaned back, then glanced around. The level of background noise in the museum food court was high and all their neighbors seemed to be otherwise preoccupied. "What else could I do? Beltaigne is nearly five months away, and I'm not going to let the bastards stampede me."

"But the other place, this new one—" Iris sounded distracted—"doesn't it take you a whole day to go each way, even if you have somewhere to stay at the other end?"

"There's no point going off half-cocked, Ma." Miriam idly opened a tube of sugar crystals and stirred them into her latte. "Look, if Baron Hjorth wants to declare me incompetent, he's going to have to come up with some evidence. He might shove it through if I'm not there to defend myself, but I figure the strongest defense I can get is proof that there's a conspiracy out there—a conspiracy that murdered my birthmother and is trying to murder me, too, not just the petty shit he and my—grandmother—are shoveling at me. A second-strongest defense is evidence that I may be erratic, but I've come up with something valuable. Now, the assassin's locket takes me to this other world—call it world three—and I've got to wonder. Does this mean they're not part of the Clan or families? They're working on the other side and in world three, while the Clan works on the other side and here, call *here* world two and Niejwein is part of world one. I'm, I guess, the first member of the Clan to actually become aware of world three and be able to get over there. That means that I can see about finding whoever's sending the killers—see defense one, above—or see about opening up a whole new trade opportunity—see defense two, above. I'm going to tie the whole story up with a bow and hand it to them. And mess up Baron Hjorth's game into the bargain." She rolled up the empty sugar tube into a tight little wad and threw it at the back of the booth.

"That sounds like my daughter," Iris said thoughtfully. She grinned. "Don't let the bastards realize you've got the drop on them until it's too late for them to dodge." She put the smile aside. "Morris would be proud of you."

"Um." Miriam nodded, unable to trust her tongue. "How have you been? How did you get away from them tonight?"

"Well, you know, I haven't had much trouble with being under surveillance lately." Iris sipped her coffee. "Funny how they don't seem to be able to tell one old woman in a motorized blue wheelchair from another, isn't it?"

"Ma, you shouldn't have!"

"What, give some of my friends an opportunity for a little adventure?" Iris snorted and pushed her bifocals up her nose. Slyly: "Just because my daughter thinks she can go haring off to other worlds, running away from her problems—"

"It's the source of my goddamn problems, not the solution," Miriam interrupted.

"Well good, just as long as you understand that." Iris met her eyes with a coolly unreadable expression that slowly moderated into one of affection. "You're grown up now and there's not a lot I can teach you. Just as well really, one day I won't be around to do the teaching and it'd be kind of embarrassing if—"

"—Mother!"

"Don't you 'mother' me! Listen, I raised you to face facts and deal with the world as it really is, not to pretend that if you stick your head in the sand problems will go away. I'm in late middle age and I'm damned if I'm not going to inflict my hard-earned wisdom on my only daughter." She looked mildly disgusted. "Come to think of it, I wish someone had beaten it into me when I was a child. Pah. But anyway. You're playing with fire, and I would really hate it if you got burned. You're going to try and track down these assassins from another universe, aren't you? What do you think they are?"

"I think—" Miriam paused. "They're like the Clan and the families," she said finally. "Only they travel between world one and world three, while the Clan travel between world one and world two, our world. I figure they decided the Clan were a threat a long time ago and that's probably something to do with, with why they tried to nail my mother. All those years ago. And they're smaller and weaker than the Clan, that much seems obvious, so I can maybe set up in world three, their stronghold, before they notice me. I think."

"Ambitious." Iris didn't crack a smile. "What did I tell you when you were young, about not jumping to conclusions?"

"Um. You know better? Is there something you haven't been telling me?"

Iris nodded sharply. "Can you permit your mother to keep one or two things to herself?"

"Guess so." Miriam shrugged uncomfortably. "Can you give your daughter any hints?"

"Only this." Iris met her gaze unflinchingly. "Firstly, do you really think you'd have been hidden from the families for all these years without someone over there covering your trail?"

"Ma—"

"I can't tell you for sure," she added, "but I think someone may have been watching over you. Someone who didn't want you dragged into all this—at least not until you were good and ready to look out for yourself."

Miriam shook her head. "Is that all? You think I've got a fairy godmother?"

"Not exactly." Iris finished her coffee. "But here's a 'secondly' for you to think about. Shortly after you surfaced, the strangers, these assassins, started hunting for you. To say nothing of the second bunch who tried to wipe out this Olga person. Doesn't that suggest something? What about that civil war among the families that you told me about?"

"Are you trying to suggest it's part of some sixty-year-old feud?" Miriam demanded. "Or that it isn't over?"

"Not exactly. I'm wondering if the sixty-year-old feud wasn't part of *this* business, if you follow my drift. Like, started by outsiders meddling for their own purposes."

"That's—" Miriam paused for thought—"Paranoid! I mean, *why*—"

"What better way to weaken a powerful enemy than to get it fighting itself?" Iris asked.

"Oh." Miriam was silent for a while. "You're saying that because of who I am—nothing more, just because of who my parents were—I'm the focus of a civil war?"

"Possibly. And you may just have reignited it by crawling out of the woodwork." Iris looked thoughtful. "Do you have any better suggestions? Are you involved in anything else that might explain what's going on?"

"Roland—" Miriam stopped. Iris stared at her. "You said not to trust any of them," Miriam continued slowly, "but I think I can trust him. Up to a point."

Iris met her eyes. "People do the strangest things for money and love," she said, a curious expression on her face. "I should know." She chuckled humorlessly. "Watch your back, dear. And . . . call me if you need me. I don't promise

I'll be there to help—with my health that would be rash—
but I'll do my best."

The next morning Paulette arrived back at the house around
noon, whistling jauntily. "I did it!" she declared, startling
Miriam out of the history book she was working up a
headache over. "We move in tomorrow!"

"We do?" Miriam shook her head as Brill came in behind
Paulie and closed the door, carefully wiping the snow off her
boots on the mat just inside.

"We do!" Paulette threw something at her; reaching out
instinctively, Miriam grabbed a bunch of keys.

"Where to?"

"The office of your dreams, madam chief high corporate
executive!"

"You found somewhere?" Miriam stood up.

"Not only have I *found* somewhere, I've rented it for six
months up front." Paulette threw down a bundle of papers on
the living room table. "Look. A thousand square feet of not-
entirely-brilliant office space not far from Cambridgeport.
The main thing in its favor is a downstairs entrance and a
backyard with a high wall around it, and access. On-street
parking, which is a minus. But it was cheap—about as cheap
as you can get anything near the waterfront for these days,
anyway." Paulie pulled a face. "Used to belong to a small
and not very successful architect's practice, then they moved
out or retired or something and I grabbed a three-year lease."

"Okay." Miriam sighed. "What's the damage?"

"Ten thousand bucks deposit up front, another ten thousand in rent. About eight hundred to get gas and power
hooked up, and we're going to get a lovely bill from We the
Peepul in a couple of months, bleeding us hard enough to
give Dracula anemia. Anyway, we can move in tomorrow. It
could really use a new carpet and a coat of paint inside, but
it's open plan and there's a small kitchen area."

"The backyard looked useful," Brill said hesitantly.

"Paulie took you to see it?"

"Yeah." Brill nodded. *Where'd she pick that up from?* Miriam wondered: Maybe she was beginning to adjust, after all.

"What did you think of it?" Miriam asked as Paulette hung her coat up and headed upstairs on some errand.

"That it's where ordinary people *work*? There's nowhere for livestock, not enough light for needlework or spinning or tapestry, not enough ventilation for dyeing or tanning, not enough water for brewing—" She shrugged. "But it looks *very* nice. I've slept in worse palaces."

"Livestock, tanning, and fabric all take special types of building here," Miriam said. "This will be an office. Open-plan. For people to work with papers. Hmm. The yard downstairs. What did you think of that?"

"Well. First we went in through a door and up a staircase like that one there, narrow—the royal estate agent, is that right? took us up there. There's a room at the top with a window overlooking the stairs, and that is an office for a secretary. I thought it rather sparse, and there was nowhere for the secretary's guards to stand duty, but Paulie said it was good. Then there is a short passage past a tiny kitchen, to a big office at the back. The windows overlooking the yard have no shutters, but peculiar plastic slats hung inside. And it was dim. Although there were lights in the ceiling, like in the kitchen here."

"Long lighting tubes." Miriam nodded. "And the back?"

"A back door opens off the corridor onto a metal fire escape. It goes down into the yard. We went there and the walls are nearly ten feet high. There is a big gate onto the back road, but it was locked. A door under the fire escape opens into a storage shed. I could not see into any other windows from inside the yard. Is that what you wanted to know?"

Miriam nodded. "I think Paulie's done good. Probably." *Hope there's something appropriate on the far side, in "world three,"* she thought. "Okay, I'm going to start on a shopping list of things we need to move in there. If it works out, I'll start ferrying stuff over to the other side—then make a trip through to the far side, to see if we're in the right place." She grinned. "If this works, I will be *very* happy." *And I won't have to fork out a second deposit for somewhere more useful,* she noted mentally.

"How was your reading?" Paulie asked, coming downstairs again.

"Confusing." Miriam rubbed her forehead. "This history book—" she tapped the cover of the "legal" one—"is driving me nuts."

"Nuts? What's wrong with it?"

"Everything!" Miriam raised her hands in disgust. "Okay, look. I don't know much about English history, but it's got this civil war in the sixteen-forties, goes on and on about some dude called the Lord Protector, Oliver Cromwell. I looked him up in Encarta and yes, he's there, too. I didn't know the English had a civil war, and it gets better: They had a revolution in 1688, too! Did you know that? I sure didn't, and it's not in Encarta—but I didn't trust it, so I checked Britannica and it's kosher. Okay, so England has a lot of history, and it's all in the wrong order."

She sat down on the sofa. "Then I got to the seventeen-forties and everything went haywire."

"Haywire. Like, someone discovered a time machine, went back, and killed their grandfather?"

"Might as well have." Miriam rolled her eyes. "The Young Pretender—look, I'm not making these names up—sails over from France in 1745 and invades Scotland. And in *this* book, he got to crown himself king in Edinburgh."

"Young pretender—what did he pretend to be?"

"King. Listen, in *our* world, he did the same—then he marched on London and got himself spanked, hard, by King George. That's George the first, not the King George the thingummy who lost the war of Independence."

"I think I need an aspirin," said Paulette.

"What this means is that in the far side, England actually lost Scotland in 1745. They fought a war with the Scots in 1746, but the French joined in and whacked their fleet in the channel. So they whacked the French back in the Caribbean,

and the Dutch joined in and whacked the Spanish—settling
old scores—and then the Brits, while their back was turned.
It's all a crazy mess. And somewhere in the middle of this
mess things went wrong, wrong, *wrong*. According to Britannica, Great Britain got sucked into something called the
Seven Years' War with France, and signed a peace treaty in
1763. The Brits got to keep Canada but gave back
Guadaloupe and pissed off the Germans, uh, Prussians.
Whatever the difference is. But according to this looking-
glass history, every time the *English*—not the Brits, there's
no such country—started getting somewhere, the king of
Scotland tried to invade—there were three battles in as
many years at some place called New Castle. And then
somewhere in the middle of this, King George, the *second*
King George, gets himself killed on a battlefield in Germany, and is succeeded by King Frederick, and I am totally
confused because there is *no* King Frederick in Britannica."

Miriam stopped. Paulette was looking bright, fascinated—
and a million miles away. "That was when the French invaded," she said.

"Huh?" Paulie shook her head. "The French? Invaded
where?"

"England. See, Frederick was the crown prince, right? He
got sent over here, to the colonies as a royal governor or
something—"Prince of the Americas"—because his step-
mother the queen really hated him. So when his father died
he was over here in North America—and the French and
Scottish simultaneously invaded England. Whose army, and
previous king, had just been whacked. And they *succeeded*."

"Um, does this mean anything?" Paulette looked puzzled.

"Don't you see?" demanded Miriam. "Over on the far
side, in world three, there is no United States of America:
Instead there's this thing called New Britain, with a king-
emperor! And they're at war with the French Empire—or
cold war, or whatever. The French invaded and conquered
the British Isles something like two hundred and fifty years
ago, and have held it ever since, while the British royal family moved to North America. I'm still putting it all together.

Like, where we had a constitutional congress and declared independence and fought a revolutionary war, *they* had something called the New Settlement and set up a continental parliament, with a king and a house of lords in charge." She frowned. "And that's as much as I understand."

"Huh." Paulette reached out and took the book away from her. "I saw you look like that before, once," she said. "It was when Bill Gates first began spouting about digital nervous systems and the net. Do you need to go lie down for a bit? Maybe it'll make less sense in the morning."

"No, no," Miriam said absently. "Look, I'm trying to figure out what *isn't* there. Like, they've had a couple of world wars—but fought with wooden sailing ships and airships. There's a passage at the end of the book about the 'miracle of corpuscular transsubstantiation'—I think they mean atomic power but I'm not sure. They've got the germ theory of disease and steam cars, but I didn't see any evidence of heavier-than-air flight or antibiotics or gasoline engines. The whole industrial revolution has been delayed—they're up to about the 1930s in electronics. And the social thing is weird. I saw an opium pipe in that pawnbroker's, and I passed a bar selling alcohol, but they're all wearing hats and keeping their legs covered. It's not like our 1920s, at least not more than skin-deep. And I can't get a handle on it," she added frustratedly. "I'll just have to go over there again and try not to get myself arrested."

"Hmm." Paulette pulled up a carrier bag and dumped it on the table. "I've been doing some thinking about that."

"You have? What's about?"

"Well," Paulie began carefully, "first thing is, nobody can arrest you and hold you if you've got one of these lockets, huh? Or the design inside it. Brill—"

"It's the design," Brilliana said suddenly. "It's the family pattern." She glanced at Paulette. "I didn't understand the history either," she said plaintively. "Some of the men . . ." she tailed off.

"What about them?" Asked Miriam.

"They had it tattooed on their arms," she said shyly. "They said so, anyway. So they could get away if someone caught them. I remember my uncle talking about it once. They even shaved their scalp and tattooed it there in reverse, then grew their hair back—so that if they were imprisoned they could shave in a mirror and use it to escape."

Miriam stared at her in slack-jawed amazement. "That's brilliant!" she said. "Hang on—" her hand instinctively went to her head. "Hmm."

"You won't have to shave," said Paulie, "I know exactly what to do. You know those henna temporary tattoos you can get? There's this dot-com that takes images you upload and turns them into tattoos, then sends them to you by mail order. They're supposed to last for a few days. I figure if you put one on the inside of each wrist, then wear something with sleeves that cover it—"

"Wow." Miriam instinctively glanced at the inside of her left wrist, smooth and hairless, unblemished except for a small scar she'd acquired as a child. "But you said you'd been thinking about something else."

"Yup." Paulette upended her shopping bag on the table. "Behold: a pair of digital walkie-talkies, good for private conversations in a ten-mile radius! And lo, a hands-free kit."

"This is going to work," Miriam said, a curious fixed smile creeping across her face. "I can feel it in my bones." She looked up. "Okay. So tell me, Paulie, what do you know about the history of patent law?"

It took Miriam another day to work up the nerve to phone Roland. Before she'd gone back to Niejwein, to the disastrous plot and counterplot introduction to court life that had culminated in two attempts to murder her on the same night, they'd exchanged anonymous mobile phones. If she went outside she could phone him, either his voice mail or his own real-life ear, and dump all the unwanted complexities of her new life on a sympathetic shoulder. He'd understand: That was half the attraction that had sparked their whirlwind affair. He probably grasped the headaches she was facing better than anyone else, Brill included. Brill was still not much more than a teenager with a sheltered upbringing. But Roland knew just how nasty things could get. *If I trust him,* she thought wistfully. *Someone* had murdered the watchman and installed the bomb in the warehouse. She'd told Roland about the place, and then . . . *correlation does not imply causation,* she told herself.

In the end she compromised halfway, taking the T into town and finding a diner with a good range of exit options before switching on the phone and dialing. That way, even if someone had grabbed Roland and was actively tracing the call, they wouldn't find her before she ended the call. It was raining, and she had a seat next to the window, watching the slug-trails of rain on the glass as her latte cooled while she tried to work up her nerve to call him.

When she dialed, the phone rang five times before he picked it up, a near-eternity in which she changed her mind about the wisdom of calling him several times. But it was too late: She was committed now. "Hello?" he asked.

"Roland. It's me."

"Hello, you." Concern roughened his voice: "I've been really worried about you. Where are—"

"Wait." She realized she was breathing too fast, shallow breaths that didn't seem to be bringing in enough oxygen. "You're on this side. Is anyone with you?"

"No, I'm taking a day off work. Even your uncle gives his troops leave sometimes. He's been asking about you, though. As if he knows I've got some kind of channel to you. When are you going to come in? What have you been doing? Olga had the craziest story—"

"If it's about the incident in her apartment, it's true." Miriam stopped, glanced obliquely at the window to check for reflections. There was nobody near her, just a barrista cleaning the coffee machine on the counter at the other side of the room. "Is Edsger around? He hasn't gone missing or anything?"

"Edsger?" Roland sounded uncertain. "What do you know about—"

"Edsger. Courier on the Boston–New York run." Quickly Miriam outlined her departure from the Clan's holdings in the capital city Niejwein, her encounter with the courier on an Accela express. "Did he arrive alright?"

"Yes. I think so." Roland paused. "So you're telling me somebody tried to kill you in the warehouse as well?" A note of anger crept into his voice. "When I find out who—"

"You'll do nothing," Miriam interrupted. "And you're not going to tell me you can provide security. There's a mole in the organization, Roland, they'd work around you—and I've found out something more interesting. There's a whole bunch of world-walkers you don't know about, and they're coming in from yet another world, where everything's different. What we were talking about, the whole technology transfer thing, it can work there, too. In fact, that's what I'm doing now, with Brill. The politics—do you know anything about Baroness Hildegarde's interests? Olga said she's going to try to get the Clan committee to declare me incompetent. Before that happens I want to be able to make her look like an idiot. I'm working on the other side, Roland, in the third world, building a front company. So I'm going to stay out of touch for quite a bit longer."

"That makes sense. Can I see you?" he asked. A pause: "I really think we've got a lot to work out. I don't know about you." Another pause, "I was hoping we could . . ."

This was the hardest part. "I don't think so," Miriam heard herself saying. "I'd love to spend some time with you, but I've got so much to do. And there isn't enough time to do it. I can't risk you being followed, or Angbard deciding to reel me in too soon. I want to, but—"

"I get it." He sounded distant.

"I'm not dumping you! It's just I, I need some time." She was breathing too fast again. "Later. Give me a week to sort things out, then we'll see."

"Oh. A week?" The distant tone vanished. "Okay, a week. I'll wait, somehow. You'll take care of yourself? You're sure you're safe where you are?"

"For now," Miriam affirmed, crossing her fingers. "And I'll have a lot more to tell you then, I'll need your advice." *And everything else.* The urge to drop her resolve, grab any chance to see him, was so strong she had trouble resisting. *Keep it businesslike, for now.* "I love you," she said impulsively.

"Me too. I mean, I love you, too." It came out in a tongue-tied rush, followed by a silence pregnant with unspoken qualifications.

"I'd better go," she said at last.

"Uh. Okay, then."

"Bye." She ended the call and stared bleakly at the rain outside the window. Her coffee was growing cold. *Now why did I really say that?* She wondered, puzzled: *Did I really mean it?* She'd said those words before, to her husband—now ex-husband—and she'd meant them at the time. Why did this feel different?

"Damn it, I'm a fool," she told herself gloomily, muttering under her breath so that the waitress at the far end of the bar took pains to avoid looking at her. *I'm a fool for love, and if I don't handle this carefully, I could end up a dead fool. Damn it, why did I have to take that locket in the first place?*

The raindrops weren't answering, so she finished her latte hurriedly and left.

They spent the next three days exercising Miriam's magic credit card discreetly. Angbard hadn't put a stop on it. Evidently the message had gotten through: *Don't bug me, I'm busy staying alive.* A garden shed, a deluxe shooting hide, and enough gas-powered tools to outfit a small farm vanished into the trunk of Miriam's rental car in repeated runs between Home Depot and Costco and the new office near Cambridgeport. Miriam didn't much like the office—it had a residual smell of stale tobacco and some strange coffee-colored stains on the carpet that not even an industrial carpet cleaner could get rid of—but she had to admit that it would do.

They moved a couple of sofa beds into the rear office, and paid a locksmith to come around and beef up the door frame with deadbolts, and install an intruder alarm and closed-circuit TV cameras covering the yard and both entrances. A small fridge and microwave appeared in the kitchen, a television set and video in the front office. Paulette and Miriam groaned at each other about their aches and pains, and even Brill hesitantly joined in the bitching and moaning after they unloaded the flat-pack garden shed. "This had better be worth it," Miriam said on day three as she swallowed a Tenolol tablet and a chaser of ibuprofen on the back of her lunchtime sub.

"You're going across this afternoon?" asked Paulie.

"I'm going in half an hour," Miriam corrected her. "First trip to see if it's okay. Then as many short ones as I can manage, to ferry supplies over. I'll take Brill through to help get the shed up and covered, then come back to plot expedition one. You happy with the shopping list?"

"I think so." Paulette sighed. "This isn't what I was expecting when we got started."

"I know." Miriam grinned. "But I think this is going to work out. Listen, you've been going crazy with the both of us living on top of you for the past week, but once we're gone we'll be out of your hair for at least five days. Why don't you kick back and relax? Get in some of that partying you keep moaning about missing?"

"Because it won't be the same without you! I was planning on showing you some of the good life. Get you hitched up with a date, anyway."

Miriam sobered. "I don't need a date right now," she said, looking worried—and wistful.

"You're—" Paulette raised an eyebrow. "You still hooked on him?"

Miriam nodded. "It hasn't gone away. We spoke yesterday. I keep wanting to see him."

Paulette caught her arm. "Take it from me: don't. I mean, really, *don't*. If he's for real, he'll be waiting for you. If he isn't, you'd be running such a huge risk—"

Miriam nodded, wordlessly.

"I figured that was what it was," Paulie said softly. "You want him whether or not he's messed up with the shits who're trying to kill you or disinherit you, is that right?"

"I think he's probably got his reasons," Miriam said reluctantly. "Whatever he's doing. And I don't think he's working for them. But—"

"Listen, *no one* is worth what those fuckers want to do to you. Understand?"

"But if he *isn't*—" it came out as more of a whine than Miriam intended. She shook her head.

"Then it will all sort itself out, won't it?" said Paulette. "Eventually."

"Maybe."

They broke off as the noise of the door opening downstairs reached them. Two pairs of eyes went to the camera. It was Brill, coming in from the cold: She'd been out shopping on foot, increasingly sure-footed in the social basics of day-to-day life in the twenty-first century. "I look at her, and I think she'll be like you when she's done some growing up," Paulette commented quietly.

"Maybe." Miriam stood up. "What've you got?" she called down the stairwell.

"Food for the trip." Brill grinned. Then her smile turned thoughtful: "Do you have a spare gun?" she asked.

"Huh? Why?"

"There are wild animals in the hills near Hasleholm," she said matter-of-factly.

"Oops." Miriam frowned. "Do you really think it's a problem?"

"Yes." Brill nodded. "But I can shoot. He is very conservative, my father, and insisted I learn the feminine virtues— deportment, dancing, embroidery, and marksmanship. There are wolves, and I'd rather have a long gun for dealing with them."

Paulette rolled her eyes.

"Okay. Then I guess we'll have to look into getting you a hunting rifle as soon as possible. In the meantime, there's the pistol I took from the courier. Where did you stash it?"

"Back at Paulette's home. But I really could use something bigger in case of wolves or bears," Brill said seriously. She shoved her hair back out of the way and sniffed. "At least a pistol will protect me from human problems."

"Deep joy. Try not to shoot any Clan couriers, huh?"

"I'm not stupid." Brill sniffed again.

"I know: I just don't want you taking any risks," Miriam added. "Okay, kids, it's time to move. And I'm *not* taking you through just yet, Brill." She reached for her heavy hiking jacket, pulled it on, and patted the right pocket to check her own gun was in place. "Wish me luck," she said, as she walked toward the back door and the yard beyond.

CLEANING THE AIR

Miriam snapped into awareness teetering on the edge of an abyss. She flung herself sideways instinctively, grabbing for a tree branch—caught it, took two desperate strides as the ground under her feet crumbled, then felt her boots grip solid ground that didn't crumble under her feet.

"Shit." She glanced to her left. A large patch of muddy soil lay exposed in the middle of the snowscape, exposed on the crest of a steep drop to a half-frozen streambed ten feet below and twenty feet beyond what would be the side of the yard. "Oh shit." She gasped for breath, icy terror forcing her to inhale the bitterly cold air. Horrified, she looked down into the stream. *If we'd rented the next unit over, or if I'd carried Brill over*—a ducking in this sort of weather could prove fatal. *Or could I have come through at all?* She glanced up. She'd been lucky with the tree, a young elm that grew straight and tall for the first six feet. The forest hereabouts was thin. *I need to ask Brill what else she hasn't thought to tell me about world-walking,* she realized. Perhaps her mother was right about her being over-confident. A vague memory floated up from somewhere, something about much of Boston being built on landfill reclaimed from the bay. *What if I'd tried this somewhere out at sea?* she thought, and leaned against the tree for a minute or two to catch her breath. Suddenly, visions of coming through with her feet embedded in a wall or hovering ten feet above a lake didn't seem comical at all.

She closed her locket and carefully pocketed it, then looked around. "It'll do," she muttered to herself. "As long as I avoid that drop." She stared at it carefully. "Hmm." She'd gone through about a foot away from the left-hand wall of their yard: The drop-off was steepest under the wall. The yard was about twelve feet wide, which meant—

"Right here." She took out her knife and carved a blaze on the tree around head height. Then she dropped her backpack and turned around, slowly, trying to take in the landscape.

The stream ran downhill toward the river a quarter of a mile away, but it was next to invisible through the woods, even with the barren winter branches blocking less of the view than the summer's profusion of green. In the other direction trees stretched away as far as she could see. "I could walk for miles in this, going in circles," Miriam told herself. "Hmm."

She carved another blaze on a tree, then began cautiously probing into the woods, marking trees as she went. After an hour she'd established that there was no sudden change in the landscape for a couple of hundred yards in two directions away from her little backyard. Sheer random chance had brought her through in nearly the worst possible place.

"Okay," she told herself, squeezing her forehead as if she could cram the headache back inside the bones of her skull. "Here goes." And this time, she pulled down her left sleeve and looked at the chilly skin on the inside of her wrist—pale and almost blue with cold, save for the dark green-and-brown design stippled in dye below the pulse point.

It worked.

That night, Miriam didn't sleep well. She had a splitting headache and felt sick to her stomach, an unfamiliar nausea for one who didn't suffer migraines. But she'd managed a second trip after dark, only four hours after the first, and returned after barely an hour with aching back and arms (from lifting the heavy shooting hide and a basic toolkit) and a bad case of the shivers.

Brilliana fussed over her, feeding her moussaka and grilled octopus from a Greek take-out she'd discovered somewhere—Brill had taken to exploring strange cuisines with the glee of a suddenly liberated gastronome—and readied her next consignment. "I feel like a Goddamn mule," Miriam complained over a bottle of wine. "If only there were two of us!"

"I'd do it if I could," Brill commented, stung. "You know I would!"

"Yes, yes . . . I'm sorry. I didn't mean it that way. It's just—I can carry eighty pounds on my back, just. A hundred and twenty? I can't even pick it up. I wish I could take more. I should take up weight lifting . . ."

"That's what the couriers all do. Why don't you use a walking frame?" asked Brill.

"A walking—is this something the Clan does that I don't know about?"

Brill shook her head. "I'm not sure," she said, "I never saw how they operate the post service. But surely—if we get a very heavy pack ready, and lift it so you can walk into it backwards then just lock your knees, wouldn't that work?"

"It might." Miriam pulled a face. "I might also twist an ankle. Which would be bad, in the middle of nowhere."

"What happens if you try to go through with something on the ground?" Brill asked.

"I don't." Miriam refilled her glass. "It was one of the first things I tried. If you jump on my back I can just about carry you for thirty seconds or so before I fall over—that's long enough. But I tried with a sofa a while ago. All that happened was, I got a splitting headache and threw up in the toilet. I don't know how I managed it the first time, sitting in a swivel chair, except maybe it was something to do with its wheels—there wasn't much contact with the floor."

"Oh, right."

"Which says interesting things about the family trade," Miriam added. "They're limited by weight and volume in what they can ship. Two and a half tons a week. If we open up 'world three' that'll go down, precipitously, although the three-way trade may be worth more. We've got to work out how to run an import/export business that doesn't run into the mercantilist zero-sum trap."

"The what?" Brill looked blank.

Miriam sighed. "Old, old theory. It's the idea that there are only a finite quantity of goods of fixed value, so if you ship them from one place to another, the source has to do without. People used to think all trade worked that way. What happens is, if you ship some commodity to a place where it's scarce, sooner or later the price drops—deflates— while you're buying up so much of the supply that the price rises at the source."

"Isn't that the way things always work?" Brill asked.

"Nope." Miriam took a sip of wine. "I'm drinking too much of this stuff, too regularly. Hmm, where was I? This guy called Adam Smith worked it out about two centuries ago, in this world. Turns out you can create value by working with people to refine goods or provide services. Another guy called Marx worked on Smith's ideas a bit further a century later, and though lots of people dislike the prescription he came up with, his analysis of how capitalism works is quite good. Labor— what people do—enhances the value of raw materials. This table is worth more than the raw timber it's made out of, for example. We can create value, wealth, what-have-you, if we can just move materials to where the labor input on them enhances their value the most." She drifted off, staring at the TV set, which was showing a talk show with the volume muted. (Brill said it made more sense that way.) "The obvious thing to move is patents," she murmured. "Commercially valuable ideas."

"You think you can use the talent to create wealth, instead of moving it around?" Brill looked puzzled.

"Yes, that's it exactly." Miriam put her glass down. "A large gold nugget is no use to a man who's dying of thirst in a desert. By the same token, a gold nugget may be worth a lot more to a jeweler, who can turn it into something valuable and salable, than it is to someone who just wants to melt it down and use it as coin. Jewelry usually sells for more than its own weight in raw materials, doesn't it? That's because of the labor invested in it. Or the scarcity of the end product, a unique work of art. The Clan seems to have gotten hung up on shipping raw materials around as a way of making money. I want to ship ideas around, instead, ideas that people can use to create value locally—in each world—actually *create* wealth rather than just cream off a commission for transporting it."

"And you want to eventually turn my world into this one," Brilliana said calmly.

"Yes." Miriam looked back at her. "Is that a good thing or a bad thing, do you think?"

Brill gestured at the TV set. "Put one of *those*, showing *that*, in every peasant's house? Are you kidding? I think it's the most amazingly wonderful thing I've ever heard of!" She frowned. "My mother would say that's typical of me, and my father would get angry and perhaps beat me for it. But I'm right, and they're wrong."

"Ah, the self-confidence of youth." Miriam picked up her glass again. "Doesn't the idea of, like, completely wiping out the culture of your own people worry you? I mean, so much of what we've got here is such complete shit—" She stopped. Brill's eyes were sparkling—with anger, not amusement.

"You really think so? Go live in a one-room hut for a couple of years, bearing illiterate brats half of whom will die before they're five! Without a fancy toilet, or even a thunder-mug to piss in each morning. Go do that, where the only entertainment is once a week going to the temple where some fat stupid priest invokes the blessings of Sky Father and his court on your heads and prays that the harvest doesn't fail again like it did five years ago, when two of your children starved to death in front of your eyes. *Then* tell me that your culture's shit!"

Miriam tried to interrupt: "Hey, what about—"

Brill steamed right on. "Shut *up*. Even the children of the well-off—like me—grow up living four to a room and wearing hand-me-downs. We are married off to whoever our parents think will pay best bride-price. Because we're members of the outer families we don't die of childbed fever—not since the Clan so graciously gave us penicillin tablets and morphine for the pain—but we get to bear child after child because it's our duty to the Clan! Are you insane, my lady? Or merely blind? And it's better for us in the families than for ordinary women, better by far. Did you notice that within the Clan you had rights? Or that outside the Clan, in the ordinary aristocracy, you didn't? We have at least one ability that is as important, more important, than what's between our legs: another source of status. But those ordinary peasants you feel such guilt for don't have any such thing. There's a better life awaiting me as a humble illegal immigrant in this world than there is as a lady-in-waiting to nobility in my own. Do you think I'd ever go back there for *any* reason except to help you change the world?"

Taken aback, Miriam recoiled slightly. "Ouch," she said. "I didn't realize all that stuff. No." She picked up her wine glass again. "It's post-colonial guilt, I guess," she added by way of explanation. "We've got a lot of history here, and it's really ugly in parts. We've got a long tradition of conquering other people and messing them up. The idea of taking over and running people for their own good got a very bad name about sixty years ago—did anyone tell you about the Second World War? So a lot of us have this cringe reflex about the whole idea."

"Don't. If you do what you're planning, you couldn't invade and conquer, anyway. How many people could you bring through? All you can do is persuade people to live their lives a better way—the one thing the families and the Clan have never bothered trying to do, because they're swimming desperately against the stream, trying to hold their own lives together. It takes an outside view to realize that if they started building fabulous buildings and machines like these at home they wouldn't be dependent on imported luxuries from the world next door. And they never—" her chest heaved—"let us get far enough away to see that clearly. Because if we did, we might not come back."

She looked depressed.

"You don't want to go back?" asked Miriam. "Not even to visit, to see your family and friends?"

"Not really." It was a statement of fact. "This is *better*. I can find new friends here. If I go there, and you fail—" she caught Miriam's gaze. "I might never be able to come back here."

For a moment, looking at this young woman—young enough to be at college but with eyes prematurely aged by cynicism and the Clan's greedy poverty of riches— Miriam had second thoughts. The families' grip on their young was eggshell-thin, always in danger of bursting. If they ever got the idea that they could just take their lockets or tattoos or scraps of paper and leave, the Clan would be gone within a generation. *Am I going to end up making this family tyranny stronger?* she wondered. *Because if so, shouldn't I just give up now . . . ?* "I won't fail you," she heard herself saying. "We'll fix them."

Brill nodded. "I know you will," she said. And Miriam nodded right back at her, her mind awash with all the other family children, her distant relatives—the siblings and cousins she'd never known, might never have known of, who would live and die in gilded poverty if she failed.

A woman dressed in black stepped out of the winter twilight.

She looked around curiously, one hand raised to cover her mouth. "I'm in somebody's garden by the look of things. Hedge to my left, dilapidated shed in front of me—and a house behind. Can't be sure, but it looks a mess. The hedge is wildly overgrown and the windows are boarded up."

She glanced around, but couldn't see into the neighboring gardens. "Seems like an expensive place." She furtively scratched an arrowhead on the side of the shed, pointing to the spot she'd arrived on, then winced. "This light is hurting my head. *Ow . . .*" She hitched her coat out of the grayish snow then stumbled toward the house, crouching below the level of the windows.

She paused. "It looks empty," she muttered to the dictaphone. "Forward ho." She walked around to the front of the house, where the snow was banked in deep drifts before the doors and blank-eyed wooden window shutters. Nobody had been in or out for days, that much was clear. There was a short uphill driveway leading to a road, imposing iron gates chained in front. "Damn. How do I get out?" She glanced round, saw a plaque on the front of the house— BLACKSTONES, 1923. A narrow wooden gate next to the pillar supporting one of the cast-iron gates was bolted on the inside. Miriam waded toward it, shivering from the snow, shot the bolt back, and glanced round one final time to look at the house.

It was *big*. Not as big as the palace in Niejwein, or Angbard's fortress, but bigger than anything she'd ever lived in. And it was clearly mewed up, shutters nailed across those windows that weren't boarded, gates chained tight. She grinned, gritting her teeth against the cold. "Right, you're mine." Then she slipped through the wooden door and onto the sidewalk. The street here was partially swept. On the other side of it lay an open field in the middle of what was dense forest in world one and downtown Cambridge in world two. She could see other big town houses on the other side of the field, but that didn't matter. She turned left and began walking toward the crossroads she could see at the far corner of the quadrangle.

Her teeth were chattering by the time she reached the clock tower on the strange traffic circle at the crossroads. There was almost no traffic on this bitterly cold morning. A lone pony-trap clattered past her, but the only vehicles she saw out and about were strange two-deck streetcars, pantographs sparking occasionally as they whirred down the far side of the field and paused at a stand in the middle of the traffic circle. Miriam blinked back the instinctive urge to

check her watch. *What day is it?* she wondered. A sign in
heavy classical lettering at the empty tram stop answered
her question: Sunday service only. *Oh.* Below it was a
timetable as bemusingly exact as anything she'd seen at an
airport back home—evidently trams from this stop ran into
the waterfront and over something called Derry Bridge once
every half hour on Sundays, for a fare of 3d, whatever that
meant. She shivered some more and stepped inside the
wooden shelter, then fidgeted with the handful of copper
change that she had left. Second thoughts began to occur to
her. Was it normal for a single woman to catch a tram, unaccompanied, on a Sunday? What if Burgeson's shop was
closed? What if—

A streetcar pulled up beside the shelter with a screech of
abused steel wheels. Miriam plucked up her courage and
climbed aboard. The driver nodded at her, then without warning moved off. Miriam stumbled, almost losing her footing
before she made it into the passenger cabin. She sat down
without looking around. The wooden bench was cold but
there seemed to be a heater running somewhere. She surreptitiously examined her fellow passengers, using their reflections in the windows when she couldn't look at them directly
without being obvious. They were an odd collection—a fat
woman in a ridiculous bonnet who looked like a Salvation
Army collector, a couple of thin men in oddly cut, baggy
suits with hats pulled down over their ears, a twenty-
something mother, bags under her eyes and two quietly bickering children by her side, and a man in what looked like a
Civil War uniform coming toward her, a ticket machine hung
in front of his chest. Miriam took a deep breath. *I'm going to
manage this,* she realized.

"I'm going to Highgate, for Holmes Alley. How much is
it, please, and what's the closest stand? And what's this stop
called?"

"That'll be fourpence, miss, and I'll call you when it's
your stop. This is Roundgate interchange." He looked at her
slightly oddly as she handed him a sixpence, but wound off a

strip of four penny tickets and some change, then turned away. "*Tickets,* please."

Ouch. Miriam examined the tickets in her hand. *Is nothing simple?* she wondered. Even buying streetcar tickets was a minor ordeal of anticipation and surprise. *Brill did very well,* she began to realize. *Maybe too well. Hmm. That would explain why Angbard is letting me run . . .*

The tram trundled downhill at not much better than walking pace, the driver occasionally ringing an electric bell then stopping next to a raised platform. The houses were much closer together here, in terraces that shared side walls for warmth, built out of cheap red brick stained black from smoke. There was an evil smell of half-burned coal in the air, and chimneys belched from every roofline. She hadn't noticed it in the nob hill neighborhood of Blackstones, but the whole town smelled of combustion, as if there'd been a house fire a block away. The air was almost acrid, a nasty sour taste undercutting the cold and coating her throat when she tried to breathe. Even the cloud above was yellowish. The tram turned into a main road, rattled around a broad circle with a snow-covered statue of a man on a horse in the middle, then turned along an alarmingly skeletal box-section bridge that jutted out over the river. Miriam, watching the waterfront through the gray-painted girders, felt a most unsettling wave of claustrophobia—as if she was being taken into police custody for a crime she hadn't committed. She forced herself to shrug it off. *Everything will be alright,* she told herself.

The town center was almost empty compared to its state the last time she'd visited. It smelled strongly of smoke— chimneys on every side bespoke residents in the upstairs flats—but the shop windows were dark, their doors locked. A distant church bell clattered numbly. Scrawny pigeons hopped around near the gutter, exploring a pile of horse dung. The conductor tapped Miriam on the shoulder, and she started. "You'll be wanting the next stop," he explained.

"Thank you," she replied with a wan smile. She stood up, waiting on the open platform as the stop swung into view, then pulled the string threaded through brass eyeholes that she'd seen the other passengers use. A bell dinged behind in the driver's partition and he threw on the brakes. Miriam hopped off the platform, shook her coat out, hiked her bag up onto her shoulder, and stepped back from the tram as it moved off with a loud whirr and a gurgle of slush. Then she took stock of her surroundings.

Everything looked different in the chilly gloom of a Sunday morning. The shop fronts, comparatively busy last time she'd been here, looked like vacant eyes, and the peddlars hawking roast chestnuts and hand-warmers had disappeared. *Do they have Sunday trading laws here?* she wondered vaguely. That could be a nuisance—

Burgeson's shop was closed, too, a wooden shutter padlocked into place across the front window. But Miriam spotted something she hadn't noticed before, a solid wooden door next to the shop with a row of bell-pull handles set in a tarnished plaque beside it. She peered at them. *E. Burgeson, esq.* "Aha," she muttered, and pulled the handle.

Nothing happened. Miriam waited on the doorstep, her toes freezing and feeling increasingly damp, and cursed her stupidity. She put her hand on the knob and yanked again, and this time heard a distant tinkling reward. Then the door scraped inward on a bare-walled corridor. "Yes?"

"Mr. Burgeson?" she smiled hopefully at him. "I'm back."

"Oh." He was dressed as he had been in the shop, except for a pair of outrageous purple slippers worn over bare feet. "You again." A faint quirk tugged at the side of his upper lip. "I suppose you'll be wanting me to open the shop."

"If it's convenient."

He sniffed. "It isn't. And this is rather irregular—although something tells me you don't put much stock by regularity. Still, if you'd care to grace my humble abode with your presence and wait while I find my galoshes—"

"Certainly."

She followed him up a tightly spiraling stone-flagged staircase that opened out onto a landing with four stout-looking doors. One of them stood open, and he went inside without waiting for her. Miriam began to follow, then paused on the threshold.

"Come on, come on," he said irritably. "Don't leave the door open, you'll let the cold in. Then I'll have to fetch more coal from the cellar. What's keeping you?"

"Oh, nothing," she said, stepping forward and shutting the door behind her. The hall had probably once been wide enough for two people to stand abreast in, and it was at least ten feet high, but now it felt like a canyon. It was walled from floor to ceiling with bookcases, all crammed to bursting. Burgeson had disappeared into a kitchen—at least Miriam supposed it was a kitchen—in which a kettle was boiling atop a cast-iron stove that looked like something that belonged in a museum. The lights flickered as the door closed, and Miriam abruptly realized that they weren't electric. "I see you've got more books up here than you have down in the shop."

"That's work, this is pleasure," he said. "What did you come to disturb my Sunday worship for, this time?"

"Sunday worship? I don't see much sign of that around here," Miriam let slip. She backed up hastily. "I'm sorry. I hope I didn't cause you any trouble?"

"Trouble, no, no trouble, not unless you count having the King Street thief-taker himself asking pointed questions about my visitor of the other morning." His back was turned to her, so Miriam couldn't see his expression, but she tightened her grip on her bag, as she suddenly found herself wishing that the pockets of her coat were deep enough to conceal her pistol.

"That wasn't my doing," she said evenly.

"I know it wasn't." He turned to face her, and she saw that he was holding a somewhat tarnished silver teapot. "And you'd taken the Marx, so it wasn't as if it was lying around for him to trip over, was it? For which I believe I owe you thanks enough to cancel out any ill will resulting from his unwelcome visit." He held up the pot. "Can I offer you some refreshment, while you explain why you're here?"

"Sure." She glanced in the opposite direction. "In there?"

"The morning room, by all means. I will be but a few moments."

Miriam walked into Burgeson's morning room and got a surprise. The room was perfectly round. Even the window frames and the door were curved in line with the wall, and the plaster moldings around the ceiling described a perfect circle twelve feet in diameter. It was also extremely untidy. A huge and dubious Chesterfield sofa with stuffing hanging out of its arms hulked at one side, half submerged beneath a flood of manuscripts and books. An odd-looking upright piano, its scratched lid supporting a small library, leaned drunkenly against the wall. There was a fireplace, but the coals in it barely warmed the air immediately in front of it, and the room was icy cold. A plate with the remnants of a cold lunch sat next to the fireplace. Miriam sat gingerly on the edge of the sofa. The sofa was cold too, so that it seemed to suck the heat right through her layers of heavy clothing.

"How do you take your tea?" Burgeson called. "Milk, sugar?"

He was moving in the hall. She slipped a hand into her bag and pulled out her weapon, and pointed its spine at him. "Milk, no sugar," she replied.

"Very good." He advanced, bearing a tray, and laid it down in front of the fireplace. There were, she noticed, bags under his eyes. He looked tired, or possibly ill. "What's that?" He asked, staring at her hand.

"One good history book deserves another," she said evenly.

"Oh dear." He chuckled hoarsely. "You know I can't offer you anything for it. Not on a Sunday. If the police—"

"Take it, it's a gift," she said impatiently.

"A *gift*?" From his expression Miriam deduced that the receipt of presents was not an experience with which Erasmus Burgeson was well acquainted—he made no move to take it. "I'm touched, m'dear. Mind if I ask what prompted this unexpected generosity?" He was staring at her warily, as if he expected her to sprout bat wings and bite him.

"Sure," she said easily. "If you would pour the tea before

it gets cold? Is it always this cold here in, uh, whatever this city is called?"

He froze for a moment, then knelt down and began pouring tea from the pot into two slightly chipped Delft cups. "Boston."

"Ah, Boston it is." She nodded to herself. "The cold?"

"Only when a smog notice is in effect." Burgeson pointed at the fire. "Damned smokeless fuel ration's been cut again. You can only burn so much during a smog, or you run out and then it's just too bad. Especially if the pipes burst. But when old father smog rolls down the Back Bay, you'd rather not have been born, lest pipes of a different kind should go pop." He coughed for effect and patted his chest. "You speak the King's English remarkably well for someone who doesn't know a blessed thing. Where are you from, really?"

She put the book down on the heap on the sofa. "As far as I can tell, about ten miles and two hundred years away," she said, feeling slightly light-headed at the idea of telling him even this much.

"Not France? Are you sure you don't work for the dauphin's department?" He cocked his head on one side, parrotlike.

"Not France. Where I come from they chopped his head off a long time ago." She watched him carefully.

"Chopped his *head* off? Fascinating—" He rose on one knee, and held out a cup to her.

"Thank you." She accepted it.

"If this is madness, it's a most extraordinary delusion," he said, nodding. "Would you be so good as to tell me more?"

"In due course. I have a couple of questions for you, however." She took a decorous sip of the tea. "Specifically, taking on trust the question of your belief in my story, you might want to contemplate some of the obstacles a traveler from, um, another world, might face in creating an identity for themselves in this one. And especially in the process of buying a house and starting a business, when one is an unaccompanied female in a strange country. I don't know much about the legal status of women here other than that it differs quite significantly from where I come from. I think I'm probably going to need a lawyer, and possibly a proxy. Which is why I thought of you."

"I see." Burgeson was almost going cross-eyed in his attempts to avoid interrupting her. "Pray tell, why me?"

"Because an officer of the law recommended you." She grinned. "I figure a fence who is also an informer is probably a safer bet than someone who's so incompetent that he hasn't reached a working accommodation with the cops." There were other reasons too, reasons connected with Miriam's parents and upbringing, but she wasn't about to give him that kind of insight into her background. Trust went only so far, after all.

"A fence—" He snorted. "I'm not dishonest or unethical, ma'am."

"You just sell books that the Lord Provost's Court wants burned," she said, with an amused tone. "And the police recommend you. Do I need to draw a diagram?"

He sighed. "Guilty as charged. If you aren't French, are you sure you aren't a Black Chamber agent playing a double game?"

"What's the Black Chamber?"

"Oh." Abruptly he looked gloomy. "I suppose I should also have sold you an almanac."

"That might have been a good idea," she agreed.

"Well, now." He brushed papers from the piano stool and sat on it, opposite her, his teacup balanced precariously on a bony knee. "Supposing I avoid saying anything that might incriminate myself. And supposing we take as a matter of faith your outrageous claim to be a denizen of another, ah, world? Like this one, only different. No *le Roi Francaise,* indeed. What, then, could you be wanting with a humble dealer and broker in secondhand goods and wares like myself?"

"Connections." Miriam relaxed a little. "I need to establish a firm identity here, as a woman of good character. I have some funds to invest—you've seen the form they take—but mostly . . . hmm. In the place I come from, we do things differently. And while we undoubtedly do some things worse, everything I have seen so far convinces me that we are far, *far* better at certain technical fields. I intend to establish a type of company that as far as I can tell doesn't exist here, Mister Burgeson. I am limited in the goods I can carry back and forth, physically, to roughly what I can carry on my back—but *ideas* are frequently more valuable than gold bricks." She grinned. "I said I'd need a lawyer, and perhaps a proxy to sign documents for my business. I forgot to mention that I will also want a patent clerk and a front man for purposes of licensing my inventions."

"Inventions. Such as?" He sounded skeptical.

"Oh, many things." She shrugged. "Mostly little things. A machine for binding documents together in an office that is cheap to run, compact, and efficient—so much so that where I come from they're almost as common as pens. A better design of brake mechanism for automobiles. A better type of wood screw, a better kind of electric cell. But one or two big things, too. A drug that can cure most fulminating infections rapidly and effectively, without side effects. A more efficient engine for aviation."

Burgeson stared at her. "Incredible," he said sharply. "You have some proof that you can come up with all these miracles?"

Miriam reached into her bag and pulled out her second weapon, one that had cost her nearly its own weight in gold, back home, a miniature battery-powered gadget with a four-inch color screen. "When I leave, you can start by looking at that book. In the meantime, here's a toy we use for keeping children quiet on long journeys where I come from. How about some light Sunday entertainment?" And she hit the "start" button on the DVD player.

Three hours and at least a pint of tea later, Miriam stepped down from a hackney carriage outside the imposing revolving doors of the Brighton Hotel. Behind her, the driver grunted as he heaved her small trunk down from the luggage rack—"if you're going to try to pass in polite society you'll need one, no lady of quality would travel without at least a change of day wear and her dinner dress," Burgeson had told her as he gave her the trunk—"and you need to be at least respectable enough to book a room." Even if the trunk had been pawned by a penniless refugee and cluttered up a pawnbroker's cellar for a couple of years, it looked like luggage.

"Thank you," Miriam said as graciously as she could, and tipped the driver a sixpence. She turned back to the door to see a bellhop already lifting her trunk on his handcart. "I say! You there."

The concierge at the front desk didn't turn his nose up at a single woman traveling alone. The funereal outfit Burgeson had scared up for her seemed to forbid all questions, especially after she had added a severe black cap and a net veil in place of her previous hat. "What does milady require?" he asked politely.

"I'd like to take one of your first-class suites. For myself. I travel with no servants, so room service will be required. I will be staying for at least a week, and possibly longer while I seek to buy a house and put the affairs of my late husband in order." *I hope Erasmus wasn't stringing me along about getting hold of a new identity,* she thought.

"Ah, by all means. I believe room fourteen is available, m'lady. Perhaps you would like to view it? If it is to your satisfaction . . ."

"I'm sure it will be," she said easily. "And if it isn't you'll see to it, I'm sure, won't you? How much will it be?"

He stiffened slightly. "A charge of two pounds and eleven shillings a night applies for room and board, ma'am," he said severely.

"Hmm." She sucked on her lower lip. "And for a week? Or longer?"

"I believe we could come down from that a little," he said, less aggressively. "Especially if provision was made in advance."

"Two a night." Miriam palmed a huge, gorgeously colored ten-pound note onto the front desk and paused. "Six shillings on top for the service."

The concierge smiled and nodded at her. "Then it will be an initial four nights?" he asked.

"I will pay in advance, if I choose to renew it," she replied tonelessly. *Bastard,* she thought angrily. Erasmus had primed her with the hotel's rates. Two pounds flat was the norm for a luxury suite: This man was trying to soak her. "*If* it's satisfactory," she emphasized.

"I'll see to it myself." He bowed, then stepped out from behind his desk. "If I may show you up to your suite myself, m'lady?"

Once she was alone in the hotel suite, Miriam locked the door on the inside, then removed her coat and hung it up to dry in the niche by the door. "I'm impressed," she said aloud. "It's huge." She peeled off her gloves and slung them over a brass radiator that gurgled beneath the shuttered windows, then unbuttoned her jacket and collar and knelt to unlace her ankle boots—her feet were beginning to feel as if they were molded to the inside of the damp, cold leather. *Chilblains as an occupational hazard for explorers of other worlds?* she thought whimsically. She stepped out of her shoes then carried them to the radiator, stockinged feet feeling almost naked against the thick pile of the woolen carpet.

Dry at last, she walked over to the sideboard and the huge silver samovar, steaming gently atop a gas flame plumbed into the wall. She poured a glass full of hot water and dunked a sachet of Earl Grey tea into it. Finally, gratefully, she plopped herself down in the overstuffed armchair opposite the bedroom door, pulled out her dictaphone, and began to compose a report to herself. "Here I am, in Suite fourteen of the Brighton Hotel. The concierge tried to soak me. Getting a handle on the prices is hard—a pound seems to be equivalent to about, uh, two hundred dollars? Something like that. This is an *expensive* suite, and it shows, it's got central heating, electric lights—incandescent filaments, lots of them, dim enough you can look right at them—and silk curtains." She glanced through the open bathroom door. "The bathroom looks to be all brass and porcelain fittings and a flushing toilet. Hmm. Must check to see what their power distribution system's like. Might be an opportunity to sell them electric showers."

She sighed. "Tomorrow Erasmus will fix me up with a meeting with his attorney and start making inquiries about that house. He also said he'd look into a patent clerk and get me into the central reading library. Looks like their intellectual property framework is a bit primitive. I'll need to bring over some more fungibles soon. Gold is all very well, but I'm not sure it isn't cheaper here than it is back home. I wonder what their kitchens are short of," she added, brooding.

"Damn. I wish there was someone to talk to." She clicked off the little machine and put it down on the sideboard, frowning. Whether or not Erasmus Burgeson was trustworthy was an interesting question. Probably he was, up to a point—as long as he could sniff a way to put one over on the cops who were enforcing his unwilling cooperation. But he was most clearly a bachelor, and there was something uncomfortable, slightly strained about him when she was in his presence. *He's not used to dealing with women, other than customers in his shop,* she decided. *That's probably it.*

In any event, her head ached and she was feeling tired. *Think I'll leave the dining room for another day,* she decided. The bed seemed to beckon. Tomorrow would be a fresh start . . .

GOLD BUGS

The following morning, Miriam awakened early. It was still semi-dark outside. She yawned at her reflection in the bathroom mirror as she brushed her hair. "Hmm. They wear it long here, don't they?" It would just have to do, she thought, as she dressed in yesterday's clothes once more. She carefully sorted through her shoulder bag to make sure there was nothing too obtrusively alien in it, then pulled her boots on.

She paused at the foot of the main staircase, poised above the polished marble floor next to the front desk. "Can I help you, ma'am?" a bellhop offered eagerly.

She smiled wanly. "Breakfast. Where is it?" The realization that she'd missed both lunch and dinner crashed down on her. Abruptly she felt almost weak from hunger.

"This way, please!" He guided her toward two huge mahogany-and-glass doors set at one side of the foyer, then ushered her to a seat at a small table, topped in spotless linen. "I shall just fetch the waiter."

Miriam angled her chair around to take in the other diners as discreetly as possible. *It's like a historical movie!* she thought. One set in a really exclusive Victorian hotel, except the Victorians hadn't had a thing for vivid turquoise and purple wallpaper and the costumes were messed up beyond recognition. Men in Nehru suits with cutaway waists, women in long skirts or trousers and wing-collared shirts. Waiters with white aprons bearing plates of—fish? And bread rolls? The one familiar aspect was the newspaper. "Can you fetch me a paper?" she asked after the bellhop.

"Surely, ma'am!" he answered, and was off like a shot. He was back in a second and Miriam fumbled for a tip, before starting methodically on the front page.

The headlines in *The London Intelligencer* were bizarrely familiar, simultaneously tainted with the exotic. "Speaker: House May Impeach Crown for Adultery"—but no, there was no King Clinton in here, just unfamiliar names and a proposal to amend the Basic Law to add a collection of additional charges for which the Crown could be impeached—Adultery, Capitative Fraud, and Irreconsilience, whatever that was. *They can impeach the king?* Miriam shook her head, moved on to the next story. "Morris and Stokes to hang," about a pair of jewel thieves who had killed a shopkeeper. Farther down the page was more weirdness, a list of captains of merchantmen to whom had been granted letters of marque and reprise against "the forces and agents of the continental enemy," and a list of etheric resonances assigned for experimentation by the Teloptic Wireless Company of New Britain.

A waiter appeared at her shoulder as she was about to turn the page. "May I be of service, ma'am?"

"Sure. What's good, today?"

He smiled broadly. "The kippers are most piquant, and if I may recommend Mrs. Wilson's strawberry jam for after? Does ma'am prefer tea or coffee?"

"Coffee. Strong, with milk." She nodded. "I'll take your recommendations, please. That'll be all."

He rustled away from her, leaving her puzzling over the

meaning of a story about taxation powers being granted by
The-King-In-Parliament to the Grand Estates, and enforcement of the powers of printing rights by the Royal Excise.
Even the addition of a powerful dose of coffee and a plate of
smoked fish—not her customary start to the day, but nevertheless remarkably edible on an empty stomach—didn't
make it any clearer. *This place is so complex! Am I ever going to understand it?* She wondered.

She was almost to the bottom of her coffee when a different bellhop arrived, bearing a silver platter. "Message for the
Widow Fletcher?" he asked, using the pseudonym Miriam
had checked in under.

"That's me." Miriam took the note atop the platter—a
piece of card with strips of printed tape gummed to it.
MEET ME AT 54 GRT MAURICE ST AT 10 SEE BATES
STOP EB ENDS. "Ah, good." She glanced at the clock
above the ornate entrance. "Can you arrange a cab for me,
please? To Great Maurice Street, leaving in twenty minutes."

Folding her paper she rose and returned to her room to
retrieve her hat and topcoat. *The game's afoot,* she thought
excitedly.

By the time the cab found its way to Great Maurice Street
she'd cooled off a little, taking time to collect her thoughts
and begin to work out what she needed to do and say. She
also made sure her right glove was pulled down around her
wrist, and the sleeve of her blouse was bunched up toward
the elbow. Not that it was the ideal way to make an exit—
indeed, it would wreck her plans completely if she had to escape by means of the temporary tattoo of a certain intricate
knot—but if Erasmus had decided to sell her out to the constabulary, he'd be sorry.

Great Maurice Street was a curving cobblestoned boulevard hemmed in on either side by expensive stone town
houses. Little stone bridges leapt from sidewalk to broad
front doors across a trench which held two levels of subter-
ranean windows. The street and sidewalks had been swept
free of snow, although huge piles stood at regular intervals in

the road to await collection. Miriam stepped down from the cab, paid the driver, and marched along the sidewalk until she identified number 54. "Charteris, Bates and Charteris," she muttered to herself. "Sounds legal." She advanced on the door and pulled the bell-rope.

A short, irritated-looking clerk opened the door. "Who are you?" he demanded.

Miriam stared down her nose at him. "I'm here to see Mr. Bates," she said.

"Who did you say you were?" He raised a hand to cup his ear and Miriam realized he was half-deaf.

"Mrs. Fletcher, to see Mr. Bates," she replied loudly.

"*Oh.* Come in, then, I'll tell someone you're here."

Lawyers' offices didn't differ much between here and her own world, Miriam realized. There was a big, black, ancient-looking electric typewriter with a keyboard like a church organ that had shrunk in the wash, and there was an archaic telephone with a separate speaking horn, but otherwise the only differences were the clothes. Which, for a legal secretary in this place and time—male, thin, harried-looking—included a powdered wig, knee breeches, and a cutaway coat. "Please be seated—ah, no," said the secretary, looking bemused as a tall fellow dressed entirely in black opened the door of an inner office and waggled a finger at Miriam: "This is His Honor Mr. Bates," he explained. "You are . . . ?"

"I'm Mrs. Fletcher," Miriam repeated patiently. "I'm supposed to be seeing Mr. Bates. Is that right?"

"Ah, yes." Bates nodded congenially at her. "If you'd like to come this way, please?"

The differences from her own world became vanishingly small inside his office, perhaps because so many lawyers back home aimed for a traditional feel to their furnishings. Miriam glanced round. "Burgeson isn't here yet," she observed disapprovingly.

"He's been detained," said Bates. "If you'd care to take a seat?"

"Yes." Miriam sat down. "How much has Erasmus told you?"

Bates picked up a pair of half-moon spectacles and balanced them on the bridge of his nose. His whiskers twitched, walruslike. "He has told me enough, I think," he intoned in a plummy voice. "A woman fallen upon hard times, husband dead after years abroad, papers lost in an unfortunate pursuit—I believe he referred to the foundering of the *Greenbaum Lamplight*, a most unpleasant experience for you, I am sure—and therefore in need of the emolient reaffirmation of her identity, is that right? He vouched for you most plaintively. And he also mentioned something about a fortune overseas, held in trust, to which you have limited access."

"Yes, that's all correct," Miriam said fervently. "I am indeed in need of new papers—and a few other services best rendered by a man of the law."

"Well. I can see *at a glance* that you are no Frenchie," he said, nodding at her. "And so I can see nothing wrong with your party. It will take but an hour to draw up the correct deeds and post them with the inns of court, to declare your identity fair and square. Erasmus said you were born at Shreveport on, ah, if I may be so indelicate, the seventh of September, in the year of our lord nineteen hundred and sixty nine. Is that correct?"

Miriam nodded. *Near enough,* she thought. "Uh, yes."

"Very well. If you would examine and sign this—" he passed a large and imposing sheet of parchment to her— "and this—" he passed her another, "we will set the wheels of justice in motion."

Miriam examined the documents rapidly. One of them was a declaration of some sort; asserting her name, age, place of birth, and identity and petitioning for a replacement birth certificate for the one lost at sea on behalf of the vacant authorities of—"Why are the authorities of Shreveport not directly involved?" she asked.

Bates looked at her oddly. "After what happened during the war there isn't enough left of Shreveport to *have* any authorities," he muttered darkly.

"Oh." She read on. The next paper petitioned for a passport in her name, with a peculiar status—competent adult. "I see I am considered a competent adult here. Can you just explain precisely what that entails?"

"Certainly." Bates leaned back in his chair. "You are an adult, aged over thirty, and a widow; there is no man under whose mantle your rights and autonomy are exercised, and you are deemed old enough in law to be self-sufficient. So you may enter into contracts at your own peril, as an adult, until such time as you choose to remarry, and any such contracts as you make will then be binding upon your future husband."

"Oh," she said faintly, and signed in the space provided. *Better not marry anyone, then.* She put the papers back on his desk then cleared her throat. "There are some other matters I will want you to see to," she added.

"And what might those be?" He smiled politely. After all, the clock was ticking at her expense.

"Firstly." She held up a finger. "There is a house that takes my fancy; it is located at number 46, Bridge Park Lane, and it appears to be empty. Am I right in thinking you can make inquiries on my behalf about its availability? If it's open for lease or purchase I'd be extremely interested in acquiring it, and I'll want to move in as soon as possible."

Bates sat up straight and nodded, almost enthusiastically. "Of course, of course," he said, scribbling in a crabbed hand on a yellow pad. "And is there anything else?" he asked.

"Secondly." She held up a second finger. "Over the next month I will be wanting to create or purchase a limited liability company. It will need setting up. In addition, I will have a number of applications for patents that must be processed through the royal patent office—I need to locate and retain a patent agent on behalf of my company."

"A company, and a patents agent." He raised an eyebrow but kept writing. "Is there anything else?" he asked politely.

"Indeed. Thirdly, I have a quantity, held overseas, I should add, of bullion. Can you advise me on the issues surrounding its legal sale here?"

"Oh, that's easy." He put his pen down. "I can't, because it's illegal for anyone but the crown to own bullion." He pointed at the signet ring he wore on his left hand. "No rule against jewelry, of course, so long as it weighs less than a pound. But bullion?" He sniffed. "You can perhaps approach the mint about an import license, and sell it to the crown yourself—they'll give you a terrible rate, not worth your while, only ten pounds for an ounce. But that's the war, for you. The mint is chronically short. If I were you I'd sell it overseas and repatriate the proceeds as bearer bonds."

"Thank you." Miriam beamed at him ingratiatingly to cover up the sound of her teeth grinding together. *Ten pounds for an ounce? Erasmus, you and I are going to have strong words,* she thought. *Scratch finding an alternative, though.* "How long will this take?" she asked.

"To file the papers? I'll have the boy run over with them right now. Your passport and birth certificate will be ready to-morrow if you send for them from my office. The company—" he rubbed his chin. "We would have to pay a parliamentarian to get the act of formation passed as a private member's bill in this sitting, and I believe the going rate has been driven up by the demands of the military upon the legislature in the current session. It would be cheaper to buy an existing company with no debts. I can ask around, but I believe it will be difficult to find one for less than seventy pounds."

"Ouch." Miriam pulled a face. "There's no automatic pro-cess to go through to set one up?"

"Sadly, no." Bates shook his head. "Every company re-quires an act of parliament; rubber-stamping them is bread and butter for most MPs, for they can easily charge fifty pounds or more to put forward an early day motion for a five-minute bill in the Commons. Every so often someone proposes a registry of companies and a regulator to create them, but the backbenches won't ever approve that—it would take a large bite out of their living."

"Humph." Miriam nodded. "Alright, we'll do it your way. The patent agent?"

Bates nodded. "Our junior clerk, Hinchliffe, is just the fel-low for such a job. He has dealt with patents before, and will doubtless do so again. When will you need him?"

Miriam met Bates's eye. "Not until I have a company to employ him, a company that I will capitalize by entirely legal means that need not concern you." The lawyer nodded again, eyes knowing. "Then—let's just say, I have encountered some ingenious innovations overseas that I believe may best be exploited by patenting them, and farming out the rights to the patents to local factory owners. Do you follow?"

"Yes, I think I do." Bates nodded to himself, and smiled like a crocodile. "I look forward to your future custom, Mrs. Fletcher. It has been a pleasure to do business with such a perceptive member of the frail sex. Even if I don't believe a word of it."

Miriam spent the rest of the morning shopping for clothes. It was a disorienting experience. There were no department or chain stores: Each type of garment needed purchasing from a separate supplier, and the vast majority needed alterations to fit. Nor was she filled with enthusiasm by what she found. "Why are fashion items invariably designed to make people look ugly or feel uncomfortable?" she muttered into her microphone, after experiencing a milliner's and a corsetiere's in rapid succession. "I'm going to stick to sports bras and briefs, even if I have to carry everything across myself," she grumbled. Nevertheless, she managed to find a couple of presentable walking suits and an evening outfit.

At six that evening, she walked through the gathering gloom to Burgeson's shop and slipped inside. The shop was open, but empty. She spent a good minute tapping her toes and whistling tunelessly before Erasmus emerged from the back.

"Oh, it's you," he said distractedly. "Here." He held out an envelope.

Miriam took it and opened it—then stopped whistling. "What brought this on?" she asked, holding it tightly.

His cheek twitched. "I got a better price than I could be sure of," he said. "It seemed best to cut you in on the profits, in the hope of a prosperous future trade."

Miriam relaxed slightly. "I see." She slid the envelope into a jacket pocket carefully. The five ten-pound notes in it were more than she'd expected to browbeat out of him. "Is your dealer able to take larger quantities of bullion?" she asked, abruptly updating her plans.

"I believe so." His face was drawn and tired. "I've had some thinking to do."

"I can see that," she said quietly. Fifty pounds here was equivalent to something between three and seven thousand dollars, back home. Gold was *expensive,* a sign of demand, and what did that tell her? Nothing good. "What's the situation? Do you trust Bates?"

"About as far as I can throw him," Erasmus admitted. "He isn't a fellow traveler."

"Fellow traveler." She nodded to herself. "You're a Marxist?"

"He was the greatest exponent of my faith, yes." He said it quietly and fervently. "I believe in natural rights, to which all men and women are born equal; in democracy: and in freedom. Freedom of action, freedom of commerce, freedom of faith, just like old Karl. For which they hanged him."

"He came to somewhat different conclusions where I come from," Miriam said dryly, "although his starting conditions were dissimilar. Are you going to shut up shop and tell me what's troubling you?"

"Yes." He strode over and turned the sign in the door, then shot the bolt. "In the back, if you please."

"After you." Miriam followed him down a narrow corridor walled in pigeon holes. Parcels wrapped in brown paper gathered dust in them, each one sprouting a plaintive ticket against the date of its redemption—graveyard markers in the catacombs of usury. She kept her hand in her right pocket, tightening her grip on the small pistol, heart pounding halfway out of her chest with tension.

"You can't be a police provocateur," he commented over his shoulder. "For one thing, you didn't bargain hard enough over the bullion. For another, you slipped up in too many ways, all of them wrong. But I wasn't sure you weren't simply a madwoman until you showed me that intricate engine and left the book." He stepped sideways into a niche with a flight of wooden steps in it, leading down. "It's far too incredible a story to be a flight-of-the mind concoction, and far too . . . *expensive*. Even the publisher's notes! The quality of the paper. And the typeface." He stopped at the foot of the stairs and stared up at her owlishly, one hand clutching at a load-bearing beam for support. "And the pocket kinomagraph. I think either you're real or I'm going mad," he said, his voice hollow.

"You're not mad." Miriam took the steep flight of steps carefully. "So?"

"So it behooves me to study this fascinating world you come from, and ask how it came to pass." Erasmus was moving again. The cellar was walled from floor to ceiling in boxes and packing cases. "It's fascinating. The principles of enlightenment that your republic was founded on—you realize they were smothered in the cradle, in the history I know of? Yes, by all means, the Parliamentary Settlement and the exile were great innovations for their time—but the idea of a *republic!* Separation of Church and State, a bill of rights, a universal franchise! After the second Leveler revolt, demands for such rights became something of a dead issue here, emphasis on the *dead* if you follow me . . . hmm." He stopped in a cleared space between three walls of crates, a paraffin lamp hanging from a beam overhead.

"This is a rather big shop," Miriam commented, tightening her grip on the gun.

"So it should be." He glanced at her, saw the hand in her pocket. "Are you going to shoot me?"

"Why should I?" She tensed.

"I don't know." He shrugged. "You've obviously got some scheme in mind, one that means someone no good, whatever else you're doing here. And I might know too much."

Miriam came to a decision and took her hand out of her pocket—empty.

"And I'm not an innocent either," Erasmus added, gesturing at the crates. "I'm glad you decided not to shoot. Niter of glycerol takes very badly to sudden shocks."

Miriam took a deep breath and paused, trying to get a grip on herself. She felt a sudden stab of apprehension: The stakes in his game were much higher than she'd realized. This was a police state, and Erasmus wasn't just a harmless dealer in illegal publications. "Listen, I have *no* intention of shooting anyone if I can avoid it. And I don't care about you being a Leveler quartermaster with a basement full of explosives—at least, as long as I don't live next door to you. It's none of my damn business, and whatever you think, I didn't come here to get involved in *your* politics. Even if it sounds better than, than what's out there right now. On the other hand, I have my own, uh, political problems."

Erasmus raised an eyebrow. "So who are your enemies?"

Miriam bit her lip. *Can I trust him this far?* She couldn't see any choices at this point but, even so, taking him into her confidence was a big step. "I don't know," she said reluctantly. "They're probably well-off. Like me, they can travel between worlds—not to the one in the book I gave you, which is my own, but to a much poorer, medieval one. One in which Christianity never got established as the religion in Rome, the dark ages lasted longer, and the Norse migration reached and settled this coast, as far inland as the Appalachians, and the Chinese empire holds the west. These people will be involved in trading, from here to there—I'm not sure what, but I believe ownership of gold is something to investigate. They'll probably be a large and prosperous family, possibly ennobled in the past century or two, and they'll be rich and conservative. Not exactly fellow travelers."

"And what is your problem with them?"

"They keep trying to kill me." Now she'd said it, confiding in him felt easier. "They come from over here. This is their power base, Erasmus. I believe they consider me a threat to them. I want to find them before they find me, and order things in a more satisfactory manner."

"I think I see." He made a steeple of his fingers. "Do you want them to die?"

"Not necessarily," she said hesitantly. "But I want to know who they are, and where they came here from, and to stop their agents trying to kill me. I've got a couple of suspicions about who they are that I need to confirm. If I'm correct I might be able to stop the killing."

"I suggest you tell me your story then," said Erasmus. "And we'll see if there's anything we can do about it." He raised his voice, causing her to start. "Aubrey! You can cease your lurking. If you'd be so good as to fetch the open bottle of port and three glasses, you may count yourself in for a long story." He smiled humorlessly. "You've got our undivided attention, ma'am. I suggest you use it wisely . . ."

Back at the hotel a couple of hours later, Miriam changed into her evening dress and went downstairs, unaccompanied, for a late buffet supper. The waiter was unaccountably short with her, but found her a solitary small table in a dark corner of the dining room. The soup was passable, albeit slightly cool, and a cold roast with vegetables filled the empty corners of her stomach. She watched the well-dressed men and few women in the hotel from her isolated vantage point, and felt abruptly lonely. *Is it just ordinary homesickness?* she wondered, *or culture shock?* One or two hooded glances came her way, but she avoided eye contact and in any event nobody attempted to engage her in conversation. *It's as if I'm invisible,* she thought.

She didn't stay for dessert. Instead she retreated to her room and sought sollace with a long bath and an early night.

The next morning she warned the concierge that she would be away for a few days and would not need her room, but would like her luggage stored. Then she took a cab to the lawyer's office. "Your papers are here, ma'am," said Bates's secretary.

"Is Mr. Bates free?" she asked. "Just a minute of his time."

"I'll just check." A minute of finger twiddling passed. "Yes, come in, please."

"Ah, Mr. Bates?" She smiled. "Have you made progress with your inquiries?"

He nodded. "I am hoping to hear about the house tomorrow," he said. "Its occupant, a Mr. Soames, apparently passed away three months ago and it is lying vacant as part of his estate. As his son lives in El Dorado, I suspect an offer for it may be received with gratitude. As to the company—" He shrugged. "What business shall I put on it?"

Miriam thought for a moment. "Call it a design bureau," she said. "Or an engineering company."

"That will be fine." Bates nodded. "Is there anything else?"

"I'm going to be away for a week or so," she said. "Shall I leave a deposit behind for the house?"

"I'm sure your word would be sufficient," he said graciously. "Up to what level may I offer?"

"If it goes over a thousand pounds I'll have to make special arrangements to transfer the funds."

"Very well." He stood up. "By your leave?"

Miriam's last port of call was the central library. She spent two hours there, quizzing a helpful librarian about books on patent law. In the end, she took three away with her, giving her room at the hotel as an address. Carefully putting them in her shoulder bag she walked to the nearest main road and waved down a cab. "Roundgate Interchange," she said. *I'm going home,* she thought. *At last!* A steam car puttered past them, overtaking on the right hand side. *Back to clean air, fast cars, and electricity everywhere.*

She gazed out of the cab's window as the open field came into view through the haze of acrid fog that seemed to be everywhere today. *I wonder how Brill and Paulie have been?* She thought. *It'll be good to see them again.*

It was dusk, and nobody seemed to have noticed the way that Miriam had damaged the side door of the estate. She slunk into the garden, paced past the hedge and the dilapidated greenhouse, then located the spot where she'd blazed a mark on the wall. A fine snow was falling as she pulled out the second locket and, with the aid of a pocket flashlight, fell head-first into it.

She staggered slightly as the familiar headache returned with a vengeance, but a quick glance told her that nobody had come anywhere near this spot for days. A fresh snowfall had turned her hide into an anonymous hump in the gloom a couple of trees away. She waded toward it—then a dark shadow detached itself from a tree and pointed a pistol at her.

"Brill?" she asked, uncertainly.

"Miriam!" The barrel dropped as Brill lurched forward and embraced her. "I've been so worried! How have you been?"

"Not so bad!" Miriam laughed, breathlessly. "Let's get under cover and I'll tell you about it."

Brill had been busy; the snowbank concealed not only the hunting hide, but a fully assembled hut, six feet by eight, somewhat insecurely pegged to the iron-hard ground beneath the snow. "Come in, come in," she said. Miriam stepped inside and she shut the door and bolted it. Two bunks occupied one wall, and a paraffin heater threw off enough warmth to keep the hut from freezing. "It's been terribly cold by night, and I fear I've used up all the oil," Brill told her. "You really *must* buy a wood stove!"

"I believe I will," Miriam said thoughtfully, thinking about the coal smoke and yellow sulfurous smog that had made the air feel as if she was breathing broken glass. "It's been, hmm, three days. Have you had any trouble?"

"Boredom," Brilliana said instantly. "But sometimes boredom is a good thing. I have not been so alone in many years!" She looked slightly wistful. "Would you like some cocoa? I'd love to hear what adventures you've been having!"

That night Miriam slept fitfully, awakening once to a distant howling noise that raised the hair on her neck. *Wolves?* she wondered, before rolling over and dozing off again. Although the paraffin heater kept the worst of the chill at bay, there was frost inside the walls by morning.

Miriam woke first, sat up and turned the heat up as high as it would go, then—still cocooned in the sleeping bag—hung her jeans and hiking jacket from a hook in the roof right over the heater. Then she dozed off again. When she awakened, she saw Brill sitting beside the heater reading a book. "What is it?" she asked sleepily.

"Something Paulie lent me." Brill looked slightly guilty. Miriam peered at the spine: *The Female Eunuch.* Sitting on a shelf next to the door she spotted a popular history book. Brill had been busy expanding her horizons.

"Hmm." Miriam sat up and unzipped her bag, used the chamber pot, then hastily pulled on the now-defrosted jeans and a hiking sweater. Her boots were freezing cold—she'd left them too close to the door—so she moved them closer to the heater. "You've been thinking a lot."

"Yes." Brilliana put the book down. "I grew up with books; my father's library had five in hoh'sprashe, and almost thirty in English. But this—the style is so strange! And what it says!"

Miriam shook her head. *Too much to assimilate.* "We'll have to go across soon," she said, shelving the questions that sat at the tip of her tongue—poisonous questions, questions about trust and belief. Brill seemed to be going through a phase of questioning everything, and that was fine by Miriam. It meant she was less likely to obey if Angbard or whoever was behind her told her to point a gun at Miriam. Searching her bag Miriam came up with her tablets, dry-swallowed them, then glanced around. "Anything to drink?"

"Surely." Brill passed her a water bottle. It crackled slightly, but most of the contents were still liquid. "I didn't realize a world could be so large," Brill added quietly.

"I know how you feel," Miriam said with feeling, running fingers through her hair—it needed a good wash and, now she thought about it, at least a trim—she's spent the past four weeks so preoccupied in other things that it was growing wild and uncontrolled. "The far side is pretty strange to me, too. I *think* I've got it under control, but—" she shrugged uncomfortably. *Private ownership of gold is so illegal there's a black market in it, but opium and cocaine are sold openly in apothecary shops. Setting up a company takes an act of Parliament, but they can impeach the king.* "Let's just say, it isn't quite what I was expecting. Let's go home."

"Alright."

Miriam and Brill pulled their boots and coats on. Brill turned off the heater and folded the sleeping bags neatly then went outside to empty the chamber pot. Miriam picked up her shoulder bag, and then went outside to join Brill on the spot she'd marked on her last trip. She took a deep breath, pulled out the locket with her left hand, took all of Brill's weight on her right hip for a wobbly, staggering moment that threatened to pull her over, and focused—

On a splitting headache and a concrete wall as her grip slipped and Brill skidded on the icy yard floor. "Ow!" Brill stood up, rubbing her backside. "That was most indelicately done."

"Could be worse." Miriam winced at the pain in her temples, glanced around, and shook her head to clear the black patches from the edge of her vision. There was no sign of any intrusion, but judging by the boxes stacked under the metal fire escape—covered with polythene sheeting against the weather—Paulette had been busy. "Come on inside, let's fix some coffee and catch up on the news."

The office door opened to Miriam's key and she hastily punched in the code to disable the burglar alarm. Then she felt the heat, a stifling warmth that wrapped itself around her like a hot bath towel. "Wow," she said, "come get a load of this."

"I'm coming! I'm coming!" Brill shut and locked the door behind her and looked around. "Ooh, I haven't been this warm in *days*." She hastily opened her jacket and untied her boots, the better to let the amazing warmth from the underfloor heating get closer to her skin.

"You'll want to use the shower next," Miriam said, amused. "I could do with it too, so don't be too long." The shower in the office bathroom was cramped and cheap, but better than the antique plumbing arrangements on the far side. "I'll make coffee."

Miriam found her mobile phone in the front room. Its battery had run down while she'd been gone, so she plugged it in to recharge. She also found a bunch of useful items—

Paulette had installed a brand new desk telephone and modem line while she'd been away—and a bunch of paperwork from the city government.

She was drinking her coffee in the kitchen when the front door opened. Miriam ducked out into the corridor, hand going to her empty jacket pocket before she realized what the reaction meant. "Paulie!" she called.

"Miriam! Good to see you!" Paulette had nearly jumped right out of her skin when she saw Miriam, but now she smiled broadly. "Oh wow. You look like you've spent a week on the wild side!"

"That's exactly what I've done. Coffee?"

"I'd love some, thanks." There was someone behind her. "In the front office, Mike, it needs to come through under the window," she said over her shoulder. "We're putting a DSL line in here," she told Miriam. "Hope you don't mind?"

"No, no, that's great." She retreated back into the small kitchenette, mind blanking on what to do next. She'd been thinking about a debriefing session with Paulie and Brill, then a provisioning trip to the universe next door, then a good filling lunch—but not with a phone company installer drilling holes in the wall.

Paulette obviously had things well in hand here, and there was no way Miriam was going to get into the shower for a while. She stared at the coffee machine blackly for a while. *Maybe I should go and see Iris,* she decided. *Or . . . hmm. Is it time to call Roland again?*

"Miriam. You've going to have to tell me how it's going." Paulette waited in the kitchen doorway.

"In due course." Miriam managed a smile. "Success, but not so total." Miriam sobered up fast. "At your end?"

"Running low on money—the burn rate on this operation is like a goddamn start-up," Paulette complained. "I'll need another hundred thousand to secure all the stuff you left on the shopping list."

"And don't forget the paycheck." Miriam nodded. "Listen, I found one good thing out about the far side. Gold is about as legal there as heroin is here, and vice versa. I'm getting about two hundred pounds on the black market for a brick weighing sixteen Troy ounces, worth about three thousand, three five, dollars here. A pound goes a *lot* further than a dollar, it's like, about two hundred bucks. So three and a half thousand here buys me the equivalent of forty thousand over there. Real estate prices are low, too. The place I need to buy on the far side is huge, but it should go for about a thousand pounds, call it equivalent to two hundred grand here. In our own Boston it'd be going for upwards of a million, easily. But gold is worth so much that I can pay for it with five bars of the stuff—about eighteen thousand dollars on this side. I've found an, uh, black-market outlet who seems reasonably trustworthy at handling the gold—he's got his angles, but I know what they are. And it is *amazingly* easy to set up a new identity! Anyway, if I play this right I can build a front as a rich widow returning home from the empire with a fortune and then get the far side money pump running."

"What are you going to carry the other way?" Paulette asked, sharply.

"Not sure yet." Miriam rubbed her temples. "It's weird. They sell cocaine and morphine in drugstores, over the counter, and they fly Zeppelins, and New Britain is at war with the French Empire, and their version of Karl Marx was executed for Ranting—preaching democracy and equal rights. With no industrial revolution he turned into a leveler ideologue instead of a socialist economist. I'm just surprised he was born in the first place—most of the names in the history books are unfamiliar after about eighteen hundred. It's like a different branch in the same infinite tree of history; I wonder where Niejwein fits in it . . . let's not go there now. I need to think of something we can import." She brooded. "I'll have to think fast. If the Clan realizes their drug-money pump could run this efficiently they'll flood the place with cheap gold and drop the price of crack in half as soon as they learn about it. There's got to be some *other* commodity that's valuable over here that we can use to repatriate our profits."

"Old masters," Paulette said promptly.

"Huh?"

"Old masters." She put her mug down. "Listen, they haven't had a world war, have they?"

"Nope, I'm afraid they have," Miriam said, checking her watch to see if she could take another pain killer yet. "In fact, they've had two. One in the eighteen-nineties that cost them India. The second in the nineteen-fifties that, well, basically New Britain got kicked out of Africa. Africa is a mess of French and Spanish colonies. But they got a strong alliance with Japan and the Netherlands, which also rule most of northwest Germany. And they rule South America and Australia and most of East Asia."

"No tanks? No H-bombs? No strategic bombers?"

"No." Miriam paused. "Are you saying—"

"Museum catalogues!" Paulie said excitedly. "I've been thinking about this a lot while you've been gone. What we do is, we look for works of art dating to before things went, uh, differently. In the other place. Works that were in museums in Europe that got bombed during World War Two, works that disappeared and have never been seen since. You get the picture? Just *one* lost sketch by Leonardo . . ."

"Won't they be able to tell the difference?" Miriam frowned. "I'd have thought the experts would—" she trailed off.

"They'll be exactly the same age!" Paulette said excitedly. "They'd be the real thing, right? Not a hoax. What you do is, you go over with some art catalogues from here and when you've got the money you find a specialist buyer and you buy the paintings or marbles or whatever for your personal collection. Then bring them over here. It's about the only thing that weighs so little you can carry it, but is worth millions and is legal to own."

"It'll be harder to sell," Miriam pointed out. "A *lot* harder to sell."

"Yeah, but it's legal," said Paulie. She hesitated momentarily: "unless you want to go into the Bolivian marching powder business like your long-lost relatives?"

"Um." Miriam refilled her coffee mug. "Okay, I'll look at it." *Miriam Beckstein, dealer in fine arts,* she thought. It had a peculiar ring to it, but it was better than *Miriam Beckstein, drug smuggler.* "Hmm. How's this for a cover story? I fly over to Europe next year, spend weeks trolling around out there in France and Germany and wherever the paintings went missing. Right? I act secretive and just tell people I'm investigating something. That covers my absence. What I'll really be doing is crossing to the far side then flying right back to New Britain by airship. Maybe I'll come home in the meantime, maybe I can work over there, whatever. Whichever I do, it builds up a record of me being out of the country, investigating lost art, and I use the travel time to read up on art history. When I go public over here, it's a career change. I've gone into unearthing lost works of art and auctioning them. Sort of a capitalist version of Indiana Jones, right?"

"Love it." Paulie winked at her. "Wait till I patent the business practice, 'a method of making money by smuggling gold to another world and exchanging it for lost masterpieces'!"

"You *dare*—" Miriam chuckled. "Although I'm not sure we'll be able to extract anything like the full value of our profits that way. I'm not even sure we want to—having a world to live in where we're affluent and haven't spent the past few decades developing a reputation as organized criminals would be no bad thing. Anyway, back to business. How's the patent search going?"

"I've got about a dozen candidates for you," Paulie said briskly. "A couple of different types of electric motor that they may or may not have come up with. Flash boilers for steam cars, assuming they don't already have them. They didn't sound too sophisticated but you never know. The desk stapler—did you see any? Good. I looked into the proportional font stuff you asked for, but the Varityper mechanism is just amazingly complicated, it wouldn't just hatch out of nowhere. And the alkaline battery will take a big factory and supplies of unusual metals to start making. The most promising option is still the disk brake and the asbestos/resin brake shoe. But I came up with another for you: the parachute."

"Parachute—" Miriam's eyes widened. "I'll need to go check if they've invented them. I know Leonardo drew one, but it wouldn't have been stable. Okay!" She emptied the coffeepot into her and Paulette's mugs, stirred in some sugar. "That's great. How long until the cable guy is done?"

"Oh, he's already gone," Paulette said. "I get to plug the box in myself, don't you know?"

"Excellent." Miriam picked up her mug. "Then I can check my voice mail in peace."

She wandered into the front office as Brill was leaving the shower, wrapped in towels and steaming slightly. A new socket clung rawly to the wall just under the window. Miriam dropped heavily into the chair behind the desk, noticing the aches of sleeping on a hard surface for the first time. She picked up her phone and punched in her code. Paulette intercepted Brill, asking her something as she led her into the large back office they'd begun converting into a living room.

"You have two messages," said the phone.

"Yeah, yeah." Miriam punched a couple more buttons.

"First message, received yesterday at eleven-forty two: Miriam? Oh, Sky Father! Listen, are you alright? Phone me, *please."* It was Roland, and he didn't sound happy. Anguish rose in her chest. *Roland*—she didn't let the thought reach her tongue. "It's urgent," he added, before the click of the call ending.

"Second message, received yesterday at nine-twelve: Miriam, dear? It's me." *Iris,* she realized. There was a pause. "I know I haven't been entirely candid with you, and I want you to know that I bitterly regret it." Another, much longer pause and the sound of labored breathing. Miriam clutched the phone to her ear like a drowning woman. "I've . . . something unexpected has come up. I've got to go on a long journey. Miriam, I want you to understand that I *am* going to be alright. I know exactly what I'm doing, and it's something I should have done years ago. But it's not fair to burden you with it. I'll try to call you or leave messages, but you are *not* to come around or try to follow me. I love you." *Click.*

"Shit!" Miriam threw the mobile phone across the room

in a combination of blind rage and panic. She burst out of her chair and ran for the back room, grabbed her jacket and was halfway into her shoes by the time Paulette stuck a curious head out of the day room door. "What's going on?"

"Something's happened to Iris. I'm going to check on her."

"You can't!" Paulette stood up, alarmed.

"Watch me," Miriam warned.

"But it's under—"

"Fuck the surveillance!" She fumbled in her bag for the revolver. "If the Clan has decided to go after my mother I am going to kill someone."

"Miriam—" it was Brill—"Paulie and I can't get away the way you can."

"So you'd better be discreet about the murder business," said Paulette. She fixed Miriam with a worried stare. "Can you wait two minutes? I'll drive."

"I—yes." Miriam forced herself to unclench her fists and take deep, steady breaths.

"Good. Because if it *is* the Clan, rushing in is exactly what they'll expect you to do. And if it isn't, if it's the other guys, that's what *they'll* want you to do, too." She swallowed. "Bombs and all. Which is why *I'm* going with you. Got it?"

"I—" Miriam forced herself to think. "Okay." She stood up. "Let's go."

They went.

Paulette cruised down Iris's residential street twice, leaving a good five-minute interval before turning the rental car into the parking space at the side of her house. "Nothing obvious," she murmured. "You see anything, kid?"

"Nothing," said Miriam.

Brill shook her head. "Autos all look alike to me," she admitted.

"Great . . . Miriam, if you want to take the front door, I'm going to sit here with the engine running until you give the all-clear. Brill—"

"I'll be good." She clutched a borrowed handbag to her chest, right hand buried in it, looking like a furtive sorority girl about to drop an unexpected present on a friend.

Miriam bailed out of the car and walked swiftly to Iris's front door, noticing nothing wrong. There was no damage around the lock, no broken windows, nothing at all out of the usual for the area. No lurking Dodge vans, either, when she glanced over her shoulder as she slipped the key into the front door and turned it left-handed, her other hand full.

The door bounced open and Miriam ducked inside rapidly, with Brill right behind her. The house was empty and cold—not freezing with the chill of a dead furnace, but as if the thermostat had been turned down. Miriam's feet scuffed on the carpet as she rapidly scanned each ground floor room through their open doors, finishing in Iris's living room—

No wheelchair. The side table neatly folded and put away. Dead flowers on the mantlepiece.

Back in the hall Miriam held up a finger, then dashed up the stairs, kicking open door after door—the master bedroom, spare bedroom, box room, and bathroom.

"Nothing," she snarled, panting. In the spare bedroom she pulled down the hatch into the attic, yanked the ladder down— but there was no way Iris could have gotten up there under her own power. She scrambled up the ladder all the same, casting about desperately in the dusty twilight. "She's *not here.*"

Down in the ground floor hallway she caught up with Paulette, looking grave. "Brill said Iris is gone?"

Miriam nodded, unable to speak. It felt like an act of desecration, too monstrous to talk about. She leaned against the side of the staircase, taking shallow breaths. "I've lost her." She shut her eyes.

"Over here!" It was Brill, in the kitchen.

"What is it—"

They found Brill inspecting a patch of floor, just inside the back door. "Look," she said, pointing.

The floor was wooden, varnished and worn smooth in places. The stains, however, were new. Something dark had spilled across the back doorstep. Someone had mopped it up but they hadn't done a very good job, and the stain had worked into the grain of the wood.

"Outside. Check the garbage." Miriam fumbled with the lock then got the door open. "Come on!" She threw herself at the Dumpsters in the backyard, terrified of what she might find in them. The bins were huge, shared with the houses to either side, and probably not emptied since the last snowfall. The snow was almost a foot deep on top of the nearest Dumpster. It took her half a minute to clear enough away to lift the lid and look inside.

A dead man stared back at her, his face blue and his eyes frozen in an expression of surprise. She dropped the lid.

"What is it?" asked Paulette.

"Not Iris." Miriam leaned against the wall, taking deep breaths, her head spinning. *Who can he be?* "Check. The other bins."

"Other bins, okay." Paulette gingerly lifted the lids, one by one—but none of them contained anything worse than a pile of full garbage bags which, when torn, proved to contain kitchen refuse. "She's not here, Miriam."

"Oh thank god."

"What now?" asked Paulie, head cocked as if listening for the sound of sirens.

"I take another look while you and Brill keep an eye open for strangers." Steeling herself, Miriam lifted the lid on the bin's gruesome contents. "Hmm." She reached out and touched her hand to an icy cold cheek. "He's been dead for at least twelve hours, more likely over twenty-four." A mass of icy black stuff in front of the body proved to be Iris's dish towels, bulked up by more frozen blood than Miriam could have imagined. She gingerly shoved them aside, until she saw where the blood had come from. "There's massive trauma to the upper thorax, about six inches below the neck. Jesus, it looks like a shotgun wound. Saw a couple in the ER, way back when. Um . . . sawed-off, by the size of the entry wound, either that or he was shot from more than twenty yards away, which would have had to happen outdoors, meaning witnesses. His chest is really torn up, he'd have died instantly." She dropped the wadding back in front of the body. He was, she noted distantly, wearing black overalls and a black ski mask pulled up over his scalp like a cap. Clean-shaven, about twenty years old, of military appearance. Like a cop or a soldier—or a Clan enforcer.

She turned around and looked at the back door. Something was wrong with it; it took almost a minute of staring before she realized—

"They replaced the door," she said. "They replaced the fucking door!"

"Let's go," Paulette said nervously. "Like right now? Anywhere, as long as it's away? This is giving me the creeps."

"Just a minute." Miriam dropped the Dumpster lid shut and went back inside the house. *Iris phoned me when the shit hit the fan,* she realized distantly. *She was still alive and free, but she had to leave. To go underground, like in the sixties. When the FBI bugged her phone.* Miriam leaned over Iris's favorite chair, in the morning room. She swept her hand around the crack behind the cushion; nothing. "No messages?" She looked up, scanning the room. The mantlepiece: dead flowers, some cards . . . birthday cards. One of them said 32 TODAY. She walked toward it slowly, then picked it up, unbelieving. Her eyes clouded with tears as she opened it. The inscription inside it was written in Iris's jagged, half-illiterate scrawl. *Thanks for the memories of treasure hunts, and the green party shoes,* it said. "Green party shoes?"

Miriam dashed upstairs, into Iris's bedroom. Opening her mother's wardrobe she smelled mothballs, saw row upon row of clothes hanging over a vast mound of shoes—a pair of green high-heeled pumps near the front, pushed together. She picked them up, probed inside, and felt a wad of paper filling the toes of the right shoe.

She pulled it out, feeling it crackle—elderly paper, damaged by the passage of time. A tabloid newspaper page, folded tight. She ran downstairs to where Brill was waiting impatiently in the hall. "I got it," she called.

"Got what?" Brill asked, her voice incurious.

"I don't know." Miriam frowned as she locked the door,

then they were in the back of the car and Paulie was pulling away hastily, fishtailing slightly on the icy road.

"When your mother phoned you," Paulie said edgily, "what did she say? Daughter, I've killed someone? Or, your wicked family has come to kidnap me, oh la! What is to become of me?"

"She said." Miriam shut her eyes. "She hadn't been entirely honest with me. Something had come up, and she had to go on a journey."

"Someone died," said Brill. "Someone standing either just outside the back door or just inside it, in the doorway. Someone shot them with a blunderbuss." She was making a singsong out of it, in a way that really got on Miriam's nerves. *Stress,* she thought. *Brill had never seen a murder before last week. Now she's seen a couple in one go, hasn't she?* "So someone stuffed the victim in a barrel for Iris, went out and ordered a new door. Angbard's men will have been watching her departure. Probably followed her. Why don't you call him and ask about it?"

"I will. Once we've returned this car and rented a replacement from another hire shop." She glanced at Brill. "Keep a lookout and tell me if you see any cars that seem to be following us."

Miriam unfolded the paper carefully. It was, she saw, about the same fateful day as the first Xeroxed news report in the green and pink shoebox. But this was genuine newsprint, not a copy, a snapshot from the time itself. Most of it was inconsequential, but there was a story buried halfway down page two that made her stare, about a young mother and baby found in a city park, the mother suffering a stab wound in the lower back. She'd been wearing hippy-style clothes and was unable to explain her condition, apparently confused or intoxicated. The police escorted her to a hospital with the child, and the subeditor proceeded to editorialize on the evils of unconventional lifestyles and the effects of domestic violence in a positively Hogarthian manner. *No,* Miriam thought, *they must have gotten it wrong. She was murdered, Ma told me! Not taken into hospital with a stab wound!* She shook her head, bewildered and hurting. "I'll do that. But first I need some stuff from my house," she said, "but I'm not sure I dare go there."

"What stuff?" asked Paulie. Miriam could see her fingers white against the rim of the steering wheel.

"Papers." She paused, weighing up the relative merits of peace of mind and a shotgun wound to the chest. "Fuck it," she said shortly. "I need to go home. I need five minutes there. Paulie, take me home."

"Whoa! Is that really smart?" asked Paulette, knuckles tightening on the steering wheel.

"No." Miriam grimaced. "It's really *not* smart. But I need to grab some stuff, the goddamn disk with all your research on it. I'll be about thirty seconds. We can ditch the car immediately afterwards. You willing to wait?"

"Didn't you say they'd staked you out?"

"What does that mean?" Brill asked, confused. "What are you talking about?"

Miriam sighed. "My house," she said. "I haven't been back to it since my fun-loving uncle had me kidnapped. Roland said it was under surveillance so I figured it would be risky. Now—"

"It's even *more* risky," Paulette said vehemently. "In fact I think it's stupid."

"Yes." Miriam bared her teeth, worry and growing anger eating at her: "But I *need* that disk, Paulie, it may be the best leverage I've got. We don't have time for me to make millions in world three."

"Oh shit. You think it may come to that?"

"Yeah, 'oh shit' indeed."

"What kind of disk?" Brill asked plaintively.

"Don't worry. Just wait with the car." Miriam focused on Paulette's driving. *The answer will be somewhere in the shoebox,* she thought, desperately. *And if Angbard had my ma snatched, I'll make him pay!*

Familiar scenery rolled past, and a couple of minutes later they turned into a residential street that Miriam knew well enough to navigate blindfolded. A miserable wave of homesickness managed to penetrate her anger and worry: This was where she belonged, and she should never have left. It was her home, dammit! And it slid past to the left as Paulette kept on driving.

"Paulie?" Miriam asked anxiously.

"Looking for suspicious-acting vehicles," Paulie said tersely.

"Oh." Miriam glanced around. "Ma said there was a truck full of guys watching her."

"Uh-huh. Your mother spotted the truck. What did she miss?"

"Right." Miriam spared a sideways glance: Brill's head was swiveling like a ceiling fan, but her expression was more vacant than anything else. Almost as if she was bored. "Want to drive round the block once more? When you get back to the house stop just long enough for me to get out, then carry on. Come back and pick me up in three minutes. Don't park."

"Um. You sure that you want to do this?"

"No, I'm not sure, I just know that I have to."

Paulie turned the corner then pulled over. Miriam was out of the car in a second and Paulette pulled away. There was virtually nobody about—no parked occupied vans, no joggers. She crossed the road briskly, walked up to her front door, and remembered two things, in a single moment of icy clarity. Firstly, that she had no idea where her house keys might be, and secondly, that if there were no watchers this might be because—

Uh-oh, she thought, and backed away from the front step, watching where her feet were about to go with exaggerated caution. A cold sweat broke out in the small of her back, and she shuddered violently. But fear of trip wires didn't stop her carefully opening the yard gate, slipping around the side of the house, and up to the shed with the concealed key to the French doors at the back.

When she had the key, Miriam paused for almost a minute at the glass doors, trying to get her hammering heart under control. She peered through the curtains, thoughtfully. *They'll expect me to go in the front,* she realized. *But even so . . .* She unlocked the door and eased it open a finger's width. Then she reached as high as she could, and ran her index finger slowly down the opening, feeling for the faint tug of a lethal obstruction. Finding nothing, she opened the door farther, then repeated the exercise on the curtains. Again: nothing. And so, Miriam returned to her home.

Her study had been efficiently and brutally strip-searched. The iMac was gone, as were the boxes of CD-ROMs and the zip drive and disks from her desk. More obviously, every book in the bookcase had been taken down, the pages riffled, and dumped in a pile on the floor. It was a big pile. "Bastards," she said quietly. The pink shoebox was gone, of course. Fearing the worst she tiptoed into her own hallway like a timid burglar, her heart in her mouth.

It was much the same in the front hall. They'd even searched the phone books. A blizzard of loose papers lay everywhere, some of them clearly trampled underfoot. Drawers lay open, their contents strewn everywhere. Furniture had been pulled out from the walls and shoved back haphazardly, and one of the hall bookcases leaned drunkenly against the opposite wall. At first sight she thought that the living room had gotten off lightly, but the damage turned out to be even more extensive—her entire music collection had been turned out onto the floor, disks piled on a loose stack.

"Fuck." Her mouth tasted of ashes. The sense of violation was almost unbearable, but so was the fear that they'd taken her mother and found Paulie's research disk as well. The money-laundering leads were in the hands of whoever had done this to her. Whoever they were, they had to know about the Clan, which meant they'd know what the disk's contents meant. They were a smoking gun, one that was almost certainly pointing at the Clan's east coast operations. She knelt by the discarded CD cases and rummaged for a minute—found *The Beggar's Opera* empty, the CD-ROM purloined.

She went back into the front hall. Somehow she slithered past the fallen bookcase, just to confirm her worst fear. They'd strung the wire behind the front door, connecting one end of it to the handle. If she hadn't been in such a desperate hurry that she'd forgotten her keys, the green box taped crudely to the wall would have turned her into a messy stain on the sidewalk. *Assassin number two is the one who likes Claymore mines,* she reminded herself edgily. The cold fear was unbearable and Miriam couldn't take any more. She blundered out through the French doors at the back without pausing to lock them, round the side of the house, and onto the sidewalk to wait for Paulie.

Seconds later she was in the back of the car, hunched and shivering. "I don't see any signs of anything going on," Paulie said quietly. She seemed to have calmed down from her state at Iris's house. "What do you want to do now? Why don't we find a Starbucks, get some coffee, then you tell us what you found?"

"I don't think so." Miriam closed her eyes.

"Are you alright?" Brill asked, concern in her voice.

"No, I'm not alright," Miriam said quietly. "We've got to ditch the car, *now*. They trashed the place and left a trip-wire surprise behind the front door. Paulie, the box of stuff my mother gave me was gone. And so was the disk."

"Oh—*shit*. What are we going to do?"

"I—" Miriam stopped, speechless. "I'm going to talk to Angbard. But not until I've had a few words with Roland." She pulled an expression that someone who didn't know her might have mistaken for a smile. "He's the one who told me about the surveillance. It's time to clear the air between us."

PART 3

CAPITALISM FOR

BEGINNERS

INTERROGATIONS

The city of Irongate nestled in the foothills of the Appalachians, soot-stained and smoky by day, capped at night by a sky that reflected the red glow of the blast furnaces down by the shpping canal. From the center of town, the Great North-East Railway spur led off toward the coastline and the branches for Boston and New London. West of the yards and north of the banked ramparts of the Vauban pattern fortress sloped a gentle rise populated by the houses of the gentry, while at the foot of the slope clustered tight rows of worker's estates.

Irongate had started as a transport nexus at the crossing of the canal and the railways, but it had grown into a sprawling industrial city. The canal and its attendant lock system brought cargos from as far as the Great Lakes—and, in another time, another world, it was the site of a trading post with the great Iroquis Nation, who dominated the untamed continental interior between the Gruinmarkt and the empire of the West.

There was a neighborhood down in the valley, rubbing shoulders with the slums of the poor and the business districts, that was uncomfortable with its own identity. Some people had money but no standing in polite society, no title or prospects for social advancement. They congregated here, Chinese merchants and Jewish brokers and wealthy owners of bawdy houses alike, and they took pains to be discreet, for while New Britain's laws applied equally to all men, the enforcers of those laws were only too human.

Esau walked slowly along Hanover Street, his cane tapping the cobblestones with every other stride. It was early evening and bitterly cold with it, but the street sweepers had been at work and the electric street lamps cast a warm glow across the pavement. Esau walked slowly, forgoing the easy convenience of a cab, because he wanted time to think. It was vital to prepare himself for the meeting that lay ahead, both emotionally and intellectually.

The street was almost empty, the few pedestrians hurrying with hands thrust deep in coat pockets and hats pulled down. Esau passed a pub, a blare of brassy noise and a stench of tobacco smoke squirting from the doorway as it opened to emit a couple of staggering drunks. "Heya, slant-eye!" one of them bellowed after him. Esau kept on walking steadily, but his pulse raced and he carefully grasped the butt of the small pistol in his pocket. *Don't react,* he told himself. *You can kill him if he attacks you. Not before.* Not that Esau looked particularly Oriental, but to the Orange louts of Irongate anyone who didn't look like themselves was an alien. And reports of a white man killed by a Chinee would inflame the popular mood—building on the back of a cold winter and word of defeats in the Kingdom of Siam. The last thing Esau's superiors needed right now was a pogrom on the doorstep of their East Coast headquarters.

The betting shops were closed and the pawnbrokers shut, but between two such shops Esau paused. The tenement door was utterly plain, but well painted and solidly fitted. A row of bellpulls ran beside a set of brass plaques bearing the names of families who hadn't lived here in decades. Esau pulled the bottom-most bellpull, then the second from the top, the next one down, and the first from the bottom, in practiced series. There was a click from the door frame and he pushed through, into the darkened vestibule within. He shut the door carefully behind him, then looked up at the ceiling.

"Esh'sh icht," he said.

"Come on in," a man's voice replied in accented English. The inner door opened on light and finery—a stairwell furnished with rich hand-woven carpets, banisters of mahogany, illuminated by gilt-edged lamps in the shape of naked maidens. A ceramic lucky cat sat at one side of the staircase, opposite a guard. The guard bowed stiffly as soon as he saw Esau's face. "You are expected, lord," he said.

Esau ignored him and ascended the staircase. The tenement block above the two shops had been cunningly gutted and rebuilt as a palace. The rooms behind the front windows—visible from the street as ordinary bedrooms or kitchens—were Ames rooms barely three feet deep, their floors and walls and furniture slanted to preserve the semblance of depth when seen from outside. The family had learned the need for discretion long ago. Fabulous wealth was no social antidote for epicanthic folds and dark skins in New Britain and if there was one thing the mob disliked more than Chinee-men, it was rich and secretive criminal families of Chinee-men.

Vermin, Esau thought of the two drunks who had harangued him outside the pub. *Never mind.* At the top of the staircase he bowed once to the left, to the lacquered cabinet containing the household shrine. Then he removed his topcoat, hat, and shoes, and placed them in front of the servant's door to the right of the stairs. Finally he approached the door before the staircase, and knocked once with the head of his cane.

The door swung open. "Who calls?" asked the majordomo.

"It is I." Esau marched forward as the majordomo bowed low, holding the door aside for him. Like the guard below, the majordomo was armed, a pistol at his hip. If the mob ever came, it was their job to buy the family time to escape with their lives. "Where can I find the elder of days?"

"He takes tea in the Yellow Room, lord," said the majordomo, still facing the floor.

"Rise. Announce me."

Esau followed the majordomo along a wood-floored passage, the walls hung with ancient paintings. Some of them legacies of home, but others, in the European renaissance style, bore half-remembered names. The majordomo paused at a door just beyond a Caravaggio, then knocked. After a whispered conversation two guards emerged—guards in family uniform this time, not New British street clothes. In addition to their robes and twin swords (in the style this shadow-world called "Japanese," after a nation that had never existed in Esau's family home) they bore boxy black self-feeding carbines.

"His lordship," said the majordomo. Both soldiers came to attention. "Follow me."

The majordomo and guards proceeded before Esau, gathering momentum and a hand's count of additional followers as befitted his rank: a scribe with his scrolls and ink, a master of ceremonies whose assistant clucked over Esau's suit, following him with an armful of robes, and a gaggle of messengers. By the time they arrived outside the Yellow Room, Esau's quiet entry had turned into a procession. At the door, they paused. Esau held out his arms for the servants to hang a robe over his suit while the majordomo rapped on the door with his ceremonial rod of office. "Behold! His lordship James Lee, second of the line, comes to pay attendance before the elder of days!"

"Enter," called a high, reedy voice from inside the room.

Esau entered the Yellow Room, and bowed deeply. Behind him, the servants went to their knees and prostrated themselves.

"Rise, great-nephew," said the elder. "Approach me."

Esau—James Lee—approached his great-uncle. The elder sat cross-legged upon a cushioned platform, his wispy beard brushing his chest. He had none of the extravagant fingernails or long queue that popular mythology in this land imagined the mandarin class to have. Apart from his beard, his silk robes, and a certain angle to his cheekbones, he could pass for any beef-eating New Englishman. The family resemblance was pronounced. *This is how I will look in fifty years,* James Lee thought whenever he saw the elder. *If our enemies let me live that long.*

He paused in front of the dais and bowed deeply again, then once to the left and once to the right, where his great-uncle's companions sat in silence.

"See, a fine young man," his great-uncle remarked to his left. "A strong right hand for the family."

"What use a strong right hand, if the blade of the sword it holds is brittle?" snapped his neighbor. James held his breath, shocked at the impudence of the old man—his great-uncle's younger brother, Huan, controller of the eastern reaches for these past three decades. Such criticism might be acceptable in private, but in public it could only mean two things—outright questioning of the Eldest's authority, or the first warning that things had gone so badly awry that honor called for a scapegoat.

"You are alarming our young servant," the Eldest said mildly. "James, be seated, please. You may leave," he added, past Esau's shoulder.

The servants bowed and backed out of the noble presence. James lowered himself carefully to sit on the floor in front of the elders. They sat impassively until the doors thumped shut behind his back. "What are we to make of these accounts?" asked the Eldest, watching him carefully.

"The accounts? . . ." Esau puzzled for a moment. This was all going far too fast for comfort. "Do you refer to the reports from our agent of influence, or to the—"

"The agent." The Eldest shuffled on his cushion. "A cup of tea for my nephew," he remarked over his shoulder. A servant Esau hadn't noticed before stepped forward and placed a small tray before him.

"The situation is confused," Esau admitted. "When he first notified me of the re-emergence of the western alliance's line

I consulted with uncle Stork, as you charged me. My uncle sent word that the orders of your illustrious father were not discharged satisfactorily and must therefore be carried out. Unfortunately, the woman's existence was known far and wide among the usurpers by this time, and her elder tricked us, mingling her party with other women of his line so that the servants I sent mistook the one for the other. Now she has gone missing, and our agent says he doesn't know where."

"Ah," said the ancient woman at the Eldest's right hand. The Eldest glanced at her, but she fell silent.

"Our agent believes that the elder Angbard is playing a game within the usurper clan," Esau added. "Our agent intended to manipulate her into a position of influence, but controlled by himself—his goal was to replace Angbard. This goal is no longer achievable, so he has consented to pursue our preferences."

"Indeed," echoed Great-Uncle Huan, "that seems the wisest course of action to me."

"Stupid!" Esau jerked as the Eldest's fist landed on a priceless lacquered tray. "Our father's zeal has bound us to expose ourselves to their attack, lost a valued younger son to their guards, and placed our fate in the hands of a mercenary—"

"Ah," sighed the ancient woman. The Eldest subsided abruptly.

"Then what is to be done?" asked Huan, almost plaintively.

"Another question," said Esau's great-uncle, leaning forward. "When you sent brothers Kim and Wu after the woman they both failed to return. What of their talismans?"

James Lee hung his head. "I have no news, Eldest." He closed his eyes, afraid to face the wrath he could feel boiling on the dais before him. "The word I received from our agent Jacob is that no locket was found on either person. That the woman Miriam disappeared at the same time seems to suggest—" his voice broke. "Could she be of our line, as well?" he asked.

"It has never happened before," quavered the ancient woman next to the Eldest.

He turned and stared at her. "That is not the question,

aunt," he said, almost gently. "Could this long-lost daughter of the western alliance have come here?" he asked Esau. "None of them have ever done so before. Not since the abandonment."

James Lee took a deep breath. "I thought it was impossible," he said. "The family is divided by the abandonment. We come here, and they go . . . wherever it is that the source of their power is. They abandoned us, and that was the end of it, wasn't it? None of them ever came *here*."

"Do we know if it's possible?" asked Huan, squinting at Esau. "Our skill runs in the ever-thinning blood of the family. So does theirs. I see no way—"

"You are making unfounded assumptions," the Eldest interrupted. He turned his eyes on Esau. "The talisman is gone, and so is the woman. I find that highly suggestive. And worrying." He ran his fingers through his beard, distractedly. "Nephew, you must continue to seek the woman's demise. Seek it not because of my father's order, but because she may know our secrets. Seek her in the barbarian castles of Niejwein; also seek her here, in the coastal cities of the north-east. You are looking for a mysterious woman of means, suddenly sprung from thin air, making a place for herself. You know what to do. You must *also*—" he paused and took a sip of tea—"obtain a talisman from the usurper clan. When you have obtained one, by whatever means, compare it to your own. If they differ then I charge you to attempt to use it, both here and in the world of our ancestors. See where it takes you, if anywhere! If it is to familiar territory, then we may rest easy. But if the talent lies in the pattern instead of the bearer, we are all in terrible danger."

He glanced at the inner shrine, in its sealed cabinet on the left of the Yellow Room. "Our ancestor, revered though he be, may have made a terrible error about the cause of the abandonment. Unthinkable though that is, we must question everything until we discern the truth. And then we must find a way to achieve victory."

* * *

"Hello, Roland's voice mail. If it's still secure, meet me at the Marriott suite you rented, tonight at six p.m. Bye." She stabbed the "off" button on her phone viciously then remarked to the air, "Be there or be dead meat."

Paulette was bent over the screen of her laptop, messing around with some fine arts web sites, a browser window pointing to a large online bookstore: "Are you sure you mean that?" she murmured.

"I don't know." Miriam frowned darkly, arms crossed defensively. "Give me the car keys, I'm going for a drive. Back late."

Being behind the wheel of a car cleared Miriam's head marvelously. The simple routine of driving, merging with traffic and keeping the wheels on the icy road, distracted her from the ulcer of worry gnawing away at her guts. At Home Depot she shoved a cart around with brutal energy, slowing only when a couple of five-gallon cans of kerosene turned it into a lumbering behemoth. Afterwards she left quickly and headed for the interstate.

She was almost a hundred and thirty miles south of Boston, driving fast, haunted by evil thoughts, when her phone rang. She held it to her ear as she drove.

"Yes?"

"Miriam?" Her throat caught.

"Roland? Where are you?"

"I'm in the hotel suite right now. Listen, I'm so sorry."

You will be, if I find you're responsible, she thought. "I'll be over in about an hour, hour and twenty," she said. "You're alone?"

"Yes. I haven't told anyone else about this room."

"Good, neither have I." They'd rented the room in New York for privacy, for a safe house where they could discuss their mutual plans and fears—and for other purposes. Now all she could think of was the man in her mother's Dumpster, eyes frozen and staring. "Do you know if Angbard got my message?"

"What message?" He sounded puzzled. "The courier—"

"The message about my mother."

"I think so," he said uncertainly. "You sure you can't be here any faster?"

She chuckled humorlessly. "I'm on the interstate."

"Uh, okay. I can't stay too long—got to go back over. But if you can be here in an hour we'll have an hour together."

"Maybe," she said guardedly. "I'll see you."

She killed the phone and sped up.

It took her only an hour and ten minutes to make the last sixty miles, cross town, and find somewhere to park near the hotel. As she got out of the car she paused, first to pat her jacket pocket and then to do a double take. *This is crazy,* she thought, *I'm going everywhere with a gun!* And no license, much less a concealed-carry permit. *Better not get stopped, then.* Having to cross over in a hurry would be painful, not to say potentially dangerous; the temporary tattoos on her wrists seemed to itch as she pushed through the doors and into the lobby of the hotel.

The elevator took forever to crawl up to the twenty-second floor, then she was standing in the thickly carpeted silence of the hallway outside the room. She knocked, twice. The door opened to reveal Roland, wearing an immaculate business suit, looking worried. He looked great, better than great. She wanted to tear his clothes off and lick him all over—not an urge she had any intention of giving in to.

His face lit up when he saw her. "Miriam! You're looking well." He waved her into the room.

"I'm not looking good," she said automatically, shoulders hunched. "I'm a mess." She glanced around. The room was anonymous as usual, untouched except for the big aluminium briefcase on the dressing table. She walked over to the row of big sealed windows overlooking the city. "I've been living out of a suitcase for days on end. Why did you call me yesterday?" She steeled herself for the inevitable, ensuring that his next words came as a surprise.

"It's—" He looked drawn. "It's about Olga. She's been shot. She's stable, but—"

"Was it a shotgun?" Miriam interrupted, startled out of her scripted confrontation.

"A shotgun?" He frowned. "No, it was a pistol, at close

range. After you disappeared, ran or whatever, she started acting very strangely. Refused to let anyone anywhere near her chambers then moved into your apartment at House Hjorth, deeply disconcerting Baron Oliver—she did it deliberately to snub him, I think." He shook his head. "Then someone shot her. The servants were in the antechamber to her room, heard a scuffle and shots—she defended herself. When they went in, there was blood, but no assassin to be seen."

Miriam leaned against the wall wearily, overcome by a sense that events were spinning out of control. "After I ran. Anything about a corpse in the orangery? Or a couple more in Olga's rooms? We sure left enough bullet holes in the walls—"

"What?" Roland stood up, agitated. "I didn't hear anything about this! I got the message about you running, but not—"

"There were two assassination attempts." Miriam tugged at the curtains, pulling them shut. *You can never be sure,* she thought, chilled: even though a high building was implicitly doppelgängered, inaccessible from the other worlds, a Clan sniper in a neighboring office block could shoot and then make a clean escape as soon as they reached ground level. "The first guy wanted me in the garden. Unfortunately for their plans, Olga's chaperone Margit turned up instead. I went back to tell Olga and ran into two guys with machine pistols."

"But." Roland shut his mouth, visibly biting his tongue, as Miriam stared at him.

"I don't think they were working together," Miriam added after a brief pause. "That's why I . . . left."

"I ought to get you to a safe house right now," said Roland. "It's what Angbard will expect. We can't have random strangers trying to murder Clan heiresses. That they should have shot Olga is bad enough, but this goes far beyond anything I'd known about." He glanced at her sharply. "It's as if I'm being kept out of the loop deliberately."

"Tell me about Olga?" Miriam asked. *Well, we know just how reliable Angbard thinks you are.* "How is she being looked after? What sort of treatment is she receiving?"

"Whoa! Slowly. Baron Oliver couldn't afford to look as if

he was ignoring an attack under his own roof—he personally got her across to an emergency room in New York, and
notified the Duke while they stabilized her. Angbard had her
moved to Boston Medical Center by helicopter once she was
ready: She's in a private room, under guard." Roland looked
mildly satisfied at her expression of surprise. "She's got
round-the-clock bodyguards and hot and cold running
nurses. Angbard isn't taking any chances with her safety. We
could provide bodyguards for you, too, if you want—"

"Not an issue. But I want to visit Olga." Miriam put her
shoulder bag down on the bed. "Tonight."

"You can't. She's stable, but that doesn't mean she's taking visitors. She's on a drip and pain killers with a hole in
one arm and a head injury. Shock and blood loss—it took us
nearly two hours to get her to the emergency room. Maybe in
a couple of days, when she's feeling better, you can see her."

"You said she had a head injury?"

"Yeah. The bad guy used a small-caliber popgun, that's
why she's still alive." He looked at her. "You carry—"

Miriam pulled out her pistol. "Like this?" she asked dryly.
"Fuck it, Roland, if I was going to kill Olga, I wouldn't mess
around. You know damn well they were hoping to nail me
instead."

"I know, I know." He looked irritated and gloomy. "It
wasn't you. Nobody with half a wit says it was you, and the
fools that do don't have any pull at court. But your departure
set more tongues flapping than anything else that's happened
in years; a real scandal, say the idiots. Eloping with a lady-
in-waiting, according to the more lurid imaginations. It
doesn't look good to them, the shooting coming so soon after."

"Well, I don't give a shit whether I look good or bad to the
Clan." Miriam stared at him through narrowed eyes. "What
about my mother?" she asked.

"Your mother? Isn't she alright?" He looked surprised.
"Is she—"

"I went over there this morning. She phoned last night
while I was away. Something about going on a long journey.

Today there is a new back door in her kitchen, and a dead man's body in the Dumpster behind her house, and not a sign of her to be found. I told Angbard that if anything happened to her, heads would roll, and I meant it."

Roland sat down heavily in the room's armchair. "Your mother?" His face was pale. "This is the first I've heard of it."

Miriam pursed her lips. "Would Angbard tell you if he was going to order her abducted?"

"Abducted—" Roland began to look worried. "Someone was shot on her doorstep?"

"You're catching on. Someone was shot with a sawed-off shotgun. And *she* sure as hell didn't stuff him into a Dumpster and repair the kitchen door before leaving, or mop up the blood stains. In case you didn't know, she's got multiple sclerosis. She's in a wheelchair right now, and even when the disease is in remission she walks with crutches."

Miriam watched him go through the stages of surprise, denial, anger, and alarm with gloomy satisfaction. "That doesn't make sense!" he insisted. "Angbard put her under a protective watch! If someone had gotten through to her I would know about it!"

"Don't be so sure of yourself."

"But it can't be!" He was vehement.

"Listen, I know a shotgun wound when I see one, Roland. I stuck my finger in it and waggled it about. You know something? It was sawed-off, either that or he was shot from at least fifty feet away, and I figure that would have attracted some attention. It makes a hell of a mess. Which ward is Olga in? I have *got* to go and see her. What the hell is Angbard playing at?"

"I don't know," he said slowly. "He's not exactly been confiding in me lately." Roland's frown deepened.

Miriam took a deep breath. "I went over to my house," she said quietly.

"Oh?" Roland looked slightly stunned, but it wasn't the expression of a would-be murderer confronted by a surprisingly animated victim: He looked much the way she felt.

"Someone searched it efficiently. They left an, uh, surprise. Behind the front door. I'm not sure what kind except that it's probably explosive and it's wired to the handle. Only reason I'm here is I forgot my keys and had to use the back way in."

"Oh *shit*—" He stood up, his hand going to his pocket instinctively. "You're alright?"

"Not for want of somebody trying," she said dryly. "Seems to me that we have a pattern. First, someone tries to kill me or mess with Olga. They then try harder to kill me and succeed in killing Olga's chaperone. I shoot one killer and leave, taking Brill with me. Olga moves into my room at the palace and someone shoots her. Meanwhile, people who should know where I've gone don't, and my mother vanishes, and everywhere I'm likely to go on this side starts sprouting bombs. Can you tell me what kind of fucking pattern I am seeing here, Roland? *Can* you?"

"Someone is out to get you," he said through gritted teeth. "More than one conspiracy, by the sound of it. And they're getting Olga by mistake. Repeatedly. For some reason. And they're lying to me, too. And Angbard is treating me as a potential security leak, keeping me in the dark and feeding me shit."

"Right." She nodded jerkily. "So what are we going to do about it?" She watched him like a hawk.

"I think—" He came to some decision, because he took a step toward her. "I think you'd better come with me. I'm going to take you to Angbard in person and we'll sort out this out in person—he's over here now, taking personal control. We can accommodate you at Fort Lofstrom, a fully doppelgängered apartment, round-the-clock guards—"

She pushed his hand away. "I don't think so."

"What do you mean, you don't think so?" He looked surprised.

"I can look after myself, thank you," she said coolly. "I'm making arrangements. I'll get this sorted out by Beltaigne. One last question. Do you have any idea *who* might be trying to kill me?"

"Lots of suspects with motives, but no evidence." Puzzlement and worry mingled in his expression. For a moment he looked as if he was about to say something more, then he shook his head.

"Well then, that means I win because I *do* know roughly who's trying to kill me," she said, gloomily triumphant. "And I'm going to flush them from cover. Your clue is this: They're not part of the Clan, and a doppelgängered house on the other side is no defense—but they can't get at me while I'm here."

"Miriam," he rolled his eyes. "You're being paranoid. I'll get your mother's house checked out immediately, but you'll be a lot safer if we put a dozen armed bodyguards around you—"

"Safer from what? Safe from some blood feud that was ancient before I was born? Or safe from the idiots who think they're going to inherit my mother's estate if I can be declared incompetent next May, in front of a Clan council? Get real, Roland, the Clan is nearly as big a threat to my freedom as the world-walking assholes who shot Olga and booby-trapped the warehouse!"

"Booby-trapped—" his eyes widened.

"Yeah, a claymore mine on a tripwire in the doorway. And nobody cleared up the night watchman's body. Do you begin to get it?" She began to back away toward the door. "Someone set up the bomb, someone *inside* Angbard's security operation! And," she continued in a low voice, "you were in the right places at the right times."

Roland looked angry. "Miriam, you can't mean that!" He paced across the room restlessly. "Come on, look, let me sort everything out and it'll be okay, won't it? I'll vet your guards—"

"Roland." She shook her head, angry with him, angry with herself for wanting to give in and take him up on an offer that meant far more and went far further than words could express: "I'm gone. If you know where I'm going, the bad guys will find out—if you aren't one of them." She kept her hand in her pocket, just in case, but the idea of shooting him filled her with a numinous sense of horror.

He looked appalled. "Can't we just . . . ?"

"Just what?" she cried. "Kiss and make up? Jesus, Roland, don't be naive!"

"Shit." He stared at her. "You really mean it."

"I am going to walk out the door in a minute," she said tensely, hating herself for her own determination, "and we are not going to see each other again until next May, probably. At least, not in the next few days or weeks. We both need time out. I need to get my head together and see if I can flush the bastards who're trying to kill me. *You* need to think about who you are and who I am and where we're going before we take this any further—and you need to find whoever's wormed their way into Angbard's confidence and whoever shot Olga."

"I don't *care* about Olga! I care about *you!*" he snapped.

"That is part of the problem I've got with you right now," she said coldly, and headed for the door.

A thought occurred to her as she pulled the door open. "Roland?"

"Yes?" He sounded coldly angry.

"Tomorrow I'm going to get lost again, probably until Beltaigne. Keep checking your voice mail—there's no need to hold this room any longer."

"I wish you wouldn't do this," he said quietly. She shut the door behind her and departed, her heart infinitely heavier than it had been when she arrived.

Ring ring. There was a breeze blowing, and the park was bitterly cold: Miriam sat hunched at one end of a bench.

"Hello? Lofstrom Associates, how may I help you?"

"This is Miriam. I want to talk to Angbard."

"I'm sorry, Mr. Lofstrom is unavailable right now—"

"I said I'm *Miriam*. If you don't know the name, check with someone who does. You have five minutes to get Angbard on the line before the shit hits the fan."

"I'll see what I can do. Please hold—"

beep beep beep

"Hello?" A different voice, not Angbard's, came on the line.

"To whom am I speaking?" Miriam asked calmly.

"Matthias. And you are?"

"Miriam Beckstein. I want to talk to Angbard. Right now. This call has been logged by the front desk."

"I'm sorry, but he's in a meeting. If—"

"If I don't get him on the line *right now* I'll make sure the *Boston Globe* receives a package that will blow your East Coast courier line wide open. You have sixty seconds." Her fingers tensed on the handset.

"One moment."

Click.

"Angbard here. What's this?"

"It's me," said Miriam. "Sorry I had to strong-arm my way past your mandarins, but it's urgent."

"Urgent?" She could almost hear the eyebrows rising. "I've never seen Matthias so disturbed since—well. Unpleasant events. What did you tell him?"

"Oh, nothing much." Miriam leaned back, felt the cold bench bite through her coat, sat up straight again. "Listen. I told you something about my mother. That if anything happened to her I would be really pissed off."

"Yes?" Polite interest colored Angbard's voice.

"I'm really pissed off. Really, *really* pissed off."

"What happened?" he demanded.

"She's gone. There's a dead man in the Dumpster behind her house, killed with a shotgun. She had time to phone me to say she was going on a journey—I don't know if anyone was holding a gun to her head. Roland didn't know this. Apparently it happened at the same time that Olga was shot. And my house has been burgled and stuff taken, and somebody booby-trapped the front door."

"Come here immediately. Or if you tell me where you are I'll send a carload of guards—"

"No, Angbard, that won't work." She swallowed. "Listen. I am about to vanish more deeply than last time. Don't worry about Brilliana, she's safe. What I want you to do . . . look for my mother. By all means. Raise heaven and earth. I am going to visit Olga tomorrow and I do *not* expect to be stopped. If I don't leave that meeting and reach a certain point, unhindered, later tomorrow, unpleasant letters will go in the mail. I am serious about this, I am pissed off, and I am establishing my own power base because I believe that civil war you told me about is not over and the faction who started it is trying to fire it up again, through me."

"But Helge, that faction—" he sounded coldly angry— "they're your father's side of your family!"

"That's not the faction I'm thinking of," she said dryly. "The people I have in mind never signed on to the cease-fire. Listen, I will be in touch ahead of the Beltaigne conference. I'm going to have some really big surprises for you all, including . . . well, anyone who tries to declare me incompetent is going to get a really nasty shock. I'm going to keep in touch through Roland, but he won't know where I'm hiding. So, if you find my mother tell Roland. More to the point, don't trust your staff. Someone is not telling you everything that happens in the field. I think you've got a mole."

"Explain." The terser he became the better Miriam felt.

She thought for a moment. *Tell him about Roland?* No, but . . . "Ask Roland about the warehouse warning I phoned him. Find out why instead of cleaners calling, someone turned up and booby-trapped the place. Looks like the same style as whoever planted the bomb behind the front door of my house. You didn't know about that? Ask Matthias about the courier I intercepted on the train. Ask Olga about the previous assassination attempts. By the way, if I think her life is in danger, I reserve the right to move Olga somewhere safer. Once she's out of immediate danger."

"You're asking for a blank check," he said. "I've noticed the withdrawals. They're big."

"I'm setting up an import/export business." Miriam took a deep breath. "I'll announce it to the Clan at Beltaigne. By then, I should have a return on investment that will, um, justify your confidence in me." Another deep breath. "I'd like another million dollars, though. That would make things run smoother."

"Are you sure?" asked Angbard. He sounded almost amused, now.

"A million here, a million there, pretty soon you're talking serious money. Yes, I'm sure. It's a new investment opportunity in the family tradition. Like I said, I'm not setting up in competition—think of it as proof of concept for a whole new business area the Clan can move into. And a way of making Baron Oliver Hjorth and his backers look really stupid, if that interests you."

"Well. If you insist, I'll take your word for it." He was using the indulgent paterfamilias voice again. "It'll be in your account by the day after tomorrow. From central funds this time, not my own purse." In a considerably icier tone: "Please don't disappoint me in your investments. The Council has a very short way of dealing with embezzlement and not even your position would protect you."

"Understood. One other thing, uncle."

"Yes?"

"Why didn't you tell me about the other branch of the Clan? The one that accidentally got mislaid a couple of hundred years ago and is now blundering around in the dark trying to kill people?"

"The—" He paused. "Who told you about them?"

"Sleep well," she told him, and hit the "off" button on her phone with a considerable sense of satisfaction. She looked at the sky, saw night was pulling in already. It was time to go pick up Brill and visit the hospital. She hoped Olga would be able to talk to visitors. All she needed was confirmation of one little point and she could be on her way back to the far side, and the business empire she planned to establish.

Boston Medical Center was much like any other big general hospital, a maze of corridors and departments signposted in blue. Uniformed porters, clerical officers, maintenance staff, and lots of bewildered relatives buzzed about like a nest of bees. As they entered, Miriam murmured to Brill: "usual drill, do what I do. Okay?"

"Okay." They walked up to reception and Miriam smiled.

"Hi there, I'm wondering if it's possible to visit a patient? An Olga, uh, Hjorth—"

The receptionist, bored, shoved hair up past her ear bug. "I'll just check. Uh, what did you say your name was?"

"Miriam Beckstein. And a friend."

"Yeah, they're expecting you, go right up. You'll find her on ward fourteen. Have a nice day!"

"This place smells strange," Brill muttered as Miriam hunted for the elevators.

"It's a hospital. Full of sick people, they use disinfectant to keep diseases down."

"An infirmary?" Brill looked skeptical. "It doesn't look like one to me!"

Miriam tried to imagine what an infirmary might look like in the Gruinmarkt, and failed. *When were hospitals invented, anyway?* she wondered irrelevantly as the elevator doors slid open, and a bunch of people came out. "Come on," she said.

Ward fourteen was on the third floor, a long walk away. Brill kept glancing from side to side as they passed open doors, a hematology lab here, the vestibule of another ward there. Finally they found the front desk. "Hello?" said Miriam.

"Hello yourself." The nurse at the desk glanced up. "Visiting hours run until eight," she commented, "you've got an hour. Who are you looking for?"

"Olga Hjorth. We're expected."

"Hmm." The nurse frowned and glanced down, then her frown cleared. "Oh, yeah, you're on the list. I'm sorry," she looked apologetic. "She's only taking a few visitors; we've got orders to keep strangers out. And she's on nil by mouth right now, so if you've brought any food or drink you'll have to leave it right here at the desk."

"No, that's okay," said Miriam. "Uh, can you ask if she's willing to see my friend here? Brill?"

"That's me," said Brill, miscueing off Miriam's request.

"Oh, well—you're on the clear list." The nurse shrugged. "It's just that somebody shot her." She frowned. "She's under guard. Spooks, if you follow my drift."

Miriam gave her a sympathetic smile. "I follow. They know us both."

"That way." The nurse pointed. "Second door on the right. *Knock* before you open it."

Miriam knocked. The door opened immediately. A very big guy in dark clothes and dark glasses filled it. "Yes?" he demanded, in a vaguely central-European accent.

"Miriam Beckstein and Brill van Ost to see Olga. We're expected."

"One moment." The door closed, then opened again, this time unobstructed. "She says to come in."

It was a small anteroom and there were not one but three heavies in suspiciously bulky jackets and serious expressions hanging around. One of them was sitting down reading a copy of *Guns and Ammo,* but the other two were on their feet and they studied Miriam carefully before they opened the inner door. "Olga!" cried Brill, rushing in. "What have they done to you?"

"Careful," warned Miriam, following her.

"Hello," said Olga. She smiled slightly and shifted in the bed.

"Excuse *me*," the young nurse said waspishly. "I'll just be finishing here before you disturb her, if you don't mind?"

"Oh," said Brill.

"I don't mind," said Miriam, staring at Olga. "How are you?" she asked anxiously.

"Bad." Olga's smile warmed slightly. "Tired'n'bruised. But alive." Her eyes tracked toward the nurse, who was fiddling with the drip mounted on the side of the bed, and Miriam nodded minutely. The back of her bed was raised and there was a huge dressing over her right shoulder. Alarming-looking drain tubes emerged from it, and a bunch of wires from under the neck of her hospital gown fed into some kind of mobile monitor on a trolley. It chirped occasionally. "Damn." Half of her hair was missing, and there was another big dressing covering one side of her head, but no drain tubes—which, Miriam supposed, was a good sign. "This feels most strange."

"I'll bet it does," Miriam said with some feeling. *Wow,* she thought, thinking about Brill's first reaction to New York, *she's handling it well*. "Did they find whoever did it?"

"I'm told not." Olga glanced at the nurse again, who glanced back sternly and straightened up.

"I'll just leave you to it," she announced brightly. "Remember, no food or drink! And don't tire her out. I'll be back in fifteen minutes; if you need me before then, use the buzzer."

Miriam, Brill, and Olga watched her departure with relief. "Strange fashions here," Olga murmured. "Strange buildings. Strange everything."

"Yeah, well." Miriam glanced at the drip, the monitoring gear, everything else. Cable TV, a private bathroom, and a vase with flowers in it. Compared to the care Olga would receive in the drafty palace on the other side, this was the very lap of luxury. "What happened?"

"Ack." Olga coughed. "I was in your, your room. Asleep. He appeared out of nowhere and shot . . . well." She shifted slightly. "Why doesn't it hurt more?" she asked, sounding puzzled. "He shot at me, but I am a light sleeper. I was already sitting up. And I sleep with my pistol under my pillow." Her smile widened.

Miriam shook her head. "Did he get away?" she asked. "If not, did you get his locket?"

"I wondered when you would ask." Olga closed her eyes. "Managed to grab it before they found me. It's in the drawer there."

She didn't point at the small chest of drawers, but Miriam figured it out. Before she could blink, Brill had the top drawer open and lifted out a chain with a disk hanging from it. "Give me," said Miriam.

"Yeah?" Brill raised an eyebrow, but passed it to her all the same.

"Hmm." Miriam glanced at it, felt a familiar warning dizziness, and glanced away. Then she pulled back a cuff and looked at the inside of her right wrist. *The same*. "Same as the bastard who killed Margit. *Exactly* the same. While the other bunch of heavies who tried to roll us over at the same time didn't have any lockets. At all."

"Thought so," murmured Olga.

"Listen, they're after us both," said Miriam. "Olga?"

"I'm listening," she said sleepily. "Don't worry."

"They're after us both," Miriam insisted. "Olga, this is very important. You're probably going to be stuck here for two or three days, minimum, and it'll take weeks before you're well—but as soon as you're well enough to move, Angbard will want to take you back to his fortress on the other side. It is really important that you don't go there. I mean, it's vital. The killers can reach you on the other side, in Fort Lofstrom, even in a doppelgängered room. But they can't reach you here. Listen, I've got a friend here working for me. And Brill's here, too. You can stay with us, if you like. Or talk to Roland, get Roland to help. I'm pretty sure he's reliable—for you, at least. If you stay in Angbard's doppelgängered rooms on this side, the ones he uses to stop family members getting at him in the fort, you'll be safe from the lost family in world three, and from the other conspirators, but not from the mole. And if you go back to Niejwein, the conspirators will try to kill you."

"Wait!" Olga struggled visibly to absorb everything. "Lost family? World three? What's—"

"The assassin who killed Margit." Miriam tensed. "It's a long story. I think they're after you, now, because of me."

Olga shook her head. "But why? I mean, what purpose could that serve?"

"Because it'll discredit me, or it'll restart the civil war, and I'm fairly certain that's what the bunch from world three, the long-lost relatives, want to achieve. If I die and it can be blamed on one half of the Clan, that starts it up again. If *you* die and it looks like I've schemed with Roland to get you out of the way so I can marry him, it starts up for a different reason. Do you see?"

"Vaguely." Olga opened her eyes and looked at Miriam. "You'll have to explain it again later. Do you think they'll let me stay here?"

"Hmm." Miriam thought for a moment. "You can stay here to recover. I don't think even Angbard is stupid enough to move you while you're ill. You can lean on him to let you stay a bit longer to see what it's like, too. That might work. If he's got any sense he'll work it out from what I told him. But he isn't safe, Olga."

Brill turned around. "They abducted—or killed—Miriam's foster-mother, milady. Yesterday, at the same time they shot you."

"Oh!" Olga looked pensive. "So. What would you suggest?"

"I think you should stay here for now. When you're better, I want to—" Miriam caught Brill's eye—"introduce you to a friend of mine called Paulette. And then we'll see." She licked her lips. "I've got a business proposition in mind. One that will flush out the bastards who want us both dead, *and* make everybody involved wealthy beyond belief." She grinned at Olga. "Interested?"

AGREEMENTS

Almost exactly two weeks later, Miriam sat in front of a mirror in the Brighton Hotel, brushing her hair and pulling a face. *It's definitely getting longer,* she thought. *Damn that hairdresser!* She'd drawn the line at a wig, but even shoulder-length hair was considered eccentrically short by Boston polite society, and a reputation for eccentricity was something Miriam didn't want to cultivate—it would happen anyway, and could only get in her way. But she hadn't had hair even this long since she was a teenager. *Bloody nuisance,* she thought affectedly, then snorted with amusement. *This place is getting to me. Even the way they talk!*

The house purchase was going ahead, the conveyancing papers and legal to-ing and fro-ing well in hand. Erasmus had taken delivery of no less than ten pounds of twenty-three carat gold, an immense amount by any standard—back in Cambridge it would have paid Miriam's salary at *The Weatherman* for almost a year—and had warned his shadowy compatriots to expect much larger amounts to start flowing soon, "from a sympathetic source." His stock had risen. Meanwhile, Miriam had taken pains to quietly slip into at least two meetings of the Friendly Party to keep an eye on where the money was going. When she'd left money on the collecting tray, it had been with a sense that she was doing the right thing.

The Levelers, despite official persecution (and the imprisonment of many of their leading lights for sedition), had a political agenda she thought she understood, one not too alien from her own. High upon it was a bill of rights; the universal franchise (granting women the vote here for the first time); equal rights regardless of age, race, and sex; and separation of Church from state. That the imperial government didn't take such things for granted gave Miriam one source of comfort; if she was going to get her start here by smuggling contraband gold to fund radicals, at least they were radical democrats. The ironies in the similarity between her activities and the Clan's own business model didn't leave her untouched. She consoled herself with two thoughts: Smuggling gold to undermine a despotic monarchy wasn't in the same moral league as being the main heroin connection for the East Coast, and she intended to switch to a different business model just as soon as she could.

Miriam checked her appearance in the mirror. With earrings and a pearl choker and the right haircut and dress she could just about pass, but she still felt she was walking a knife-edge in maintaining appearances. New Britain seemed to take class consciousness almost as seriously as the feudal nobility of the Gruinmarkt. It was depressing, and the need to dive into the detail work of setting up a business here left her no time to pursue casual friendships. When she had time to think about it, she realized she was lonely. But at least she had the option of going home in a few more days. That was more than Brill had. Or Iris, wherever she was.

As she locked the jewel box, there was a knock at the door. A bellhop bobbed to her outside. "Begging your pardon, ma'am, but you have a visitor." He offered Miriam a card on a silver tray. Miriam nodded. "Please show Sir Alfred Durant to my table in the dining room. I have been expecting him, and I will join him shortly. I'm also expecting a Mr. Humphrey Bates. If you'd care to see they are offered an aperitif first."

Miriam left her room and headed downstairs, outwardly calm but inwardly tense. Paradoxically, some things were easier to do over here. The primitive state of the corporate scene made it relatively easy to mount an all-out assault on the captains of industry, for which she was deeply grateful. (An SEC-approved due diligence background check such as she'd have faced at home would have smashed through her public identity as if it was made of wet cardboard.) But other things were harder to fake. People judged your trustworthiness by a whole slew of social indicators, your class background, and the way you spoke and dressed. The equivalent of a dark suit and a PowerPoint presentation would get you precisely nowhere unless you were a member of the right clubs or had been to the correct finishing school. If you were an outsider, you needed a special edge—and you needed to be at least twice as good.

She'd spent most of the day running scenarios for how this meeting could play, ranging from the irredeemably bad to the unexpectedly good. She'd gotten her story prepared, her answers ready, her lawyer in attendance, and just about everything—except her hair—straight. Now all that remained was to see if Sir Durant would bite . . . or whether he'd turn out to be an inveterate snob, or an overbred twit whose business was run for him by self-effacing middle-class technicians.

She'd reserved the Hanover Room off the back of the carvery downstairs. Most restaurants in this city were associated with hotels, and the Brighton's was a very expensive, very exclusive one. As she came through the door, two men rose. One of them was the lawyer, Bates, and the other—she smiled at him and dipped her head briefly. "You must be Sir Alfred Durant?" she asked. "I've been looking forward to meeting you."

"A pleasure, ma'am," he said, in a hoarse, slightly gravelly voice. Durant was thin and tall, imposing but with a hauteur that spoke more of a weary self-confidence than of arrogance. His eyes were soft, brown, and deceptively tired-looking. "Please, you must call me Alfred. Mr. Bates has been pinning my ears back with stories about you."

"Indeed." Miriam's expression acquired a slightly fixed, glassy overtone as she nodded to her lawyer. "Well, and have you arrived in good health? Has anyone offered you a drink? I say, waiter—"

The waiter hurried over. "Yes, milady?"

Durant raised an eyebrow. "Gin and tonic for me," he said slowly—or was it melancholia? *He likes people to think he drives from the back seat,* Miriam noted. *Watch this one.*

"A sweet Martini for me," Bates added. Next to Sir Durant he was short, plump, and somewhat overeager.

"Certainly." Miriam relaxed slightly. "A sherry, please," she added. "If you'd like to come in, I believe our table is waiting . . . ?"

The scandalous overtones of a single woman entertaining two gentlemen to dinner in a closed room were mildly de-fused by her black dress and rumored widowhood. Bates had confirmed that there were no unsalubrious rumors about Sir Durant's personal life—or at least none she need worry about. Miriam concentrated on being a perfect hostess while pump-ing Durant for information about himself, and keeping Bates from either drying up or running off at the mouth. Durant was not the most forthcoming of interview subjects, but after the soup she found a worthwhile button to press, and triggered a ten-minute monologue on the topic of car-racing. "It is with-out doubt the wooden track that makes it so exciting," Durant droned over the salmon steak—expensively imported by air-ship from the north—"for with the embankment of the course, and the addition of pneumonic wheels, they get up to the most exhausting speeds. There was the time old Timmy Watson's brakes failed on the inside straight toward the finish line at Yeovilton—"

After the best part of two hours, both Bates and Sir Durant were reclining in their chairs. Miriam felt bloated and silently cursed the etiquette that prevented her from leaving the table for a minute, but the last-minute addition of an excellent glass of vintage port seemed to have helped loosen Alfred up. Especially after Miriam had asked a couple of leading questions about brake shoe manufacture, which veered dangerously close to discussing business.

"You seem to me to be unusually interested in brakes," Sir Durant said, cupping his glass in one hand and staring at her across the table with the expression of a well-fed and somewhat cynical vulture. "If you'll pardon me for saying this, it's a somewhat singular interest in one of the fairer sex."

"I like to think I have lots of singular interests." Miriam smiled. *Patronizing old bastard.* "I have spent much of my time traveling to far places and I'm afraid my education in the more feminine arts may be a little lacking. Business, however, is another matter."

"Ah, business." Bates nodded knowingly, and Miriam had to actively resist the temptation to kick him under the table.

"Business." Durant, too, nodded. "I noticed your purchase of a company—was it by any chance Dalkeith, Sidney and Fleming?—with interest. A fine engineering venture, once upon a time."

Miriam nodded. "I like to get my hands dirty. By proxy," she added, glancing at Bates. "It's something of a hobby. My father taught me never to take anything for granted, and I extended the lesson to the tools in his workshop."

"I see." Durant nodded. "I found the, ah, *samples* you sent me most interesting."

"Good." When she smiled this widely, Miriam's cheeks dimpled: She hated to be reminded of it, but there was no escaping the huge gilt-framed mirror hanging above the sideboard opposite. *Is that rouged harpy in the evening dress really me?* "That was the idea."

"My men applied one of the samples to a test brake engine. The results were precisely as your letter promised."

"Indeed." Miriam put her glass down. "I wouldn't waste your time, Alfred. I don't like to mince words. I'm a woman in a hurry, and I wanted to get your attention."

"Can you provide more samples?" His stare was penetrating.

"Yes. It will take about a month to provide them in significant quantities, though. And the special assembly for applying them." It had taken a week to get the chrysotile samples in the first place, and longer to set up the workshop, have them ground to powder, and set into the appropriate resin matrix. Epoxide resins were available here, but not widely used outside the furniture trade. Likewise, asbestos and rock wool—chrysotile—could be imported from Canada, but were only really used in insulating furnaces. The young industrial chemist Miriam had hired through Bates's offices, and the other three workers in her makeshift research laboratory, were initially startled by her proposal, but went along with it. The resulting grayish lumps didn't look very impressive, and could certainly do with much refinement, but the principle was sound. And she wouldn't be stopping with asbestos brakes—she intended to obsolesce it as rapidly as she'd introduced it, within a very few years, once she got her research and development department used to a steady drip feed of advanced materials from the other world. "The patents are also progressing nicely, both on the brake material and on the refinements we intend to apply to its use." She smiled, and this time let her teeth show. "The band brake and the wheel brake will be ancient history within two years."

"I'd like to know how you propose to produce the material in sufficient volume to achieve that," said Sir Durant. "There's a big difference between a laboratory experiment and—"

"I'm not going to," Miriam butted in. "*You* are." She stopped smiling. "That's what this meeting is about."

"If I disagree?" He raised his glass. Miriam caught Bates shrinking back in his chair out of the corner of her eye.

"You're not the only big fish in the pond." Miriam leaned back and stifled a yawn. "Excuse me, please, I find it rather hot in here." She met Sir Durant's gaze. "Alfred, if man is to travel faster, he will have to learn to stop more efficiently first, lest he meet with an unfortunate accident. *You* made your fortune by selling pneumonic wheels—" *tires,* she mentally translated. "If you pause to consider the matter, I'm sure you'll agree that cars that travel faster and stop harder will need more and better pneumonics, too. I'm prepared to offer you a limited monopoly on the new brake material and a system that will use it more efficiently than wheel brakes or band brakes—in return for a share in the profits. I'm going to plow back those profits into research in ways to improve automotive transport. Here and *now*—" she laid a fingertip on the table for emphasis—"there is one car for every thirty-two people in New Britain. If we can make motoring more popular, to the point where there is one car for every two people—" she broke off.

"Not very ambitious, are you?" Sir Durant asked lightly, eyes gleaming. At the other side of the table Bates was gaping at her, utterly at a loss for words.

Many thoughts collided in Miriam's mind at that moment, a multivehicle pileup of possible responses. But the one that found its way to her lips was, "not hardly!" She picked up her glass, seeing that it was nearly empty, and raised it. "I'd like to propose a toast to the future of the automobile: a car for every home!"

Miriam was able to rent premises for her company in a former engineering shop on the far side of town. She commuted to it by cab from the hotel while she waited for Bates to process the paperwork for her house purchase. She was acutely aware of how fast the luxury accommodation was gobbling her funds, but there didn't seem to be a sensible alternative—not if she wanted to keep up the front of being a rich widow, able to entertain possible investors and business partners in style. Eventually she figured she'd have to buy a steam car—but not this year's model.

The next morning she had a quick shower, dressed in her black suit and heavy overcoat, then hailed a cab outside without lingering for breakfast. The air was icy cold but thankfully clear of smog. As the cab clattered across tram rails and turned toward New Highgate, she closed her eyes, trying to get her thoughts in order.

"Two weeks," she told herself, making a curse of it. She'd been here for six nights already and it felt like an eternity. Living out of suitcases grew old fast and she'd shed any lingering ideas of the romance of travel back when she was covering trade shows and haunting the frequent flyer lounges. Now it was just wearying, and even an expensive hotel suite didn't help much. It lacked certain essential comforts—privacy, security, the sensation of not being in *public* the whole time. She was getting used to the odd clothing and weird manners but doubted she'd ever be comfortable with it. And besides, she was missing Roland, waking sometimes from vague sensual dreams to find herself alone in a foreign city. "Seven more days and I can go home!" Home, to her own damn house, if she could just lean on Angbard a bit harder—failing that, to the office, where she could lock the door, turn on the TV, and at least understand everything she was seeing.

The cab arrived. Miriam paid the driver and stepped out. The door to the shop was already unlocked, so she went straight in and opened up the office. It was small but modern, furnished in wood and equipped with electric lamps, a telephone, and one of the weird chord-key typewriters balanced precariously on one of the high, slanted writing desks. It was also freezing cold until she lit the gas fire. Only when it was blazing did she go through the mail then head for the lab.

The lab was a former woodworking shop, and right now it was a mess. Roger had moved a row of benches up against one wall, balanced glass-fronted cabinets on top of them, and made enthusiastic use of her line of credit at an instrument maker's shop. The results included a small potter's kiln—converted into a makeshift furnace—and a hole in the ceiling where tomorrow a carpenter would call to begin building a fume cupboard. Roger was already at work, digging into a wooden crate that he'd manhandled into the center of the floor. "Good morning to you," said Miriam. "How's it going?"

"I'll tell you when I get into this," Roger grunted. He was

in his late twenties, untidy even in a formal three-piece suit, and blessed with none of the social graces that would have allowed him to hang onto his job when the Salisbury Works had shed a third of their staff three months earlier. Rudeness concealed shyness; he'd been completely nonplussed by Miriam at first, and was still uneasy in her presence.

"That'll be the chrysotile from Union Quebecois," she said. "Isn't it?"

"It should be. If they haven't sent us rock salt by mistake again." He laid down his crowbar and straightened up panting, his breath steaming in the cold air.

"If they have, they'll pay for it." She grinned. "Go make yourself a pot of tea, I don't want you freezing to death on the job."

"Um, yes, Ma'am." Roger shuffled toward the other back room—the one Miriam intended to have converted into that luxury, a kitchen and indoor toilet block for the work force—that currently held only a cast-iron wood stove, a stack of lumber, and a kettle. He gave her a wide berth, as if being female in the workplace might be contagious. Miriam watched his back disappear before she knelt to pick up the crowbar, and went around the lid of the crate levering out the retaining nails. *Men*. She laid the crowbar down and dusted her skirt off before he returned, bearing a chipped mug containing some liquid as dark as coffee.

"I think you'll find it easier to open now," Miriam remarked, laying one hand on the lid. "What have you got in mind for resin processing this week?"

"I was thinking about the vulcanization process," Roger muttered. "I want to see how varying the sulfate concentration affects the stiffness of the finished mixture."

"I was asking about resins," Miriam pointed out. "In particular, the epoxide sample I suggested you look into on Thursday. Have you done anything with it yet?"

"Um, I was getting to it." Roger glanced at her face then looked away bashfully.

"That's why I suggested a timetable," said Miriam. "You can estimate how long each batch will take to run; you already do that for yourself, don't you? Put the timetable on the blackboard and I won't have to keep asking you the same questions."

"Oh, alright then." He nodded.

"I wanted the epoxide sample running as soon as possible because we have a possible customer," she added.

"A customer?" He brightened visibly.

"Yes, a customer." She kept her face sober. "But we won't have them if we don't have a suitable product, will we? They're going to want an extensive range of samples in about four weeks time, for their own materials testing people. That's why I want you to get on to the epoxide-based samples as soon as possible. If you time the kiln runs right, you can probably put your sulfate experiments through at the same time. Just as long as they don't hold up the epoxide."

Oh, right. I'll do it that way, then," he said, almost carelessly. And he would. She'd met Roger's type before, hammering keyboards into submission in dot-com start-ups. He'd work overnight if he had to, without even noticing, just to get the product ready to meet the deadline—as long as he had a target to aim for. All this thrashing about with rubber and vulcanization processes was just a distraction.

"I'm going to be in the office today," she added. "I've got an idea to work on. The carpenter will be in here tomorrow to work on the fume cupboard, and then the kitchen. Meanwhile, you wouldn't happen to know any model engineers looking for work? I have some mechanical assemblies to get started."

"Mechanical—" he almost went cross-eyed. "Why?"

"A better way of applying this wonderful high-friction material to the task of stopping a moving vehicle," she pointed out. "You think this high-friction compound will work well if you just clamp it to a pneumonic? It'll work— right until the rubber wall of the wheel wears through and it blows out. What we need is a hub-mounted disk bolted to the wheel with a block of brake material to either side, which can be clamped or released by hydraulic calipers, balanced to apply force evenly. With me so far?"

"Um, I think so." He looked abstracted. "I, I don't know any model artificers. I'm sorry. But I'm sure you'll find someone."

"Oh I think I will, indeed I do." She headed back to the office, leaving Roger wrestling a ten-kilogram lump of very high-grade rock wool onto his workbench.

The day passed in a blur. Miriam had rigged a travel transformer for her laptop, which she kept in a locked drawer in the office along with an inkjet printer and a small digitizer tablet. The CAD software was a pain to use with such a small screen, but far better than the huge draftsman's board and ink pens in the far corner of the room. Between calls she lost herself in an extruded 3D model of a brake assembly—one of her own invention, crude but recognizable as the ancestor of late twentieth-century disk brakes. Another file awaited her attention—steel radial bands for reinforcing tires. The idea was sound, but she kept having to divert into her physics and engineering textbooks. Her calculus was rustier than she was willing to admit, and she was finding some of the work extremely hard.

But perfection didn't matter. *Getting there first* mattered. Get there first and just-good-enough and you could buy the specialists to polish the design to perfection later. This was the lesson Miriam had learned from watching over the shoulders of her Silicon Valley colleagues, and from watching a myriad of biotech companies rise and fall—and it was the lesson she intended to shove up New Britain's industrialists so hard it made them squeak.

One o'clock. Miriam blinked, suddenly dizzy. Her buttocks ached from the hard stool, she was hungry, and she needed the lavatory. She stood up and put the notebook PC away, then headed for the toilet—an outhouse in the backyard. Afterwards she slipped out the front door in search of lunch. Of such elements were a working day made.

In the public environment of the hotel, or the lab, she cut an eccentric, possibly scandalous figure. On the streets she was just another woman, better dressed than most, hurrying about her errands. Anonymity of a kind: *Treasure it while you can,* she told herself as she lined up at a street corner where a baker's boy had set up a stand to sell hot bacon rolls. *It won't last.*

She returned to the office and had been busy for an hour—phoning her lawyer, then calling a commercial agent at what passed for a recruiting house—when there was a peremptory knock on the side window. "Who's there?" she demanded, standing up to open it.

"Police. Inspector Smith at your service." A bushy moustache and a suspicious, beefy face stood behind an imposing warrant card with a crown and heraldic beasts cavorting atop it chased her in through the open window. "Homeland Defense Bureau. Are you Mrs. Fletcher?"

"Uh, yes." Flustered, Miriam tried to pull herself together. "How can I be of service?"

"I'd like a word with you if I may."

"Ah, do come in, then." Miriam hurried to open the door. *Shit, what did I do wrong?* She wondered. There was a deep hollow icy feeling in her stomach as she hauled the door open and smiled, ingratiatingly. "What can I do for you, officer?" she asked, leaving the door and retreating behind the front desk.

"Ah, well." He nodded, then remembered his manners and took his hat off.

Bizarre, thought Miriam, fascinated as a bird facing a snake. To her surprise she realized that she wasn't frightened for herself—only for her plans, which depended on continuity and legality for their success.

"Been in business long?" asked the Inspector.

"No," she said, tight-lipped. "This is a new venture."

"Ah *well.*"

He looked around slowly. Luckily she'd put the computer away before lunch, and everything was much as it should be in an office. He moved to shove the door closed. "Don't do that," Miriam said quickly.

"Alright." He found the one comfortable chair in the office—a wooden swivel chair too low to work at the writing desks—and looked her in the eyes. "How long have you known Erasmus Burgeson?"

"Huh?" Miriam blinked. "Not long. A few weeks?"

"I see." Smith nodded portentiously. "How did you come to know him?"

"Is this an official investigation?"

"I'm asking the questions. How did you come to know him?"

"Uh." Miriam considered her options. *Not official,* she decided. "If this isn't an official investigation, why should I tell you?"

"Because." He looked irritated. "Little lady, if you don't want to cooperate while it's unofficial, I can go away and waste my time *making* it official. And then you'll have to cooperate, and it will be the worse for you because I won't have to knock on your door polite, like. Do I make myself clear?"

"Perfectly." She didn't smile. "I first met Erasmus Burgeson because one of your own officers directed me to him when I asked if he knew where I could find a pawnbroker. Is that what you wanted to know?"

"*Ah,* well." Smith looked even more annoyed now, but not in her direction. "You wouldn't happen to know which officer this would be?"

"Hmm. He'd have been on duty in Highgate Close on, um, the morning of Saturday the sixteenth. I think he thought I might be lost. That might be enough for you to find his notebook."

"Humph. So you asked for a pawnbroker and he gave you directions to Burgeson. Is that all? Why did you want a pawnbroker in the first place?"

The Inspector's blunt manner was beginning to annoy Miriam. *But that's what he wants,* she realized suddenly: *He wants me to make a slip. Hmm.* "I arrived on the India Line ship *Vespasian* that morning, after a crossing from Ceylon," she told him, very deliberately keeping to her story—the *Vespasian* had indeed docked that day, with some passengers aboard, but was conveniently halfway across the Atlantic by now. "I was so preoccupied with packing my posessions and getting ashore that I forgot to ask the purser to convert my scrip to honest currency. In addition, clothing suitable for the climate of Ceylon is inadequate here. So I thought a sensible first step would be to find a pawnshop and exchange an old pair of earrings and a small pearl necklace for a decent wool suit and the wherewithal to find a hotel room and cable my banker."

All of which was, very remotely, true—and indeed Erasmus had arranged, for a fee and by way of a friend of a fellow traveler, for the purser of the *Vespasian* to find a passenger of her name in the ship's manifest should anyone ask—but it was only as Miriam spun it out in front of Smith's skeptical gaze that she realized how thin a tale it sounded. If she was in Smith's shoes she could punch holes in it with very little effort. But Smith simply nodded. "I see," he said. "Your husband left you adequately provided for, didn't he?"

Miriam nodded. "Indeed." *Keep it close. Make him dig.*

"And so you dabble in manufacturing." It wasn't phrased as a question, so Miriam didn't answer. She just sat tight wearing a politely interested expression, wishing for the phone to ring or something to disturb the silence that stretched out uncomfortably.

"I said, you dabble in manufacturing."

"I do not 'dabble' in anything, Mr. Smith," Miriam finally stated in her iciest tone. "You're a police officer. You can go ask the patent office questions—I'm sure Mr. Sagetree will be able to tell you whether there is any merit in the applications I filed last week. The first *three*, Inspector, of the many I have in mind."

"Ah. I stand corrected." Smith leaned back in his chair. "Well then, may I rephrase? Do you have any opinion of Burgeson's business? Does he strike you as in any way at all being odd?"

Miriam shook her head and allowed an irritated expression to cross her face. "He's a pawnbroker," she said. "He's a very literate pawnbroker with a good line in conversation, but I imagine sitting in the back of a shop gives him a lot of time to read, don't you?"

"A literate pawnbroker. So this would explain why you have visited his establishment on three occasions?"

Shit, shit, shit—"The first time, as I've told you, I needed money and suitable attire. The second time—let me see, on my first visit I had noticed a hat that was not then out of hock. I went back to see if it was available, and also to redeem my earrings and necklace. On the *third* occasion—well, he'd shown me some of the antiquarian books various of his customers pawned when they fell upon hard times. I confess I was quite partial to a couple of them." She forced a smile. "Is that a crime?"

"No." Inspector Smith stood, unfolding smoothly to a good six feet. He was a huge, imposing man, overweight but built like a rugby player, and now she noticed that his nose had been broken, although it had set well. "But you should be careful who you associate with, Mrs. Fletcher. Some people question Mr. Burgeson's patriotism and devotion to the Crown, you know. He keeps strange company, and you would not want to be taken for one among them."

"Strange company?" She looked up at Smith.

"Strangers." He wore a peculiar tight, smug expression. "Frenchies, some of 'em. And papists. Uppity women suffragists, too." Miriam glanced past his shoulder then looked away hastily. Roger was leaning in the laboratory doorway, one hand behind his back. *I don't need this,* she thought to herself.

"He hasn't done anything to hang himself yet," Smith continued, "but there's always a first time." He nodded to himself. "I see *my* job as ensuring there isn't a second, if you catch my drift. And that the first 'appens as soon as possible."

Miriam looked past him. "Roger, go back to your workbench," she called sharply.

Roger turned and shuffled away, bashfully. Inspector Smith shook himself, the spell broken, and glanced over his shoulder.

"Huh. Another bad 'un, I shouldn't be surprised." Smith smirked at Miriam. "Wouldn't want anything to 'appen to him, would you? I really don't know what the world's coming to, a single woman running a business full of strapping young men. Huh. So, let's see. The question is, are you a good citizen?"

"Of course I'm a good citizen," Miriam said tightly, crossing her arms. "I really don't see what your point is."

"If you're a good citizen, and you were to learn something about the personal habits of a certain pawnbroker—" The inspector paused, brow wrinkled as if he'd just caught himself in an internal contradiction: "casting no aspersions on your reputation, if you follow me, ma'am." Another pause. "But if you happened to know anything that would be of *interest*, I'm sure you'd share it with the police . . ."

"I've got a business to run, inspector," Miriam pointed out coldly. "This business pays taxes which ultimately go to pay your wages. You are getting in the way. I'm a law-abiding woman, and if I find out anything you need to know you will be the first to hear of it. Do I make myself understood?"

"Ah, well." Smith cast her a sly little glance. "You will, as well, won't you? Huh." He paused in the doorway. "If you don't you'll be bleeding *sorry*," he hissed, and was gone like a bad smell.

"Oh shit," Miriam whispered, and sat down heavily in the swivel chair he'd vacated. Now the immediate threat was past, she felt weary, drained beyond belief. *The bastard!*

"Uh, ma'am?"

"Yes, Roger." She nodded tiredly. "Listen. I know you meant well, but, next time—if there is a next time—stay out of it. Leave the talking to me."

"Uh, yes." He ducked his head uncertainly. "I meant to say—"

"And leave the fucking crowbar behind. Have you any *idea* what they'll do to you for attacking a Police Inspector with a crowbar?"

"Ma'am!" His eyes bulged—at her language, not the message.

"Shit." She blinked. "Roger, you're going to have to get used to hearing me curse like a soldier if you work for me for any length of time. At least, you'll hear it when the bastards are attacking." She caught his eye. "I'm not a lady. If I was, I wouldn't be here, would I?" she added, almost plaintively. *And that's for sure, more than you'll ever know.*

"Ma'am." He cleared his throat, then carefully pretended not to have heard a single word. "It's about the furnace. I've got the first epoxide mixture curing right now, is that what you wanted?"

"Yes!" she exclaimed, relief forcing its way out of her in a shout. "That's what I wanted." She began to calm down. A thought occurred to her. "Roger. When you go home tonight, I'd like you to post a letter for me. Not from the pillar box outside, but actually into the letter box of the recipient. Will you do that?"

"Um." He blinked. "Would it be something to do with the King's man as called, just now?"

"It might be. Then again it might not. Will you?"

"Yes," he said firmly. "Don't like those folks. Not at all."

After he retreated to his workbench Miriam sat down in front of the manual typewriter and threaded some paper into it—then paused. *They can identity typewriters by their typeface, can't they?* she remembered. *Sort of like a fingerprint. And they lift messages off used ribbons, too.* She pulled out the notebook computer and briefly tapped out a note, then printed it on the battery-powered inkjet printer she'd brought over with her. *Let them try and identify* that.

She took care to pull on her gloves before feeding the paper in, and before folding it and putting it in the envelope, leaving no fingerprints to incriminate. Then she addressed it and sealed it. If they were tailing Roger or had staked out Burgeson's shop it was just too bad—nothing she could do would help—but if they were still looking for information she doubted things would have gone that far. Besides which, Erasmus had agreed to make inquiries on her behalf: If the inspector nailed him for sedition, there'd go her most fruitful line of inquiry in pursuit of the hidden enemies who'd murdered her birth mother and tried to kill her.

It was only on her way home, having given the anonymous tip to Roger, that she realized she'd stepped over the line into active collusion with the Leveler quartermaster.

SNARK HUNTING

One week and two new employees later (not to mention a signed, formal offer for the house), Miriam practiced her breaking-and-entering skills on the vacant garden for what she hoped would be the last time. After spending two uncomfortable hours in the hunting hide, she felt well enough to risk an early crossing.

Paulette was in the back office doing something with the fax machine when Miriam came in through the door. "What on earth—" She looked her up and down. "Jesus, what's that you're wearing?"

"Everyday office outfit in Boston, on the other side." Miriam dropped her shoulder bag, took her hat and topcoat off, then pulled a face. "Any word on my mother?" she asked.

"Nothing I've heard," said Paulie. "I put out a wire search, like you said. Nothing's turned up." She looked at Miriam worriedly. "She may be alright," she said.

"Maybe." Black depression clamped down on Miriam. She'd been able to keep it at bay while she was on the far side, with a whole different set of worries, but now she was home she couldn't hide it anymore. "I'm going to the bathroom. I may be some time. Taking this stuff off's a major engineering undertaking."

"Want me to make you some coffee?" Paulette called around the door.

"Yes! Thanks!"

"So you have to play dress-up all the time?" Paulie asked around the door.

"It's only dress-up if you can stop after a couple of hours," Miriam said as she came back out, wearing her bathrobe. She accepted a coffee mug from Paulette. "What you're wearing now would get you arrested for indecent exposure over there." Paulette was in jeans and a plaid shirt unbuttoned over a black T-shirt.

"I think I get the picture. Sounds like a real bundle of laughs." Paulette eyed her thoughtfully. "Two thoughts strike me. One, you've got a hell of a dry cleaning bill coming up. Secondly, have you thought about putting artificial fibers on your to-do list?"

"Yeah." Miriam nodded fervently. "Starting with rayon, that came first I think. Then the overlocking sewing machine, nylon, and sneakers." She yawned, winced at her headache, then stirred the coffee. "So tell me, how have things been while I've been away?"

"Well." Paulie perched on the desktop beside the fax. "I've got the next gold shipment waiting for you. Brill is doing fine, and those, uh, feelers—" She looked furtive. "Let's just say she's going to be from Canada. Right?"

"Right," Miriam echoed. "What else has she been up to?"

"She's been visiting your friend Olga in the hospital. Once she spotted someone trying to tail her on the T, but she lost him quick. Olga is out of intensive and recovering nicely, but she's got a scar under her hairline and her arm's in a sling. The guards—" Paulie shrugged. "What is it with those guys?"

"What's what?"

"Last time she went, she said one of them said she ought to come home. Any idea what that's about?"

"Uh, yes, probably he was a relative of hers. You say she's visiting Olga now?"

"Why, sure." Paulette frowned. "I've just got an odd feeling about her. Great kid, but she's hiding something. I think."

"If she wanted me out of the way she's had more than enough opportunities to do it quietly."

"There is that," Paulette agreed. "I don't think she's out to get you. I think it's something else."

"Me too. I just want to know for sure what she's hiding. The way she and Kara were planted on me by Angbard's office, she's probably just reporting back to him—but if she's working for someone else . . ." The fax machine bleeped and began to emit a page of curling paper. "Hmm. Maybe I should check my voice mail."

She didn't, not at first. Instead she went back into the bathroom and spent almost an hour standing in the cramped shower cubicle, at first washing and thoroughly cleaning her hair with detergents of a quality unimaginable in New Britain, even for the rich—then just standing there, staring at her feet beneath a rain the temperature of blood, wondering if she'd ever feel clean again. Thinking about the expression on Roger's face when he'd been ready to murder a secret policeman for her, and about Burgeson's kindly face, high ideals, and low friends. Friends who believed fervently in political ideals Miriam took for granted, and who were low subversives destined for the gallows if Smith and his friends ever caught up with them. Gallows where whoever had kidnapped or murdered Iris belonged—and that in turn led Miriam to think about her mother and how little time she'd spent with her in the past year, and how many questions she'd never asked. And more questions for Roland, and his face as he'd turned away, hurt by her rejection; a rejection he didn't understand because it wasn't anything personal, it was a rejection of the world he would unintentionally lock her into, rather than the person he was.

Miriam had lots of things to think of—all of them bleak. She finished with the shower in much the same black mood she'd been in that fateful evening when she'd first opened the locket and unhitched a mind-gate leading to a world where things turned out to be paradoxically worse. *Why bother?* She wondered. *Why do I keep going?* True love would be a great answer if she believed in it. But she was too much the realist: While she'd love to find Roland in her bed and fuck him senseless—the need for him sometimes brought her awake from frustrated dreams in the still small hours—there wasn't a cozy little cottage for two at the end of that primrose path. Miriam had held her daughter in her arms, once, twelve years ago, kissed her on the head and given her up for adoption. Over the next few years she'd spent nights agonizing over the decision, trying to second-guess the future, to decide whether she'd done the right thing.

The idea of bringing another child, especially a daughter, into the claustrophobic scheming of the Clan filled her with horror. She was a big girl now, and the idea of expecting a man to protect her didn't strike her as cool. That wasn't what she'd gone through pre-med and college and divorce and most of med school and the postgraduate campus of hard knocks for. But facing all this on her own was so daunting that sometimes it made her lie awake wondering if there was any point.

She wandered through into the bedroom and sat on the futon beneath the platform bed in the corner. Her phone was still sitting on the floor next to it, plugged in to charge but switched off. She picked it up, switched it on, waited for it to log on, then hit her mailbox.

"You have messages. Message one . . ." A gravelly voice, calling from ten days ago. "Miriam?" She sat up straight: It was Angbard! "I have been thinking very deeply and I have concluded that you are right."

Her jaw dropped. "Holy shit," she whispered.

"What you said about my security is correct. Olga is at evident risk. For the time being she remains in the hospital, but when you return, I release her into your care until Beltaigne, when I expect you *both* to appear before the Clan council to render an account of your persecution."

Miriam found herself shaking. "Is there anything else?"

"There's no news about your mother. I will continue to search until I find something positive to report to you. I am sorry I can't tell you anything more about her disappearance. Rest assured that no stone will go unturned in hunting for her assailants. You may call me at any time, but bear in mind that my switchboard might—if you are correct—be intercepted. Good-bye."

Click. "Message two—" Miriam shook her head. "Hello! This is a recorded greeting from Kleinmort Baintree Investments! Worried about your pension? You too—" Miriam hit the delete button.

"Message three: Call me. Please?" It was Roland, plaintive. She hit 'delete' again, feeling sick to her stomach. *"Message four*: Miriam? You there? Steve, at *The Herald.* Call me. Got work for you."

It was the last message. Miriam stared at her phone for a good few seconds before she moved her thumb to the delete key. It only traveled a millimeter, but it felt like miles. She hung up. "Did I just hear myself do that?" she asked the empty room; "did I just decide to ignore a commission from *The Herald?*"

She shook her head, then began to rummage through the clothes in her burnished suitcase, looking for something to wear. They felt odd, and once dressed she felt as if she'd forgotten something, but at least it was comfortable and nothing pinched. "Weird," she muttered and went back out into the corridor just as the front door banged open, admitting a freezing gust of cold air.

"Miriam!" Someone in a winter coat leapt forward and embraced her.

"Brill!" There was someone behind—"Olga! What are you doing here?"

"What do you think?" Olga looked around curiously. "What kind of house do you call this?"

"I don't. It's going to be a doppelgängered post office, though. Brill, let go, you're freezing!"

"Oh, I'm sorry," she said earnestly. "The duke, he sent a message to you with lady Olga—"

"Yo! Coffee?" Paulie took one look at them and ducked back into the kitchenette.

"Come in. Sit down. Then tell me everything," Miriam ordered.

They came in, stripping off outdoor coats: Olga had acquired a formal-looking suit from somewhere, which contrasted oddly with her arm in a sling. She shivered slightly. "How strange," she remarked, looking round. "Charming: quaint! What's that?"

"A fax machine. Everything feeling strange?" Miriam looked at her sympathetically. "I know that sensation—been having it a lot, lately."

"No, it's how *familiar* it feels! I've been seeing it on after-dinner entertainments for so long, but it's not the same as being here."

"Some of those tapes are quite old," Miriam remarked. "Fashions change very fast over here."

"Well." Olga attempted a shrug, then winced. "Oh, coffee." She accepted the offered mug without thanks. Paulie cast her a black look.

"Uh, Olga." Miriam caught her eye.

"What?"

"This is Paulette. She's my business manager and partner on this side."

"Oh!" Olga stood up. "Please, I'm so sorry! I thought you were—"

"There aren't any servants here," Brill explained patiently.

"Oh, but I was so rude! I shouldn't have—"

"It's okay," said Paulette. She glanced at Miriam. "Is this going to happen every time? It could get old fast."

"I hope not." Miriam pulled a face. "Okay, Olga. What did Uncle A have to say for himself?"

"He came to visit me shortly after you left. I'd had time to think on your explanations, and they made uncommon sense. So much sense, in truth, that I passed them on to him in a most forthright manner."

Brill cracked up.

"Care to share the joke?" Miriam asked carefully.

"Oh, it was mirthful!" Brill managed to catch her breath for a moment before the giggles came back. "She told him, she told—"

Olga kept her face carefully neutral. "I pointed out that my schooling was incomplete, and that I had been due to spend some time here in any case."

"She *pointed* out—"

"Uh." Miriam stared at Olga. "Did she by any chance have something pointed to do the pointing out with?"

"There was no need, he took the message," Olga explained calmly. "He also said that desperate times required desperate measures, and your success was to be prayed for by want of avoiding—" she glanced at Paulette—"the resumption of factional disputes."

"Civil war, you mean. Okay." Miriam nodded. "How long have you been out of the hospital?"

"But Miriam, this was *today*," said Brilliana.

"Oh," she said, hollowly. "I think I'm losing the plot." She rubbed her forehead. "Too many balls in the air, and some of them are on fire." She looked around at her audience; Paulie was watching them in fascination. "Olga, did you keep the locket you took from the gunman?"

"Yes." Olga looked uncertain.

"Good." Miriam smiled. "In that case, you may be able to help me earn more than the extra million dollars I borrowed from Angbard last month." She pretended to ignore Paulette's sharp intake of breath. "The locket doesn't work in this world," she explained, "but if you use it on the other side, it takes you to yet another place—more like this one than your home, but just as different in its own way."

She took a mouthful of coffee. "I'm setting up a business in, uh, world three," she told Olga. "It's going to set the Clan on its collective ear when they find out. It's also going to flush out our mystery assassins, who live in world three. Right out of wherever they're hiding. The problem is, it takes a whole day for me to world-walk across in each direction. Running a business there is taking all my time."

"You want me to be a courier?" asked Olga.

"Yes." Miriam watched her. "In a week or two I'll own a house in world three that is in exactly the same place as this office. And we've already got the beginnings of a camp in world one, in the woods north of Niejwein, on the same spot. Once I've got the house established, it'll be possible to go from here to there without having to wander through a strange city or know much about local custom—"

"Are you trying to tell me I'm not fit to be allowed out over there?" Olga's eyes blazed.

"Er, no! No!" Miriam was taken aback until she noticed Brill stifling laughter. "Er. That is, only if you want to. Have you seen enough of Cambridge yet? Don't you want to look around here, first, before going to yet another world?"

"Do I want—" Olga looked as if she was going to explode: "yes!" she insisted. "I want it all! Where do I sign? Do you want it in blood?"

Early evening, a discreet restaurant on the waterfront, glass windows overlooking the open water, darkness and distant lights. It was six-thirty precisely. Miriam nervously adjusted her bra strap and shivered, then marched up to the front desk.

"Can I help you?" asked the concierge.

"Yes." She smiled. "I'm Miriam Beckstein. Party of two. I believe the person I'm expecting will already be here. Name of Lofstrom."

"Ah, just a moment—yes, please go in. He's at a window table, if you'd just come this way—"

Miriam went inside the half-deserted restaurant, still filling up with an upmarket after-work crowd, and headed for the back. After weeks in New Britain she felt oddly exposed in a black minidress and tux jacket, but nobody here gave her a second glance. "Roland?"

He'd been studying the menu, but now he rocketed to his feet, confusion in his face. "Miriam—" He remembered to put the menu down. "Oh. You're just—"

"Sit down," she said, not unkindly. "I don't want you to

offer me a seat or hold doors open when it's easier for me to do it myself."

"Uh." He sat, looking slightly flustered. She felt a sudden surge of desire. He was in evening dress, like the first time. Together they probably looked as if they were heading for a night at the opera. A couple.

"It's been how long?" she asked.

"Four weeks and three days," he said promptly. "Want the number of hours, too?"

"That would be—" She stopped and looked at the waiter who'd just materialized at her elbow. "Yes?"

"Would sir et madame care to view the wine list?" he asked stuffily.

"You go ahead," she told Roland.

"Certainly. We'll have the Chateau Lafitte '93, please," he said without pause. The waiter scurried away.

"Come here often?" she asked, amused despite her better judgment.

"A wise man said, when you're planning a campaign, preparation is everything." He grinned wryly.

"Are we safe here?" she asked. "Really?"

"Hmm." His smile slipped. "Angbard sent a message. Your house appears to be clear, but it might be a bad idea to sleep over there. It's not doppelgängered, and even if it was, he couldn't vouch for its security. Apart from *that*—" He looked at her significantly. "I made sure nobody back at the office knows where I am tonight. And I wasn't tailed here."

The wine arrived, as did the waiter. They spent a minute bickering good-naturedly over the relative merits of a warming chowder against the chef's way with garlic mushrooms. "What has Angbard got you doing?" she asked.

"Well." He looked ruefully out of the window. "After our last meeting it was like you'd thrown a hornet's nest through his window. Everybody got to walk around downtown Cambridge in the snow, looking for a missing old lady in a powered wheelchair, you know? I ended up spending a week spying on a private security firm we'd hired. Didn't find much except a few padded expenses claims. Then Angbard quietly started shuffling people around—again, nothing turned up except a couple of guards on the take. So then he put me back on regular courier duty in the post room, with a guard assignment or two on the side, moved himself to a high-rise in New York—real estate above the thirtieth floor is going cheap these days—left Matthias running Fort Lofstrom and Angus in Karlshaven, and declared that the search for your foster-mother couldn't go on any longer. Uh, he figured we weren't going to find anything new after that much time. Well." He shrugged. "I can't tell you any specifics about my current assignments, but his lordship told me that if you got in touch, I was to—" He paused.

"I think I can guess," she said dryly.

"No, I promise! Angbard doesn't know about us," he said firmly. "He thinks we're just friends."

The appetizers arrived. Miriam took a sip of her chowder. The news about the hunt for Iris depressed her, but came as no real surprise. "Angbard. Does not know. That we, uh, you know." Somehow the thought made her feel free and sinful, harboring personal secrets—as well as strategic information about the third universe—that the all-powerful intelligence head didn't. She paused for a moment and studied the top of his head, trying to memorize every hair.

"I never told him," Roland said, putting down his soup spoon. "Did you think I would?"

"You can keep secrets when it suits you," Miriam noted.

He looked up. "I am an obedient servant to your best interests," he said quietly. "If Angbard finds out he'll kill us. If you want me to apologize for not giving him grounds to kill us, I apologize."

She met his eyes. "Apology noted." Then she went back to her soup. It was deliciously fresh and lightly seasoned, and Miriam luxuriated in it. She stretched out her legs, and nearly spilled soup everywhere as she found his ankle rubbing against hers. Or was it the other way around? It didn't matter. Nearly two months of lonely nights was coming to the boil. "What would you do for me?" she whispered to him over the remains of the appetizer.

"Anything." He met her eyes. "Almost anything."

"Well, I'd like that. Tonight. On one condition." The waiter removed their bowls, discreetly avoiding the line of sight between them—obviously couples behaving this way were a well-understood phenomenon in his line of work.

"What?"

"Don't, whatever you do, talk about tomorrow," she said.

"Okay. I promise." And it was that simple. He surrendered before the main course, a sirloin steak for him and a salmon cutlet for her, and Miriam felt something tight unwind inside her, a subliminal humming tension that had been building up for what felt like forever. She barely tasted the food or noticed as they finished the bottle of wine. He paid, but she paid no attention to that, either. "Where to?" he asked.

"Do you still have an apartment here?" she replied.

"Yes." She heard the little catch in his throat.

"Is it safe? You're sure nobody's, uh—"

"I sleep there. No booby traps. Do you want to—"

"Yes." She knew it was a bad idea, but she didn't care about that—at least, not right now. What she cared about, as she pulled her jacket on and allowed him to take her arm, was the warmth at the base of her spine and the sure knowledge that she could count on tonight. All the tomorrows could take their chances.

He drove carefully, back to his apartment in a warehouse redevelopment not far from the restaurant. Miriam leaned back, watching him sidelong from the passenger seat of the Jaguar. "This is it," he said, pulling into the underground garage. "Are you sure?" he asked, turning off the engine.

She leaned forward and bit his lower lip, gently.

"Ow—" Their mouths met. "Not here," he panted.

"Okay. Upstairs."

They worked their way into the elevator without getting too disheveled. It stopped on a neat landing with three doors. Roland freed up a hand to unlock one, and punched a code into a beeping alarm system. Then they were inside. He locked the door, put a chain across it, then bolted it—and she tackled him.

"Not here!"

"Where, then?"

"There!" He pointed through an open door into the living room, dimly lit by an old seventies lava lamp that shed moving patterns of orange and red light across a sofa facing the uncurtained window.

"That'll do." She dragged him over, and they collapsed onto the sofa. He was ready for her, and it was all Miriam could do to force herself to unwrap a condom before she launched herself at him. There was no time to pull off his clothes. She straddled him, felt his hands working under her dress, and then she was—

—an hour later, sitting on the toilet, giggling madly as she watched him shower. Both of them frog-naked and sweaty. "We've got to stop this happening to us!" she insisted.

"Come again?"

She threw the toilet roll at him.

"You're violent," he complained: "That isn't in *The Rules*."

"You *read* that?"

"Olga's elder sister had a copy. I sneaked a peek."

"Ugh!" Miriam finished with the toilet. "Move over, you're not doing that right."

"I've been showering myself for years—"

"Yes, that's what's wrong. Stand up." She stepped into the bathtub with him and pulled the shower curtain across.

"Hey! This wasn't in the rules either!"

"Where's the soap?"

"It does, doesn't—ow!"

Morning came late. Miriam stirred drowsily, feeling warm and secure and unaccountably bruised. There was something wrong with the pillow: It twitched. She tensed. *An arm! I didn't, did I . . . ?*

Memory returned with a rush. "Your apartment is too big," she said.

"It is?"

"Too many rooms."

"What do you mean?"

She squirmed backwards slightly until she felt his crotch

behind her. "We managed the living room, the bathroom, and the bedroom. But you've got a kitchen, haven't you? And what about the back passage?"

"I, uh." He yawned, loudly. She could feel him stiffening. "Need the toilet," he mumbled.

"Oh shit." She rolled over and watched him stand up, fondly. *Aren't they funny in the morning?* she thought. *If only . . .* Then the numb misery was back. It was tomorrow, already.

Damn, she thought. *Can't keep it together for even a night! What's* wrong *with me?*

"Would you like some coffee?" he called through the open doorway.

"Yeah, please." She yawned. Waking up in bed with him should feel momentous, like the first day of the rest of her life. But it didn't, it just filled her with angst—and a strong desire to spit in the faces of the anonymous sons of bitches who'd made it so. She *wanted* Roland. She wanted to wake up this way forever. She'd even think about the marriage thing, and children, if it was just about him. But it wasn't, and there was no way she'd sacrifice a child on the altar of the Clan's dynastic propositions. *Romeo and Juliet were just stupid dizzy teenagers,* she thought morosely. *I know better. Don't I?*

She stood up and pulled her dress on. Then she padded into Roland's small kitchen. He smiled at her. "Breakfast?" he asked.

"Yeah." She smiled back at him, brain spinning furiously. *Okay, so why don't you give him a chance?* she asked herself. *If he* is *hiding something, let's see if he'll get it off his chest. Now.* She knew full well why she didn't want to ask, but not knowing scared her. Especially while Iris remained missing. On the other hand, a plausible bluff might make him tell her whatever it was, and if it was about Iris, that mattered. Didn't it? *So what can I use—oh.* It was obvious. "Listen," she said quietly. "I know you're holding out on me. It doesn't take a genius to figure it out. You haven't told Angbard. So who knows about us?"

She wasn't sure what she'd been expecting: denial,

maybe, or laughter; but his face crumpling up like a car wreck wasn't on the list. "Damn," he said quietly. "Shit."

Her mouth went dry. "Who?" she asked.

Roland looked away from her. "He showed me pictures," he said quietly. "Pictures of us. Can you believe it?"

"Who? Who are you talking about?" Miriam took a step back, suddenly feeling naked. *Ask and ye shall learn.*

Roland sat down heavily on a kitchen chair. "Matthias."

"Jesus, Roland, you could have told me!" Anger lent her words the force of bullets: He winced before them. "What—"

"*Cameras.* All the cameras in Fort Lofstrom. Not just the ordinary security ones—he's got bugs in some of the rooms, hidden and wired into the surveillance net. You can't sweep for them, they don't show up, and they're not supposed to be there. He's a spider, Miriam. We were in his web." Roland's face was turned toward her, white and tortured. "If he tells the old man—"

"Damn." Miriam shook her head in disgust. "When?"

"After you disappeared, I swear it. Miriam, he's black-mailing me. Not you, you might survive. Angbard'd kill me. He'd be honor-bound to, if it came out."

Miriam glared at him. "What. What did he ask. You to do?"

"*Nothing!*" Roland cried out. He was right on the edge. *I'm scaring him,* she realized, an echo of grim satisfaction cutting through the numbness around her. *Good.* "At least, nothing yet. He says he wants you out of the picture. Not dead, just out of the Clan politics. Invisible. What you're doing now—he thinks I'm behind it."

"Give me that coffee," Miriam demanded.

"When you called about the body in the warehouse, I told Matthias because he's in charge of internal security," Roland explained as he poured a mug from the filter machine. "Then when you told me there was a bomb, I couldn't figure it out. Because if he wants to blackmail me he needs you to be alive, don't you see? So I can't see why he'd plant it, but at the same time—"

"Roland."

"Yes?"

"Shut up. I'm trying to think."

Shit. Matthias. Cameras everywhere. She remembered the servant's staircase. Roland's bedroom. *So Matthias wants us out of the way?* It was tempting. "Two million dollars."

"Huh?"

"We could go a long way on two million bucks," she heard herself say. "But not far enough to outrun the Clan."

"You want to—"

"Shut up." She glared at Roland. He'd been holding out on her. For what sounded like good reasons, she admitted—but the thought made her blood run cold. Roland was no knight in shining armor. The Clan had broken him. Now all it took was Matthias pushing his buttons to make him do whatever they wanted. She wanted to hate him for it, but found that she couldn't. The idea of going up against an organization with billions of dollars and hundreds of hands was daunting. Roland had done it once already, and paid the price. *Okay, so he's not brave,* she thought. *Where does that leave me? Am I brave, or crazy?* "Are you holding out anything else on me?" she asked.

Roland took a deep breath. "No," he said. "Honest. The only person who's got anything on me is Matthias." He chuckled bitterly, ending in a cough. "Nobody else. No other girlfriends. No boyfriends, either. Just you."

"If Matthias has primed you for blackmail, he must want something you can do for him," she pointed out. "He knows he could get rid of both of us by just giving us a shitload of money and covering our trail. And if he was behind these attempts to kill me, I'd be dead, wouldn't I? So what does he want to do that involves me and needs you—and that he figures he needs a blackmail lever for?"

"I—don't know." Roland pulled himself together, visibly struggling to focus on the problem. "I feel so stupid. I haven't been thinking rationally about this."

"Yeah, well, you'd better start, then." Miriam took a mouthful of coffee and looked at him. "What does Matthias want?"

"Advancement. Recognition. Power." Roland answered immediately.

"Which he can't get, because . . . ?"

"He's outer family."

"Right." Miriam stared at him. "Do you see a pattern here?" she asked.

"He can't get it, from the Clan. Not as long as it's run the way it is right now."

"So." Miriam stood up. "We've been stupid, Roland. Shortsighted."

"Huh?" He looked at her uncomprehendingly, lost in his private self-hatred.

"I'm not the target. You're not the target. *Angbard* is the target."

"Oh shit." He straightened up. "You mean Matthias wants to take over the whole Clan security service. Don't you?"

Miriam nodded, grimly. "With whoever his mystery accomplices are. The faction who murdered my mother and kept the family feuds going with judicious assassinations over a thirty-year period. The faction from world three. Leave aside Oliver and that poisonous dowager granny and the others who'd like me dead, Matthias is in league with those assassins. And before he makes his move—"

"He'll tell Angbard about us, whatever we do. To get us out of the frame before he rolls the duke up. Miriam, I've been a fool. But we can't go to Angbard with it—we'd be openly admitting past disloyalty, hiding things from him. What are we going to *do?*"

PART 4

STAKEOUT

TIP OFF

I t was a Friday morning late in January. The briefing
room in the police fortress was already full as the inspector entered, and there was a rattle of chairs as a
dozen constables came to their feet. Smith paused for a moment, savoring their attentive expressions. "At ease, men,"
he said, and continued to the front of the room. "I see you're
all bright and eager this morning. Sit down and rest your feet
for a while. We've got a long day ahead, and I don't want
you whining about blisters until every last one of our pigeons is in the pokey."

A wave of approving nods and one or two coughs swept
the room. Sergeant Stone stayed on his feet, off to one side,
keeping an eye on his men.

"You'll all be wondering what this is all about, then," began Smith. "Some of you'll 'ave heard rumors." He glanced
around the room, trying to see if anyone looked surprised.
Rumors were a constable's stock in trade, after all. "If any of
'em turns out to be true, I want to know about it, because if

you've heard any rumors about what I'm telling you now, odds are the pigeons've heard it too. An' today we're going to smash a nest of rotten eggs."

He scanned his audience for signs of unease: Here and there a head nodded soberly, but nobody was jumping up and down. "The name of the game is smuggling," he said dryly. "In case you was wondering why it's our game, and not the Excise's, it turns out that these smugglers have a second name, too: Godwinite scum. The illegal press we cracked last week was bankrolled from here, in *my* manor, by a Leveler quartermaster. We ain't sure where the gold's coming from, but my money is on a woman who's lately moved into town and who smells like a Frog agent to me. At least, if she ain't French she's got some serious explaining to do."

Smith clapped his hands together briskly to warm them up.

"You men, your job is to help me give our little lady an incentive to sing like a bird. We are going to run this by shifts and you are going to stick to her like glue. Two tailing if she goes out, two on the manor, four hours on, four off, but the off team ready to go in if I says so. We are going to keep this up until she makes contact with a known seditionist or otherwise slips up, or until we get word that more gold is coming. Then we're going to get our hands on her and find out who her accomplices are. When that happens we are going to get them back here, make them talk, and cut out the disease that has infected Boston for the past few years. A lot of traitors to the crown are going to go for a long walk to Hudson Bay, a bunch more are going to climb the nevergreen tree, and *you* are going to be the toast of the town." Smith grinned humorlessly. "Now, sergeant. If you'd like to run through the work details, we can get started . . ."

A few hours later, a woman stepped out from behind a hedge, kicked the snow from her boots, and glanced around the dilapidated kitchen garden.

"Hmm." She looked at the slowly collapsing greenhouse,

where holes in the white curtain revealed the glass panes that had fallen in. Then she saw the house, most of its windows dark and gloomy. "Hah!"

She strode up the garden path boldly, a huge pack on her shoulders: When she came to the side door she banged on it with a confident fist. "Anyone at home?" she called out.

"Just a minute there!" The door scraped ajar. "Who be you, and what d'you want, barging into our garden—"

"That's enough, Jane, she's expected." The door opened wide. "Olga, come in!"

The maid retreated, looking suspiciously at the new arrival as she stepped inside and shut the door. Miriam called: "Wait!"

"Yes'm?"

"Jane, this is Olga, my young cousin. She'll be staying here from time to time and you're to treat her as a guest. Even if she has an, uh, unusual way of announcing her arrival. Is that understood?"

"Yes'm." The kitchen maid bobbed and cast a sullen glance at Olga. Olga didn't react. She was used to servants.

"Come on in and get out of the cold," Miriam told her, retreating through the scullery and kitchen into a short corridor that led to the huge wooden entrance hall. "Did you have a good trip? Let's get that pack stowed away. Come on, I'll show you upstairs." There was only one staircase in this house, with a huge window in front of it giving a panoramic view of the short drive and the front garden. Miriam climbed it confidently and gestured Olga toward a door beside the top step. "Take the main guest bedroom. Sorry if it looks a bit underfurnished right now—I'm still getting myself moved in."

The bedroom was huge, uncarpeted, and occupied by a single wardrobe and a high-canopied bed. It could have come straight out of House Hjorth, except for the gurgling brass radiators under the large-paned windows, and the dim electric candles glowing overhead. "This is wonderful," Olga said with feeling. She smiled at Miriam. "You're looking good."

"Huh." Miriam shrugged. "I'm taking a day out from the office, slobbing around here to catch up on the patent paperwork." She was in trousers and a baggy sweater. "I'm afraid I scandalized Jane. Had to tell her I was into dress reform."

"Well, what does the help's opinion matter? *I* say you look fine." Olga slid out from under her pack and began to unbutton her overcoat. "Do you have anything I can take for a headache?"

"Sure, in the bathroom. I'll show you." Miriam paused. "How would you like a guided tour of the town?" she asked.

"I'd love it, when the headache is sorted." Olga rubbed her forehead. "This cargo had better be worth it," she said as Miriam knelt and began to work on the pack. "I feel like a pack mule."

"It's worth it, believe me." Miriam worked the big, flattish box loose from the top of Olga's pack. "A decent flat-panel monitor will make *all* the difference to running AutoCAD, believe me. And the medicine and clothes and, uh, other stuff." *Other stuff* came in a velvet bag and was denser than lead, almost ten kilograms of gold in a block the size of a pint of milk. "Once I've stored this safely and changed, we can go out. We'll need to buy you another set of clothes while you're over here."

"It can wait." Olga reached into her coat pocket and pulled out a pistol, held it out to Miriam. "I brought this along, by the way. Lady Brilliana is waiting on the other side."

"She is, is she?" Miriam pulled a mirthless smile. "Good. Did she bring that cannon of hers?"

"Yes." Olga nodded.

"You'd better put that away," Miriam warned. "People don't go armed here, except the police. You don't want to attract attention."

"Yes. I noticed that in your world, as well." Olga found an inner pocket in her coat and slid the gun into it carefully. "Who's to defend you?"

"The thief-takers and constables, in theory. Ordinary thief-takers are mostly safe, but the police constabulary are somewhat different here—their job is to defend the state against its own subjects." Miriam picked up the dense velvet bag with both hands and carried it to the doorway, glanced either way, then ducked through into the next room.

"This is your bedroom?" asked Olga.

"Yes." Miriam grunted. "Here, help me move the bed." There was a loose panel in the skirting board behind the bed. Miriam worried it loose, to reveal a small safe which she unlocked. The bag of bullion was a tight fit because the safe was already nearly full, but she worked it closed eventually and put the wooden slat back before shoving the bed up against it. "That's about ten thousand pounds," Miriam commented—"enough to buy this house nine times over."

Olga whistled appreciatively. "You're doing it in style."

"Yeah, well, as soon as I can liquidate it, I'm going to invest it." Miriam shrugged. "You're sure Brill is alright?" she asked.

"Brilliana is fine," Olga said dismissively. "I don't believe you have anything to worry about on her part."

"I don't believe she's a threat." Miriam shook her head. "A snoop planted by Angbard is another matter."

"Hmm." Olga looked skeptical. "I see."

"Give me ten minutes? I need to get decent."

"Certainly." Olga retreated to the bathroom—opposite the guestroom—to play with the exotic fixtures. They weren't as efficient as those in Miriam's office or Fort Lofstrom, but they'd do.

Miriam met her on the landing, dressed for a walk in public and wearing a ridiculous-looking bonnet. "Let's head to the tram stop," she suggested. "I'll take you by the office and introduce you to people. Then there's a friend I want you to meet."

Miriam couldn't help but notice the way Olga kept turning her head like a yokel out in the big city for the first time. "Not like Boston, is it?" she said, as the tram whined around the corner of Broad Street and narrowly avoided a costermonger's cart with a screech of brakes and an exchange of curses.

"It's—" Olga took a deep breath: "smellier," she declared. She glanced around. "Smaller. More people out and about. Colder. Everyone wears heavier clothing, like home, but well cut, machine-made. Dark fabrics."

"Yes," Miriam agreed. "Clothing here costs much more than in world two because the whole industrial mass-production thing hasn't taken off. People wear hand-me-downs, insist on thicker, darker fabrics that wear harder, and fashion changes much more slowly. It used to be like that back home; in 1900 a pair of trousers would have cost me about four hundred bucks in 2000 money, but clothing factories were already changing that. One of the things on my to-do list is introducing new types of cloth-handling machines and new types of fabric. Once I've got a toe-hold chiseled out. But don't assume this place is wholly primitive—it isn't. I got some nasty surprises when I arrived."

Something caught her eye. "Look." She pointed up into the air, where a distant lozenge shape bearing post from exotic Europe was maneuvering toward an airfield on the far side of town.

"Wow. That must be huge! Why don't your people have such things?"

Miriam pulled a wry face. "We tried them, long ago. They're slow and they don't carry much, but what really killed them was politics. Over here they've developed them properly—if you want to compare airships here with airships back home, they've got the U.S. beat hands-down. They sure look impressive, don't they?"

"Yes."

Miriam stood up and pulled on the bell cord, and the tram slid to a halt. "Come on," she urged. They stepped off the platform into shallow slush outside a street of warehouses with a few people bustling back and forth. "This way."

Olga followed Miriam—who waited for her to catch up—toward an open doorway. Miriam entered, and promptly turned right into a second doorway. "Behold, the office," Miriam said. "Declan? This is Miss Hjorth. Olga, meet Declan McHugh."

"Pleased to meet you, ma'am." Declan was a pale-faced draftsman somewhere in his late twenties, his face spotted badly by acne. He regarded Olga gravely from beside his board: Olga smiled prettily and batted her eyelashes, hamming it up. Behind Declan two other youths kept focused on their blueprints. "Will you be in later, ma'am?" he asked Miriam. "Had a call from O'Reilly's works regarding the wood cement."

"I'll be in tomorrow," Miriam replied thoughtfully. "I'm showing Olga around because she will be in and out over the next few months. She's carrying documents for me and talking to people I need to see on my behalf. Is that clear?"

"Er, yes." Declan bobbed his head. "You'll be wanting the shoe-grip blueprints tomorrow?"

"Yes. If you could run off two copies and see that one gets to Mr. Soames, that would be good. We'll need the first castings by Friday."

"I will do that." He turned back to his drawing board and Miriam withdrew.

"That," she explained quietly, "is the office. *There* is the lab, where Roger and Martin work: They're the chemistry team. Around that corner is going to be the metal shop. Soames and Oswald are putting it together right now, and the carpenter's busy on the kitchen. But it'll be a while before everything is in shape. The floor above us is still half derelict, and I'm going to convert a couple of rooms into paper storage and more drafting offices before we move the office work to new premises. Currently I've got eight men working here full-time. We'd better introduce you to all of them."

She guided Olga into a variety of rooms, rooms full of furnaces, rows of glass jars, a lathe and drill press, gas burners. Men in suits, men in shirts and vests, red-faced or pale, whiskered or clean-shaven: men who stood when she entered, men who deferred to Miriam as if she was royalty or management or something of both.

Olga shook her head as they came out of the building. "I wouldn't have believed it," she said quietly. "You've done it.

All of them, followers, all doing your bidding respectfully. How did you manage it?"

Miriam's cheek twitched. "Money," she murmured. "And being right, but mostly it was the money. As long as I can keep the money coming and seem to know what I'm talking about, they're mine. I say, cab! Cab!" She waved an arm up and down and a cabbie reined his nag in and pulled over.

"Greek Street, if you please," Miriam said, settling into the cab beside Olga.

Olga glanced at her, amused. "I remember the first time you met a carriage," she said.

"So do I." Miriam pulled a face. "These have a better suspension. And there are trains for long journeys, and steam cars if you can afford the expense and put up with the unreliability and noise."

The cab dropped them off at Greek Street, busy with shoppers at this time of day. Miriam pulled her bonnet down on her head, hiding her hair. "Come on, my dear," she said, in a higher voice than normal, tucking Olga's hand under her arm. "Oh, cab! Cab, I say!" A second cab swooped in and picked them up. "To Holmes Alley, if you please."

Miriam checked over her shoulder along the way. "No sign of a tail," she murmured as the cab pulled up. "Let's go." They were in the door of the pawn shop before Olga could blink, and Miriam whipped the bonnet off and shook her hair out. "Erasmus?"

"Coming, coming—" A burst of loud wet coughing punctuated his complaint. "Excuse me, please. Ah, Miriam, my friend. How nice of you to visit. And who is this?"

"Olga, meet Erasmus Burgeson." Miriam indicated the back curtain, which billowed slightly as Erasmus tried to stifle his coughing before entering. "Erasmus, meet my friend Olga."

"Charmed, I'm sure," he said, and stepped out from behind the curtain. "Yes, indeed I *am* charmed, I'm absolutely certain, my dear." He bowed stifly. "To what do I owe the honor of this occasion?"

Miriam turned around and flipped the sign in the door to

4, then shot the bolt. She moved deeper into the shop. "You got my letter?"

"It was most welcome." Burgeson nodded. "The fact of its existence, if not its content, I should say. But thank you, anyway."

"I don't think we were observed," Miriam stated, "but I think we'd better leave by the cellar."

"You trust her?" Burgeson raised an eyebrow.

"Implicitly." Miriam met his eyes. "Olga is one of my business associates. And my bodyguard. Show him, Olga."

Olga made her pistol appear. Burgeson's other eyebrow rose. She made it disappear again. "Hmm," said Burgeson. "A fine pair of Amazon women!" He smiled faintly. "Nevertheless, I hope you don't need to use that. It's my experience that however many guns you bring to a fight, the Crown can always bring more. The trick is to avoid needing them in the first place."

"This is your agent?" Olga asked Miriam, with interest.

"Yes, exactly." Miriam turned to Burgeson. "I brought her here because I think it may be impossible for me to visit in person in the future. In particular, I wanted to introduce her to you as an alternative contact against the time when we need to be publicly seen in different places at the same time. If you follow."

"I see." Burgeson nodded. "Most prudent. Was there anything else?"

"Yes. The consignment we discussed has arrived. If you let us know where and how you want it, I'll see it gets to you."

"It's rather, ah, large." Burgeson looked grim. "You know we have a lot of use for it, but it's hard to make the money flow so freely without being overseen."

"That would be bad," Miriam agreed. Olga looked away, then drifted toward the other side of the shop and began rooting through the hanging clothes, keeping one ear on the conversation. "But I can give you a discount for bulk: say, another fifteen percent. Think of it as a contribution to the cause, if you want."

"If I want." Burgeson chuckled humorlessly: It tailed off

in a hoarse croak. "They hanged Oscar yesterday, did you hear?"

"Oscar?"

"The free librarian who fenced me the Marx you purchased. Two days before Inspector Smith searched my domicile."

"Oh dear." Miriam was silent for a moment. Olga pulled an outfit out to examine it more closely.

"It wouldn't be so bad if Russell hadn't shot Lord Dalgleish last year," Burgeson mused. "You wouldn't know about that. But the revolution, in that history book you gave me, the one in the Kingdom of Russ, the description all sounds exceedingly familiar, and most uncomfortably close to the bone. In particular, the minister named Stolypin, and the unfortunate end he came to." He coughed damply.

Olga cleared her throat. "Is there somewhere I can try this on?" she asked.

"In the back," said Burgeson. "Mind the stove on your way through." He paused for breath as Olga squeezed past.

"Is she serious?" he asked Miriam quietly.

"Serious about me, and my faction." Miriam frowned. "She's not politicized, if that's what you're asking about. Sheltered upbringing, too. But she's loyal to her friends and she has nothing to gain from the Emergency here. And she knows how to shoot."

"Good." Erasmus nodded gravely. "I wouldn't want you to be placing your life in the hands of a dizzy child."

"Placing my—*what*?"

"Two strangers. Not constabulary or plainclothes thief-takers, one of them looking like a Chinee-man. They've been drinking in the wrong establishments this past week, asking questions. Some idiots, the kind who work the wrong side of the law—not politicals—these idiots have taken their money. Someone has talked, I'm sure of it. A name, Blackstones, was mentioned, and something about tonight. I wrote to you but obviously it hasn't arrived." He stared at her. "It's a very deep pond you're swimming in."

"Erasmus." She stared right back. "I am going to make

this world fit to live in by every means at my disposal. Believe me, a couple of gangsters playing at cracksman won't stop me."

The curtain rustled. Olga stepped out, wearing a green two-piece outfit. "How do I look?" she asked, doing a twirl.

"Alright," said Miriam. "I think. I'm not the right person to ask for fashion tips."

"You look marvelous, my dear," Erasmus volunteered gallantly. "With just a little work, a seamstress will have the jacket fitting perfectly. And with some additional effort, the patching can be made invisible."

"That's about what I thought." Olga nodded. "I'd rather not, though." She grinned impishly. "What do you say?"

"It's fine," said Miriam. She turned back to Burgeson. "Who leaked the news?" she asked.

"I want to find out." He looked grim.

"Write to me, as I did to you, care of this man." She wrote down Roger's address on a scrap of card. "He works for me and he's trustworthy."

"Good." Erasmus stared at the card for a moment, lips working, then thrust it into the elderly cast-iron stove that struggled to heat the shop. "Fifty pounds weight. That's an awful lot."

"We can move it in chunks, if necessary."

"It won't be," he said absent-mindedly, as if considering other things.

"Miriam, dear, you really ought to try this on," called Olga.

"Oh, really." Miriam rolled her eyes. "Can't you—"

"Did you ever play at avoiding your chaperone as a child?" Olga asked quietly. "If not, do as I say. The same man has walked past the outside window three times while we've been inside. We have perhaps five minutes at the outside. Maybe less."

"Oh." She looked at Olga in surprise. "Okay, give it to me." She turned to Burgeson. "I'm sorry, but I'm going to have to abuse your hospitality. I hope you don't have anything illegal on the premises?"

"No, not me. Not now." He smiled a sallow smile. "My

lungs are giving me trouble again, that's why I locked up shop, yes? You'd better go into the back."

Olga threw a heavy pinafore at Miriam. "Quick, take off your jacket, put this on over your dress. That's right. Lose the bonnet." She passed Miriam a straw hat, utterly unsuited to the weather and somewhat tattered. "Come on, take this overcoat. You don't mind?" She appealed to Burgeson.

"My dear, it's an education to see two different women so suddenly." He smiled grimly. "You'd better put your old outfit in this." He passed Miriam a Gladstone bag.

"But we haven't paid—"

"The devil will pay if you don't leave through the cellar as fast as you can," Burgeson hissed urgently, then broke up in a fit of racking coughs. Miriam blinked. *He needs antibiotics,* she thought absent-mindedly.

"Good-bye!" she said, then she led Olga—still stuffing her expensive jacket into the leather case—down the rickety steps into the cellar, just as the doorbell began to ring insistently.

"Come on," she hissed. Glancing round she saw Olga shift the bag to her left hand. Shadows masked her right. "Come *on,* this way."

She led Olga along a narrow tunnel walled with mildewed books, past a row of pigeonholes, and then an upright piano that had seen better days. She stopped, gestured Olga behind her, then levered the piano away from the wall. A dank hole a yard in diameter gaped in the exposed brickwork behind it, dimly lit from the other side. "Get in," she ordered.

"But—"

"Do it!" She could already hear footsteps overhead.

Olga crawled into the hole. "Keep going," Miriam told her, then knelt down and hurried after her. She paused to drag the piano back into position, grunting with effort, then stood up.

"Where are we?" Olga whispered.

"Not safe yet. Come *on.*" The room was freezing cold, and smelled of damp and old coal. She led Olga up the steps at the end and out through the gaping door into a larger cellar, then immediately doubled back. Next to the doorway there was another one, this time closed. Another two stood opposite. Miriam opened her chosen door and beckoned Olga inside, then shut it.

"Where—"

"Follow me." The room was dark until Miriam pulled out a compact electric flashlight. It was half full of lumber, but there was an empty patch in the wall opposite, leading back parallel to Burgeson's cellar. She ducked into it and found the next tunnel, set in the wall below the level of the stacked firewood. "You see where we're going? Come on."

The tunnel went on and on, twisting right at one point. Miriam held the flashlight in her mouth, proceeding on hands and knees and trying not to tear her clothes. She was going to look like a particularly grubby housemaid when she surfaced, she decided. She really hoped Olga was wrong about the visitor, but she had a nasty hunch that she wouldn't be seeing Burgeson again for some time.

The tunnel opened up into another cellar, hidden behind a decaying rocking horse, a broken wardrobe, and a burned bed frame with bare metal springs like skeletal ribs. Miriam stood up and dusted herself off as best she could, then made room for Olga. Olga pulled a face. "Ugh! That was filthy. Are you alright?"

"Yes," Miriam said quietly.

"It was the same man," Olga added. "About six and a half feet tall, a big bull with a bushy moustache. And two more behind him dressed identically in blue. King's men?"

"Probably. Sounds like Inspector Smith to me. Hmm. Hold this." Miriam passed her the flashlight and continued to brush dirt and cobwebs out of the pinafore: It had started out white, and at best it would be gray by the time she surfaced. "Right, I think we're just about ready to surface."

"Where?"

"The next street over, in a backyard." Miriam pulled the door open to reveal wooden steps leading up toward daylight. "Come on. Put the flashlight away and for God's sake hide the gun."

They surfaced between brick walls, a sky the color of a slate roof above them. Miriam unlatched the gate and they slipped out, two hard-faced women, one in a maid's uniform and the other in a green much-patched suit that had seen better days. They were a far cry from the dignified widow and her young companion who had called on Burgeson's emporium twenty minutes earlier.

"Quick." Miriam guided Olga onto the first tram to pass. It would go sufficiently close to home to do. "Two fourpenny tickets, please." She paid the conductor and sat down, feeling faint. She glanced round the tram, but nobody was within earshot. "That was too close for comfort," she whispered.

"What was it?" Olga asked quietly, sitting next to her.

"We weren't there. They can't prove anything. There's no bullion on Erasmus's premises, and he's a sick man. Unless we were followed from the works to his shop . . ." Miriam stopped. "He said some housebreakers were going to hit on us tonight," she said slowly. "This is *not* good news."

"Housebreakers." Olga's face was a mask of grim anticipation. "Do you mean what I think you intend to say? Blackguards with knives?"

"Not necessarily. He said two men were asking around a drinking house for bravos who'd like to take their coin. One of them looked Oriental."

Olga tensed. "I see," she said quietly.

"Indeed." Miriam nodded. "I think tonight we're going to see some questions answered. Oriental, huh?" She grinned angrily. "Time to play host for the long-lost relatives . . ."

The big stone house was set well back from the curving road, behind a thick hedge and a low stone wall. Its nearest neighbors were fifty yards away, also set back and sheltered behind stone walls and hedges. Smoke boiled from two chimneys, and the lights in the central hall burned bright in the darkness, but there were no servants. On arriving home

Miriam had packed Jane and her husband Ronald the gardener off to a cheap hotel with a silver guinea in hand and the promise of a second to come against their silence. "I want no questions asked or answered," Miriam said firmly. "D'you understand?"

"Yes'm," said Jane, bobbing her head skeptically. It was clear that she harbored dark suspicions about Olga, and was wondering if her mistress was perhaps prone to unspeakable habits: a suspicion that Miriam was happy to encourage as a decoy from the truth.

"That'll do," Miriam said quietly, watching from the landing as they trudged down the road toward the tram stop and the six-fifteen service into town. "No servants, no witnesses. Right?"

"Right," Olga echoed. "Are you sure you want me to go through with this?"

"Yes, I want you to do it. But do it fast, I don't want to be alone longer than necessary. How are your temporary tattoos?"

"They're fine. Look, what you told me about Matthias. If Brill's working for—"

"She isn't," Miriam said firmly. "If she wanted me dead I'd be dead, okay? Get over it. If she's hiding anything, it's something else—Angbard, probably. Bring her over here and if the bad guys don't show we'll just dig out a bottle of wine and have a late-morning lie-in tomorrow, alright?"

"Right," Olga said dubiously. Then she headed downstairs, for the kitchen door and the walk to the spot beside the greenhouse where Miriam had cleared the snow away.

Miriam watched her go, more apprehensive than she cared to admit. Alone in the house in winter, every creak and rustle seemed like a warning of a thief in the night. The heating gurgled ominously. Miriam retired to her bedroom and changed into an outfit she'd brought over on her last trip. The Velcro straps under her arms gave her some trouble, but the boots fitted well and she felt better for the bulletproof vest. With her ski mask on hand, revolver loaded and sitting on her hip, and night vision goggles strapped to her forehead, she felt even more like an imposter than she did when she was dressed up to the nines to meet the nobs. *Just as long as they take me as seriously,* she thought tensely. Then she picked up her dictaphone and checked the batteries and tape one last time—fully charged, fully rewound, ready for action. *I hope this works.*

The house felt dreadfully empty without either the servants or Olga about. *I've gotten used to having other people around,* Miriam realized. *When did* that *happen?*

She walked downstairs slowly, pausing on the landing to listen for signs of anything amiss. At the bottom she opened the door under the staircase and ducked inside. The silent alarm system was armed. Ronald the gardener had grumbled when she told him to bury the induction wire a foot underground, just inside the walls, but he'd done as she'd told him to when she reminded him who was paying. The control panel—utterly alien to this world—was concealed behind a false panel in the downstairs hall. She turned her walkie-talkie on, clipped the hands-free earphone into place, and continued her lonely patrol.

It all depended on Brill, of course. And on Roland, assuming Roland was on the level and wasn't one of *them* playing a fiendishly deep inside game against her. Whoever *they* were. She was reasonably sure he wasn't—if he was, he'd had several opportunities to dispose of her without getting caught, and hadn't taken any of them—but there was still a question mark hanging over Brill. But whatever game she was playing wasn't necessarily hostile, which was why Olga had gone back over to the hunting hide to fetch her. The idea of not being able to trust *Olga* just made Miriam's head hurt. *You have to start somewhere, haven't you?* she asked herself. If she assumed Olga was on her side and she was wrong, *nothing* she did would make any difference. And Olga vouched for Brill. And three of them would be a damn sight more use than two when the shit hit the fan, as it surely would, sometime in the small hours.

The big clock on the landing ticked the seconds away slowly. Miriam wandered into the kitchen, opened the door on the big cast-iron cooking range set against the interior wall, and shoveled coal into it. Then she turned the airflow up. It was going to be an extremely cold night, and even though she was warm inside her outdoor gear and flak jacket, Miriam felt the chill in her bones.

Two men, one of them Chinese-looking, in the wrong pubs. She shook her head, remembering a flowering of blood and a long, curved knife in the darkness. The feel of Roland's hands on her bare skin, making her go hot and cold simultaneously. Iris looking at her with a guarded, startled expression, as unmotherly as Angbard's supercillious crustiness. *These are some of my favorite things,* butter-pat sized lumps of soft metal glowing luminous in the twilight of a revolutionary quartermaster's shop: *Glock automatics and diamond rings . . .*

Miriam shook herself. "Damn, if I wait here I'll doze off for sure." She stood up, raised the insulating lid on the range, and pushed the kettle onto the hot plate. A cup of coffee would get her going. She picked up her dictaphone and re-wound, listening to notes she'd recorded earlier in the day.

"The family founder had six sons. Five of them had families and the Clan is the result. The sixth—what happened to him? Angbard said he went west and vanished. Suppose—suppose he did. Reached the western empire, that is, but did so poor, destitute, out of luck. Along the way he lost his talisman, the locket with the knotwork. If he had to re-create it from memory, so he could world-walk, would be succeed? Would I? I know what happens when I look at the knot, but can I remember exactly what shape it is, well enough to draw it? Let's try."

Whirr. Click. New memo. "Nope. I just spent ten minutes and what I've drawn does nothing for me. Hmm. So we know that it's not that easy to re-create from memory, and I know that if you look at the other symbol you go here, not home. Hmm again."

Whirr. Click. New memo. "I just looked at both lockets. Should have done it earlier, but it's hard to see them without zoning out and crossing over to the other world. The knots—

in the other one, there's an arc near the top left that threads over the outer loop, not under it, like in the one Iris gave me. So it looks like the assassin's one is, yeah, a corruption of the original design. So maybe the lost family hypothesis is correct."

Whirr. Click. New memo. "Why didn't they keep trying different knots until they found one that worked? One that let them make the rendezvous with the other families?"

Whirr. Click. New memo. "It's a bloodline thing. If you know of only one other universe, and if you know the ability to go there runs in the family, would you necessarily think in terms of multiple worlds? Would you realize you'd mis-remembered the design of the talisman? Or would you just assume—the West Coast must have looked pretty much the same in both versions, this world and my own back then—that you'd been abandoned by your elder brothers? Scumbags."

Whirr. Click. New memo. "Why me? Why Patricia? What was it about her ancestry that threatened them? As opposed to anyone else in the Clan? Did they just want to kill her to restart the blood feuds, or was there something else?"

Whirr. Click. New memo. "What do they want? And can I use them as a lever to get the Clan to give me what *I* want?"

The door around the back of the scullery creaked as it opened.

Miriam was on her feet instantly, back to the wall beside the cooker, pistol in her right hand. *Shit, shit*—she froze, breath still, listening.

"Miriam?" called a familiar voice, "are you there?"

She lowered her gun. "Yes!"

Olga shuffled inside, looking about a thousand years older than she had an hour before. "Oh, my *head,*" she moaned. "Give me drugs, give me strong medicine, give me a bone saw!" She drew a finger across her throat, then looked at Miriam. "*What* is that you're wearing?" she asked.

"Hello." Brilliana piped up behind her. "Can I come in?" She looked around dubiously. "Are you *sure* this is another world?" she asked.

"Yes," Miriam said tersely. "Here. Take two of these now. I'll give you the next two when it's time." She passed the capsules to Olga, who dry-swallowed them and pulled a face. "Get a glass of water." Miriam looked at Brill. "Did you bring—"

Brill grinned. "This?" she asked, hefting a stubby looking riot gun.

"Uh, yeah." Miriam froze inside for a moment, then relaxed. She fixed Brill with a beady eye. "You realize an explanation is a bit overdue?"

"An explan—oh."

"It doesn't wash, Brill," she said evenly. "I know you're working for someone in Clan security. Or were you going to tell me you found that cannon in a cupboard somewhere?"

Olga had taken a step back. Miriam could see her right hand flexing. "Why don't you go upstairs and get dressed for the party?" Miriam suggested.

"Ah, if you think so." Olga looked at her dubiously.

"I do." Miriam kept her eyes on Brill, who stared back unwavering as Olga swept past toward the staircase. "Well?"

"I got word to expect you two days before you arrived in Niejwein," Brill admitted. "You didn't really expect Angbard to hang you out to dry, did you? He said, and I quote, 'Stick to her like glue, don't let her out of your sight on family territory, and especially don't give Baron Hjorth an opportunity to push her down a stairwell.' So I did as he said," she added, her self-satisfaction evident.

"Who else was in on it?" Miriam asked.

"Olga." Brill shrugged. "But not as explicitly. She's not an *agent*, but . . . you didn't think she was an accident, did you? The duke sent you down to Niejwein with her because he thought you'd be safer that way. And to add to the confusion. Conspirators and murderers tend to underestimate her because of the giggling airhead act." She shrugged.

"So who do you report to?" said Miriam.

"Angbard. In person."

"Not Roland?"

"Roland?" Brill snorted. "Roland's useless at this sort of thing—"

"So you world-walk? Why did you conceal it from me?"

"Because Angbard told me to, of course. It wasn't hard: You don't know enough about the Clan structure to know who's likely to be outer family and who's going to have the talent." She took a deep breath. "I used to be a bit of a tear-away. When I was eighteen I tried to join the Marine Corps." She frowned. "I didn't make the physical, though, and my mother had a screaming fit when she heard about it. She told Angbard to beat some sense into me and he paid for the bodyguard training and karate while I made up my mind what to do next. Back at court, my job—" she swallowed— "if we ever had to bring the hammer down on Alexis, I was tasked with that. Outside the Clan, nobody thinks a lady-in-waiting is a threat, did you know that? But outside the Clan, noble ladies aren't expected to be able to fight. Anyway, that's why Angbard stuck me on you as a nursemaid. If you ran into anything you couldn't handle . . ."

"Er." The kettle began to hiss. Miriam shook her head, suffering from information overload. *My lady-in-waiting wants to be a marine?* "Want some coffee?"

"Yes. Please. Hey, did you know you look just like your Iris when you frown?"

Miriam stopped dead. "You've seen her?" she demanded.

"Calm down!" Brilliana held up her hands in surrender. "Yes, I've seen her in the past couple of days, and she's fine. She just needed to go underground for a bit. Same as you, do you understand? I met up with her when you left me in Boston with Paulie and nothing to do. After you shot your mouth off at Angbard, I figured he needed to know what had you so wound up. He takes a keen interest in her well-being, and not just because you threatened to kill him if he didn't. So of *course* I went over to see her. In fact, I visited every couple of days, to keep an eye on her. I was there when—" Brill fell silent.

"It was you with the shotgun," Miriam pushed.

"Actually, no." Brill looked a little green. "She kept it taped under her chair, the high-backed one in the living room. I just called the Clan cleaners for her afterwards. It was during your first trip over here when she, she had the incident. She phoned your office line, and I was in the office, so I picked up the phone. As you were over here I went around to sort everything out. I found—" She shuddered. "It took a lot of cleaning up. They were Clan security, from the New York office, you know. She was so *calm* about it."

"Let me get this straight." Miriam poured the kettle's contents into a cafetiere. Her hand was shaking, she noticed distantly. "You're telling me that *Iris* gunned down a couple of intruders?"

"Huh?" Brill looked puzzled. "Oh, *Iris*. That's right. Like 'Miriam.' Listen, she said, 'it gets to be a habit after the third assassination attempt. Like killing cockroaches.' "

"Urk." Miriam sat down hard and waited for the conceptual earthquake to stop. She fixed Brill with the stare she kept in reserve for skewering captains of industry she was getting ready to accuse of malfeasance or embezzlement. "Okay, let me get this straight. You are telling me that my mother just *happens* to keep a sawn-off shotgun under her wheelchair for blowing away SWAT teams, a habit which she somehow concealed from me during my childhood and upbringing while she was a political activist and then the wife of a radical bookstore manager—"

"No!" Brill looked increasingly annoyed. "Don't you get it? This was the first attempt on her life in over thirty years—"

Miriam's walkie-talkie bleeped at her urgently.

"We've got company." Miriam eyed the walkie-talkie as if it might explode. *My mother is an alien,* she thought. *Must have been in the Weather Underground or something.* But there was no time to worry about that now. "Is that thing loaded?"

"Yes."

"Right. Then wait here. If anyone comes through the garden door, shoot them. If anyone comes through the other door, it'll be either me and Olga, or the bad guys. I'll knock first. Back in a second."

Miriam dashed for the hall and took the stairs two at a time. *"Zone two breach,"* the burglar alarm chirped in her ear. Zone two was the east wall of the garden. "Olga?" she called.

"Here." Olga stepped out onto the landing. Her goggles made her look like a tall, angular insect—a mantis, perhaps.

"Come on. We've got visitors."

"Where do you want to hold out?"

"In the scullery passage and kitchen—the only direct way in is via the front window, and there are fun surprises waiting for them in the morning room and dining room."

"Right." Olga hurried downstairs, a machine pistol clutched in one hand.

"Brill," Miriam called, "we're coming in." She remembered to knock.

Once in the kitchen she passed Brill a walkie-talkie with hands-free kit. "Put this in a pocket and stick the headphone in. Good. Olga? You too." She hit the transmit button. "Can you both hear me?"

Two nods. "Great. We've—"

"*Attention. Zone four breach.*"

"—That's the living room. *Wait* for it, dammit!"

"*Attention. Zone five breach.*"

"Dining room," Miriam whispered. "Right. Let's go."

"Let's—what?"

She switched her set to a different channel and pressed the transmit button.

"*Attention. Zone four smoke release. Attention. Zone five smoke release. Attention. Zone six smoke release.*"

"What—"

"Smoke bombs. Come on, the doors are locked on the hall side and I had the frames reinforced. We've got them bottled up, unless they've got demolition charges. Here." Miriam passed Brill a pair of handcuffs. "Let's go. Remember, we want to get the ringleader alive—but I don't want either of you to take any risks."

Miriam led them into the octagonal hallway. There was a muffled thump from the day room door, and a sound of coughing. She waved Olga to one side, then prepared to open the door. "Switch your goggles on," she said, and killed the lights.

Through the goggles the room was a dark and confusing jumble of shapes. Miriam saw two luminous green shadows moving around her—Brill and Olga. One of them gave her a thumbs-up, while the other of them raised something gun-shaped. "On my mark. I'm going to open the door. Three, two, one, *mark*." Miriam unlocked the door and shoved it open. Smoke billowed out, and a coughing figure stumbled into the darkened hall. Olga's arm rose and fell, resulting in a groan and a crash. "I'm in." Miriam stepped over the prone figure and into the smoke-filled room. It was chilly inside, and her feet crackled on broken glass. *Bastards,* she thought angrily. Something vague and greenish glowed in the smoke at the far corner, caught between the grand piano and the curtains. "Drop your gun and lie down!" Miriam shouted, then ducked.

Bang-bang: The thud of bullets hitting masonry behind her was unmistakable. Miriam spat, then knelt and aimed deliberately at the shooter. *Can I do this*—rage filled her. *You tried to kill my mother!* She pulled the trigger. There was a cry, and the green patch stretched up then collapsed. She froze, about to shoot again, then straightened up.

"Stop! Police!" Whistles shrilled in the garden. *"Attention. Zone three breach."*

"That's the south wall! What the fuck?" Miriam whispered. She keyed her walkie-talkie. "Status!"

"One down." Brill, panting heavily. "Olga's got the guy in the hall on the floor. They tried to shoot me."

"Listen." Whistles loud in the garden, flashlight beams just visible through the smoke. "Into the hall! Brill, can you drag the fucker? Get him upright? You take him and I'll carry Olga."

The sound of breaking glass came from the kitchen. Miriam darted back through the doorway and nearly ran straight into Olga.

"Quick!" Olga cried. "I can't do it, my head's still split-ting. You'd better—"

"Shut the fuck up." Miriam pushed her goggles up, grabbed Olga around the waist, and mashed a hand against the light switch. She fumbled with her left sleeve, saw the blurry outline clearly for a moment, tried to focus on it, and tightened her grip on Olga painfully. "Brill?"

"Do it!" Brill's voice was edgy with tension and fear. More police whistles then a cry and more gunshots, muffled by the wall.

Miriam tensed and lifted, felt Olga grab her shoulders, and stared at her wrist. Her knees began to buckle under the weight: *Can't keep this up for long,* she thought desperately. There was a splintering sound behind her, and the endless knotwork snake that ate its own tail coiling in the darkness as it reached out to bite her between the eyes. She fell forward into snow and darkness, Olga a dead weight in her arms.

FACING THE MUSIC

Miriam was freezing. She had vague impressions of ice, snow, and a wind coming in off the bay that would chill a furnace in seconds. She stumbled to her feet and whimpered as pain spiked through her forehead.

"Ow." Olga sat up. "Miriam, are you alright?"

Miriam blinked back afterimages of green shapes moving at the far end of the room. She remembered her hot determination, followed by a cry of pain. She doubled over abruptly and vomited into the snow, moaning.

"Where's the hut?" Olga demanded in a panicky voice. "Where's the—"

"Goggles," Miriam gasped. Another spasm grabbed her stomach. *This cold could kill us,* she thought through the hot and cold shudders of a really bad world-walk. "Use your goggles."

"Oh." Olga pulled them down across her eyes. "Oh!"

"Miriam?" Brill's voice came from behind a tree. "Help!"

"Aaarh, aarh—"

Miriam stumbled over, twigs tearing at her face. It was snowing heavily, huge flakes the size of fingernails twisting in front of her face and stinging when they touched her skin. Brill was kneeling on top of something that thrashed around. "Help me!" she called.

"Right." Miriam crashed to her knees in front of Brill, her stomach still protesting, and fumbled at her belt for another set of restraints. Brill had handcuffed the prisoner but he'd begun kicking and she was forced to sit on his legs, which was not a good position for either of them. "Here."

"Lay *still*, damn you—"

"We're going to have to make him walk. It's that or we carry him," Olga commented. "How big is he?"

"Just a kid. Just a goddamn kid."

"Watch *out*, he may have friends out here!"

Miriam stood up and pulled her night-vision goggles back down. Brill and the prisoner showed up as brilliant green flames, Olga a hunched figure a few feet away. "Come on. To the cabin." Together with Brill she lifted the prisoner to his feet—still moaning incoherently in what sounded like blind panic—and half-dragged him toward the hunting blind, which was still emitting a dingy green glow. The heat from the kerosene heater was enough to show it up like a street light against the frigid background.

It took almost ten minutes to get there, during which time the snow began to fall heavily, settling over their tracks. The prisoner, apparently realizing that the alternative was freezing to death slowly, shut up and began to move his feet. Miriam's head felt as if someone was whacking on it with a hammer, and her stomach was still rebelling from its earlier mistreatment. Olga crept forward and hunted around in the dark, looking for signs of disturbance, but as far as Miriam could see they were alone in the night and darkness.

The hut was empty but warm as Brill and Miriam lifted the youth through the door. With one last effort they heaved him onto a sleeping mat and pulled the door shut behind them to keep the warmth in. "Right," said Miriam, her voice shaking with exhaustion, "let's see what we've got here." She stood up and switched on the battery-powered lantern hanging from the roof beam.

"Please don't—" He lay there shaking and shivering, trying to burrow away into the corner between the wall and the mattress.

"It speaks," Brill observed.

"It does indeed," said Miriam. He was shorter than she was, lightly built with straight dark hair and a fold to his eyes that made him look slightly Asian. And he didn't look more than eighteen years of age.

"Check him for an amulet," said Miriam.

"Right, you—got it!" A moment of struggle and Brill straightened up, holding out a fist from which dangled a chain. "Which version is it?"

Miriam glanced in it, then looked away. "The second variation. For world three." She stuffed it into a pocket along with the other. "You." She looked down at the prisoner. "What's your name?"

"Lin—Lin."

"Uh-huh. Do you have any friends out in this storm, Mr. Lin Lin?" Miriam glanced at the door. "Before you answer that, you might want to think about what they'll do to you if they found us here. Probably shoot first and ask questions later."

"No." He lay back. "It's Lee."

"Lin, or Lee?"

"I'm Lin. I'm a Lee."

"Good start," said Brill. She stared malevolently at him. "What were you doing breaking into our house?"

Lin stared back at her without saying anything.

"Allow me," Miriam murmured. Her headache was beginning to recede. She fumbled in her jacket, pulled out a worryingly depleted strip of tablets, punched one of them out, and swallowed it dry. It stuck in her throat, bitter and unwanted.

"Listen, Lin. You invaded my house. That wasn't very clever, and it got at least one of your friends shot. Now, I have some other friends who'd like to ask you some questions, and they won't be as nice about it as I am. In about an hour we're going to walk to another world, and we're going to take you with us. It's a world your family can't get to, because they don't even know it exists. Once you're there, you are going to be *stuck*. My friends there will take you to pieces to get the answers they want, and they will probably kill you afterwards, because they're like that."

Miriam stood up. "You have an hour to make up your mind whether you're going to talk to me, or whether you're going to talk to the Clan's interrogators. If you talk to me, I won't need to hurt you. I may even be able to keep you alive. The choice is yours."

She glanced at Brill. "Keep an eye on him. I'm going to check on Olga."

As she opened the door she heard the prisoner begin to weep quietly. She closed it behind herself hastily.

Miriam keyed her walkie-talkie. "Anyone out there? Over."

"Just me," replied Olga. "Hey, this wireless talkie thing is great, isn't it?"

"See anyone?"

"Not a thing. I'm circling about fifty yards out. I can see you on the doorstep."

"Right." Miriam waved. "I just read our little housebreaker the riot act."

"Want me to help hang him?"

"No." Miriam could still feel the hot wash of rage at the intruder in her sights, and the sense of release as she pulled the trigger. Now that the anger had cooled, it made her feel queasy. The first time she'd shot someone, the killer in the orangery, she'd barely felt it. It had just been something she had to do, like stepping out of the path of an onrushing juggernaut: He'd killed Margit and was coming at her with a knife. But this, the lying in wait and the hot rush of righteous anger, left her with a growing sense of appalled guilt the longer she thought about it. *It was avoidable, wasn't it?* "Our little housebreaker is just a chick. He's crying for momma already. I think he's going to sing like a bird as soon as we get him to the other side."

"How are you doing?" asked Olga. "You came through badly."

"Tell me about it." Miriam shuddered. "The cold seems to be helping my head. I'll be ready to go again in about an hour. Yourself?"

"I wish." Olga hummed to herself. "I never had that headache pill."

"Come over here, then," said Miriam. "I've got the stuff."

"Right."

They converged on a tree about five yards from the hut. Miriam stripped off a glove and fumbled in her pocket for the strip of beta blockers and the bottle of ibuprofen. "Here. One of each. Wash it down with something, huh?"

"Surely." Miriam waited in companionable silence while Olga swallowed, then pulled out a small hip flask and took a shot.

"What's that?"

"Spiced hunter's vodka. Fights the cold. Want some?"

"Better not, thanks." Miriam glanced over her shoulder at the hut. "I'm giving him an hour. The poor bastard thinks I'm going to give him to Angbard to torture to death if he doesn't tell me everything I want to know immediately."

"You aren't going to do that?" Olga's expression was unreadable behind her bulky headset.

"Depends how angry he makes me. There's been too much killing already, and it's been going on for far too long. We're going to have to stop sooner or later, or we'll run out of relatives."

"What do you mean, relatives? He's the enemy—"

"Don't you get it yet?" Miriam said impatiently. "These guys, the strangers who pop out of nowhere and kill—they've got to be blood relatives somewhere down the line. They're world-walkers too, and the only reason they go between this world and New Britain, instead of this world and the USA, is because that's the pattern they use. I'm thinking they're descended from that missing branch of the first family, the brother who went west and disappeared, right after the founder died."

Olga looked puzzled. "You think they're the sixth family?" she asked.

"I'm not sure, and I don't yet know why they're trying to start up the civil war again. But don't you think we owe it to ourselves to find out what's going on before we hand him over to the thief-takers for hanging?"

Olga rubbed her head. "This is going to be the most *fascinating* Clan council in living memory," she said.

"Come on." Miriam waved at the hut. "Let's get moving. I think it's time we dragged Roland into this."

One o'clock in the morning. *Ring ring* . . . "Hello?" Roland's voice was furred with sleep.

"Roland? It's me."

"Miriam, you do pick your times—"

"Not now. Got a family emergency."

"Emergency? What kind?" She could hear him waking up by the second.

"Get a couple of soldiers who you trust, and a safe house. *Not* Fort Lofstrom or its doppelgänger, it needs to be somewhere anonymous but secure on this side. It *must* be on this side. We've got a prisoner to debrief."

"A prisoner? What kind—"

"One of the assassins. He's alive, terrified, and spilling his guts to Olga right this moment." Olga was in the back office with Lin and Miriam's dictaphone, playing Good Cop. Lin was chattering, positively manic, desperate to tell her everything she wanted. Lin wasn't even eighteen. Miram felt ashamed of herself until she thought about what he'd been involved in. Boy soldiers, bright-eyed and bushy-tailed, recruited to defend their family's honor against the children of the hostile elder brothers—elder brothers who had stolen their birthright many generations ago, abandoning them to the nonexistent mercy of the western empire.

"He needs to be kept alive, and that means keeping him away from the security leak in Angbard's operation. And, uh, your little friend, assuming they're not one and the same person. Someone there is working with this guy's people. And here's another thing: I want a full DQ Alpha typing run on a blood sample, and I want it compared to as many members of the Clan—full members—as you can get. I want to know if he's related, and if so, how far back it goes."

And I want him out of here before Paulette shows up in the morning, Miriam thought. Paulie was a good friend and true, but some things weren't appropriate for her to be involved in. Like kidnapping.

"Okay, I'll sort it. Where do I go?"

"You come here." Miriam rattled off directions, mentally crossing her fingers. "I've got a new amulet for you, one that takes you from the other side to world three, my hideaway. Watch out, it is *very* different, as different from this world as you can imagine."

"Okay—but you'd better be able to explain why if the duke starts asking questions. I'll roust Xavier and Mort out of bed and be round in an hour. They'll keep their mouths shut. Is there anything else you need?"

"Yeah." Miriam licked her lips. "Is Angbard over here?"

"I think so."

"I've got to call him right away. Then I'm probably going to be gone before you get here. Got to go back to the far side to clean up the mess when the little prick broke into my house."

"He broke in—hey! Are you alright?"

"I'm alive. Olga and Brill can fill you in. Got to go. Stay safe." She rang off before she could break down and tell him how much she wanted to see him. *Cruel fate . . .* the next number was preprogrammed as well.

"Hello?" A politely curious voice.

"This is Helge Lofstrom-Hjorth. Get me Angbard. This is an emergency."

"Please hold." No messing around this time, Miriam noted. Someone was awake at the switchboard.

"Angbard here." He sounded amused rather than tired. "What is it, Miriam? Having trouble sleeping?"

"Perhaps. Listen, the Clan summit on Beltaigne is three

months away. Is there a procedure for bringing it forward, calling an extraordinary general meeting?"

"There is, but it's most unusual—nobody has done it in forty years. Are you sure you want me to do this for you? Without a good reason, there are people who would take it as a perfect opportunity to accuse you of anything they can think of."

"Yes." Miriam took a deep breath. "Listen. I know you've got my mother." Dead silence on the phone. She continued: "I don't know why you're holding her, but I'm going to give you the benefit of the doubt—for now. But I need that meeting, and she needs to be there. If she isn't, you're going to be in deep shit. I'm going to be there, too, and it has to be *now,* in a couple of days' time, not in two months, because we've got a prisoner and if you've not found your leak yet the prisoner will probably be dead before Beltaigne."

"A prisoner—" he hissed.

"You told me about a child of the founder who went west," Miriam said, very deliberately. "I've found his descendants. They're the ones who tried to kill Patricia and who've been after Olga and me. And I figure they may be messed up with the mole in your security staff. You want to call this emergency meeting, Angbard, you *really* want to do this."

"I believe you," he said after a momentary pause, in a tone that said he wished he didn't. "How extraordinary."

"When is it going to be ready?"

"Hmm." A pause. "Count on it in four days' time, at the Palace Hjorth. Any sooner is out of the question. I'll have to clear down all nonessential mail to get the announcement out in time—this will cost us a lot of goodwill and money. Can you guarantee you'll be there? If not, then I can't speak for what resolutions will be put forward and voted through by the assembled partners. You have enemies."

"I will be there." She hesitated for a moment. "If I don't make it, it means I'm dead or incapacitated."

"But you're not, now."

"Thank Brilliana and Olga," she said. "They were good choices."

"My Valkyries." He sounded amused.

"I'll see you in four days' time," Miriam said tersely. "If you need to know more, ask Olga, she knows what I'm doing." Then she hung up on him.

Two days later, Miriam looked up from her office ledger and a stack of official forms in response to a knock on the office window. "Carry on," she told Declan, who looked up inquiringly from his drafting board. "Who is it?" she demanded.

"Police, ma'am."

Miriam stood up to open the door. "You'd better come in." She paused. "Ah, Inspector Smith of the Homeland Defense Bureau. Come to tell me my burglars are a matter of national security?" She smiled brightly at him.

"Ah, well." Smith squeezed into the room and stood with his back to the cupboard beside the door where she kept the spare stationery. The constable behind him waited in the hall outside. "It was a most peculiar burglary, wasn't it?"

"Did you *catch* any of the thieves?" she asked sharply.

"You were in New London all along," he said, accusingly. "Staying in the *Grange Mouth Hotel*. Into which you checked in at *four o'clock* in the morning the day after the incident."

"Yes, well, as I told the thief-taker's sergeant, I dined in town then caught the last train, and my carriage threw a wheel on its way from the railway station. And I stayed with it because cabs are thin on the ground at two o'clock."

"Humph." Smith looked disappointed, to her delight. *Gotcha!* She thought. She'd set off from her office in Cambridge at midnight, floored the accelerator all the way down the near-empty interstate, and somehow managed not to pick up any speeding tickets. There were no red-eye flights in New Britain, nor highways you could drive along at a hundred five miles an hour with one hand on the wheel and the other clutching an insulated mug of coffee. In fact, the fastest form of land travel was the train—and as she'd be happy to point out to the inspector, the last train she could have caught from Boston to arrive in New London before 4 a.m. had left at eight o'clock the night before.

It had been a rush. She'd parked illegally in New York—her New York, not the New London the inspector knew—and changed into her rich widow's weeds in the cramped confines of the car. Then she'd crossed over and banged on a hotel door in the predawn light. She'd been able to establish an alibi by the skin of her teeth, but only by breaking the New Britain land speed record on a type of highway that didn't exist in King John the Fourth's empire . . .

"We haven't identified the Chinee-man who was asking after you," Smith agreed. "Nor the unknown assailant who fled—who we are investigating with an eye for murder," he added with relish.

Miriam sagged slightly. "Horrible, horrible," she said quietly. "Why me?"

"If you turn up in town flashing money around, you must expect to pick up unsavory customers," Smith said sarcastically. "Especially if you willingly mix with low-lifes and Levelers."

"Levelers?" Miriam glared at him. "Who do you have in mind?"

"I couldn't possibly say." Smith looked smug. "But we'll get them all in the end, you'll see. I'll be going now, but first I'd like to introduce you to Officer Fitch from the thief-taker's office. I believe he has some more questions to ask about your burglar."

Fitch's questions were tiresome, but not as tiresome as those of the city's press—two of whose representatives had already called. Miriam had pointedly referred them to her law firm, then refused to say anything until Declan and Roger had escorted them from the premises with dire threats about the law of trespass. "We will call you if we arrest anyone," Fitch said pompously, "or if we recover any stolen property." He closed his notebook with a snap. "Good day to you, Miss." And with that he clumped out of her office.

Miriam turned to Declan and rolled her eyes. "I can live without these interruptions. How's the self-tightening mechanism coming along?"

Declan looked a trifle startled, but pointed to a sketch on his drafting board. "I'm working on it . . ."

Miriam left the office in late afternoon, earlier than usual but still hours after she'd ceased being productive. She caught a cab home, feeling most peculiar about the whole business—indignant and angry, and sick to her stomach at what she'd done—but not guilty. The morning room was a freezing mess, the glaziers still busily working on the shattered window frames. The elderly one tugged his forelock at her as she politely looked over his shoulder and tut-tutted, trying to project the image of a house-proud lady bearing up under one of life's little indignities.

She found Jane in the kitchen. "Is the dining room going to be ready by this evening?" she asked.

"No, ma'am." Jane shrugged. "It is a mess. They broke two chairs and scratched the dining table!"

"Well, at least nobody was hurt. Piece of luck, sending you away, wasn't it?" Miriam shook her head. She'd forgotten about the dining room. The windows were boarded up, but the furniture—"I think I'm going to have to hire a butler, Jane."

"Oh *good*," Jane said, startling Miriam.

"Well, indeed." Miriam left the kitchen and was about to climb the staircase when a bell began to jangle from the hall. It was the household telephone. She stalked over and picked up the earpiece, then leaned close to the condenser and said, "Hello?"

"Fletcher residence?" The switchboard operator's voice was tinny but audible. "Call from 87492, do you want to accept?"

"Yes," said Miriam. *Who can it be?* She wondered.

"Hello?" asked a laid back, slightly jovial man's voice. "Is Mrs. Fletcher available?"

"Speaking."

"Oh I'm sorry, I wasn't expecting you so soon. Durant here. Are you well, I hope? I read about your little unpleasantness."

"I'm quite alright," Miriam managed through gritted teeth. Suddenly her heart was right up at the base of her throat, threatening to fly away. "The burglars damaged some furniture, then they appear to have fallen out among themselves. It is all most extraordinarily distressing, and a very good thing for me that I was visiting my sister up in New London at the weekend. But I'm bearing up."

"Oh, good for you. I trust the thief-takers are offering you all possible assistance? If you have any trouble at all I can put in a word with the magistrate-in-chief—"

"I don't think that'll be necessary, but I'm very grateful," Miriam said warmly. "But can we talk about something else, please?"

"Certainly, certainly. I was telephoning to say—ah, this is such a spontaneous, erratic medium!—that I've been reviewing your proposal carefully. And I'd like to proceed."

Miriam blinked, then carefully sat down on the stool next to the telephone. Her head was swimming.

"You want to go ahead?" she said.

"Yes, yes. That's what I said. My chaps have been looking at the brake assembly you sent them and they say it's quite remarkable. When the other three are available we'll fit them to a Mark IV carriage for testing, but they say they're in no doubt that it's a vast step forward. However did you come up with it, may I ask?"

"Feminine intuition," Miriam stonewalled. *Oh wow,* she thought. *So close to success . . .* "How do you want to proceed?"

"Well," said Durant, and paused.

"Royalty basis or outright purchase of rights? Exclusive or nonexclusive?"

He whistled quietly past the condenser. "I believe a royalty basis would do the job," he said. "I'll want exclusive rights for the first few years. But I'll tell you what else. I should like to invest in your business if you're open to the idea. What do you say to that?"

"I say—" she bit the tip of her tongue carefully, considering: "I think we ought to discuss this later. I will not say yes, definitely, but in principle I am receptive to the idea. How large an investment were you thinking of?"

"Oh, a hundred thousand pounds or so," Sir Durant said airily. Miriam did the conversion in her head, came up with a figure, double-checked it in disbelief. *That's thirty million dollars in real money!*

"I want to retain control of my company," she said.

"That can be arranged." He sounded amused. "May I invite you to dine with me at, let's say, the Brighton's Hanover Room, a week on Friday? We can exchange letters of interest in the meantime."

"That would be perfect," Miriam said with feeling.

They made small talk for a minute, then Durant politely excused himself. Miriam sat on the telephone stool for several minutes in stunned surprise, before she managed to get a grip on herself. "He really said it," she realized. "He's really going to buy it!" Back home, in another life, this was the kind of story she'd have covered for *The Weatherman*. Bright new three-month-old start-up gets multimillion-dollar cash injection, signs rights deal with major corporation. *I'm not covering the news anymore, I'm making it.* She stood up and slowly climbed the stairs to her bedroom. *Two more days to go,* she remembered. *I wonder how Olga and Brill are doing?*

The next morning Miriam telephoned her lawyer. "I'm going to be away for a week from tomorrow," she warned Bates. "In the meantime, I need someone to handle the payroll and necessary expenditures. Can you recommend a clerk who I can leave things with?"

"Certainly." Bates muttered something, then added, "I can have my man Williams sit in for you if you want. Will that do?"

"Yes, as long as he's reliable." They haggled over a price, then agreed that Williams would show up on that afternoon for her to hand him the reins.

Later in the morning, a post boy knocked on the door. "Parcel for Fletcher?" he piped to Jane, who accepted it and carried it to Miriam, then waited for her to open the thing.

"Curiosity," Miriam said pointedly, "is not what I pay you for." Jane left, and Miriam stared at her retreating back before she reached for a paper knife from her desk and slit the string. *If I've got to have servants around, I need ones who can keep their mouths shut,* she thought gloomily. *It wasn't like this with Brill and Kara.* The parcel opened up before her to reveal a leatherbound and clearly very old book. Miriam opened the flyleaf. *A True and Accurate History of the Settlement of New Britain,* it said, by some author whose name didn't ring any bells. A card was slipped into the pages. She pulled it out and saw the name on it, blinked back sudden tears of relief. "You're alright," she mumbled. "They couldn't pin anything on you." Suddenly it was immensely important to her to know that Burgeson was safe and out of the claws of the political police. A sense of warm relief filled her. For a moment, all was right with the world.

The doorbell rang yet again at lunchtime. "Oh, ma'am, it'll be a salesman," said Jane, hurrying from the kitchen to pass Miriam, who sat alone in the dining room, toying with a bowl of soup and reading the book Erasmus had sent, her thoughts miles away. "I'll send him—"

Footsteps. "Miriam?"

Miriam dropped her spoon in the soup and stood up. "Olga?"

It was indeed Olga, wearing the green outfit she'd bought from Burgeson by way of disguise. She smiled broadly as she entered the dining room and Miriam met her halfway in a hug. "Are you alright?" Olga asked.

"Yes. Have you eaten?"

"No." Olga rubbed her forehead.

"Jane, another place setting for my cousin! How good of you to call." As Jane hurried to the kitchen, Miriam added, "We can talk upstairs while she's washing up." Louder, "I was just preparing for my trip to New London tomorrow. Are you tied down here, or do you fancy the ride?"

"That's why I came," said Olga, sitting down and leaning back as the harried maid planted a place setting before her. "You didn't think I'd let you go there all on your own, did you, cuz?" Jane rushed out, and Olga winked at Miriam. "You're not getting out of it so easily! What did you *say* to put the Iron Duke in such a mood?"

"It's going to be such a party tomorrow night!" Miriam said enthusiastically, then waited for Jane to place a bowl before Olga and withdraw to the scullery. Quietly, "I told him his little shell game was up. Why didn't you tell me?"

"Tell you what?" Olga paused, blowing on a spoon full of hot broth.

"That Angbard had planted you on me. As a bodyguard."

"A what?" Olga shook her head. "This is intelligence of a rare and fantastic nature. Not me, Helge, not me." She grinned. "Who's been spinning you these tales?"

"Angbard," said Miriam. She shook her head. "Are you certain you don't work for him?"

"Certain?" Olga frowned. "About as certain as I am that the sun rises in the east. Unless—" She looked annoyed. "—you are telling me that he has been using me?"

"I couldn't possibly comment," Miriam said, then changed the subject as fast as possible. *Let's just say Angbard's definition of someone who works for him doesn't necessarily match up to the definition of an employee in federal employment law.* "I suppose you know about the extraordinary meeting?"

"I know he's called one." Olga looked at Miriam suspiciously. "That's most unusual. Is it your fault?"

"Yup. Did you bring the dictaphone?"

"The what? Oh, your recording angel? Yes, it is in my bag. Paulie gave it to me, along with these battery things that it eats. Such a sweet child he is," she added. "A shame we'll have to hang him."

"We—" Miriam caught herself. "Who, the Clan? Lin, or Lee, or whatever he's called? I don't think that's a good idea."

"He knows too much about us," Olga pointed out calmly. "Like the fact that we're operating here. Even if he's from the lost family, that's not enough to save his life. They've been trying to kill you, Miriam, they've picking away at us for decades. They *did* kill Margit, and I have not forgiven them for that."

"Lin isn't guilty of that. He's a kid who was drafted into his family's politics at too early an age, and did what they told him to. The one who killed Margit is dead, and if anyone else deserves to get it in the neck it's the old men who sent a boy to do a man's job. If you think the Clan should execute him, then by the same yardstick his family had a perfect right to try to murder you. True?"

"Hunh." Miriam watched a momentary expression of uncertainty cross Olga's face. "This merciful mood ill becomes you. Where does it come from?"

"I told you the other day, there's been too much killing," Miriam repeated. "Family A kills a member of Family B, so Family B kills a Family A member straight back. The last killing is a justification for the next, and so it goes on, round and about. It's got to stop somewhere, and I'd rather it didn't stop with the extinction of all the families. Hasn't it occurred to anyone that the utility of world-walking, if you want to gain wealth and power, is proportional to the square of the number of people who can do it? Network externalities—"

Olga looked at her blankly. "What are you talking about?" she asked.

Miriam sighed. "The mobile phones everyone carries in Cambridge. You've seen me using one, haven't you?"

"Oh yes!" Olga's eyes sparkled. "Anything that can get Angbard out of bed in the middle of the night—"

"Imagine I have a mobile phone with me right now, here on the table." She pointed to the salt shaker. "How useful is it?"

"Why, you could call—oh." She looked crestfallen. "It doesn't work?"

"You can only call someone else who has a phone," Miriam told her. "If you have the only phone in the world, it might as well be a salt shaker. If I have a phone and you have a phone we can talk to each other, but nobody else. Now, if *everyone* has a phone, all sorts of things are possible. You can't do business without one, you can't even live without one. Lock yourself out of your home? You call a locksmith round to let you in. Want to go to a restaurant? Call your friends and tell them where to meet you. And so on. The usefulness of a phone relates not to how many people have got them, but to how many lines you can draw between those people. And the Clan's one real talent is—" she shrugged— "forget cargo, we can't shift as much in a day as a single ox-drawn wagon. The *real* edge the Clan has got is its ability to transmit messages."

"Like phones."

Miriam could almost see the light bulb switch on over her head. "Yes. If we can just break out of this loop of killing, even if it costs us, if we can just start trading . . . think about it. No more messing around with the two of us running errands. No more worries about the amount we can carry. And nobody trying to kill us, which I'd call a not-insignificant benefit—wouldn't you?"

"Nice idea," said Olga. "It's surely a shame the other side will kill you rather than listen."

"Isn't that a rather defeatist attitude?"

"They've been trying to keep the civil war going," Olga pointed out. "Are you sure they did not intrigue it in the first place? A lie here and a cut throat there, and their fearsome rivals—we families—will kill each other happily. Isn't that how it started?"

"It probably did." Miriam agreed. "So? What's your point? The people who did that are long since dead. How long are you going to keep slaughtering their descendants?"

"But—" Olga stopped. "You really *do* want him alive," she said slowly.

"Not exactly. What I *don't* want is him dead, adding to the bad blood between the families. As a corpse he's no use to anyone. Alive, he could be a go-between, or an information source, or a hostage, or something."

Miriam finished with her soup. "Listen, I have to go to the office, but tomorrow evening I need to be in Niejwein. At the Castle Hjorth. Lin, whoever he is, was from out of town. Chances are we can get there from here without being noticed by anyone in this world, at least anyone but Inspector Smith. This afternoon I'm going to the office. I suggest that tomorrow morning we catch the train to New London. That's

New York in my world. When we get there—how well do you know Niejwein? Outside of the palaces and houses?"

"Not so well," Olga admitted. "But it's nothing like as large as these huge metropoli."

"Fine. We'll go to the railway terminal, cross over, and walk in bold as brass. There are two of us and we can look after each other. Right?"

Olga nodded. "We'll be back in my apartment by afternoon. It will be a small adventure." She put her spoon down. "The council will meet on the morrow, won't it? I'm not sure whether that's good or bad."

"It'll have to be good," Miriam assured her. "It can't be anything else."

EXTRAORDINARY MEETING

Two women sat alone in a first-class compartment as the morning train steamed through the wintry New England countryside. Puffs of smoke coughed past from the engine, stained dirty orange by the sun that hung low over icy woods and snow-capped farmland. The older woman kept her nose buried in the business pages of *The London Intelligencer,* immune to the rattle of track joints passing underneath the carriage. The younger woman in contrast started at every strange noise and stared out at the landscape with eyes eager to squeeze every detail from each passing town and village. Church steeples in particular seemed to fascinate her. "There are *so many* people!" Olga exclaimed quietly. "The countryside, it's so packed!"

"Like home." Miriam stifled a yawn as she read about the outrageous attempts of a consortium of robber barons from Carolingia to extract a royal monopoly on bituminous path-making, and the trial of a whaler's captain accused of barratry. "Like home, ninety years ago." She unbuttoned her jacket; the heating in the carriage was efficient but difficult to control.

"But this place is so rich!"

Miriam folded her paper. "Gruinmarkt will be this rich too, and within our lifetimes, if I have my way."

"But how does it *happen*? How do you make wealth? Nobody here knows how the other world got so rich. Where does it come from?"

Miriam muttered to herself, "teach a mercantilist dog new tricks . . ." She put the paper aside and sat up to face Olga. "Look. It's a truism that in any land there is so much gold, and so much iron, and so much timber, and so many farmers, isn't it? So that if you trade with a country, anything you take away isn't there anymore. Your gain is their loss. Right?"

"Yes." Olga nodded thoughtfully.

"Well, that's just plain wrong," said Miriam. "That idea used to be called mercantilism. Discarding it was one of the key steps that distinguishes my world from yours. The essential insight is that human beings *create* value. A lump of iron ore isn't as valuable as a handful of nails, because it takes human labor to turn it into nails and nails are more useful. Now, if you have iron ore but no labor, and I have labor but no iron ore, *both* of us can profit by trade, can't we? I can take your iron ore, make nails, give you some of them in payment, and we're both better off, because before we had no nails at all. Isn't that right?"

"I think I see." Olga wrinkled her brow. "You're telling me that we don't trade? That the Clan has the wrong idea about how to make money—"

"Yes, but that's only part of it. The Clan doesn't add value, it simply moves it around. But another important factor is that a peasant farmer is less good at creating value than, say, a farmer who knows about crop rotation and soil maintenance and how to fertilize his fields effectively. And a man who can sit down all day and make nails is less productive than an engineer who can make a machine that takes in wire feedstock at one end and spits out nails at the other. It's more productive to make a machine to make nails, and then run it, than to make the nails yourself. Educated people can think of ways to make such machines or provide valuable services—but to get to the wealth, you've got to have an educated population. Do you see that?"

"What you're doing, you're taking ideas where they're needed, and teaching people with iron ore to make nails and, and do other things, aren't you?"

"Yes. And while I can't easily take the fruits of that trade home with me, I can make myself rich over here. Which in turn should serve to give me some leverage with the Clan, shouldn't it? And there's another thing." She looked pensive. "If the goal is to modernize the Gruinmarkt, the land where the Clan holds so much power, it's going to be necessary to import technologies and ideas from a world that isn't as far ahead as the United States. There's less of a gap to jump between New Britain and the eastern kingdoms. What I want to do is to develop riches in this realm, and use them to finance seed investments in the kingdoms. If the Clan won't let me live away from them, at least I can try to make my life more comfortable. No more drafty medieval castles!"

"Castles." Olga looked wistful for a moment. "You'd build a house like your own near Niejwein? Bandits, the southern kingdoms—"

"No bandits," said Miriam, firmly. "First, we need to improve the efficiency of farming. What I saw looked—no offense—like the way things were done five or six hundred years ago in Europe. Strip cultivation, communal grazing, no reaping or sowing machines. By making farming more efficient, we can free up hands for industry. By providing jobs, we can begin to produce more goods—fabric, fuel, housing, ships—and see to the policing of the roads and waterways along which trade flows. By making trade safer we make it cheaper, and increase the profits, and by increasing the profits we can free up money to invest in education and production."

Olga shook her head. "I'm dizzy! I'm dizzy!"

"That's how it happened in England around the industrial

revolution," Miriam emphasized. "That's how it happened here, from 1890 onwards, a century later than in my world. The interesting thing is that it *didn't* happen in the Gruinmarkt, or in Europe, over there. I've got this nagging feeling that knowing why it failed is important . . . still. Given half a chance we'll make it happen." She leaned toward Olga. "Roland tried to run away and they dragged him back." She took a deep breath. "If they're going to try to drag me away from civilization, I'm going to try to bring civilization with me, middle class morality and all. And then they'll be sorry."

The train began to slow its headlong charge between rows of red-brick houses.

"If you go down this path, you'll make enemies," Olga predicted. "Some of them close to home, but others . . . Do you really think the outer families will accept an erosion of their relative status? Or the king? Or the court? Or the council of lords? *Someone* will think they can only lose by it, and they'll fight you for it."

"They'll accept it if it makes them rich," Miriam said. She glanced at the window, sniffed, and buttoned her jacket up. "Damn, it's cold out there." A thought struck her. "Will we be alright on the other side?"

"We're always at risk," Olga remarked. She paused for a moment. "But, on second thoughts, I think we are at no more risk than usual." She nudged the bag at her feet. "As long as we don't linger."

The train sneaked along a suburban platform and stopped with a hissing of steam; doors slammed and people shouted, distant whistles shrilling counterpoint. "Next stop?" Miriam suggested tensely. She pulled out a strip of tablets, took one, and offered another to Olga.

"Thanking you—yes."

The train pulled away into a deep cutting, its whistle hooting. Buildings on either side cast deep shadows across the windows, then Miriam found herself watching the darkness of a tunnel. "I'm worried about the congress," Miriam admitted.

"Hah. Leave that to the duke. Do you think he would have called for it if he didn't trust you?"

"If anything goes wrong, if we don't get there, if Brill was lying about my mother being safe—"

The train began to slow again. "Our stop!" Olga stood up and reached for her coat.

They waited at one end of the platform while the huge black and green behemoth rumbled away from the station. A handful of tired travelers swirled around them, making for the footbridge that led over the tracks to the main concourse. Miriam nodded at a door. "Into the waiting room." Olga followed her. The room was empty and cold. "Are you ready?" Miriam asked. "I'll go across first. If I run into trouble, I'll come right back. If I'm not back inside five minutes, you come over too."

Olga discreetly checked her gun. "I've got a better idea. You're too important to risk first." She pulled out her locket and picked up her bag: "See you shortly!"

"Wait—" It was too late. Miriam squinted at the fading outline. *Funny,* she thought, irritated, *I've never seen someone else do that.* "Damn," she said quietly, pulling out her own compact and opening it up so that she could join Olga. "You'd better not have run into anything you can't handle—"

Ouch. Miriam took a step back and a branch whacked her on the back of the head.

"Are you alright?" Olga asked anxiously.

"Ouch. And again, ouch. How about you?"

"I'm fine, except for my head." Olga looked none the worse for wear. "Where are we?"

"I should say we're still some way outside the city limits." Miriam put her bag down and concentrated on breathing, trying to get the throbbing in her head under control. "Are you ready for a nice bracing morning constitutional?"

"Ugh. Mornings should be abolished!"

"You will hear no arguments from this quarter." Miriam bent down, opened her bag, and removed a cloak from it to cover her alien clothes. "That looks like clear ground over there. How about we try to pick up a road?"

"Lead on," sighed Olga.

* * *

They'd come out in deciduous woodland, snow lying thick on the ground between the stark, skeletal trees; it took them the best part of an hour to find their way to a road, and even that was mostly dumb luck. But, once they'd found it, Niejwein was already in sight. And what a sight it was.

Miriam hadn't appreciated before just how crude, small, and just plain smelly the city was. It stood on a low bluff overlooking what might, in a few hundred years, mutate into the Port Authority. Stone walls twenty feet high followed the contours of the ground for miles, bascules sprouting ominously every hundred yards. Long before they reached the walls, she found herself walking beside Olga in a cloud of smelly dust, passing rows of windowless tumbledown shacks. Scores of poor-looking countryfolk— many in clothes little better than layered rags—drove heavily laden donkeys or small herds of sheep toward the city gates. Miriam noticed that they were picking up a few odd looks, especially from the ragged mothers of the barefoot urchins who cast stones across the icy cobbles, but she avoided eye contact and nobody seemed interested in approaching two women who knew where they were going. Especially after Olga pointedly allowed the barrel of her gun to slip from under her cloak, in response to an importuning rascal who attempted to get too close. "Hmm, I see why you always travel by—" Miriam stopped and squinted at the gatehouse. "Tell me that's not what I think it is, on the wall," she said.

"Not what—oh, that." Olga looked at her oddly. "What else would you have them do with bandits?"

"Um." Miriam swallowed. "Not that." The city gates were wide open and nobody seemed to be guarding them. "Is there meant to be anyone on watch?"

"Invasion comes from the sea, most often."

"Um." *I've got to stop saying that,* Miriam told herself. Her feet were beginning to hurt with all the walking, she was picking up dust and dirt, and she was profoundly regretting not making use of the dining carriage for breakfast. Or crossing all the way over, phoning for Paulie to pick them up, and driving all the way in the back of an air-conditioned car. "Which way to the castle?"

"Oh, that's a way yet." Olga beamed as a wagon laden with bales of hay clattered past. "Isn't it grand? The largest city in the Gruinmarkt!"

"Yes, I suppose it is," Miriam said hollowly. She'd seen something like this before, she realized. Some of the museum reconstructions of medieval life back home were quite accurate, but nothing quite captured the reek—no, the overwhelming stench—of open sewers, of people who bathed twice a year and wore a single set of clothes all the time, of houses where the owners bedded down with their livestock to share warmth. *Did I really say I was going to modernize this?* she asked herself, aghast at her own hubris. *Why yes, I think I did. Talk about jumping in with both feet . . .*

Olga steered her into a wide boulevard without warning. "Look," she said. Huge stone buildings fronted the road at intervals, all the way up to an imposing hill at the far end, upon which squatted a massive stone carbuncle, turretted and brooding. "You see? There is civilization in Niejwein after all!"

"That's the palace, isn't it?"

"It is indeed. And we'll be much better off once we are inside its walls." A hundred yards more and Olga waved Miriam into what at first she mistook for an alleyway— before she worked out that it was the drive leading to the Hjorth Palace.

"I didn't realize this—" Miriam stopped, coming to a halt behind Olga. Two men at arms were walking toward them, hands close to their sword hilts.

"Chein bethen! Gehen'sh veg!"

"Ver she mishtanken shind?" said Olga, drawing herself up and glaring at them icily.

"Ish interesher'ish nish, when sheshint the Herzogin von Praha—" said one, sneering contemptuously.

"Stop right there," Miriam said evenly, pulling her right hand inside her cloak. "Is Duke Lofstrom in residence?"

The sneering one stopped and gaped at her. "You . . . say, the duke?" he said slowly in broken English. "I'll *teach* you—"

His colleague laid a hand on his arm and muttered something urgent in his ear.

"Fetch the duke, or one of his aides," Miriam snapped. "I will wait here."

Olga glanced at her sidelong, then turned her cloak back to reveal her gun and her costume. What she wore would be considered respectable in New London: Over here it was as exotic as the American outfits the Clan members wore in private.

"I take you inside," said the more prudent guard, trying to look inoffensive. "Gregor, *gefen she jemand shnaill'len, als if foor leifensdauer abhngt fon ihm,*" he told his companion.

Olga grinned humorlessly. "It does," she said.

A carriage rattled up the drive behind them; meanwhile, booted feet hurried across the hall. A man, vaguely familiar from Angbard's retinue, glanced curiously at Miriam. "Oh great Sky Father, it's *her,*" he muttered in a despairing tone. "Please, come in, come in! You came to see the duke?"

"Yes, but I think we should freshen up first," said Miriam. "Please send him my compliments, tell these two idiots to let us in, and we will be with him in half an hour."

"Certainly, certainly—"

Olga took Miriam's hand and led her up the steps while the duke's man was still warming up on the hapless guards. A couple more guards, these ones far more alert-looking, fell in behind them. "Your apartment," said Olga. "I took the liberty of moving some of my stuff in. I hope you don't mind?"

"Not at all." Miriam shrugged, then winced. "I'll need more than half an hour to freshen up."

"Well, you'll have to do it fast." Olga rapped on the huge double doors by the top of the main stairs. "The duke detests being kept waiting."

"Indeed—Kara!—oof!"

"My lady!"

Miriam pushed her back to arm's length. "You've been alright?" she asked anxiously. "No murderers lurking in your bedroom?"

"None, milady!" Kara flushed and let go of her. "Milady! What *is* that you're wearing? It's so frumpy! And you, lady Olga? Is this some horrid new fashion from Paris that we'll all be wearing in a month? Has somebody been biting your neck, that you've got to hide it?"

"I hope not," Miriam said dryly. "Listen." She towed Kara into the empty outer audience chamber. "We're going to see Angbard in half an hour. *Half* an hour. Get something for me to wear. And warn Olga's maids. We've been on the road half a day."

"I shall!" She bounced away toward the bedchamber.

Miriam rubbed her forehead. "Youth and enthusiasm." She made a wry curse of it.

Her bedroom was as she'd left it four months ago—Olga had taken the Queen's Room, for there were four royal rooms in this apartment—and for once Miriam didn't drive Kara out. "Help me undress," she ordered. "Aah, that's better. Um. Fetch the pot. Then would you mind getting me a basin of hot water? I need to scrub my face."

Kara, for a wonder, left Miriam alone to wash herself—then doubled the miracle by laying out one of Miriam's trouser suits and retiring to the outer chamber. "She's learning," Miriam noted. "Hmm." It felt strange to be dressing for an ordinary day in the office world, doubly strange to be doing so with medieval squalor held at bay outside by guards with swords. "What the hell." She looked at herself in the mirror. Her hair was past shoulder length, there were worry lines around her eyes that hadn't been there six months ago, and her jacket was loose at the waist. "Not bad." Then she spotted a couple of white hairs. "Damn. Bad." She combed it back hard, held it in place with a couple of pins, and turned her back on the mirror. "Hostile takeover time, kid. Go kill 'em."

There were no simple chambers for the duke. He'd taken over the royal apartment in the west wing, occupying half of the top floor, and his guards had staked out the entire floor below as a security measure. Nor was it possible for Miriam to pay a quiet visit on him. Not without first picking up a retinue of a palace majordomo, a bunch of guards led by a nervous young officer, and an overexcited teenager. Kara fussed around behind Miriam as she climbed the stairs. "Isn't it exciting?" she squealed.

"Hush." Miriam cast her eye over the guards with a jaundiced eye. Their camouflage jackets and submachine guns sounded a jarring note. Strip them from the scene and this might merely be some English stately home, taken over for the duration of a rich multinational's general meeting. "Am I always supposed to travel with this much protection?"

"I wouldn't know," Kara said artlessly.

"Make a point of finding out, then," Miriam said sharply as she climbed the last few steps toward the separate guard detachment outside Angbard's residence.

Two soldiers came to attention on either side of the door to the royal apartment. Their sergeant strode forward. "Introduce me," Miriam hissed at the majordomo.

"Ahem! May I present my lady, her excellency the countess Helge Thorold-Hjorth, niece of the duke Angbard of that family, who comes to pay her attendance on the duke?" The man ended on a strangled squeak.

The sergeant checked his clipboard. "Everything is as expected." He saluted, and Miriam nodded acknowledgment at him. "Ma'am. If you'd like to come this way." His eyes lingered on Kara. "Your lady-in-waiting may attend. The guards—"

"Very well," said Miriam. She glanced over her shoulder: "Wait here, I'm not expecting my uncle to try to kill me," she told her retinue. *Yet,* she added silently. The doors swung open and she stepped through into a nearly empty audience chamber. The doors slammed shut behind her with a solid thud of latches, and she would have paused to look around but for the sergeant, who was already halfway across the huge expanse of hand-woven carpet.

He paused at the inner door and knocked twice: "Visitor

six-two," he muttered to a peephole, then stood aside. The inner door opened just wide enough to admit Miriam and Kara. "If you please, ma'am."

"Hmm." Miriam entered the room, then stopped dead. "Mother!"

"Miriam!" Iris smiled at her from her wheelchair, which stood beside the pair of thrones mounted at one end of the audience room. A pair of crutches leaned against one of them.

Miriam crossed the room quickly and leaned down to hug her mother. "I've missed you," she said quietly, mind whirling with shock. "I was so worried—"

"There, there." Iris kissed her lightly on the cheek. "I'm alright, as you can see." Miriam straightened up. "You look as if you're keeping well!" Then she noticed Kara's head in the doorway, jaw agape. "Oh dear, another one come to stare at me," she sighed. "I suppose it can't be helped. It'll all be over by this time tomorrow, anyway, isn't that the case, Angbard?"

"I would not make any assumptions," said the duke, turning away from the window. His expression was distant. "Helge, Miriam."

"So, *it is* true," said Miriam. She glanced at Iris. "He brought you here?" She rounded on Angbard: "You should be ashamed of yourself!"

"Nonsense." He looked offended.

"Don't blame him, Miriam." Iris looked at her strangely. "Drag up a seat, dear. It's a long story."

Miriam sat down beside her. "Why?" she asked, her thoughts whirling so that she couldn't make her mind up what word to put next. "What is she doing here then, if you didn't kidnap her?" she asked, looking at Angbard. "I thought it was against all your policies to take people from—"

"Policies?" Angbard asked, raising his nose. He shrugged dismissively then looked at Iris. "Tell her."

"Nobody kidnapped me," said Iris. "But after a party or parties unknown tried to kill me, I phoned Angbard and asked for help."

"Uh." Miriam blinked. "You *phoned* him?"

"Yes." Iris nodded encouragingly. "Isn't that how you normally get in touch with someone?"

"Well yes, but, but . . ." Miriam paused. "You had his number," she said accusingly. "How?"

Iris glanced at the duke, as if asking for moral support. He raised his eyebrows slightly, and half-turned away from Miriam.

"Um." Iris froze up, looking embarrassed.

Miriam stared at her mother. "Oh no. Tell me it isn't true."

Iris coughed. "I expected you to look at the papers, use the locket or not, then do the sensible thing and ask me to tell you all about it. I figured you'd be fairly safe, your house being in the middle of open woodland on this side, and it would make explaining everything a lot easier once you'd had a chance to see for yourself. Otherwise—" She shrugged. "If I'd broken it to you cold you'd have thought I was crazy. I didn't expect you to go running off and getting yourself shot at!" For a moment she looked angry. "I was so worried!"

"Ma." She had difficulty swallowing. "You're telling me you knew about. The Clan. All along."

A patient sigh from the window bay. "She appears to be having some difficulty. If you would allow me—"

"No!" Iris snapped, then stopped.

"If you can't, I will," the duke said firmly. He turned back to face Miriam. "Your mother has had my number all along," he explained, scrutinizing her face. "The Clan has maintained emergency telephone numbers—a nine-eleven service, if you like—for the past fifty years. She only saw fit to call me when you went missing."

"Ma—" Miriam stopped. Glanced at Angbard again. "My *mother*," she said thoughtfully. "Not, um, foster-mother, is it?"

Angbard shook his head slightly, studying her beneath half-hooded eyes.

Miriam glared at Iris. "Why all the lies, then?" she demanded.

Iris looked defensive. "It seemed like a good idea at the

time, is all I can say." She shuffled deeper into her chair. "Miriam?"

"Yeah?"

"I know I brought you up not to tell lies. All I can say is, I wish I could have lived up to that myself. I'm sorry."

Angbard took a step forward, then moved to stand behind Iris's wheelchair.

"Don't go too hard on her," he said warningly. "You have no idea what she's—" He stopped, and shook his head. "No idea," he echoed grimly.

"So explain," said Miriam. Her gaze slid past Iris to focus on Kara, who was doing her best imitation of a sheet of wallpaper—wallpaper with a fascinated expression. "Whoa. Kara, please wait outside. Now."

Kara skidded across the floor as if her feet were on fire: "I'm going, I'm going!" she squeaked.

Miriam stared at Iris. "So why did you do it?"

Iris sighed. "They'd shot Alfredo, you know."

She fell silent for a moment.

"Alfredo?"

"Your father."

"Shot him, you said."

"Yes. And Joan, my maid, they killed her too. I got across but they'd done a good job on me, too—I nearly bled to death before the ambulance got me to a hospital. And then, and then . . ." She trailed off. "I was in Cambridge, unidentified, in a hospital, with no chaperone and no guards. Can you understand the temptation?"

Miriam looked sideways: Angbard was watching Iris like a hawk, something like admiration in his eyes. Or maybe it was the bitterness of the dutiful brother who stuck to his post? It was hard to tell.

"How did you meet Morris?" she asked her mother, after a momentary pause.

"He was a hospital visitor." Iris smiled at the recollection. "Actually he was writing for an underground newspaper at the time and came to see if I'd been beaten up by the pigs. Later he sorted out our birth certificates—mine and yours, that is, including my fake backstory leading out of the country, and the false adoption papers—when we moved around. Me being a naturalized foreigner was useful cover. There was a whole underground railroad going on in those days, left over from when the SDS and the Weather Underground turned bad, and it served our purpose to use it. Especially as the FBI wasn't actually looking for us."

"So I—I—" Miriam stopped. "I'm not adopted."

"Does it make any difference to you?" Iris asked, sounding slightly puzzled. "You always said it didn't. That's what you told me."

"I'm confused," Miriam admitted. Her head was spinning. "You were rich and powerful. You gave it all up—brought your daughter up to think she was adopted, went underground, lived like a political radical—just to get away from the in-laws?"

Angbard spoke. "It's her mother's fault," he said grimly. "You met the dowager duchess, I believe. She has always taken a, ah, utilitarian view of her offspring. She played Patty like a card in a game of poker, for the highest stakes. The treaty process, re-establishing the braid between the warring factions. I think she did so partially out of spite, to get your mother out of the way, but she is not a simple woman. Nothing she does serves only a single purpose." His expression was stony. "But she is untouchable. Unlike whoever tried to ruin her hand by murdering my cousin and her husband."

Iris shifted around, trying to make herself more comfortable. "Don't trouble yourself on my account. If you ever find Alfredo's body, you'd best not tell me where it's buried—I'd have a terrible time getting back into my wheelchair after I pissed on it."

"Patricia," his smile was razor-thin, "I usually find that death settles all scores to my complete satisfaction. Just as long as they stay dead."

"Well, I don't agree. And you weren't married to Alfredo."

"Mother!" Miriam stared at both of them in shock: Just as she was certain Angbard was serious, she was more than half afraid that her mother was, too.

"Don't you 'mother' me!" Iris chided her. "I was mooning at the national guard before you were out of diapers. I'm just not very mobile these days." She frowned and turned to Angbard. "We were speaking of *mother,*" she bit out.

"I can't keep her out forever," said Angbard, his frightening smile vanishing as rapidly as it had appeared. "You two clearly need more time together, but I have an audience with his majesty in an hour. Miriam, can you fill me in quickly?"

Miriam took a deep breath. "First, I need to know where Roland is."

"Roland—" Angbard looked at his watch, his face intent. Then back at Miriam. "He's been looking after Patty for the past month," he said, his tone neutral. "Right now he's in Boston, minding the shop. You don't need to worry about his reliability."

For a moment Miriam felt so dizzy that she had to shut her eyes. She opened them again when she heard her mother's voice. "Such a suitable young man." She glared at Iris, who smiled lazily at her. "Don't let them get together, Angbard, or they'll be over the horizon before you have time to blink."

"It's not. That." Miriam was having difficulty breathing. "There's a hole in your security," she said as calmly as she could. "It's at a very high level. I told Roland to do something about a corpse in an inconvenient place and instead a bunch of high explosives showed up. It turns out that Matthias has been blackmailing him." She felt dizzy with the significance of the moment.

"Roland? Are you sure?" Angbard leaned forward. His face was expressionless.

"Yes. He told me everything." She felt as if she were floating. "Listen, it was on the specific understanding that I would intercede with you to clean it up. Your secretary has been running his own little game and seems to have decided that getting a handle on Roland would help him cover his traces."

"That was a mistake," Angbard said, his voice deceptively casual. His expression was immobile, except for his scarred left cheek, which twitched slightly. "How did you find out?"

"It happened in the warehouse my chamber is doppelgängered onto here. Most of this pile is colocated with a bonded warehouse, but one wing sticks out into a real hole-in-the-wall shipping operation." She swallowed, then forced herself to speak. "There was a night watchman. Emphasis on the *was*." She explained what had happened when she'd first carried Brill through to New York.

"Roland, you say," said Angbard. "He's been blackmailed?"

"I want your word," Miriam insisted. "No consequences."

A sharp intake of breath. "Well—" Angbard started to pace. "Did he betray any secrets?"

Miriam stood up. "Not as far as I know," she said.

"And did anyone die as a result of his actions?"

Miriam paused for a moment before answering: "again, not as far as I know. Certainly not directly. And certainly not as a result of anything he knew he was doing."

"Well, well. Maybe I will not have to kill him." Angbard stopped again, behind Iris's chair. "What do you think I should do?" he asked, visibly tense.

"I think." Miriam chewed her lower lip. "Matthias has tapes. I think you should hand the tapes over to me, unwatched. I'll burn them. In front of you both, if you want." She paused. "You'll want to remove all his responsibilities for security operations, I guess."

"This blackmail material," Iris prodded. "These tapes—is it something personal? Or has he been abusing his position in any way?"

"It's absolutely personal. I can swear to it. Matthias just got the drop on Roland's private life. Nothing illegal; just, uh, sensitive."

Iris—Patricia, the long-lost countess—stared at her knowingly for a moment, then turned to look at her half-brother. "Do as she says," she said firmly.

Angbard nodded, then cast her a sharp look. "We'll see," he said.

"No, we won't!" Iris snapped. She continued quietly but with emphasis: "If your secretary has been building up private dossiers on nobles, you're in big trouble. You need all the friends you can get, bro. Starting by pardoning anyone

who isn't an active enemy will clear the field. And make
damn sure you burn those tapes *without* watching them, because for all you know some of them are fabrications that
Matthias concocted just in case you ever stumbled across
them. It's untrustworthy evidence, all of it." She turned to
Miriam. "What else have you dug up?" she demanded.

"Well." Miriam leaned against a priceless lacquered
wooden cabinet and managed to muster up a tired smile to
conceal her gut-deep sense of relief. "I'm pretty sure
Matthias is in league with whoever was running the prisoner."

"The prisoner," Angbard echoed distantly. By his expression, he was already wrapped up in calculating the requirements of the coming purge.

"What prisoner?" asked Iris.

"Something your daughter's friends dragged in a couple
of days ago," Angbard dropped offhandedly. To Miriam he
added, "He's downstairs."

"Have you worked out who he is, yet?" Miriam interrupted.

"What, that he's a long-lost cousin? And so are the rest of
his family, stranded with a corrupt icon that takes them to
this new world you have opened up for our trade? Of course.
Your suggestion that we do DNA fingerprinting made it
abundantly clear."

"Cousins? New world?" Iris echoed. "Would one of you
please back up a bit and explain, before I have to beat it out
of you with my crutches?"

Angbard stood up. "No, I don't think so." He grinned
mirthlessly. "You kept Miriam in the dark for nearly a third
of a century, I think it's only fair that we keep you in suspense for a third of a day."

"So nobody else knows?" Miriam asked Angbard.

"That's correct." He nodded. "And I'm going to keep it
that way, for now."

"I want to talk to the prisoner," Miriam said hastily.

"You do?" Angbard turned the full force of his icy stare
on her. "Whatever for?"

"Because—" Miriam struggled for words—"I don't have
old grudges. I mean, his relatives tried to *kill* me, but . . . I

have an idea I want to test. I need to see if he'll talk to me. May I?"

"Hmm." Angbard looked thoughtful. "You'll have to be quick, if you want to collect your pound of flesh before we execute him."

Miriam swallowed bile. "That's not what I have in mind."

"Oh, really?" He raised an eyebrow.

"Give me a chance?" she asked. "Please?"

"If you insist." Angbard waved lazily. "But don't lose the plot." He stared at her, and for a moment Miriam felt her bones turn to water. "Remember not all your relatives are as liberal-minded as I am, or believe that death heals all wounds."

"I won't," Miriam said automatically. Then she looked at Iris again, a long, appraising inspection. Her mother met her gaze head-on, without blinking. "It's alright," she said distantly. "I'm not going to stop being your daughter. Just as long as you don't stop being my ma. Deal?"

"Deal." Iris dropped her gaze. "I don't deserve you, kid."

"Yes, you do." Angbard looked Miriam up and down. "Like mother, like daughter, don't you know what kind of combination that makes?" He chuckled humorlessly. "Now, if you will excuse me, Helge, you have made much work for this old man to attend to . . ."

I should have realized all castles had dungeons, Miriam thought apprehensively. If not for keeping prisoners, then for supplies, ammunition, food, wine cellars—ice. It was freezing cold below ground, and even the crude coal-gas pipes nailed to the brickwork and the lamps hissing and fizzing at irregular intervals couldn't warm it up much. Miriam followed the guard down a surprisingly wide staircase into a cellar, then up to a barred iron door behind which a guard waited patiently. Finally he led her into a well-lit room containing nothing but a table and two chairs.

"What is this?" she asked.

"I'll bring the prisoner to you, ma'am," the sergeant said

patiently. "With another guard. The gate at the front won't be unlocked again until he's back in his cell."

"Oh." Miriam sat down, feeling stupid, and waited nervously as the guard disappeared into the basement tunnels beneath the castle. *The dungeon. I put him here,* she thought apprehensively. *What must it be like?*

A clattering outside brought her back to herself, and she turned around to watch the door as it opened. The sergeant came in, followed by another soldier, and a hunched, thin figure with his arms behind his back and a hood over his head. *He's manacled,* Miriam realized.

"One moment." The guards positioned the prisoner against the wall opposite Miriam's table. The guard knelt, and Miriam heard something click into place—padlocks. "That's it," said the sergeant. He pulled off the prisoner's hood, then he and the other guard withdrew to stand beside the door.

"Hello, Lin," Miriam said as evenly as she could. "Recognize me?"

He flinched, clearly terrified, and was brought up short by his chains. *Shit,* Miriam thought, a sense of horror stealing over her. She peered at him in the dim light. "They've been beating you," she said quietly. *The things on the gatehouse walls*—no, she didn't want to be involved in this. It was all a horrible mistake. *Multiple contusions, some bleeding and inflamation around the left eye.* He stared past her left shoulder, shivering fearfully, but didn't say anything. Miriam resisted the urge to turn around and yell at the guards: She had a hopeless feeling that all it would do was earn the kid another beating when she was safely out of the way.

Her medical training wouldn't let her look away. Up until this moment she'd have sworn she was angry with him: But she hadn't expected them to treat him like this. Breaking into her house on the orders of someone placed in authority over him—sure she was angry. But the real guilty parties were a long way away, and if she didn't do something fast, this half-starved kid was going to join the grisly carcasses displayed on the gatehouse wall, for the crime of following orders. And where was the justice in that?

"I'm not going to hit you," she said.

He didn't reply: His posture said he didn't believe her.

"Fuck!" She pulled one of the chairs out from the table, turned it around, and sat down on it, her arms folded across the back. "I just want some answers. That's all. Lin of, what did you call yourself?"

"Lin. Lin Lee. My family is called Lee." He kept glancing past her, as if trying to conceal his fear: *I'm not going to hit you, but my guards—*

"That's good. How old are you?"

"Fifteen." *Fifteen! Holy shit, they're running the children's crusade!* A thought struck her. "Have they been feeding you? Giving you water? Somewhere to sleep?"

He managed a brief, painful croak: Maybe it was meant to be laughter.

Miriam looked around. "Well? Have you been feeding him?"

The sergeant shook himself. "Ma'am?"

"What food, drink, and medical attention has this child had?"

He shook his head. "I really couldn't say, ma'am."

"I see." Miriam's hands tensed on the back of the chair. She turned back to Lin. "I didn't order this," she said. "Will you tell me who sent you to my house?"

She saw him swallow. "If I do that you'll kill me," he said.

"No, that's not what I've got in mind."

"Yes you will." He looked at her with bitter certainty in his eyes. "They'll do it."

"Like you were going to kill me?" she asked quietly.

He didn't say anything.

"You were supposed to find out if I was from the Clan," she said. "Weren't you? A strange new woman showing up in town and making waves. Is that it? And if I was from the Clan, you were supposed to kill me. What was it to be? A bomb in my bedroom? Or a knife in the dark?"

"Not me," he whispered. "One of the warriors."

"So why were you there? To spy on me? Are they that short-handed?"

He looked down at the table, but not before she saw shame in his eyes.

"Ah." She glanced away for a moment, trying desperately to think of a way out of the impasse. She was hopelessly aware of the guards standing behind her, waiting patiently for her to finish with the prisoner. *If I leave him here, the Clan will kill him,* she realized, with a kind of hollow dread she hadn't expected to be able to summon up for a housebreaker. Housebreaker? What his actions said about his family, *that* was something she could get angry about. "Hell." She made up her mind.

"Lin, you're probably right about the Clan. Most of them would see you dead as soon as look at you. There've been too many years of their parents and grandparents cutting each other's throats. They're suspicious of anything they don't understand, and you're going to be high on any list of mysteries. But I'll tell you something else."

She stood up. "You know how to world-walk, don't you?"

Silence.

"I said." She stopped. "You ought to know when you can stop holding it in," she said tiredly. Thinking back to Angbard, and how she'd managed to face him down over Roland: *Don't look too deep. Everything on the surface.* The familes all worked that way, didn't they? "Nothing you say to me can make your position worse. It might make it better, though."

Silence.

"World-walking," she said. "We *know* you can do it, we got the locket you carried. So why lie?"

Silence.

"The Clan can world-walk too, you know," she said quietly. "It isn't a coincidence. Your family are relatives, aren't they? Lost for a long time, and this shit—the killing, the feuding, the attempts to reopen old wounds—isn't in anyone's interests."

Silence.

"Why do they want me dead?" she asked. "Why are you people killing your own blood relatives?"

Maybe it was something in her expression—frank curiosity, perhaps—but the youth looked away at last. The silence stretched out for a long moment, lengthened toward a minute, punctuated only by the sound of one of the guards shifting position.

"You betrayed us," he whispered.

"Uh?" Miriam shook her head. "I don't understand."

"In the time of the loyal sons," said Lin. "All the others. They abandoned my ancestor. The promise of a meeting in the world of the Americans. Reduced to poverty, he took years to gain his freedom, then he spent his entire life searching for them. But never did they come."

"This is all news to me," Miriam said quietly. "He was reduced to poverty?"

Lin nodded convulsively. "This is the tale of our family," he said, in sing-song tones. "That of the brothers, it was agreed that Lee would go west, to set up a trading post. And he did, but the way was hard and he was reduced to penury, his caravan scattered, his goods stolen by savages, abandoned by his servants. For seven years he labored as a bond servant, before buying his freedom: He lost everything, from his wife to the first talisman of the family. Finally he forged a new talisman, working from memory, earned his price, and bought himself liberty. He was a very determined man. But when he walked to the place assigned for meeting, nobody was there to wait for him. Every year, at the appointed day and hour, he would go there; and never did anyone come. His brothers had abandoned him, and over the years his descendants learned much of the eastern Clan. The betrayers, who profited from his estate."

"Ah," said Miriam, faintly. *Oops, a betrayal-for-a-legacy myth. So he accidentally mangled the knotwork and ended up going to New Britain instead of*—she blinked.

"You've seen my world," she said. "Do you know, that's where the Clan have been going all along? Where you go when you world-walk, it's all set up by the, uh, talisman. Your illustrious ancestor re-created it wrong. Sending himself over to, to, New Britain. For all you know, the other brothers thought that your ancestor had abandoned *them*."

Lin shrugged. "When are you going to kill me?" he asked.

"In about ten seconds if you don't shut up about it!" She glared at him. "Don't you see? Your family's reasons for feuding with the Clan are bogus. They've been bogus all along!"

"So?" He made a movement that might have been a shrug if he hadn't been wearing fetters. "Our elders, now dead, laid these duties upon our shoulders. We must obey, or dishonor their memory. Only our eldest can change our course. Do you expect me to betray my family and plead for mercy?"

"No." Miriam stood up. "But you may not need to beg, Lin. There is a Clan meeting coming up tomorrow. Some—most—of them will want your head. But I think it might be possible to convince them to let you go free, if you agree to do something."

"No!"

She rolled her eyes. "Really? You don't *want* to go home and deliver a letter to this elder of yours? I knew you were young and silly, but this is ridiculous."

"What kind of letter?" he asked hesitantly.

"An offer of terms." She paused. "You need it more than we do, I hasten to add. Now we can get into *your* world—" He flinched—"and there are many more of us, *and* there's the other world you saw, the one the Clan's power is based in. Did you see much of America?" His eyes went wide: He'd seen enough. "From now on, in any struggle, we can win. There is no 'maybe' in that statement. If the eldest orders your family to fight it out, they can only lose. But I happen to have a use for your family—I want to keep them alive. And you. I'm willing to settle this thing between us, the generations of blood and murder, if your eldest is willing to accept that declaring war on the Clan was wrong, that his ancestor was not deliberately abandoned, and that ending the war is necessary. So I'm going to do everything I can to convince the committee to send you home with a cease-fire proposal."

He stared at her as if she'd sprouted a second head.

"Will you carry that message?" she asked.

He nodded, slowly, watching her with wide eyes.

"Don't get your hopes up," she warned. She turned to the door. "Take this one back to his cell," she said. "I want you to make sure he's given food and water. And take good care of him." She leaned toward the sergeant. "There is a chance that he is going to run an errand for us. I do *not* want him damaged. Do you understand?"

Something in her eyes made the soldier tense: "Yes, ma'am," he grunted warily. "Food and water." His companion pulled the door open, staring at the wall behind her, trying to avoid her gaze.

"See that you do."

She came out of the cellars shivering into the evening twilight, and headed upstairs as fast as she could, to get back to a warm fireplace and good company. But it was going to take more than that to get the chill of the dungeon out of her bones, and out of her dreams.

PART 5

MELTDOWN

escape plans

he's done *what*?" demanded Matthias, in a tone of rising disbelief .

The duke's outer office in Fort Lofstrom was home to the duke's secretary, and during Angbard's lengthy absence it served as a headquarters from which the Clan's operations in Massachusetts were coordinated. One of a chain of nine such castles up and down the eastern seaboard (in the Gruinmarkt, but also in the free kingdoms to the north and south), it coordinated the transshipment of Clan cargo along the entire eastern continental coast. Half a dozen junior Clan members were stationed there at any time, each shuttling back and forth at eight-hour intervals. Every three hours a message packet would arrive from Cambridge, and Matthias would be the first to open it and read any confidential dispatches.

This packet had contained a couple of letters, and a terse coded message. It was the latter that had whetted Matthias's curiosity, then raised his ire.

The youth standing in front of his desk looked very frightened, but held his ground. "It came over the wireless just now, sir, an order to shut down. A blanket order, for the duration of the extraordinary general meeting, sir." He cleared his throat. "Isn't that unusual?"

"Hmm." Matthias looked at him hard. "Well, Poul." The lad was barely out of his teens, still afflicted by acne and a bad case of deference to authority—especially the kind of deadly, self-confident authority that Matthias exuded—but for all that he was brave. "We'll just have to shut down the postal service, won't we?" He allowed his expression to relax infinitesimally, determined not to give the youth any hint of the turmoil he felt.

"Are those your orders, sir?" Poul asked eagerly.

"No." Matthias cocked his head. A Clan extraordinary meeting, held without warning . . . it didn't smell good. In fact, it smelled extraordinarily bad to him. Ever since Esau's asshole relatives had started trying to rub out the long-lost countess and another bunch of interlopers had joined in, things had looked distinctly unstable. "It sounds to me as if there's something very big going on," Matthias said slowly. "On that basis, I don't think suspending the post is sufficient. We have assets on the other side who may not have got the warning. I'll need you to make one more crossing to deliver a message, as soon as possible. *Then* we shut down. Meanwhile, it will be necessary to secure the fort."

"Secure the—sir? Do you know what's going on?"

Matthias fixed the young man with a grim stare. "I have a notion that it's no good. The civil war, lad, that's what this is about. Pigeons are coming home to roost and promises made thirty years ago are about to be delivered on." He snorted. "Idiots," he muttered bitterly. "Wait here. I have to go and get the special dispatches out of the duke's office. Then I'll go over what you have to do to deliver them."

Matthias rose and let himself through the door into the duke's inner study. Everything was as it had been when Angbard departed, a week ago. Matthias closed the door, then leaned his head against the wall and cursed silently. *So close, so damned close!* But he couldn't just sit here. Not with that bitch about to spill her guts at the meeting. Esau's confession—that the eldest had authorized repeated attempts on Helge's life—had shaken him. He'd had Helge, Miriam, in his sights: She was a natural fellow traveler for his plans. He'd been getting positioned to bring her into his orbit until the idiot fanatics started trying to kill her, making her suspicious of everyone and everything. With no friends but that weakling Roland, she'd been easy meat before. But now—

He read through his illicit decrypt one more time. The original message wasn't addressed to him, but that had never stopped Matthias in the past; as Angbard's secretary he was used to reading the duke's mail—and also mail for other people on station that passed through the mail room. People such as Sir Huw Thoms, lieutenant of the guard, who right now was over on the other side, making a delivery run. And he had access to the code books, too.

ACTION THIS DAY STOP ARREST MATTHIAS
VAN HJORTH ANY MEANS NECESSARY STOP
CHARGES OF TREASON TO FOLLOW STOP

Shit. Matthias crumpled the letter in his fist, his face a tight mask of anger. *Bitch,* he thought. Either his hold on Roland wasn't as strong as he'd believed, or she was more ruthless than he'd thought. But the old man has made a mistake. Poul, the callow messenger, was in the next room. That gave him an edge, if he could only work out how to use it.

He went back out to his own office, and opened another desk drawer. He smiled to himself at the thought of Angbard's reaction should he discover what Matthias kept in it, the use to which Matthias had put his access to the duke's personal files. But right now there wasn't much time for self-indulgent daydreams. What Matthias needed was a smoke-screen to cover his own disappearance, and smokescreens didn't come any thicker than this one.

First, Matthias removed the most recent addition from the safe: an anonymous CD, the enigmatic phrase "deep throat" scrawled on it in a feminine hand. Obtaining it had taken him a lot of detective work; only the hints turned up by the duke's background checks on Miriam had kept him searching until it came to light, buried in her music collection. Next, he removed three small stamped, addressed envelopes, each containing a covering letter and a floppy disk. When he left his office a minute later, the drawer was locked and empty of incriminating evidence. And the letters were on the first stage of their journey to Cambridge, Massachusetts, by Clan courier.

Letters addressed to local FBI and DEA offices.

The huge ballroom at the back of the Clan's palace could, when the situation demanded it, be converted into a field hospital—or a boardroom large enough to hold all the voting members of an ancient and prolific business partnership. It was only when she saw it filled that Miriam began to grasp the sheer scale of the power the Clan wielded in the Gruinmarkt.

The room was dominated by a table at one end, behind which sat a row of eight chairs: three for administrative officers of the committee, and one for each head of one of the families. Rows of green leather-topped benches had been installed facing the table, the ones farther back raised to give their occupants a view of the front. The huge glass doors that in summer would open onto the garden were closed, barricaded outside by heavy oak shutters.

The main entrance to the room was guarded by soldiers in black helmets and body armor, armed with automatic rifles. They stood impassively by as Miriam entered, Kara trailing her. "Ooh, look! It's your uncle!" Kara whispered.

"Tell me something new. Like, where do I sit?" Angbard occupied one of the three raised chairs at the middle of the table, a black robe drawn over his suit. His expression was as grim as a hanging judge's. The room was already beginning to fill, men and women in business attire seeking out their benches and quietly conversing. The only anomalous touch was their attendants, decked out in archaic finery.

"Excuse me, where should milady sit?" Kara simpered at a uniformed functionary who, now that Miriam was getting her bearings, seemed to be one of many who were unobtrusively directing delegates and partners to one side or another.

"Thorold-Hjorth—that would be there. Left bench, second row if she is to be called."

Miriam drifted toward the indicated position. *Like a company's annual general meeting,* she noted. It was oddly familiar, but in no way comforting. She looked up at the front table and saw that three of the high seats had already been filled—one of them by Oliver Hjorth, who caught her watching and glared at her. The other two held dusty nonentities, elderly men who looked half-asleep already as they leaned heads together to talk. *I wish Roland were here,* she thought uneasily. *Or—no, I just wish I wasn't facing this alone. Roland would be supportive, but he wouldn't be much use. Would he?*

"May I join you?" Someone asked. Miriam glanced up.

"Olga? Yeah, sure! Did you have a good night?"

Olga sat down next to her. "No intruders," she said smugly. "A pity. I was rather hoping."

"Hoping?"

"To test my new M4-Super 90. Ah well. Oh, look, it's Baron Gruinard." She indicated one of the dried sticks at the board table.

"Is that good or bad?"

"Depends if he's sitting for the Royal Assizes and you're brought up in front of him. At most other times he's rather harmless, but one hears the most frightful things when his court is in session."

"Um." Miriam noticed another familiar figure, an elderly dowager in a blue twin-set and pearls. Her stomach twisted. "I spy a grandmother."

"Don't make a habit of it." Olga beamed in the direction of the elderly duchess, who spotted Miriam and frowned, horribly. "Isn't she impressive?"

"Is that meant to be a compliment?"

The duchess cast Olga a hideous glare and then diverted

her attention elsewhere, to a balding middle-aged man in a suit who fawned and led her toward the far side of the room.

"Where's—"

"Hush," said Olga. Angbard had produced a gavel from somewhere. He rapped it on the edge of the table peremptorily.

"We are gathered today for an extraordinary meeting," Angbard announced conversationally. He frowned and tapped the elderly looking microphone. "We are gathered . . . state of emergency." The sound system cut in properly and Miriam found that she no longer had to make an effort to hear him. "Thirty-two years ago, Patricia Thorold-Hjorth and Alfredo Wu were attacked on their way to this court. The bodies of Alfredo and his guards were found, but that of Patricia remained lost. Until very recently it was believed that she and her infant daughter had perished."

A quiet ripple of conversation swept the hall. Angbard continued after a brief pause. "Four months ago an unknown woman appeared in the wilds of Nether Paarland. She was apprehended, and a variety of evidence—backed up by genetic fingerprinting, which my advisors tell me is infallible for this purpose—indicated that she was the long-lost infant, Helge Thorold-Hjorth, grown to majority in the United States."

The conversational ripple became a cascade. Angbard brought his gavel down again and again. "Silence, I say silence! I will have silence."

Finally the room was quiet enough for him to continue. "A decision was taken to bring Helge into the Clan. I personally took responsibility for this. Her, ah, induction, was not an immediate success. Upon her arrival here a number of unexpected events transpired. In particular, it appears that someone wanted her dead—someone who couldn't tell the difference between a thirty-two-year-old countess and a twenty-three-year-old chatelaine, traveling together. In the interests of clarity I must add that *nobody* in this room is presently under suspicion."

Miriam's scalp prickled. Glancing aside she realized that half the eyes in the room were pointed at her. She sat up and looked back at Angbard.

"I believe we now have evidence enough to confirm the identity of the parties behind the attacks on Patricia and Alfredo, *and* on Patricia's daughter, Helge. These same parties are accused of fomenting the civil war that split this Clan into opposing factions fifty-seven years ago—" Uproar. Angbard sat back and waited for almost a minute, then brought his gavel down again—"Silence, please! I intend to present the witnesses that Clan Security has uncovered before you in due course. The floor will then be opened for motions bearing on the matter at hand." He turned to his neighbor, an elderly gentleman who until this point appeared to have been half asleep on his throne. "Julius, if you please? . . ."

"Aha!" The old scarecrow bolted upright, raised a wobbling hand, and declaimed: "calling the first witness—" He peered at a paper that Angbard slid before him, and muttered—"can't call her, she's dead, dammit!"

"No, she isn't," retorted Angbard.

"Oh, alright then. Think I'm senile, do you?" Julius stood up. "Calling Patricia Thorold-Hjorth."

Half the room were on their feet shouting as the side door behind the table opened. Miriam had to stand, too, to see over heads to where Brilliana was entering the room, pushing a wheelchair containing her mother. Who looked bemused and rather nervous at being the focus of such uproarious attention.

"Did they take her motorized chair away to stop her running?" Miriam asked Olga.

"Oh, no—"

"Order! Order or I shall have the guards—order I say!"

Slowly order was restored. "That's odd," quavered Julius, "I was sure she was dead." A ripple of laughter spread.

"So was I," Iris—Patricia—called from her chair. Brill steered her over to one side of the table.

"Why did you run away?" asked Oliver Hjorth, leaning sideways so he could see her, an unpleasant expression of impatience on his face.

"What, *uns gefen mine mudder en geleg'hat Gelegenheit,*

mish'su 'em annudern frau-clapper weg tu heiraten?" Iris asked dryly. There was a shocked titter from somewhere in the audience: "obviously not. And if you have to ask that question I also doubt very much that you've ever had a gang of assassins trying to murder you. A pity, that. You could benefit from the experience."

"What's she saying?" Miriam nudged Olga. *I really must try to learn the language,* she thought despairingly.

"Your mother is convincingly rude," Olga replied, *sotto voce.*

"This is an imposter!" someone called from the floor. Miriam craned her neck; it might be the dowager duchess, but she couldn't be certain. "I demand to see—"

"Order!" Angbard whacked his hammer down again. "You will be polite, madam, or I will have you escorted out of this room."

"I apologize to the chair," Iris responded. "However, I assure you I'm no imposter. Mother dearest, by way of proof of my identity, would you like me to repeat what I overheard you telling Erich Wu in the maze at the summer palace gardens at Kvaern when I was six?"

"You—you!" The old dowager stumbled to her feet, shaking with rage.

"I believe I can prove my case adequately, with or without blood tests," Iris said dryly, addressing the gallery. "As any of you who have consulted the register of proxies must be aware, my mother has a strong motive for refusing to acknowledge me. Unfortunately, as in so many other circumstances, I must disobey her wishes."

"Nonsense!" blurted the duchess, an expression of profound horror settling on her face. She sat down quickly.

"I can attest that she is no imposter," said Angbard. "If anyone requests independent verification, this can be arranged. Does any party to this meeting so desire?" He glanced around the room, but no hands went up. "Very well." He rapped on the table again with his gavel. "I intend to bring up the issue of Lady Thorold-Hjorth's absence again, but not at this session. Suffice to say, *I* am convinced of her authenticity. As you have just seen, her mother appears to be convinced, too." Spluttering from the vicinity of the dowager failed to break his poise. "Now, we have more urgent matters to consider. My reason for reintroducing Lady Patricia to this body was to, ah, make it clear where the next matter is coming from."

"Clear as mud," the elderly Julius remarked to nobody in particular.

"I'd like to call the next witness before the committee," Angbard continued, unperturbed. "Lady Olga Thorold has been the subject of outrageous attempts upon her person, and has had her lady-in-waiting murdered, very recently— while traveling in the company of Lady Helge. All of this has occurred in the past six months. Please approach the table."

Olga rose and walked to the front of the table. The room was silent.

"In your own words, would you please tell us about the series of attacks on your person, when and where they began, and why they were unsuccessful?"

Olga cleared her throat. "Last December I was summoned to spend time with Duke Lofstrom at his castle. I had for a year before then been petitioning him for an active role, in the hope that he could find a use for me in the trade. He asked me to escort Helge Thorold-Hjorth, newly arrived and ignorant of our ways, both to educate her and to ensure that no harm came to her. I do not believe he anticipated subsequent events when we arrived at this house—" She continued to enumerate intrusion after intrusion, outrage by outrage, pausing only when interrupted from the floor by a burst of voices demanding further explanation.

Miriam watched in near-astonishment. "Is everyone here something to do with Clan Security?" she asked Kara quietly.

"Not me, milady!" Kara's eyes were wide.

Olga finished by recounting how Miriam had brought her to a new world, and how they had been assaulted there, too, by strangers. A voice from the floor called out. "Wait! How do you know it was another world? Can't it possibly have been another region of 'Merica?"

"No, it can't," Olga said dismissively. "I've seen America, and I've seen this other place, and the differences are glaringly obvious. They both sprang from the same roots, but clearly they have diverged—in America, the monarchy is not hereditary, is it?" She frowned for a moment. "Did I say something wrong?"

Uproar. "What's all this nonsense about?" demanded Earl Hjorth, red-faced. "It's clear as day that this can't be true! If it was, there might be a whole new world out there!"

"I believe there is," Olga replied calmly.

The gavel rose and fell on the resulting babble. "Silence! I now call Helge Thorold-Hjorth, alias Miriam Beckstein. Please approach the table."

Miriam swallowed as she stood up and walked over.

"Please describe for the Clan how you come to be here. From the day you first learned of your heritage."

"We'll be here all day—"

"Nevertheless, if you please."

"Certainly." Miriam took a deep breath. "It started the day I lost my job with a business magazine in Cambridge. I went to visit my mother—" a nod to Iris "—who asked me to fetch down a box from her attic. The box was full of old papers . . ."

She kept going until she reached her patent filing in New Britain, the enterprise she was setting up, and Olga's shooting. Her throat was dry and the room was silent. She shook her head. "Can I have a glass of water, please?" she asked. A tumbler appeared next to her.

"Thank you. By this time I had some ideas. The people who kept trying to murder Iris—sorry, Patricia—and who kept going after me, or getting at Olga by mistake—they had to be relatives. But apart from one attempt, there was never any sign of them on the other side, in America that is. I remembered being told about a long-lost brother who headed west in the earliest days of the Clan. You know—we learned—that they, too, use a pattern to let them world-walk,

however they can travel only from here to New Britain, to
the place I've just been telling you about.

"What I've pieced together is something like this. A very
long time ago one of the brothers headed west. He fell on
hard times and lost his amulet. In fact, he ended up as an in-
dentured slave and took nearly ten years to save the cash to
buy his freedom. Once free, he had to reconstruct the knot
design from memory. Either that, or his was deliberately
sabotaged by a sibling. Whichever, the knot he painted was
different. I can't emphasize that strongly enough; where you
go when you world-walk depends on the design you use as a
key. We now know of two keys, but there's another fact—the
other one, this lost brother's knot, doesn't work in America.
Our America. The one we go to.

"Anyway. he crossed over repeatedly, because it had been
arranged that at regular intervals he should check for his
brothers. They evidently intended to send a trade caravan to
meet him, somewhere in Northern California perhaps. But
he never found his business partners waiting for him, because they were elsewhere, traveling to another world where,
presumably, they interpreted his absence as a sign that he'd
died. He was cut off completely, and put it down to betrayal."

"Preposterous!" Someone in the front row snorted,
prompting Angbard to bring down the gavel again. Miriam
took the opportunity to help herself to a glass of water.

"This brother, Lee, had a family. His family was less numerous, less able to provide for themselves, than the Clan.
Just as the ability was lost to your ancestors for a generation
or two, so it was with his descendants—and it took longer
before some first cousins or cousins married and had an infant with renewed ability. They prospered much as you have,
but more slowly. The New British don't have a lot of time for
Chinese merchants, and as a smaller family they had far
fewer active world-walkers to rely on.

"Now, the Lees only found the Clan again when the family Wu moved west, less than a century ago. The Lees
reacted—well, I think it was out of fear, but they basically
conducted the campaign of assassinations that kicked off the

feud. Everyone in the Clan knew that the murders could only have been carried out by world-walkers, so the attacks on the western families were blamed—understandably—on their cousins back east."

She paused. The level of conversation breaking out in the benches made continuing futile. Angbard raised his gavel but she held up a hand. "Any questions?" she asked.

"Yes! What's this business—"

"—How did you travel—"

"—We going to put up with these lies?"

Bang. Miriam jumped as Angbard brought down the gavel. "One at a time," he snapped. "Helge, if you please. You have the floor."

"The new world, where the other family—the Lees—go, is like the one I grew up in, but less well developed. There are a number of reasons for this, but essentially it boils down to the apparent fact that it diverged historically from my own about two hundred and fifty years ago. If you want evidence of its existence I have witnesses, Lady Olga and Brilliana d'Ost, and video recordings. I can even take you over there, if you are willing to accept my directions—remember, it is a very different country from the United States, and if you don't bear that in mind you can get into trouble very easily. But let me emphasize this. I believe *anyone* who is sitting in this room now can go there quite easily, by simply using a Lee family talisman instead of a Clan one. You can verify this for yourselves. I repeat: It appears that if you have the ability to world-walk, you can go to different worlds simply by using a different kind of talisman.

"New Britain only had an industrial revolution a century ago. I've established a toehold over there, by setting up an identity and filing some basic engineering patents on the automobile. They'll be big in about five to ten years. My business plan was to leverage inventions from the U.S.A. that haven't been developed over there, rather than trading in physical commodities or providing transportation. But by doing this, I attracted the Lee family's attention. They worked out soon enough that I'd acquired one of their lockets and was setting up on their territory. As Olga told you, they attempted to black-bag my house and we were waiting for them." She glanced at Angbard for approval. He nodded to her, so she went on. "We took a prisoner, alive. He was in possession of an amulet and he's indisputably a world-walker, but he's not of the Clan. I asked for some medical tests. Ah, my lord?"

The duke cleared his throat. "Blood tests confirm that the prisoner is a very distant relative. And a world-walker. It appears that there are six families, after all."

Now he resorted to his hammer again, in earnest—but to no avail. After five minutes, when things began to quieten down, Angbard signaled for the sergeant at arms to bring order to the hall. *"Order!"* he shouted. "We will recess for one hour, to take refreshments. Then the meeting will resume." He rose, scowling ominously at the assembled Clan shareholders. "What you've heard so far is the background. There is more to come."

Morning on the day shift in Boston. The office phones were already ringing as Mike Fleming swiped his badge and walked in past security.

"Hi, Mike!" Pete Garfinkle, his officemate, waved on his way back from the coffee machine.

"'Lo." Mike was never at his best, early in the morning. Winter blues, one of his ex-girlfriends had called it in a forgiving moment. (Blues so deep they were ultraviolet, the same girlfriend had said as she was moving out—blues so deep she'd gotten radiation burns.) "Anything in?"

"What? On the—" Pete waved a finger.

"Office. Okay, give me five minutes."

Mike wandered along to the vending machine, passing a couple of suits from the public liaison office, and collected a mug of coffee. Traffic was bad this morning, really bad. And he hadn't shaved properly either. It was only nine but he already had a five o'clock shadow, adding to his bearish appearance. *Don't mess with me.*

Pete was already nose-deep in paperwork that had come in the morning mail when Mike finally made it to his desk. Pete was a morning guy, always frazzled by six o'clock—when Mike was just hitting his stride. "Tell me the news," Mike grunted. "Anything happening?"

"On the Hernandez case? Judge Judy has it on her docket." Pete grinned humorlessly.

"Judge Judy couldn't find his ass with a submarine's periscope and a map." Mike pulled a face, put his mug of coffee down, and rubbed his eyes. The urge to yawn was nearly irresistible. "Judge Judy is about the *least* likely to sign a no-knock—"

"Yeah, yeah, I know all about your pissing match with hi-zonner Stephen Jude. Can it, Mike, he works for Justice, it's his *job* to gum up the works. No point taking it personal."

"Huh. That fucker Julio needs to go down, though. I mean, the goddamn Pope knows what he's at! What the hell else do we need to convince the DA he's got a case?"

"Fifty keys of crack and a blow job from the voters." Pete leaned his chair perilously far back—the office was so cramped that a sideswipe would risk demolishing piles of banker's boxes—and snorted. "Relax, dude. We'll get him."

"Huh. Give me that." Mike held out a huge hand and Pete dumped a pile of mail into it. "Ack." Mike carefully put it down on his desk, then picked up his coffee and took a sip. "Bilge water."

"One of these days you'd better try and kick the habit," Pete said mildly. "It can't be doing your kidneys any good."

"Listen, I *run* on coffee," Mike insisted. "Lessee—"

He thumbed rapidly through the internal mail, sorting administrative memos from formal letters—some branches still ran on paper, their intranets unconnected to the outside world—and a couple of real, honest, postal envelopes. He stacked them in three neat piles and switched on his PC. While he waited for it to boot he opened the two letters from outside. One of them was junk, random spam sent to him by name and offering cheap loans. The other—

"Holy *shit*!"

Pete started, nearly going over backwards in his chair. "Hey! You want to keep a lid—"

"*Holy* shit!"

Pete turned around. Mike was on his feet, a letter clutched in both hands and an expression of awe on his face. "What?" Pete asked mildly.

"Got to get this to forensics," Mike muttered, carefully putting the letter down on his desk, then carefully peering inside the envelope. A little plastic baggie with something brown in it—

"Evidence?" asked Pete, interestedly: "Hey, I thought that was external?"

"You're not kidding!" Mike put it down as delicately as if it was made of fine glass. "Anonymous tip-offs 'R' us!"

"Explain."

"This letter." Mike pointed. "It's fingering the Phantom."

"You're sure about that?" Pete looked disbelieving. Mike nodded. "Jesus, Mike, you need to learn some new swear words, holy shit doesn't cut it! Show me that thing—"

"Whoa!" Mike carefully lifted the envelope. "Witness. You and me, we're going down to the lab to see what's in this baggie. If it's what the letter says, and it checks out, it's a sample from that batch of H that hit New York four months ago. You know? The really big one that coincided with that OD spike, pushed the price down so low they were buying it by the ounce? From the Phantom network?"

"So?" Pete looked interested. "Somebody held onto a sample."

"*Somebody* just sent us a fucking tip-off that there's an address in Belmont that's the local end of the distribution chain. Wholesale, Pete. Name, rank, and serial number. Dates—we need to check the goddamn dates. Pete, this is an *inside* job. Someone on the inside of the Phantom wants to come in from the cold and they're establishing their bona fides."

"We've had falsies before. Anonymous bastards."

"Yeah, but this one's got a sample, and a bunch of supple-mentaries. From memory, I think it checks out—at least, there's not anything obviously wrong with it at first glance. I want it dusted for fingerprints and DNA samples before we go any further. What do you think?"

Pete whistled. "If it checks out, and the dates match, I figure we can get the boss to come along with us and go lean on Judge Judy. A break on the Phantom would be just too cool."

"My thoughts exactly." Mike grinned ferociously. "How well do you think we can resource this one?"

"If it's the Phantom? Blank check time. Jesus, Mike, if this is the Phantom, I think we've just had the biggest break in this office in about the last twenty years. It's going to be all over *Time* Magazine if this goes down!"

In the hallway outside the boardroom, the palace staff had busied themselves setting up a huge buffet. Cold cuts from a dozen game animals formed intricate sculptures of meat depicting their animate origins. Jellied larks vied with sugar-pickled fruit from the far reaches of the West Coast, and exotic delicacies imported at vast expense formed pyramids atop a row of silver platters the size of small dining tables. Hand-made Belgian truffles competed for the attention of the aristocracy with caviar-topped crackers and brightly colored packets of M&Ms.

Despite the huge expanse of food, most of the Clan shareholders had other things in mind. Though waiters with trays laden with wine glasses circulated freely—and with jugs of imported coffee and tea—the main appetite they exhibited seemed to be for speech. And speech with one or two people in particular.

"Just keep them away from me, please," Miriam said plaintively, leaning close to Olga. "They'll be all over me."

"You can't avoid them!" Olga insisted, taking her arm and steering her toward the open doors onto the reception area. "Do you want them to think you're afraid?" she hissed in Miriam's ear. "They're like rats that eat their own young if they smell weakness in the litter."

"It's not that—I've got to go." Miriam pulled back and

steered Olga in turn, toward the door at the back of the boardroom where she'd seen Angbard pushing her mother's wheelchair, ahead of the crush. Kara, her eyes wide, stuck close behind Miriam.

"Where are you going?" asked Olga.

"Follow." Miriam pushed on.

"Eh, I say! Young woman!"

A man Miriam didn't recognize, bulky and gray-haired, was blocking her way. Evidently he wanted to buttonhole her. She smiled blandly. "If you don't mind, sir, there'll be time to talk later. But I urgently need to have words with—" She gestured as she slid past him, leaving Kara to soothe ruffled feathers, and shoved the door open.

"Ma!"

It was a small side room, sparsely furnished by Clan standards. Iris looked around as she heard Miriam. Angbard looked round, too, as did a cadaverous-looking fellow with long white hair who had been hunched slightly, on the receiving end of some admonition.

"Helge," Angbard began, in a warning tone of voice.

"Mother!" Miriam glared at Iris, momentarily oblivious.

"Hiya, kid." Iris grinned tiredly. "Allow me to introduce you to another of your relatives. Henryk? I'd like to present my daughter." Iris winked at Angbard: "Cut her a little slack, alright?"

The man who'd been listening to Angbard tilted his head on one shoulder. "Charmed," he said politely.

The duke coughed into a handkerchief and cast Miriam a grim look. "You should be circulating," he grumbled.

"Henryk was always my favorite uncle," Iris said, glancing at the duke. "I mean, there had to be one of them, didn't there?"

Miriam paused uncomfortably, unwilling to meet Angbard's gaze. Meanwhile, Henryk looked her up and down. "I see," she said after a moment. "Well, that's all right then, isn't it?"

"Helge." Angbard refused to be ignored. "You should be out front. Mixing with the guests." He frowned at her. "You know how much stock they put in appearances." *Harrumph.* "This is their first sight of you. Do you want them to think you're a puppet? Conspiring with the bench?"

"I *am* conspiring with you," she pointed out. "And anyway, they'd eat me alive. You obviously haven't done enough press conferences. You don't throw the bait in the water if you want to pull it out intact later, do you? You've got to keep these things under control."

Angbard's frown intensified. "This isn't a press conference; this is a beauty show," he said. "If you do not go out there and make the right moves they will assume that you cannot. And if you can't, what are you good for? I arranged this session at your request. The least you can do is not make a mess of it."

"There's going to be a vote later on," Iris commented. "Miriam, if they think you're avoiding them it'll give the reactionary bastards a chance to convince the others that you're a fraud, and that won't go in your favor, will it?"

Miriam sighed. "That's what I like about you, Ma, family solidarity."

"She's right, you know," Henryk spoke up. "Motions will go forward. They may accept your claim of title, but not your business proposals. Not if names they know and understand oppose it, and you are not seen to confront them."

"But they'll—" Miriam began.

"I have a better idea!" Olga announced brightly. "Why don't you both go forth to charm the turbulent beast?" She beamed at them both. "That way they won't know who to confront! Like the ass that starved between two overflowing mangers."

Iris glanced sidelong at Miriam. Was it worry? Miriam couldn't decide. "That would never do," she said apologetically. "I couldn't—"

"Oh yes you can, Patricia," Angbard said with a cold gleam in his eye.

"But if I go out there Mother will make a scene! And then—"

Miriam caught herself staring at Iris in exasperation,

sensing an echo of a deeper family history she'd grown up shielded from. "The dowager will make a scene, will she?" Miriam asked, a dangerous note in her voice: "Why shouldn't she? She hasn't seen you for decades. Thought you were dead, probably. You didn't get along with her when you were young, but so what? Maybe you'll both find the anger doesn't matter anymore. Why not try it?" She caught Angbard's eye. Her uncle, normally stony-faced, looked positively anesthetized, as if to stifle an image-destroying outburst of laughter.

"You don't know the old bat," Iris warned grimly.

"She hasn't changed," Angbard commented. "If anything, she's become even more set in her ways." *Harrumph.* He hid his face in his handkerchief again.

"She's been getting worse ever since she adopted that young whipper-snapper Oliver as her confidante," Henryk mumbled vaguely. "Give me Alfredo any day, we'd have straightened him out in time—" He didn't seem to notice Iris's face tightening.

"Ma," Miriam said warningly.

"Alright! That's enough." Iris pushed herself upright in her wheelchair, an expression of grim determination on her face. "Miriam, purely for the sake of family solidarity, *you* push. You, young lady, what's your name—"

"Olga," Miriam offered.

"—I know that, dammit! Olga, open the doors and keep the idiots from pushing me over and letting my darling daughter sneak away. Angbard—"

"I'll start the session again in half an hour," he said, shaking his head. "Just remember." He turned a cool eye on Miriam, all trace of levity gone: "It cost me a lot to set this up for you. Don't make a mess of it."

GOING POSTAL

Own in the post office in the basement of Fort Lofstrom, two men waited nervously for their superior to arrive. Both of them were young—one was barely out of his teens—and they dressed like law firm clerks or trainee accountants. "Is this for real?" the younger one kept asking, nervously. "I mean, has it really happened? Why does nobody tell us anything? Shit, this sucks!"

"Shut up and wait," said the elder, leaning against a wall furnished with industrial shelving racks, holding a range of brightly colored plastic boxes labeled by destination. "Haven't you learned anything?"

"But the meeting! I mean, what's going on? Have the old guys finally decided to stop us going over—"

"I said, shut the fuck up." The older courier glared at the kid with all the world-weary cynicism of his twenty-six years. Spots, tufts of straggly beard hair—*Sky Father, why do I get to nurse the babies?* "Listen, nothing is going to go wrong."

He nudged the briefcase at his feet. Inside its very expensive aluminium shell was a layer of plastic foam. Inside the plastic foam nestled a bizarrely insectile-looking H&K submachine gun. The kid didn't need to know that, though. "When the boss man gets here, we do a straight delivery run then lock down the house. *You* stay with the boss and do what he says. *I* get the fun job of telling the postmen to drop everything and yelling at the holiday heads to execute their cover plans. Then we arrest anyone who tries to drop by. Get it? The whole thing will be over in forty-eight hours, it's just a routine security lockdown."

"Yes, Martijn." The kid shook his head, puzzled. "But there hasn't been an extraordinary meeting in my lifetime! And this is an emergency lockdown, isn't it? Shutting down everything, telling all our people on the other side to go hide, that sucks. What's going on?"

The courier looked away. *Hurry up and get the nonsense out of your system,* he thought. "What do you think they're doing?" he asked.

"It's obvious: They envy us, don't they? The old dudes. Staying over, fitting in. You know I'm going back to college in a couple of weeks, did I tell you about the shit my uncle Stani's been handing out about that? I've got a girlfriend and a Miata and a place of my own and he's giving me shit because he never had that stuff. What do you need to learn reading for if you've got scribes? he told me. And you know what? Some of them, if they could stop us going back—"

The door opened, stemming his tirade in full flood. The older courier straightened up; the young one just flushed, his mouth running down in a frightened stammer. "Uh, yessir, uh, going back, uh—"

"Shut up," Matthias said coldly.

One more squeak and the kid fell silent. Matthias nodded at Martijn, the older one. "You ready?" he asked.

"Yes, my lord."

"Very well." Matthias didn't smile, but some of the tension went out of his shoulders. He wore a leather flying jacket and jeans, with gloves on his hands and a day pack slung over one arm. "Kid. You are going to carry me across. Ready?"

"Uh." Gulp. "Yessir. Yes. Sir."

"Hah." Matthias glanced at the older one. "Go on, then." He advanced on the youth. "I'm heavier than any load you're used to. You will need to have your key ready in one hand. When you are ready, speak, and I'll climb on your back. Try not to break."

"Yessir!"

A minute later they were in another post room. This one was slightly smaller, its shelves less full, and a row of wheeled suitcases were parked on the opposite wall inside an area painted with yellow stripes. The kid collapsed to his knees, gasping for breath while Matthias looked around for the older courier. "Martijn. You have your orders?"

"Yes. My lord."

"Execute them."

Matthias removed a briefcase from the rack on one wall then walked toward the exit from the room. He unlocked it then waved Martijn and the younger courier through. Once they were in the elevator to the upper floors, Matthias shut the door—then turned on his heel and headed for the emergency stairs to the garage.

The silver-blue BMW convertible was waiting for him, just as he'd ordered. Finally, Matthias cracked a smile, thin-lipped and humorless. There was barely room for the briefcase in the trunk, and his day pack went on the passenger seat. He fired up the engine as he hit the "door open" button on the dash, accelerating up the ramp and into the daylight beyond.

"Fifteen minutes," he whispered to himself as he merged with the traffic on the Cambridge turnpike. "Give me fifteen minutes!"

The time passed rapidly. Waiting at an intersection, Matthias pulled out a cheap anonymous mobile phone and speed-dialed a number. It rang three times before the person at the other end answered.

"Who is this?" they asked.

"This is Judas. Listen, I will say this once. The address you want is . . ." he rattled through the details of the location he'd just left. "Got that?"

"Yes. Who are you and—"

Matthias casually flipped the phone out of the half-open window then accelerated away. Moments later, an eighteen-wheeler reduced it to plastic shrapnel.

"Fuck *you* very much," he muttered, a savage joy in his eyes. "You can't fire me: I quit!"

It wasn't until he was nearly at the airport with his wallet full of bearer bonds and a briefcase full of Clan secrets that he began to think about what to do next.

A ghastly silence fell across the grand hall as Miriam stepped out of the doorway. She took a deep breath and smiled as brightly as she could. "Don't mind me!" she said.

"That's right," Iris whispered, "mind *me,* you back-stabbing faux-aristocratic bastards!"

"Mother!" she hissed, keeping a straight face only with considerable effort.

"Oligarchic parasites. Hah." Louder: "Steer *left,* if you please, can't you tell left from right? That's better. Now, who do I have to bribe to get a glass of Pinot Noir around here?"

Iris's chatter seemed to break an invisible curtain of suspense. Conversations started up again around the room, and a pair of anxious liveried servants hurried forward, bearing trays with glasses.

Iris hooked a glass of red wine with a slightly wobbly hand and took a suspicious sniff. "It'll pass," she declared. "Help yourself while you're at it," she told Miriam. "Don't just stand there like a rabbit in the headlights."

"Um. Are you sure it's wise to drink?"

"I've always had difficulty coping with my relatives sober. But yes, I take your point." Iris took a moderate sip. "I won't let the side down."

"Okay, Mom." Miriam took a glass. She looked up just in time to see Kara across the room, looking frightened, standing beside an unfamiliar man in late middle age. "Hmm. Looks like the rats are deserting or something. Olga?"

Beside her and following her gaze, Olga had tensed. "That's Peffer Hjorth. What's she doing talking to *him*, the minx?"

"Peffer Hjorth?"

"The baron's uncle. Outer family, not a member."

Iris whistled tunelessly. "Well, well, well. One of yours?" she asked Miriam.

"I thought so." Miriam took a sip of wine. Her mouth felt bitter, ashy.

"Lady Helge, what a story! Fascinating! And your mother—why, Patricia? It's been such a long time!"

She looked around, found Iris craning her neck, too. "Turn me, please, Miriam—" Iris was looking up and down: "Mors Hjalmar! Long time indeed. How are you doing?"

The plumpish man with a neatly trimmed beard and hair just covering his collar—like a middle-aged hippy uncomfortably squeezed into a dark suit for a funeral or court appearance—grinned happily. "I'm doing well, Patricia, well!" His expression sank slightly. "I was doing better before this blew up, I think. They mostly ignore me." He rubbed his left cheek thoughtfully. "Which is no bad thing." He looked at Olga, askance. "And who do I have the pleasure of meeting?"

"This is Lady Olga Thorold," Iris offered.

"And you are of the same party as these, ah, elusive Thorold-Hjorths?"

"Indeed I am!" Olga said tightly.

"Oh. Well, then." He shrugged. "I mean no offense, but it's sometimes hard to tell who's helping who, don't you know?"

"Lady Olga has only our best interests at heart," Miriam replied. "You knew my mother?"

Iris had been looking up at Mors all this time, her mouth open slightly, as if surprised to see him. Now she shook her head. "Thirty years," she muttered darkly. "And they haven't murdered you yet?" Suddenly she smiled. "Maybe there's hope for me after all."

"Do *you* know what she means?" Miriam asked Olga, puzzled.

"I, ahem, led an eccentric life many years ago," said Mors.

Iris shook her head. "Mors was the first of our generation to actually demand—and get—a proper education. Yale Law School, but they made him sign away his right of seniority, if I remember rightly. Wasn't that so?" she asked.

"Approximately." Mors smiled slightly. "It took them a few years to realize that the Clan badly needed its own attorney on the other side." His smile broadened by inches.

"*What?*" Iris looked almost appalled. "No, I can't see it."

"So don't." He looked slightly uncomfortable. "Is it true?" His eyes were fixed on Iris.

"If she says it's true, it's true," Iris insisted, jerking her head slightly in Miriam's direction. "A credit to the family." She pulled a face. "Not that that's what I wanted, but—"

"—We don't always get what we want," Mors finished for her, nodding. "I think I see." He looked thoughtful. Then he looked at Miriam. "If you need any legal advice, here's my card," he said.

"Thank you," said Miriam, pocketing it. "But I think I may need a different kind of help right now." *All too damned true,* she thought, seeing what was bearing down on them. Nemesis had two heads and four arms, and both heads wore haughty expressions of utmost disdain, carefully tempered for maximum intransigence.

"Well, if it isn't the runaway," snorted head number one, Baron Hjorth, with a negligent glance in Miriam's direction.

"Imposter, you mean," croaked head number two, glaring at her like a Valkyrie fingering her knife and wondering who to feed to the ravens next.

"Hello, mother." Iris *smiled,* a peculiar expression that Miriam had seen only once or twice before and which filled her with an urgent desire to duck and cover. "Been keeping well, I see?"

"I'll just be off," Mors started nervously—then stopped as Iris clamped a hand on his wrist. In any case, the gathering cloud of onlookers made a discreet escape impossible. There was only one conversation worth eavesdropping in this reception, and this was it.

"I was just catching up on old times with Mors," Iris cooed sweetly, her eyes never leaving the dowager's face. "He was telling me all about your retirement."

Ooh, nasty. Miriam forced herself to smile, glanced sideways, and saw Olga glaring at head number one. The baron somehow failed to turn to stone, but his hauteur seemed to melt slightly. "Hello, Oliver," said Miriam. "I'm glad to see you're willing to talk to me instead of sneaking into my boudoir when I'm not about."

"I have never—" he began pompously.

"—Stow it!" snapped Iris. "And *you,* mother—" she waved a finger at her mother, who was gathering herself up like a serpent readying to strike—"I gather you've been encouraging this odious person, have you?"

"Who I encourage or not is none of your business!" Hildegarde hissed. "You're a disgrace to family and Clan, you whore. I should have turned you out the day I gave birth to you. As for your bastard—"

"—I believe I understand, now." Miriam nodded, outwardly cordially, at Baron Hjorth. Startled, he pretended to ignore her words: "Your little plan to get back the Clan shares ceded to trust when my mother vanished—I got in the way, didn't I? But not to worry. An insecure apartment, a fortune-seeking commoner turned rapist, and an unlocked door on the roof would see to that. Wouldn't it?" *If not a couple of goons with automatic weapons,* she added mentally. *Just by way of insurance.*

The duchess gasped. "I don't know what you're talking about!"

"Quite possibly you don't," Miriam agreed. She jabbed a finger: "*He* does, don't you, you vile little turd?"

Baron Oliver had turned beet-red with her first accusation. Now he began to shake. "I have *never* conspired to blemish the virtue of a Clan lady!" he insisted. The duchess glared at him. "And if you allege otherwise—"

"Put up or shut up, I'd say," Iris said flatly. "Mors, wouldn't you say that any accusations along those lines would require an indictment? Before the committee, perhaps?"

"Mmm, possibly." Mors struck a thoughtful pose, seeming to forget his earlier enthusiasm to be elsewhere. "Were there witnesses? Unimpeachable ones?"

"I don't think any charges against the baron could be made to stick," Miriam said slowly, watching him. He watched her right back, unblinking. "And you will note that I made no allegation of involvement in a conspiracy to commit rape on your part," she added to Hjorth. *Or to send gunmen round to Olga's rooms.* "Although I might change my mind if you supplied the cause." She smiled.

"You bitch," he snarled.

"Just remember where I got it from." She nodded at her grandmother, who, speechless with rage, hung on Hjorth's arm like an overripe apple, ruddy-faced and swollen with wasps. "We really must get together for a family reunion one of these days," she added. "I'm sure you've got a lot of poison recipes to share with me."

"I'd stop, if I were you," Iris observed with clinical interest. "If you push her any further the only reunion you'll get is over her coffin."

"You treacherous little minx! . . ." Hildegarde was shaking with fury.

"So it's treachery now, is it? Because I had higher standards than you and didn't want to marry my way to the top of the dung heap?" Iris threw back at her.

"Children," Miriam sighed. She caught Olga's eye.

"I didn't notice you making an effort to find any suitable alternatives!" the duchess snapped. "And it got the Wu and Hjorth factions to stop murdering each other. Would you rather the feuding had continued? We'd both be dead a dozen times over by now!" She was breathing deeply. "You've got no sense of duty," she said bitterly.

"The feuding, in case you've been asleep, was caused by forces outside our control," Iris retorted. "You gained precisely nothing, except for a wife-beating son-in-law. Your *granddaughter,* now, has actually done something useful for the first time in living memory in this Clan of parasites. She's actually uncovered some of the reasons *why* we've been messed up for so long. The least you could do is apologize to her!"

"There's nothing to apologize for," Hildegarde said stiffly. But Miriam saw her grip on Hjorth's arm tighten.

"Don't worry, my dear," Oliver Hjorth muttered in her ear: "You're quite right about them." He cast a poisonous stare at Miriam. "Especially *that* one."

"You—" Miriam was brought up short by Olga's hand on her shoulder.

"Don't," Olga said urgently. "He wants you to react."

For the first time, Hjorth smiled. "She's right, you know," he said. "On that note, I shall bid you adieu, ladies. If I may conduct you back to civilized conversation, madam?" he added to the dowager.

Iris stared bleaky at the receding back of her mother. "I swear she'll outlive us all," Iris muttered. Then she glanced at Miriam. "There's no justice in this world, is there, kid?"

"What was she talking about?" Miriam asked slowly. "The treachery thing."

"An old disagreement," said Iris. She sounded old and tired. "A bit like picking at scabs. Most families have got the odd skeleton in the closet. We've got a whole damn graveyard in every wardrobe, practicing their line dancing. Don't sweat it."

"But—" Miriam stopped. She remembered her wine glass and took a mouthful. Her hand was shaking so badly that she nearly spilled it.

"You won," Olga said thoughtfully.

"Huh?"

"She's right. You went eyeball to eyeball with the baron, and he blinked. They'll know you've got balls now. That counts for everything here. And I—" Iris stopped.

"You got your mother on the defensive," said Miriam. "Didn't you?"

"I'm not sure," Iris said uncertainly. "Old iron-face must be rusting. Either that, or there's a deep game I don't know about. She never used to concede *anything*."

"Iron-face?"

"What we called her. Me and your aunt Elsa."

"I have an aunt, too?"

"Had. She died. Olga, if you don't mind taking over my chair? Miriam seems to be having trouble."

"Died—"

"You didn't think I had it in for the old bat just because of how she treated *me,* did you?"

"Oh." Miriam bolted back the rest of her wine glass, sensing the depths she was treading water over. "I think I need another glass now."

"Better drink it quick, then. Things are about to get interesting again."

There was a low bed with a futon mattress on it. It occupied most of a compact bedroom on the third floor of an inconspicuous building in downtown Boston. The bed was occupied, even though it was late morning; Roland had been awake for most of the night, working on the next month's courier schedule, worrying and reassigning bodies from a discontinued security operation. In fact, he'd deliberately worked an eighteen-hour shift just to tire himself out so that he could sleep. The worries wouldn't go away. *What if they find her incompetent?* was one of them. Another was, *What if the old man finds out about us?* In the end he'd slugged back a glass of bourbon and a five-milligram tab of diazepam, stripped, and climbed into bed to wait for the pharmaceutical knockout.

Which was why, when the raid began, Roland was unconscious: dead to the world, sleeping the sleep of the truly exhausted, twitching slightly beneath the thin cotton sheet.

A faint bang shuddered through the walls and floor. Roland grunted and rolled over slowly, still half-asleep. Outside his door, a shrill alarm went off. "Huh?" He sat up slowly, rubbing at his eyes to clear the fog of night, and slapped vaguely at the bedside light switch.

The phone began to shrill. "Uh." He picked up the handset, fumbling it slightly: "Roland here. What is it?"

"We're under attack! Some guys just tried to smash in the front door and the rooftop—"

The lights flickered and the phone died. Somewhere in the building the emergency generator cut in, too slowly to keep the telephone switch powered. "Shit." Roland put the handset down and hastily dragged on trousers and sweater. He pulled his pistol out of the bedside drawer, glanced at the drawn curtains, decided not to risk moving them, and opened the door.

A young Clan member was waiting for him, frantic with worry. "Wh-what are we going to do, boss?" he demanded, jumping up and down.

"Slow down." Roland looked around. "Who else is here?"

"Just me!"

"On site, I mean," he corrected. He shook his head again, trying to clear the Valium haze. At least he could world-walk away, he realized. He never removed his locket, even in the shower. "Is the door holding?"

"The door, the door—" The kid stopped shaking. "Yessir. Yessir. The door?"

"Okay, I tell you what I want you to do." Roland put a hand on the kid's shoulder, trying to calm him. He was vibrating like an overrevved engine. "Calm down. Don't panic. That's first. You have a tattoo, yes?"

"Y-yessir."

"Okay. We are going to go below then, and—when did you last walk?"

"Uh, uh, hour ago! We brought the lord secretary over—"

"The secretary?" Roland stopped dead. "Shit. Tell me you didn't." The kid's expression was all the confirmation Roland needed.

"Wh-what's wrong?"

"Maybe nothing," Roland said absently. *Shit, shit,* he thought. *Matthias.* It was a gut-deep certainty, icy cold, that Matthias was behind this. Whatever was going on. "Follow me. Quickly!" Roland grabbed his jacket on the way out and rummaged in one pocket for a strip of pills. With his hair uncombed and two day's growth of beard, he probably looked a mess, but he didn't have time to fix that now. He dry-swallowed, pulling a face. "Go down the stairs all the way to the bottom, fast. When you get to the parcel room, pick up all the consignments in bin eleven that you can grab and cross over immediately. If men with guns get the drop on you, either cross immediately or surrender and let them take you, then cross as soon as you can, blind. Don't try to resist; you're not trained."

"You, sir?" The kid's eyes were wide.

"Me neither." Roland shrugged, tried a grin, gave up. "C'mon. We've got to get word out."

He clattered down the concrete emergency stairwell taking the steps two at a time, stopping at the ground floor. He motioned the kid on down. "Send word as soon as you get through," he called. Then he stopped, his heart hammering.

"Sir?" He looked up. It was Sullivan, one of the outer family guards who lived on the premises.

"What's going on?" he demanded. "Tell me!"

A hollow boom rattled through the corridor and Sullivan winced. "We're on skeleton strength," he said. "They're trying to batter down the door!" The front door was armored like a bank vault, and the walls were reinforced. A normal ram wouldn't work, it would take explosives or cutting tools to get through it.

"Who?" Roland demanded.

"Cops."

"How many we got here?"

"Nine."

"I just sent the kid away. Walkers?"

Sullivan just looked at him.

"Shit." Roland shook his head, dumbfounded. "There's *nobody*?"

"Martijn and young Poul came in with the lord secretary this morning. They're the only walkers who've come over since Marissa and Ivar finished their shift last night. And I can't find Martijn or his lordship's proxy."

"Oh." Everything became clear to Roland. "How long can we hold out?"

"Against the feds?" Sullivan shrugged. "We're buttoned up tight; it'll take them time to bring in explosives and cutting gear, and shields. At least, it will if we risk shooting back."

"The escape tunnel—"

"—Someone sealed it at the other end. I don't think it would help, anyway."

"Let's hit the control room." Roland started walking again. "Have I got this straight? We're under siege and I'm the only walker who knows. The lord secretary came over, but he went missing before the siege began. So did his number-one sidekick. The outer rooms are shuttered and locked down and we've got supplies, power, and ammo, but no way out because somebody's blown the escape tunnel. Is that it?"

"Pretty much so," Sullivan agreed. He looked at Roland tensely. "What are you going to do?"

"What am I going to do?" Roland paused in the office doorway. "Shit, what *can* I do?" He opened the door and went in. The control room had desks with computer monitors around the wall. CCTV screens showed every approach to the building. Everything looked normal, except for the lack of vehicular traffic and the parked vans on every corner. And the van parked right up against the front door. Obviously the ram crew had used it for cover.

"We have half a ton of post in transit at any one time," Roland thought aloud. "There's about fifty kilos of confidential memos, documents, shit like that—enough to flame out the entire East Coast circuit." There was a knock on the door. Sullivan waved in the man outside, one of the colorless back-office auditors the Clan employed to keep an eye on things. "We've got another quarter of a ton of produce in transshipment. It was due out of here next week. That's enough to bankroll our ops for a year, too."

Sullivan looked pissed. "Is that your priority?" he demanded.

"No." Roland waved him down. "My priority is number one, getting all of us out of here, and number two, not letting

that fucker Matthias take down our entire operation." Sullivan subsided, leaning back against the door frame with a
skeptical expression. "It's going to take eighteen walks to
pull everyone out—more than I could do in a week. And
about the same to pull out the goods." Roland pulled out a
chair and sat. "We can't drive away or use the tunnel. How
long for them to get in? Six hours? Twelve?"

"I think it'll be more like three, unless we start shooting,"
Sullivan opined.

"Shooting—" Roland froze. "You want me to authorize you
to shoot at FBI or DEA agents. Other than in self-defense."

"It's the only way," said the auditor, looking a little green.

"Huh. I'll table it." Roland unfrozen, drummed his fingers
on the nearest desk. "I *really* don't like that option, it's too
much like sticking your dick in a hornet's nest. They can always point more guns at us than we can point back at them.
Has anyone phoned the scram number?"

"Huh?" Sullivan looked puzzled. "Bill?"

"Tried it five minutes ago, sir," the auditor said with
gloomy satisfaction. "Got a number-unavailable tone."

"I am beginning to get the picture. Have you tried your
cell phone?"

"They've got a jammer. And snipers on the rooftops."

"Shit." *I* am *going to have to make a decision,* Roland
thought. *And it had better be one I can live with,* he realized
sickly.

"Someone needs to walk over and yell like hell," Roland
said slowly. Sullivan tensed. "But, I'm working on the assumption that this is deliberate. That bastard Matthias, I've
been watching him." It was easy to say this, now. "I sent the
kid, what's his name?"

"Poul," Bill offered.

"I sent him over alone." Roland's eyes went wide. "Shit."

"What are you thinking?" Sullivan leaned forward.

"My working assumption right now is that Matthias has betrayed the Clan. This is all preplanned. He rigged this raid to
cover his escape. So he isn't going to want any random courier
walking into Fort Lofstrom and raising the alarm, is he?"

Sullivan's eyes narrowed as Roland stood up. "You and I," he announced, trying to keep his voice from shaking, "are going to cross over together. I know what you've been thinking. Listen, Matthias will have left some kind of surprise. It's going to be a mess. Your job is to keep me alive long enough to get out of the fort. Then there's a, a back route. One I can use to get word to the Clan, later today. It'll take me about six or seven hours to get from Fort Lofstrom to Niejwein, and the same again to come back with a bunch of help—every damn courier I can round up. I'm assuming Matthias sent everyone away from the fort before pulling this stunt. Can you hold out for twenty-four hours? Go into the sub-basement storm shelter with all the merchandise and blow the supports, bring the building down on top of you?" He addressed the last question to Bill, the auditor.

"I think so," Bill said dubiously.

"Right. Then you're going to have to do that." Roland met his eyes. "We can't afford for the feds to lay hands on you. And whatever you think I'm thinking, I figure you're too valuable to write off. *Any* family member, inner or outer, is not expendable in my book. Sullivan, think you can handle that?"

Sullivan grinned humorlessly at him. "I'll do my best." He nodded at the auditor: "He'll be back. Trust me on this."

The extraordinary meeting resumed with an argument. "The floor is open for motions," quavered the ancient Julius. "Do I hear—"

"I have a motion!" Miriam raised her hand.

"Objection!" snapped Baron Hjorth.

"I think you'll find she already has the floor," Angbard bit out. "Let her speak first, then have your say."

"Firstly, I'd like to move that my venture into New Britain be recognized as a Clan subsidiary," Miriam said, carefully trying to keep a still face. It was bitterly disappointing to risk ceding control, but as Olga had pointed out, the Clan took a very dim view of members striking out on their own. "As part of this motion I'd like to resolve that the issue of this sixth family be dealt with by participants in this subsidiary, because clearly they're the members most directly affected by the situation."

"Objection!" Shouted someone at the back of the hall. "Clan feud takes precedence!"

"Are you saying the Clan can afford to lose more people?" asked Miriam.

"Damn the blood! What about our dead? This calls for revenge!" Ayes backed him up: Miriam forced herself to think fast, knowing that if she let the heckling gather pace she could very easily lose control of the meeting.

"It seems to me that the lost family is sorely depleted," she began. "They had to send a child to supervise an adult's job. You know, as I know, that the efficiency of a postal service like the one responsible for the Clan's wealth is not just a function of how many world-walkers we have. It's also a function of the number of routes we can send packages over. They're small, and isolated, and they're not as numerous as we are. However, rooting them out in the name of a feud will uncover old wounds and risk depleting our numbers for no gain. I'm going to stick my neck out and assert that the next few years are going to be far more dangerous for the Clan than most of you yet realize."

"Point of order!" It was Baron Hjorth again. "This is rubbish. She's trying to frighten us. Won't you—"

"Shut *up*," grated Angbard. "Let her finish a sentence, damn your eyes."

Miriam waited a moment. "Thank you," she said. "Factors to think about. Firstly, a new world. This is going to be important because it opens up new opportunities for trade and development, as I've already demonstrated. Secondly, the state of the Clan's current business. I don't know how to approach this subtly so I won't: You're in *big* trouble.

"To be perfectly blunt, your current business model is obsolescent. You can keep it running for another two to five years, but then it'll go into a nosedive. In ten years, it'll be dead. And I'm not just talking about heroin and cocaine shipments. I mean *everything*.

"You'll have noticed how hard it has become to launder the proceeds of narcotics traffic on the other side in the past few years. With the current anti-terrorist clampdown and the beefing up of police powers, life isn't going to get any easier. Things are changing very fast indeed.

"The Clan used to be involved in different types of commerce: gold smuggling, gemstones, anything valuable and lightweight. But those businesses rely on anonymity, and like I said, the anti-terrorist clampdown is making anonymity much harder to sustain. Let me emphasize this, the traditional business models *don't work anymore* because they all rely on the same underlying assumption that you can be anonymous.

"Many of you probably aren't aware of the importance of electronic commerce, or e-commerce. I've been working with specialists covering the development of the field. What you need to know is that goods and services are going to be sold, increasingly, online. This isn't an attempt to sell you shares in some fly-by-night dot-com; it's just a statement of fact—communications speed is more important than geographical location, and selling online lets small specialist outfits sell to anyone on the planet. But with the shift to on-line selling, you can expect cash money to become obsolete. High-denomination euro banknotes already come with a chip, to allow transactions to be traced. How long do you think it'll be before the greenbacks you rely on stop being anonymous?

"The fat times will be over—and if you've spent all your resources pursuing a blood feud, you're going to be screwed. No money on the other side means no imports. No imports mean no toys, antibiotics, digital watches, whatever to buy the compliance of the landowners. No guns to shoot them with, either. If you try to ignore reality you will be screwed by factors outside your control.

"But this isn't inevitable. If you act now, you can open up new lines of revenue and new subsidiaries. Take ancient patents from my world, the world you're used to using as a toy chest, and set up companies around them in the new world, in New Britain. Take the money you raise in New Britain and import books and tools *here*. Set up universities and schools. Build, using your power and your money to establish factories and towns and laboratories over here. In a couple of generations, you can pull Gruinmarkt out of the mire and start an industrial revolution that will make you a true world power, whether or not you depend on the family talent.

"You can change the world—if you choose to start now, by changing the way you think about your business."

There was total silence in the hall. A puzzled silence, admittedly, but silence—and one or two nodding heads. *Just let them keep listening,* Miriam thought desperately. Then voices began to pipe up.

"I never heard such a—"

"—What would you have us put our money into?"

"—Hear, hear!"

"—Gather that educating the peasants is common over—"

"Silence," Angbard demanded testily. "The chair has a question."

"Uh. I'm ready." Feeling tensely nervous, Miriam crossed her fingers behind her back.

"Describe the business you established in the new world. What did you take with you to start it? And what is it worth?"

"Ah, that's an interesting one." Miriam forced herself to keep a straight face, although the wave of relief she felt at Angbard's leading question nearly made her go weak at the knees. "Exchange rate irregularities—or rather, the lack of them—make it hard to establish a true currency conversion rate, and I'm still looking for a means of repatriating value from the new world to the United States, but I'd have to say that expenditure to date is on the order of six hundred thousand dollars. The business in New Britain is still working toward its first contract, but that contract should be worth on the order of fifty thousand pounds. Uh, near as I can pin it down, one pound is equivalent to roughly two to three hundred dollars. So we're looking at a return on investment of three hundred percent in six months, and that's from a cold start."

A buzz of conversation rippled through the hall, and Angbard made no move to quell it. The figures Miriam had come up with sounded like venture capitalist nirvana—especially with a recession raging in the other world, and NASDAQ in the dumps. "That's by selling a product that's been obsolete for thirty years in the U.S.," Miriam added. "I've got another five up my sleeve, waiting for this first deal to provide seedcorn capital for reinvestment. In the absence of major disruptive factors—" *like a war with the hidden family,* she added mentally "—I figure we can be turning over ten to a hundred million pounds within ten to fifteen years. That would make us the equivalent of IBM or General Motors, simply by recycling ideas that haven't been invented yet over there."

The buzz of conversation grew louder. "I've done some more spreadsheet work," Miriam added, now more confident. "If we do this, we'll push the New British economic growth rate up by one or two percent per annum over its long-term average. We could do the same, though, importing intermediate technologies from there to here. There's no point trying to train nuclear engineers or build airports in the Gruinmarkt, not with a medieval level of infrastructure, and a lot of the technologies up for sale in the U.S. are simply too far ahead to use here. Those of you who've wired up your estates will know what I'm talking about. But we can import tools and ideas and even teachers from New Britain, and deliver a real push to the economy over here. Within thirty years you could be traveling to your estates by railway, your farmers could be producing three times as much food, and your ships could dominate the Atlantic trade routes."

Angbard rapped his gavel on the wooden block in front of him for attention. "The chair thanks Countess Helge," he said formally. "Are there any more questions from the floor?"

A new speaker stood up: a smooth-looking managerial type who smiled at Miriam in a friendly manner from the bench behind her grandmother. "I'd like to congratulate my cousin on her successful start-up," he began. "It's a remarkable achievement to come into a new world and set up a business, from scratch, with no background." *Oh shit,* Miriam thought uneasily. *Who is this guy, and when's he going to drop the hammer?* "And I agree completely with everything she says. But clearly, her efforts could be aided by an infusion of support and experience. If we accept her motion to transfer the new business to the Clan as a subsidiary enterprise, it can clearly benefit from sound management—"

"Which it already has," Miriam snapped, finally getting his drift. "If you would like to discuss employment opportunities—" *and a pound of flesh in return for keeping out of my way, you carpetbagger* "—that's all very well— but this is not the time and place for it. We have an immediate problem, which is relations with the sixth family. I'll repeat my proposal; that the new business venture be recognized as a Clan business, that membership in it be open to the Clan, and that handling the lost family be considered the responsibility of this business. Can we put this to a vote?"

Oliver Hjorth made to interrupt, but Angbard caught his hand and whispered something in his ear. His eyes narrowed and he shut up.

"I don't see why we can't settle it now," muttered Julius. "Show of hands! Ayes! Count them, damn your eyes. Nays!" He brought his own hammer down briskly. "The Ayes have it," he announced. He turned to Miriam. "It's yours."

Is that it? Miriam wondered dumbly, feeling as if something vast and elusive had passed her by in an eyeblink while her attention was elsewhere.

"Next motion," said Angbard. "Some of you have been misinformed that I announced that I was designating Helge as my heir. I wish to clarify the issue: I did not do so. However, I *do* intend to change my designated successor—to Patricia Thorold-Hjorth, my half-sister. Can anyone dispute my right to do so?" He looked around the room furiously. "No?" He nudged Julius. "See it minuted so."

Miriam felt as if a great weight had lifted from her shoulders—but not for long. "A new motion," said Oliver Hjorth. He frowned at Miriam. "The behavior of this long-lost niece gives me some cause for concern," he began. "I am aware that she has been raised in strange and barbarous lands, and allowances must be made; but I fear she may do herself an injury if allowed to wander around at random. As her recent history of narrow scrapes shows, she's clearly accident-prone and erratic. I therefore move that she be declared incompetent to sit as a member of the Clan, and that a suitable guardian be appointed—Baroness Hildegarde—"

"Objection!" Miriam turned to see Olga standing up. "Baron Hjorth, through negligence, failed to see to the subject's security during her residence here, notionally under his protection. He is not fit to make determinations bearing on her safety."

Oliver rounded on her in fury. "You little minx! I'll have you thrown out on the street for—"

Bang! The gavel again. "Objection sustained," Julius quavered.

Oliver glared at him. "Your time will come," he growled, and subsided into grim silence.

"I am an adult," Miriam said quietly. "I am divorced, I have created and managed a Clan subsidiary, and I am *not* prepared to surrender responsibility for my own security." She looked around the hall. "If you try to railroad me out of the New London operation, you'll find some nasty surprises in the title deeds." She stared at Oliver: "or you can sit back and wait for the profits to roll in. It's your choice."

"I withdraw my motion," Oliver growled quietly. Only his eyes told Miriam that he resented every word of it. There'd be a reckoning, they seemed to say.

"Check your gun."

"I don't need to."

"I said, check it. Listen. I told Poul to go for help. Think he'll have made it?"

"I don't see why not." Sullivan looked dubious, but he ejected the magazine and worked the slide on his gun, then reloaded and safed it.

"Matthias believes in belt and braces." For a moment, Roland looked ill. "I think he'll have left a surprise or two for us."

"So?" Sullivan nodded. "You ready?"

"Ready?" Roland winced, then flipped his locket open. "Yes. Come on. On my back—Sky Father, you're heavy! Now—"

Roland's vision dimmed and his head hammered like a drum. His knees began to give way and he fell forward, feet slipping on the damp floor. Sullivan rolled off him with a shout of dismay. "What's—"

Roland fell flat, whimpering slightly as one knee cracked hard on the concrete. Red, everything seemed to be *red* with bits of white embedded in it, like an explosion in an abattoir. He rolled over, sliding slightly, smelling something revolting and sweet as the noise of Sullivan being violently sick reached his ears.

The pounding headache subsided. Roland sat up, dismayed, staring at the wall behind him. It was chipped and battered, stained as if someone had thrown a tin of blackish paint at it. *The smell.* Roland leaned forward and squeezed his eyes shut. The blackness stayed with him, behind his eyelids. "Belt and braces."

Sullivan stopped heaving. The stench refused to clear. Roland opened his eyes again. The post room in the basement of Fort Lofstrom had been painted with blood and bits of flesh and bone, as if a live pig or sheep had been fed through a wood chipper. There were small gobbets of stuff everywhere. On his hands, sticking to his trousers where he'd fallen down. He pulled a hunk of something red with hairs sprouting from it off the back of his hand. The furniture was shredded, and the door hung from its hinges as if an angry bull had kicked it.

"Belt and braces," Roland repeated hoarsely. "Shit."

Sullivan straightened up. "You sent Poul into this," he said flatly. He wiped his mouth with the back of one hand.

"Shit." Roland shook his head. A pair of legs, still wearing trousers, still attached at the hips, had rolled under the big oak table in the middle of the room. A horrified sense of re-alization settled over him. "Why hasn't someone—"

"Because they are all fucking *dead*," Sullivan hissed, moving to the side of the door and bringing his gun up. "Shut up!"

Silence. The stink of blocked sewers and slaughterhouse blood and recent vomit filled Roland's nostrils. His skull pounded, bright diamond-flashes of light flickering in his left eye as the edges of his visual field threatened to col-lapse. He'd walked too soon after taking the beta blocker, and now he was going to pay the price. "Matthias planted a claymore mine on a wire at least once before," he said qui-etly. "Well, someone did—and my guess is Matthias. Sloppy work, using the same trick over. Think there'll be another one, or will he have used something else?"

"Shut *up*." Sullivan darted around the corner and stopped, his back visible: Roland cringed, but there was no explosion. "Yeah. Looks like it was an M18A1, we keep about a dozen in the armory. This here's the clacker. Bastard."

"See any more?" Roland shuffled forward slowly, still woozy and in pain from the too-hasty transfer.

"No, but—wait." Sullivan came back into the devastated post room and looked around twitchily, ignoring Roland.

"What are you after?"

"Some kind of pole. Lightweight. And a flashlight."

"Let me." Roland shambled over to the curtain-covered sigil and yanked hard on the curtain. The curtain rail bent and he grabbed it, pulled it away from the wall. "Will this do?" he asked, carefully not looking at the knotwork design on the wall behind it.

"Yeah." Sullivan took the rod and went back out into the corridor, advancing like an arthritic sloth. "Fuck me, that was bad."

A thought struck Roland. "Are there any explosives in the armory, apart from the mines? And detonators?"

"Are you kidding?" Sullivan barked something that in bet-

ter times might have been a laugh. "About a hundred kilos of
C4, for starters! And gunpowder. Shitloads of it. Some of his
farms, they've been, well, productive. Matthias took a serious interest in blowing things up, you know?"

"Gunpowder." Roland digested the unpleasant possibili-
ties this news opened up. "The fort should be locked down.
Where *is* everybody?"

"Like I said, dead or gone." Sullivan looked around at
him. "What are you going to—"

Roland pushed past him. "Follow me."

"Hey wait! There might be mines—"

"There won't be." Roland dashed down the corridor.
There was a servant's staircase at the end. He took the steps
two at a time, until he was gasping for breath. "He dismissed
the help. Good of him." The staircase surfaced in the
scullery, and the door was shut. "If I'm right, he's put the
whole damn fort on a time fuse. It could blow any minute."

"A bomb? There could be more than one, couldn't there?"

Roland opened the door half an inch, running a finger up
and down the crack to make sure there were no wires. "It's
clear."

"If you do that too fast—"

"Come on!" Through the scullery and up another short
flight of steps, round a corner, then into the main ground-floor
hallway. The fort was eerily empty, cold and desolate. Roland
didn't bother with the main door, but instead opened an
arched window beside it and scrambled through. "Stables!"

Matthias might have sent the servants away, but he sure as
hell hadn't thought about the livestock. Sullivan and Roland
saddled up a pair of mares, and the guard worked one of the
big gates open while Roland waited, clutching a blanket
around his shoulders. "You go get help," Sullivan panted up
at Roland. "I'll go see if the armory is wired. I might be able
to stop it."

"But you'll—"

"Shut the fuck up and listen for once! If you get help,
you'll need a safe post room to walk through, won't you?
I'm not doing this for you, I'm doing it for the others. Go get

the gods-damned Clan and get back here as fast as you can. I'll see it's safe for you."

Roland paused for a moment. "Take my keys," he said, and tossed them to the guard. "They're a master set—only place they won't get you into is the old man's office." Sullivan took the keys, then watched until Roland disappeared around the first bend in the road before he turned and headed back into the compound thoughtfully. He hadn't expected it to be this easy: He hadn't even had to hint about the place being booby-trapped. Now all he needed was time to complete the boss's business, and a lift home, then he could claim his reward.

The meeting was winding down in a haze of fatigue, recriminatory posturing, and motions to hear trivial complaints. Miriam slumped back in her seat tiredly. *Please, let this be over,* she thought, watching Iris from the other side of the room. If she was aching and bored, her mother must be feeling it ten times worse.

Baron Horst of Lorsburg had the floor, and was using it for all it was worth. "While the provisions of article eighteen of the constitution are still valid, I'd like to raise a concern about paragraph six," he droned, in the emolient tones of a lay preacher trying to get across the good message without boring his flock into catatonia in the process. "The issue of voting partners failing to attend to bills of—"

He was interrupted by a tremendous banging on the outer door. "What's that?" demanded Julius the ancient. "Sergeant! Have silence outside the room!"

The sergeant-at-arms marched over to the door, yanked it open, prepared to berate whoever was outside—but instead took a step back.

Roland lurched into the room. He was dressed for the road in a battered gray coat and a hat pulled down over his face: His expression was deathly. Miriam had another surprise coming: Brill was right behind him. "Permission to approach the Dean of Security?" he rasped.

"Approach," Angbard called. "And explain yourself. Assuming the news is fit for public hearing."

Roland glanced round the room. "Don't see why not." He passed Miriam without any indication that he'd seen her. "Big problem," he announced tersely, and Miriam swallowed her anger as she realized he was exhausted and out of breath, walking painfully, as if his clothes chafed.

"We've been betrayed. Fort Lofstrom is cut off, here *and* on the other side. What's worse is, they've got the February shipment from Panama sitting in Boston along with the post, and someone has told the Feds—there's a DEA stakeout in progress." He nodded at Angbard. "Looks like our traitor has identified himself. Bad news is, he got away and he's decided to take down the entire Massachusetts end. I only just got out by the skin of my teeth. We've got nine outer family members trapped on the other side with a SWAT team on their doorstep. To make matters worse, there are booby traps in Fort Lofstrom—at least one bomb. We lost Poul, Poul of Hjalmar. He walked into a claymore mine."

"Order! Order!" Angbard leaned down and stared at Roland. "Let's get this straight. Fort Lofstrom on this side has been barred to us. On the other side, its doppelgänger is under siege. There is a huge consignment sitting over there, and family members who lack the talent to extricate themselves. Is that broadly correct?"

"Yeah." Roland slumped against the table. "I worldwalked into the Fort. Blood all over the walls of the post room. Sullivan got me a horse and, and I rode over to a place Miriam told me about. Used the spare locket she gave me, the one she took from the enemy." The room was in uproar, half the Clan on their feet. "Lady Brilliana got me on a train in the new world, from Boston to New London. That's how I got here so fast. The shit hit the fan yesterday. By now, we're either looking at a pile of rubble on the other side with our people trapped under it and the FBI digging toward them, or something worse." He rubbed his head carefully, as if unsure whether it was still there. "I had to make three crossings in the past twelve hours."

"Security summit, clear the room!" called the sergeant-at-arms. "By your leave, sir," he told Julius apologetically.

"Can we get in from the far side? From New Britain?" asked Miriam.

Angbard stared at her. "You know more about that than we would, I think," he said. "Your opinion?"

"Hmm." Miriam thought for a moment. "You're sure it was Matthias?" she asked Roland.

Roland nodded wordlessly. "Sir?" He looked up at Angbard, tiredly.

"Yes," Angbard said darkly. "I've been keeping an eye on him. I've had my suspicions for a while now." He paused, looking as if he'd tasted something unpleasant. "Obviously I haven't been watching him closely enough. That's not a mistake I'm going to repeat." He glanced at Miriam. "Do you have anything to add?" he demanded.

"I don't know, but I don't believe in coincidences, and the way the hidden families kept going after me—" she glanced at Baron Hjorth, who stared back at her for a moment, then looked away. "I think it's clear who he was in the pay of." She shrugged. "It doesn't change my position. I think you should release Lin, send the kid home with a message offering a cease-fire. If they accept, it means your Keeper of the Secrets is cut off with no retreat and no friends. If they refuse, we're no worse off. It might make them think we're weak, but that can only be an advantage right now."

"I'll think about it," Angbard said coolly. "But right now it's not a priority. What would you suggest doing about Boston? If you have any ideas, that is."

"Uh." She paused. "Two or three crossings a day: If we do more we'll be in no condition for anything, and this needs to be fixed quick. I think we'll have to cross over to New London, won't we? If Olga and I and a bunch of others go, it'll take us a bit longer to get to Boston by steam train, but from there it's one hop into Fort Lofstrom by the back door. Faster than going by stagecoach, anyway. We'll have to carry some extras, who'll need to go over into the basement under siege and pull in our people before the FBI and DEA dig through to them. Think that would work?"

"I think it's our only chance." Roland looked worried. He seemed to be avoiding eye contact with her.

"Do it," said Iris, unexpectedly. "It's your future." She met Miriam's gaze. "I'll be alright."

"I know *you* will." Miriam walked toward her. "Please be here when I get back," she said. "We've got a lot of talking to do."

Brill cleared her throat. "I'm coming," she said calmly.

"You can't—oh." Miriam turned back to Angbard. "She can come."

"She'll have to. How many copies of the lost family's sign have you got?"

"More than you thought, bro," Iris butted in. She reached into a pocket and pulled out a battered-looking locket. "I took this off the one who killed my husband and maid and tried to cut your throat," she told Miriam. She grinned, humorlessly. "It never occurred to me to look inside it until you tipped me off. Not that I'm in any condition to use it."

"Ah. Then we've got—" Miriam did a quick stock-take. Hers, Brill's, Olga's, the one she'd given Roland, now this one. Plus the smudged and fading temporary tattoos she and Olga wore. "Only five reliable ones. Any more?"

Iris snorted. "Here." She pulled out a bunch of glossy photographs. "What the hell did you think Polaroid cameras were invented for?" Miriam gaped. "Close your mouth, kid, you'll catch a fly," Iris added.

"Get some muscle," Miriam told Roland. "Ones who can world-walk with us. We'll need guns and medicine. And clothing that can pass at a distance in New London or on the train—" She paused. "And a plan of the Fort Lofstrom doppelgänger, and a compass and map of the area. We can pick one up in New London and find where its doppelganger location is, and then someone to get us in—" another pause. "Why are you all looking at me like that?" she asked.

*   *   *

Another day, another first-class compartment—this one crammed with seven bodies, plus another seven in the compartment behind them—with the window open to let the heat out. "How conspicuous are we going to be?" asked the guy with the toothbrush moustache.

"Just as long as you don't stop, Morgan," said Miriam. "Your suit's all wrong, your coat isn't a fashion item, and—hell, your hat isn't right either. They'll probably take you for a foreigner." The train clattered over points as it began to slow.

"She's not kidding," said Brill. "It's not like Boston at all, under the surface."

"Be over soon," said Roland, staring out the window at the passing countryside. "It all looks like something out of a history book—"

"May you live in interesting times," muttered Olga, raising a startled glance from Brill.

"Miriam's been corrupting you."

"You say that like it's a bad thing."

"Ladies, ladies!" They turned and glared as one at Roland. "Is this our stop?" he asked plaintively. He looked decidedly off-color. Miriam decided to forgive him—her own headache wasn't getting any better, and four trips in thirty-six hours was more than anyone should ever have to make, even with beta blockers and pain killers.

"Not yet." Miriam refolded the map she'd bought at the station near where Niejwein would be in this world.

"Let me see that." Ivor, short and squat, leaned over. "Ah." A stubby finger followed the line into town. "This is Cambridgeport, in Cambridge. The Fort was built on a bluff overlooking the river almost exactly here. That's—"

"Blackshaft. A rookery," said Miriam. "Next to Holmes Alley." She bit her knuckle. "What happens if you try to worldwalk somewhere where you'd come out underground?"

"You get a headache." Roland looked at her curiously. "Why?"

"Nothing," she said, watching him sidelong.

Brill caught her eye. "Nothing." She snorted. "It's that revolutionary friend of yours, isn't it?"

"Well." Miriam sighed. "I suppose so."

"What's this?" asked Ivor.

"Miriam's got dodgy friends," said Olga. "Why is it that we only seem to do business with *criminals*?"

"I don't think he's a criminal; the law disagrees with me, but the law is an ass," said Miriam. "Anyway, he's got access to cellars. Lots of cellars and backyards running into the rookery. I think we can go down there, then try to cross over. If we can't, we can't. If we succeed we'll be somewhere in the basement levels. How'd that work out?"

"Angbard gave me some of his keys." Roland patted his pocket. "We can give it a try. The only thing worrying me is the time it's taking."

Liar, thought Miriam, watching him in side-profile. *You and me, when this is over, we're going to need to clear the air between us.* She focused on the line of his jaw and for some reason her heart tried to skip a beat. *See if we can catch some quality time together with nobody trying to kill me or blackmail you.* For a moment she felt a deep stab of longing. *We've got a lot to talk about. Haven't we?* But not right now, in the middle of a compartment full of Clan couriers, serious-faced and wound up for action.

The train slowed, slid into a suburban station, and paused. Then it was off again, for its final destination—the royal station, five minutes down the line. "Go tell the others, we want the next stop," said Miriam. "Remember, follow my lead and try not to say anything. It's not far, but we look like a mob, and a weird one at that. If we hang around we'll pick up unwanted attention."

Olga raised an eyebrow. "If you say so."

"I do." The train hissed and shuddered as it lurched toward the platform. "Hats on and spirits up. This shouldn't take long."

The walk to the pawnbroker's shop seemed to take forever, a frightening eternity of hanging on Roland's arm—steering discreetly and trying to look carefree, while keeping an eye open for the others—but Miriam made it, somehow. "This is it?" he asked dubiously.

"Yeah. Remember he's a friend." Miriam opened the shop door, shoved him gently between the shoulder blades, turned to catch Morgan and Brill's eyes, then went inside.

"Hello? Can I help—"

"I'm sure you can." Miriam smiled sweetly at the man behind the counter—a stranger she'd never seen before in her life. "Is Inspector Smith here?"

"No." He straightened up. "But I can get him if you want."

"That won't be necessary." Miriam drew her pistol. "Lie down. Hands behind your back." She stepped forward. "Come on, tie him!" she snapped at Roland.

"If you say so." The doorbell jangled and he glanced up at her as Olga and the two other guards entered the shop, followed rapidly by Brill and Ivor, and then the rest of the group. With fourteen youngish Clan members inside, it was uncomfortably packed. "What are you going to do with him?" asked Olga.

"Take him with us, stash him in Fort Lofstrom. Got a better idea?"

"You're making a big mistake," the man on the floor said quietly.

"You're a constable," said Miriam. "Aren't you? Where's Burgeson?" He didn't say anything. "Right," she said grimly, lifting the counter and walking behind it. *I hope he's alright,* she thought distantly. *Another spell in His Majesty's concentration camps will kill him, for sure.* "You two, carry this guy along. The rest of you, follow me."

They trooped down the steep wooden steps in the back of the shop, along an alley hemmed in with pigeonholes filled with sad relics, individually tagged and dated with their owners' hopes and fears. Miriam looked round. "This will do," she said. "I'm going to try the crossing. If I succeed and there's trouble, I'll come right back. If I'm not back in five minutes, the rest of you come over. Roland, carry Brill. You, carry Olga. Brill, Olga, you carry us over to the far side, to world two: I don't want anybody making two successive crossings without a rest between. Be ready for trouble."

She took her coat off. Beneath it she wore her hiking gear

and a bulky bulletproof vest from the Clan's Niejwein armory. It looked out of place here, but might be a lifesaver on the other side. She barely noticed the captive policeman's eyes go wide as he watched the cellar full of strangers strip down to combat fatigues and body armor. "Are you sure about this?" asked Roland as she picked up her shoulder bag again.

"I'm sure." Miriam grimaced. "Time to go."

"You'll never get away with this," the secret policeman mumbled as she pulled out her locket and, taking a deep breath, focused on it.

Everything went black and a spike of pain seemed to split her skull. *Buried alive!* she thought, appalled—then reached out a hand in front of her. *No, just in the dark.* She took another breath, smelling mildew, and swallowed back bile that threatened to climb her throat. Her heart pounded. *The flashlight—*

She fumbled for a moment over the compact LED flashlight, then managed to get enough light to see by. She was in a cellar alright, a dusty and ancient wine store with bottle racks to either side. "Phew," she said aloud. She took a second or two to let her racing heart slow down toward normal, then marched toward the door at the end of the tunnel.

The light switches worked, and the cellar flooded with illumination—bright after a minute of flashlight. "Do I wait?" she asked herself. "Like hell. We've got people to rescue." She turned the handle and cautiously entered the passage that led to the servants' stairs.

Her head ached furiously. It had been aching for days now, it seemed, and she felt worse than sick. If she stood up fast, or moved suddenly, her vision went dark. *I can't do this again,* she thought to herself, leaning against the corridor wall. *It'll kill me.*

Two hops in a day—one from Niejwein to New London, then another into Fort Lofstrom's dingy cellars. If she made a return trip to Boston now, she was sure she'd pop an artery. *Cerebral hemorrhage, what a way to go.* Half of the others were piggybacking, staying fresh as long as possible.

For her sins she'd carried Brill through on the first trip. Now she was paying the price in aching muscles and a borderline migraine.

"Matthias," she said aloud, with a flash of rage. *Bastard thought he could use me, did he?* Well, she'd see about that. Once the crisis was under control, and once she'd repossessed Paulie's stolen CD-ROM. She was certain Matthias had it, and there were only two things to do with it that made sense. Send it to the FBI, or leave it on Angbard's desk, along with the photos of her and Roland—a potentially lethal embarrassment if Angbard interpreted it as a plot by the lovers to elope and blackmail the Clan into silence. Miriam's money was on the latter. Once the immediate business was sorted, she fully intended to give Paulie a discreet request and a bunch of cash: enough to hire some private detectives. There were ways and means of finding people who didn't want to be found, when your resources and patience were unlimited, and she was willing to bet that a spider like Matthias wouldn't be able to camouflage himself as well as he thought once he left the center of his web. She'd spend whatever it took to find him, and then he'd be sorry.

After a couple of minutes she sighed, then pushed herself upright. She dry-swallowed a painkiller, which stuck uncomfortably in her throat. She was light-headed, but not too light-headed to find her way up to the basement level. Passing the scullery, she ducked inside to grab a glass of water to help the pill go down. Something caught her eye: The door to the cold store lay ajar. She looked inside.

"Oh shit. Oh shit." She breathed fast as she leaned over the top of the pile—three, maybe four corpses sprawling and stiff, not yet livid—and saw the cruel edges of bullet wounds. "Shit." She pushed herself upright and looked to the entrance. "Cameras—"

Matthias has a little helper, she realized. *How many people did he kill?* A great house like this, you couldn't send *all* of the servants away—but murdering the skeleton staff bespoke a degree of extreme ruthlessness. Angbard hadn't been suspicious enough of his own deputy: He'd let Matthias

pick and choose staff assignments. Now it looked like she
was going to be stuck paying the price.

"Matthias always has a backup plan," she muttered to herself. "If I was a sick spider sitting at the center of a web,
waiting to sting my employer, what would I do?"

She opened the door cautiously. "Roland was afraid of
bombs—" She stopped. *Where?* "The armory is where you
store explosives. It's built to contain a blast. But if Matthias
had an *accomplice* the explosive might be human—"

She panted, taking in shallow breaths. *Stop that. Matthias
blackmailed people. How many? And what could he make
them do—wait for the Clan rescue expedition to show up,
then bring the house down on them?*

The pantry was empty, a door standing ajar on the
kitchen and servants' stairwell at the end of the hallway.
Miriam hit the stairs. It corkscrewed upstairs dizzyingly,
halls branching off it toward each wing of the family accommodation. She climbed it carefully, revolver in hand,
cautiously scanning the steps ahead for signs of a tripwire.
Hoping that the dead servants meant that there'd be no eyes
left to watch the video screens. *Second floor, east wing,
through the security doors on the left,* she repeated to herself, hoping that the surveillance, if it existed at all, would
prove to be habit-blind.

The east wing corridor was as silent as a crypt, as empty
as the passages of a high-class hotel in the small hours of the
morning while the guests sleep. Any guests here were liable
to be dead in their beds. Miriam came out of the servant's
stairwell and darted down the side of the corridor, crouching
instinctively. She paused at the solid wooden doors at one
side of the passage and swiped the card-key she'd borrowed
from Roland through the scanner at one side. When she
heard the latch click, she pushed one door open with a toe
and stepped through. *This is the security zone?* It looked like
more rooms, opening off a short corridor—offices, maybe,
and Angbard's outer office door right ahead.

She paused before the door. Her heart was pounding. *You.*
She looked at it. Someone was inside. Whoever killed the ser-

vants. A ticking human bomb. Growing anger made her feel dizzy. She carefully moved to one side and raised her gun.

"I really wouldn't do that," said a sad voice right behind her left ear. "Put the gun down and turn around *slowly*."

She froze, then dropped the pistol and turned around. "Why?" she asked.

A nondescript man leaned against the wall behind her. He was unshaven, and although he was wearing a suit—standard for a courier—his tie was loose. He looked tired, but also content. "It's about time," he said.

His gun, Miriam realized. It was pointed at her stomach. She couldn't identify it. Bizarrely complex, it sprouted handles and magazines and telescopic sights seemingly at random. It looked like a movie prop, but something in his manner said he had complete confidence in it. The sights glowed red, a dot tracking across her chest.

"It's about time," she echoed. "What the hell is that supposed to mean?"

The gunman grinned humorlessly. "The boss told me a lot about you. You're the new countess, aren't you? He's got tapes, you know. *And* a disk."

She moved toward him, froze as the gun came up to point at her head. "You were responsible for what's in the cellar—"

"No, actually." He shook his head. "Not me. He's . . . Matthias likes to hunt. He stalks wild animals. Stalks his enemies, too, looking for a weak point to bring them down." He looked worried for a moment, then he grinned. "He showed me the tapes he took of you. Looking for a weak spot."

Her vision hazed over for a moment, turning black with a mixture of rage and the worst headache she'd ever experienced. "What do you fucking *want*?" she demanded.

"Simple. I'm the rear guard. Your arrival means the Clan rescue party is on its way, doesn't it?" She didn't say anything, but his grin widened just the same. "Knew it. You're my ride out of here, y'know? Little pony. We'll just be leaving by the back steps, then blow the house down. And I'll ride out on you. There's a meeting spot, ready and surveyed and waiting for me. *Nice* pony."

"Listen," she said, trying to focus through her blinding headache, "have you actually *done* anything for Matthias? Killed anyone? Planted any bombs?"

The gunman stopped smiling. "Shut the fuck up. *Now*," he snarled. *"Kneel! Move!"*

Miriam knelt slowly. Everything seemed to be happening in slow motion. Her head pounded and her stomach, even though it was empty, seemed about to make a bid for freedom through her mouth. "Whatever he paid you—" she began.

" 'S'not money. Fucking Clan bitch. It's who we *are*. Got it, yet?"

"You and Matthias?"

"That's right." He kicked the gun away. "Keep your hands on the floor. Lean forward. *Slowly* put your wrists together in front. I'll kill you if you fuck up." He carefully kept the gun on her as he pulled a looped cable tie out of a back pocket. "*Nice* pony, we're going to go riding together. Over to Boston, and then maybe out west to the ranch to see some of my friends. You won't like it there, though."

"Shoot me and you won't get away alive," she heard someone say in the distance, through a throbbing cloud bank of darkness.

"What the fuck." He yanked the cable tie tight around her wrists. "You think I give a shit about that, you bitch? Live fast, die young." He grabbed her hair and pulled, and she screamed. "Leave a pretty corpse."

Miriam tried to stand: Her legs had turned to jelly somewhere along the line. *This is crazy,* she thought vaguely. *Can't let him blow up the fort with everyone under it, or on the other side—* She leaned drunkenly, almost falling over.

"Stand, bitch!" Someone was slapping someone else's face. Suddenly there was a hand under her armpit. "Fuck, what's wrong with you?"

"Three jumps, two hours," she slurred drunkenly.

"Crap." A door opened and he shoved her forwards. "Fucking get over it or I'll start on your fingernails. You think your head hurts, you don't know shit."

"What do you *want*?" she mumbled.

"Freedom." He pushed her toward the low leather-topped sofa opposite Matthias's desk. "Freedom to travel. Freedom to live away from this fucking pesthole. A million bucks and the wind in my hair. The boss looks after his own. Drop the fort and deliver you and I've got it made. Loads of money."

He pushed her down onto the sofa. "Now you and me are going to sit tight until your friends are over on the other side." He waved at the CCTV monitor on Matthias's workstation. "Then I set a timer and we leave by the back door." He cleared his throat. "Meantime, there's something I've been wondering. Do you give good head?" he inquired, leaning over her.

Something flickered at the edge of Miriam's vision. She focused past his shoulder, saw the door open and Roland standing there with a leveled pistol. The gunman turned, and something made a noise like a sewing machine, awfully loudly. Hot metal rain, cartridge cases falling. A scream. Miriam kicked out, catching him on one leg. Then the back of his head vanished in a red mist, and he collapsed on top of her.

"Oh Miriam, you really are no good at this!" trilled Olga, "but thank you for drawing his attention! That creep, he makes me *so* angry . . ." Then her voice changed: "Dear Lightning Child! What's happened to Roland?"

"I—" Miriam tried to sit up, but something was pinning her down. Everything was gray. "Where is he?"

"Oh dear." Olga knelt in the doorway, beside something. Someone. "Are you wounded?" she asked urgently, standing up and coming toward Miriam. "It was his idea to follow you—"

Miriam finally sat up, shoving the deadweight aside. Strangely, her stomach wasn't rebelling. "Get. Others. Go across and finish off. I'll look after him." Somehow she found herself on the other side of the room, cradling Roland. "He'll be alright."

"But he's—"

She blinked, and forced herself to focus as Olga leaned over her, face white. "He'll be alright in a minute," Miriam heard herself explain. "Scalp wounds are always bloody, aren't they?" Somewhere a door opened and she heard Olga explaining something to someone in urgent tones, something about shock. "Aren't they?" she asked, still confused but frightened by Olga's tone. She tried to rub her sore eyes, rendered clumsy by her tied hands, but they were covered in blood. Then Brill rolled up her sleeve and slid a needle into her arm.

"What a mess," Brill told someone else, before the blessed darkness stifled her screams.

EPILOGUE

F ourteen of them, you say?" said Inspector Smith, raising an eyebrow.

"Yessir. Nine coves and five queans all went into the shop mob-handed, like."

"Fourteen." The other eyebrow rose to join it. "Jobson never reported back."

"There's no sign of blood, sir, or even a struggle," the inspector's visitor said apologetically. "And they wasn't in the premises when me and my squad went in, ten minutes later. Weren't in the basement, neither. Nor any of the tunnels we've explored."

"Fourteen," Smith said with a tone of increasing disbelief.

"Sir, we took fingerprints." The visitor sounded annoyed. "None of them except the Fletcher woman are in our files, and her prints were old. But we had a spook watching as they went in. The count is reliable: fourteen in and none of them came out again! It's a very rum do, I'll agree, but unless you have reason to suspect that a crime has been committed—"

"I have, dammit! Where's Jobson?" Smith stood up, visibly annoyed. "Are you telling me that one of my agents has disappeared and the people responsible aren't to be found? Because if so, that sounds like a pretty bad sign to me, too."

"I'll stand by it, sir." The regular thief-taker stood firm. "We took the entire block apart, brick by brick. *You* had the pawnbroker in custody at the time, need I remind you? And his lawyer muttering about habeas corpus all the while. There is, I repeat, no evidence of anything—except fourteen disappearing persons unknown, and a constable of the Defense Bureau who's nowhere to be seen. Which is not entirely unprecedented, I hope you'll concede."

"Bah!" The inspector snorted. "Did you take the cellar walls apart?" His eye gleamed, as if he expected to hear word of an anarchist cell crouched beneath every block.

"We used Mister Moore's new sound-echo apparatus." The thief-taker stood up. "There are no hollow chambers, sir. You can have my hat and my badge if you uncover any, as I stand by my word."

"Bah. *Get out*." Smith glared at the superintendent of thief-takers. "I have a call to make." He waited for the door to bang shut behind the other man before he added, "Sir Roderick is going to be very annoyed. But I'll make sure that damned woman gets her comeuppance soon enough . . ."

Weeks passed: days of pain, days of loss, days of mourning. Finally, an evening clear of snow beneath the winter skies over New London found Miriam standing in the foyer of the Brighton Hotel, dressed to the nines in black, smiling at the guests with a sweet solicitude she hardly felt. "*Hello,* Lord Macy! And *Hello* to you too, Mrs. Macy! How have you been? Well, I trust?" The line seemed to stretch around the block, although the red carpet stopped at the curb—many of the visitors were making a point of showing up in new Otto cars, the ones the Durant Motor Company was fitting with the new safety brakes.

"Hello, my dear lady! You're looking fine."

Her smile relaxed a bit, losing its grim determination. "I think I am, indeed," she admitted. "And yourself? Is this to your satisfaction?"

"I think—" Sir Durant raised one eyebrow—"it will do, yes." He grinned, faintly amused. "It's your party: Best enjoy it as much as you can. Or are you going to stand by your widowhood forever and a day?" He tipped his hat to her and ambled inside, to the dining room that Miriam's money had taken over for a night of glittering celebration, and she managed to keep on smiling, holding the line against desolation and guilt. The party was indeed glittering, packed with the high and the mighty of the New London motor trade, and their wives and sons and daughters, and half the board of trade to boot.

Miriam sighed quietly as the carpet emptied and the doors stopped revolving for a moment. "Busy, isn't it?" Brill remarked cheerfully behind her.

"I'll say." Miriam turned to face her. "You're looking beautiful tonight," she mimicked, and pulled a face. "Anyone would think I was selling them pin-up calendars, not brake shoes."

Brill grinned at her cheekily. "Oh, I don't know," she began. "If you put out a calendar with yourself on it, that might improve sales—" She held out a full glass of something sparkling.

"Here, give me that. It's not suitable for young ladies!" Miriam took it and raised it. "To . . . something or other." Her daringly bare shoulders slumped tiredly. "Success."

Brill raised the other glass: "Success. Hey, this isn't bad." She took a big mouthful, then wiped her lips with the back of one lace glove. "Do you think they're enjoying it?"

"They will." Miriam looked at the dining room doors, then back at the front: It was almost time for the meal to begin. "Or else," she added bitterly.

"You haven't seen Lady Olga yet?" asked Brill.

"No—" Miriam caught her eye. "Why?"

"Oh, nothing. It was meant to be her surprise, that's all. I shan't give it away." Brill did her best impression of an innocent at large, nose in the air and glass in hand. "Success," she muttered. "*Most* women would be after true love or a rich husband, but this one wants to own skyscrapers."

"True love and a helmet will stop bullets," Miriam said bitterly.

"You weren't to know." Brill looked at her askance. "Was it *really* true love?"

"How the fuck should I know?" Miriam drained her glass in one gulp, so that she wouldn't have to explain. *Was it?* she wondered, confused. *Damn it, he should be here, now. We had so much to talk about.*

"Owning skyscrapers makes the need for a rich husband irrelevant," Brill pointed out. "And anyway, you're still young. True love is bound to—" She stopped. Another car was pulling up outside, and a small crowd of partygoers was climbing out.

"Here, take this," Miriam said, passing her her empty glass. "Got to be the hostess again."

"That's okay, don't mind me." Brill took a step back as Miriam straightened her back and tried to bend her face into a welcoming mask once more. *Only another five minutes.*

The door opened. "Olga!" she exclaimed.

"My dear!" Olga swept forward and insisted on planting a kiss on her cheek. "I brought you a present!"

"Huh?" Miriam looked past her. The door was still revolving—slowly, for the occupant seemed to be having some trouble. Finally he shuffled out and slowly advanced. "Uncle, you aren't supposed to be out—"

"Miriam." He stopped in front of her, looking faintly amused. His costume was, as ever, impeccable, even though he must have found it passing strange. "I thought I should come and see the new business that the prodigal has built for us." His smile slipped. "And to apologize for nursing that viper. I understand he cost you more than money can ever repay."

"Oh hell." She frowned at him. *Easy for you to be gracious, now Roland's dead and you don't have to worry about your precious braids anymore*—But somehow the harsh thought didn't have any fire behind them. She crossed the six feet between them. "Uncle." He did his best to return the hug, although he winced somewhat. She leaned her chin on his shoulder. "I'm pleased to see you. I think."

"It was all her idea," he said, jerking his chin over his shoulder.

"Her? Why—mother!"

The revolving door ejected another late guest who seemed to be walking with a slight limp. Bundled in a voluminous gown and leaning heavily on a cane, she glowered truculently about the hall for a moment, then spotted Miriam and beamed.

"Hello, dear! You're looking every inch the princess tonight."

"Hah." Miriam walked forward and kissed her mother on the forehead. "Wait till you meet my disreputable friends."

"I wouldn't miss it for the world, dear. We've got a family tradition to uphold, haven't we?"

"Indeed." A thought struck Miriam. "Where are you staying tonight? I've got a suite here. Olga, if you don't mind—"

"I *do* mind," said Olga. "If you want me to give up the guest room, I demand the imperial suite here!"

"But you know that's booked—" Miriam began, then the doors revolved again and her eyes widened. "What are *you* doing here?"

"Is that any way to greet a friend?" Paulette grinned widely as she looked around. "Hey, plush! I thought this was going to be all horse manure and steam engines!"

"This is Brill's fault," Olga confided. "When she heard about the party, she began plotting—"

"Yeah!" Paulie agreed enthusiastically. "We couldn't let you keep the limelight all to yourself. Say, is that really a gaslight chandelier? Isn't that amazing?"

"Children, you'll be late for dinner!" Brill interrupted. "Take it up some other time, huh? I don't want to miss Sir

Brakepad's speech. Isn't he cute?" She gently moved them in the direction of the dining room, steering Angbard discreetly. Miriam followed behind, arm in arm with her mother, and for the first time in months she dared to hope that the worst was behind her.

A preview of

THE
CLAN
CORPORATE

CHARLES STROSS

Now available in paperback
from Tom Doherty Associates

1. TIED DOWN

Nail lacquer, the woman called Helge reflected as she paused in the antechamber, always did two things to her: it reminded her of her mother, and it made her feel like a rebellious little girl. She examined the fingertips of her left hand, turning them this way and that in search of minute imperfections in the early afternoon sunlight slanting through the huge window behind her. There weren't any. The maidservant who had painted them for her had poor nails, cracked and brittle from hard work: her own, in contrast, were pearlescent and glossy, and about a quarter-inch longer than she was comfortable with. There seemed to be a lot of things that she was uncomfortable with these days. She sighed quietly and glanced at the door.

The door opened at that moment. Was it coincidence, or was she being watched? Liveried footmen inclined their heads as another spoke. "Milady, the duchess bids you enter. She is waiting in the Day Room."

Helge swept past them with a brief nod—more acknowledgement of their presence than most of her rank would bother with—and paused to glance back down the hallway as her servants (a lady in waiting, a court butler, and two hard-faced, impassive bodyguards) followed her. "Wait in the hall," she told the guards. "*You* can accompany me, but wait at the far end of the room," she told her attendant ingénue. Lady Kara nodded meekly. She'd been slow to learn that Helge bore an uncommon dislike for having her conversations eavesdropped on: there had been an unfortunate incident some weeks ago, and she had not yet recovered her self-esteem.

The hall was perhaps sixty feet long and wide enough for a royal entourage. The walls, panelled in imported oak, were occupied by window bays interspersed with oil paintings and a few more recent daguerreotypes of noble ancestors, the scoundrels and skeletons cluttering up the family tree. Uniformed servants waited beside each door. Helge paced across the rough marble tiles, her spine rigid and her shoulders set defensively. At the end of the hall an equerry wearing the polished half-armor and crimson breeches of his calling bowed, then pulled the tasselled bell-pull beside the double doors. "The Countess Helge voh Thorold d'Hjorth!"

The doors opened, ushering Countess Helge inside, leaving servants and guards to cool their heels at the threshold.

The day room was built to classical proportions—but built large, in every dimension. Four windows, each twelve feet high, dominated the south wall, overlooking the regimented lushness of the gardens that surrounded the palace. The ornate plasterwork of the ceiling must have occupied a master and his journeymen for a year. The scale of the architecture dwarfed the merely human furniture, so that the chaise longue the duchess reclined on, and the spindly rococo chair beside it, seemed like the discarded toy furniture of a baby giantess. The duchess herself looked improbably fragile: gray hair growing out in intricately coiffed coils, face powdered to the complexion of a china doll, her body lost in a court gown of black lace over burgundy velvet. But her eyes were bright and alert—and knowing.

Helge paused before the duchess. With a little moue of concentration she essayed a curtsey. "Your grace, I are— am—happy to see you," she said haltingly in hochsprache. "I—I—oh *damn*." The latter words slipped out in her native tongue. She straightened her knees and sighed. "Well? How am I doing?"

"Hmm." The duchess examined her minutely from head to foot, then nodded slightly. "You're getting better. Well enough to pass tonight. Have a seat." She gestured at the chair beside her.

Miriam sat down. "As long as nobody asks me to dance," she said ruefully. "I've got two left feet, it seems—" she plucked at her lap. "And as long as I don't end up being cornered by a drunken backwoods peer who thinks not being fluent in his language is a sign of an imbecile. And as long as I don't accidentally mistake some long-lost third cousin seven times removed for the hat check clerk and resurrect a two hundred year old blood feud. And as long as—"

"Dear," the duchess said quietly, "do please shut up."

The countess, who had grown up as Miriam but who everyone around her but the duchess habitually called Helge, stopped in mid-flow. "Yes, mother," she said meekly. Folding her hands in her lap she breathed out. Then she raised one eyebrow.

The duchess looked at her for almost a minute, then nodded minutely. "You'll pass," she said. "With the jewellery, of course. And the posh frock. As long as you don't let your mouth run away with you." Her cheek twitched. "As long as you remember to be Helge, not Miriam."

"I feel like I'm acting all the time!" Miriam protested.

"Of course you do." The duchess finally smiled. "Imposter syndrome goes with the territory." The smile faded. "And I didn't do you any favors in the long run by hiding you from all this." She gestured around the room. "It becomes harder to adapt, the older you get."

"Oh, I don't know." Miriam frowned momentarily. "I can deal with disguises and a new name and background, I can even cope with trying to learn a new language, it's the sense of permanence that's disconcerting. I grew up an only child, but *Helge* has all these—relatives—I didn't grow up with, and they're real. That's hard to cope with. And *you're* here, and part of it!" Her frown returned. "And now this evening's junket. If I thought I could avoid it, I'd be in my rooms having a stomach cramp all afternoon."

"That would be a Bad Idea." The duchess still had the habit of capitalizing her speech when she was waxing sarcastic, Miriam noted.

"Yes, I know that. I'm just—there are things I should be doing do that are more important than attending a royal garden party. It's all deeply tedious."

"With an attitude like that you'll go far." Her mother paused. "All the way to the scaffold if you don't watch your lip, at least in public. Do I need to explain how sensitive to social niceties your position here is? This is not America—"

"Yes, well, more's the pity." Miriam shrugged minutely.

"Well, we're stuck with the way things are," the duchess said sharply, then subsided slightly. "I'm sorry dear, I don't mean to snap. I'm just worried for you. The sooner you learn how to mind yourself without mortally offending anyone by accident the happier I'll be."

"Um." Miriam chewed on the idea for a while. *She's stressed*, she decided. *Is that all it is, or is there something more . . . ?* "Well, I'll *try*. But I came here to see how you are, not to have a moan on your shoulder. So how are you keeping?"

"Well, now that you ask—" Her mother smiled and waved vaguely at a table behind her chaise longue. Miriam followed her gesture: two aluminium crutches, starkly functional, lay atop a cloisonné stand next to a pill case. "The doctor says I'm to reduce the prednisone again next week. The Copaxone seems to be helping a lot, and that's just one injection a day. As long as nobody accidentally forgets to bring me next week's prescription I'll be fine."

"But surely nobody would—" Miriam's whole body quivered with indignation.

"—Really?" The duchess glanced back at her daughter,

her expression unreadable. "You seem to have forgotten what kind of a place this is. The meds aren't simply costly in dollars and cents: someone has to bring them across from the other world. And courier time is priceless. Nobody gives me a neatly itemized bill, but if I want to keep on receiving them I have to pay. And the first rule of business around here is, don't piss off the blackmailers."

Miriam's reluctant nod seemed to satisfy her, because she nodded: "Remember, a lady never unintentionally gives offense—especially to people she depends on to keep her alive. If you can hang onto just one rule to help you survive in the Clan, make it that one. But I'm losing the plot. How are *you* doing? Have there been any after-effects?"

"After-effects?" Miriam caught her hand at her chin and forced herself to stop. She flushed, pulse jerking with an adrenalin-surge of remembered fear and anger. "I—" She lowered her hand. "Oh, nothing *physical*," she said bitterly. "Nothing . . ."

"I've been thinking about him a lot lately, Miriam. He wouldn't have been good for you, you know."

"I know." The younger woman—youth being relative, she wouldn't be seeing thirty again—dropped her gaze. "The political entanglements made it a messy prospect at best," she said bitterly. "Even if you discounted his weaknesses." The duchess didn't reply. Eventually Miriam looked up, her eyes burning with emotions she'd experienced only since learning to be Helge. "I haven't forgiven him, you know."

"Forgiven *Roland*?" The duchess's tone sharpened.

"No. Your goddamn half-brother. He's meant to be in charge of security! But he—" her voice began to break.

"Yes, yes, I know. And do you think he has been sleeping well lately? I'm led to believe he's frantically busy right now. Losing Roland was the least of our problems, if you'll permit me to be blunt, and Angbard has a major crisis to deal with. Your affair with him can be ignored, if it comes to it, by the Council. It's not as if you're a teenage virgin to be despoiled, damaging some aristocratic alliance by losing your honor—and you'd better think about that some more in future, because honor is *the* currency in the circles you move in, a currency that once spent is very hard to regain—but the deeper damage to the Clan that Matthias inflicted—"

"Tell me about it," Miriam said bitterly. "As soon as I was back on my feet they told me I could only run courier assignments to and from a safe house. And I'm not allowed to go home!"

"Matthias knows you," her mother pointed out. "If he mentioned you to his new employers—"

"I understand." Miriam subsided in a sullen silence, arms crossed before her and back set defensively. After a moment she started tapping her toes.

"Stop that!" Moderating her tone, the duchess added: "if you do that in public it sends entirely the wrong message. Appearances are everything, you've *got* to learn that."

"Yes, mother."

After a couple of minutes, the duchess spoke. "You're not happy."

"No."

"And it's not just—him."

"Correct." Her hem twitched once more before Helge managed to control the urge to tap.

The duchess sighed. "Do I have to drag it out of you?"

"No, Iris."

"You shouldn't call me that here. Bad habits of thought and behavior, you know."

"Bad? Or just inappropriate? Liable to *send the wrong message*?"

The duchess chuckled. "I should know better than to argue with you, dear!" She looked serious. "The wrong message in a nutshell. *Miriam can't go home, Helge*. Not now, maybe not ever. Thanks to that scum-sucking rat-bastard defector the entire Clan network in Massachusetts is blown wide open and if you even *think* about going—"

"Yeah, yeah, I know, there'll be an FBI SWAT team staking out my back yard and I'll vanish into a supermax prison so fast my feet don't touch the ground. If I'm lucky," she added bitterly. "So everything's locked down like a code red

terrorist alert, the only way I'm allowed to go back to our
world is on a closely supervised courier run to an underground railway station buried so deep I don't even see daylight, if I want anything—even a box of tampons—I have to
requisition it and someone in the Security Directorate has to
fill out a risk assessment to see if it's safe to obtain, and,
and . . ." Her shoulders heaved with indignation.

"This is what it was like the whole time, during the civil
war," the duchess pointed out.

"So people keep telling me, as if I'm supposed to be
grateful! But it's not as if this is my *only* option. I've got another identity over in world three and—"

"Do they have tampons there?"

"Ah." Helge paused for a moment. "No, I don't think so,"
she said slowly. "But they've got cotton wool." She fumbled
for a moment, then pulled out a pen-sized voice recorder.
"Memo: business plans. Investigate early patent filings covering tampons and applicators. Also sterilization methods—
dry heat?" She clicked the recorder off and replaced it.
"Thanks." A lightning smile that was purely Miriam flashed
across her face and was gone. "I should be over there," she
added earnestly. "World three is my project. I set up the
company and I ought to be managing it."

"Firstly, our dear long-lost relatives are over there," the
duchess pointed out. "Truce or not, if they haven't got the
message yet, you could show your nose over there and get it
chopped off. And secondly."

"Ah, yes. Secondly."

"You know what I'm going to say," the duchess said quietly. "So please don't shoot the messenger."

"Okay." Helge turned her head to stare moodily out of the
nearest window. "You're going to tell me that the political
situation is messy. That if I go over there right now some of
the more jumpy first citizens of the Clan will get the idea
that I'm abandoning the sinking ship, aided and abetted by
my *delightful* grandmother's whispering campaign—"

"Leave the rudeness to me. She's my cross to bear."

"Yes, but." Helge stopped.

Her mother took a deep breath. "The Clan, for all its failings, is a very *democratic* organization. Democratic in the original sense of the word. If enough of the elite voters agree, they can depose the leadership, indict a member of the Clan for trial by a jury of their peers—anything. Which is why appearances, manners, and social standing are so important. Hypocrisy is the grease that lubricates the Clan's machinery." Her cheek twitched. "Oh yes. While I remember, love, if you are accused of anything never, *ever*, insist on your right to a trial by jury. Over here, that word does not mean what you think it means. Like 'secretary'. Pah, but I'm woolgathering! Anyway. My mother your grandmother has a constituency, Miri—Helge. Tarnation. Swear at me if I slip again, will you, dear? We need to break each other of this habit."

Helge nodded. "Yes, Iris."

The duchess reached over and swatted her lightly on the arm. "Patricia! Say my full name."

"Ah—" Helge met her gaze. "Alright. Your grace is the honorable duchess Patricia voh Hjorth d'Wu ab Thorold." With mild rebellion: "also known as Iris Beckstein, of 34 Coffin Street—"

"That's enough!" Her mother nodded sharply. "Put the rest behind you for the time being. Until—unless—we can ever go back, the memories can do nothing but hurt you. You've got to live in the present. And the present means living among the Clan and deporting yourself as a, a countess. Because if you don't do that, all the alternatives on offer are drastically worse. This isn't a rich world, like America. Most women only have one thing to trade: as a lady of the Clan you're lucky enough to have two, even three if you count the contents of your head. But if you throw away the money and the power that goes with being of the Clan, you'll rapidly find out just what's under the surface—if you survive long enough."

"But there's no limit to the amount of shit!" She burst out, then clapped a hand to her face as if to recall the unladylike expostulation.

"Don't chew your nails, dear," her mother said automatically.

It had started in mid-morning. Miriam (who still found it an effort of will to think of herself as Helge, outside of social situations where other people expected her to *be* Helge) was tired and irritable, dosed up on ibuprofen and propranolol to deal with the effects of a series of courier runs the day before when, wearing jeans and a lined waterproof jacket heavy enough to survive a north-east passage, she'd wheezed under the weight of a backpack and a walking frame. They'd had her ferrying fifty kilogram loads between a gloomy cellar of undressed stone and an equally gloomy sub-basement of an underground car park in Manhattan. There were armed guards in New York to protect her while she recovered from the vicious migraine that world-walking brought on, and servants and maids in the palace quarters back home to pamper her and feed her sweetmeats from a cold buffet and apply a cool compress for her head. But the whole objective of all this attention was to soften her up until she could be cozened into making another run. *Two* return trips in eighteen hours. Drugs or no drugs, it was brutal: without guards and flunkies and servants to prod her along she might have refused to do her duty.

She'd carried a hundred kilograms in each direction across the space between two worlds, a gap narrower than atoms and colder than light-years. Lightning Child only knew what had been in those packages. The Clan's mercantilist operations in the United States emphasized high-value, low-weight commodities. Like it or not, there was more money in smuggling contraband than works of art or intellectual property. It was a perpetual sore on Miriam's conscience, one that only stopped chafing when for a few hours she managed to stop being Miriam Beckstein, journalist, and to be instead Helge of Thorold by Hjorth, Countess. What made it even worse for Miriam was that she was acutely aware that such a business model was stupid and unsustainable. Once, mere weeks ago, she'd had plans to upset the metaphorical apple cart, designs to replace it with a fleet of milk tankers. But then Matthias, secretary to the Duke Angbard, captain-general of the Clan's Security Directorate, had upset the apple cart first, and set fire to it into the bargain. He'd defected to the Drug Enforcement Agency of the United States of America. And whether or not he'd held his peace about the real nature of the Clan, a dynasty of world-walking spooks from a place where the river of history had run a radically different course, he'd sure as hell shut down their eastern seaboard operations.

Matthias had blown more safe houses and shipping networks in one month than the Clan had lost in all the previous thirty years. His psycho bag-man had shot and killed Miriam's lover during an attempt to cover up the defection by destroying a major Clan fortress. Then, a month later, Clan security had ordered Miriam back to Niejwein from New Britain, warning that Matthias' allies in that time-line made it too unsafe for her to stay there. Miriam thought this was bullshit: but bullshit delivered by men with automatic weapons was bullshit best nodded along with, at least until their backs were turned.

Mid-morning loomed. Miriam wasn't needed today. She had the next three days off, her corveé paid. Miriam would sleep in, and then Helge would occupy her time with education. Miriam Beckstein had two college degrees, but countess Helge was woefully uneducated in even the basics of her new life. Just learning how to live among her recently rediscovered family was a full-time job. First, language lessons in the hochsprache vernacular with a most attentive tutor, her lady in waiting Kara d'Praha. Then an appointment for a fitting with her dressmaker, whose on-going fabrication of a suitable wardrobe had something of the quality of a Sisyphean task. Perhaps if the weather was good there'd be a discreet lesson in horsemanship (growing up in suburban Boston, she'd never learned to ride): otherwise, one in dancing, deportment or court etiquette.

Miriam was bored and anxious, itching to get back to her start-up venture in the old capital of New Britain where she'd established a company to build disk brakes and pioneer automotive technology transfer. New Britain was about fifty years behind the world she'd grown up in, a land of opportunity for a sometime tech journalist turned entrepreneur. Helge, however, was strangely fascinated by the minutiae of her new life. Going from middle class middle American life to the rarefied upper reaches of a barely post-feudal aristocracy meant learning skills she'd never imagined needing before. She was confronting a divide of five hundred years, not fifty, and it was challenging.

She'd taken the early part of the morning off to be Miriam, sitting in her bedroom in jeans and sweater, her seat a folding aluminum camp chair, a laptop balanced on her knees and a mug of coffee cooling on the floor by her feet. *If I can't do I can at least* plan, she told herself wryly. She had a lot of plans, more than she knew what to do with. The whole idea of turning the Clan's business model around, from primitive mercantilism to making money off technology transfer between worlds, seemed impossibly utopian— especially considering how few of the Clan elders had any sort of modern education. But without plans, written studies and costings and risk analyses, she wasn't going to convince anyone. So she'd ground out a couple more pages of proposals before realizing someone was watching her.

"Yes?"

"Milady." Kara bent a knee prettily, a picture of instinctive teenage grace that Miriam couldn't imagine matching. "You bade me remind you last week that this eve is the first of summer twelvenight. There's to be a garden party at the Östhalle tonight, and a ball afterwards beside, and a card from her grace your mother bidding you to attend her this afternoon before-time." Her face the picture of innocence she added, "shall I attend to your party?"

If Kara organized her carriage and guards then Kara would be coming along too. The memories of what had happened the last time Helge let Kara accompany her to a court event made her want to wince, but she managed to keep a straight face: "yes, you do that," she said evenly. "Get mistress Tanzig in to dress me before lunch, and my complements to her grace my mother and I shall be with her by the second hour of the afternoon." Mistress Tanzig the dressmaker would know what she should wear in public, and more importantly, be able to alter it to fit if there were any last-minute problems. Miriam hit the Save button on her spreadsheet and sighed. "Is that the time? Tell somebody to run me a bath; I'll be out in a minute."

So much for the day off, thought Miriam as she packed the laptop away. *I suppose I'd better go and be Helge . . .*

"Have you thought about marriage?" asked the duchess.

"Mother! As if!" Helge snorted indignantly and her eyes narrowed. "It's been about, what, ten weeks? Twelve? If you think I'm about to shack up with some golden boy so soon after losing Roland . . ."

"That wasn't what I meant, dear."

Helge drew breath. "What do you mean?"

"I meant." The duchess Patricia glanced at her sharply, taking stock: "the, ah, noble institution. Have you thought about what it *means* here? And if so, what did you think?"

"I thought—" a slight expression of puzzlement wrinkled her forehead—"when I first arrived, Angbard tried to convince me I ought to make an alliance of fortunes, as he put it. Crudely speaking, to tie myself to a powerful man who could protect me." The wrinkles turned into a full-blown frown: "I nearly told him he could put his alliance right where the sun doesn't shine."

"It's a good thing you didn't," her mother said diplomatically.

"Oh, I know that! Now. But the whole deal, here, creeps me out. And then." Helge took a deep breath and looked at the duchess: "there's you, your experience. I really don't know how you can stand to be in the same room as her grace your mother, the bitch! How she could—"

"—Connive at ending a civil war?" The duchess asked sharply.

"Sell off her daughter to a wife-beating scumbag is more the phrase I had in mind." Helge paused. "Against her wishes," she added. A longer pause; "Well?"

"Well," the duchess said quietly. "Well, well. And well again. Would you like to know how she did it?"

"I'm not sure." A grimace.

"Well, whether you want to or not, I think you need to know," Iris—Patricia, the duchess Patricia, said. "Forewarned is forearmed, and no, when I was your age—and younger—*I* didn't want to know about it, either. But nobody's offering to trade you on the block like a piece of horse-flesh. I should think the worst they'll do is drop broad hints your way and make the consequences of non-cooperation irritatingly obvious in the hope you'll give in just to make them go away. You've probably got enough clout to ignore them if you want to push it—if it matters to you enough. But whether it would be *wise* to ignore them is another question entirely."

"Who are 'they'?"

"Aha! The right question, at last!" Iris laboriously levered herself upright on her chaise, beaming. "I told you the Clan is democratic, in the classical sense of the word. The marriage market is democracy in action, Helge, and as we all know, Democracy Is Always Right. Yes? Now, can you tell me who, within the family, provides the bride's dowry?"

"Why, the—" Helge thought for a moment—"well, it's the head of the household's wealth, but doesn't the woman's mother have something to do with determining how much goes into it?"

"Exactly." The duchess nodded. "Braids cross three families, alternating every couple of generations so that issues of consanguinity don't arise but the Clan gift—the recessive gene—is preserved. To organize a braid takes some kind of continuity across at least three generations. A burden which naturally falls on the eldest women of the Clan. Men don't count: men tend to go and get themselves killed fighting silly duels. Or in wars. Or blood feuds. Or they sire bastards who then become part of the outer families and a tiresome burden. They—the bastards—can't world-walk, but some of their issue might, or their grandchildren. So we must keep track of them and find something useful for them to do—unlike the rest of the nobility here we have an incentive to look after our by-blows. I think we're lucky, in that respect, to have a matrilineal succession—other tribal societies I studied in my youth, that were patrilineal, were not nice places to be born female. Whichever and whatever, the lineage is preserved largely by the old women acting in concert. A conspiracy of matchmakers, if you like. The 'old bitches' as everyone under sixty tends to call them." The duchess frowned. "It doesn't seem quite as funny now I'm sixty-two."

"Um." Helge leaned towards her mother. "You're telling me Hildegarde wasn't acting alone? Or she was being pressured by *her* mother? Or what?"

"Oh, she's an evil bitch in her own right," Patricia waved off the question dismissively. "But yes, she was pressured. She and the other ladies of a certain age don't have the two things that a young and eligible Clan lady can bargain with: they can't bear world-walkers, and they can no longer carry heavy loads for the family trade. So they must rely on other, more subtle tools to maintain their position. Like their ability to plait the braids, and to do each other favors, by way of their grandchildren. And when my mother was in her thirties—little older than you are now—she was subjected to much pressure."

"So there's this conspiracy of old women—" Helge was grasping after the concept—"who can make everyone's life a misery?"

"Don't underestimate them," warned the duchess. "They always win in the end, and you'll need to make your peace with them sooner or later. I'm unusual, I managed to evade them for more than three decades. But that almost never happens, and even when it does you can't actually win, because whether you fight them or no, you end up becoming one yourself." She raised one finger in warning. "You're relatively safe, kid. You're too old, too educated, and you've got your own power base. As far as I can see they've got no reason to meddle with you *unless* you threaten their honor. Honor is survival here. Don't *ever* do that, Miriam—Helge. If you do, they'll find a way to bring you down. All it takes is leverage, and leverage is the one thing they've got." She smiled thinly. "Think of them as Darwin's revenge on us, and remember to smile and curtsey when you pass them because until you've given them grandchildren they will regard you as an expendable piece to move around the game board. And if you *have* given them a child, they have a hostage to hold against you."